The Marriage Counselor
The Complete Version

Mistress Ivey

Copyright © 2017 Mistress Ivey
Published by: Georgia Ivey Green
All rights reserved.

ISBN-13: 978-1542561037

DEDICATION

This book is dedicated to all those fans
Who have supported my efforts to
Improve the acceptability of
Female Led Relationships
In our society.

ACKNOWLEDGMENTS

This is a work of fiction. All characters are over the age of 18. All characters, organizations, and events portrayed in this novel are either the product of the author's imagination or are used fictitiously. Any resemblance to real world events, people, actions, and organizations, are purely coincidental and are unintended.

The Marriage Counselor
(Part 1)

CONTENTS

1	A trip Through the Dungeon	1
2	Signing Up	10
3	Frank's First Lesson	17
4	Treatment Begins	25
5	A Lesson in Teasing	35
6	The Shopping Trip	46
7	Graduation Day	53
8	A Special Teasing	62
9	Happily, Ever-After	67

Chapter 1
A TRIP THROUGH THE DUNGEON

The ad read:
"Kathryn's Counseling Service.
We can save your marriage.
Success is guaranteed!
Call 555-5432"

Even though Jane was skeptical, she decided to give this woman a call. "After all," she thought, "what could it hurt?" Things had been so bad in her marriage for so long, Jane had almost given up hope of ever getting things back to the way they used be.

As she dialed the number, Jane wondered just how this marriage counseling service could possibly guarantee success.

She heard the phone on the other end of the line ring five times. Jane was ready to hang up when the ringing suddenly stopped and a voice came through her phone. "Kathryn's Counseling, how may we help you?"

Jane was taken by surprise and stumbled around for the right words. "I... Uh... I don't know if you can." Jane was suddenly very nervous and she didn't even know why. Maybe it was because she had not even spoken to her husband about marriage counseling. Or maybe it was the thought of having to tell a perfect stranger that her marriage was a failure.

"Ma'am?" It was the voice from the other end of the phone line again. "Ma'am, I am sure we can help you. We have a perfect track record. Whatever your problems are with your marriage, I am sure we can make things better."

The voice was soothing and confident. It put Jane at ease. "Well," she began, "my husband is... bored with me and our marriage, and I just don't know what to do about it. He has been bored for a long time, according to him. I think he wants a divorce."

"Yes, Ma'am," the voice said, "Believe me, we have methods that will turn his life of boredom around and make you the only woman in his life. Would you like to make an appointment?"

"Uh... I don't... Well, I don't think I can get him to go to a marriage counselor." Tears were welling up in Jane's eyes as she spoke and her voice was trembling.

"You don't have to do that right now," the voice told her. "Why don't you make yourself an appointment and we will show you our facility. We can explain how we do what we do here. How would that be?"

Jane wiped her eyes with a tissue before answering. "You can do that?" she asked.

"Of course we can," the voice said. "Most women don't understand exactly how we do what we do here. I think it would be much more reassuring if you could tour our facility. Are you available tomorrow? Say about ten?"

Still not fully recovered, emotionally, Jane answered, "Sure, I... Uh... I guess I could do that. Ten will be fine. My name is Jane Walters"

"Great!" the voice said, "We'll expect you at ten, Jane."

Jane hung up the phone with a puzzled look on her face. "I just don't understand how they can guarantee success," she said to herself. "But, what have I got lose?"

Jane was just happy that she didn't have to tell Frank anything about what she had in mind. After all, she knew how he would react the minute she even mentioned seeing a marriage counselor. She had tried to get him to go before, but he would have nothing to do with it. Frank was so against marriage counseling that he had threatened to leave Jane the last time she suggested it. But what difference would that make now? He wanted to leave her anyway. She could tell by his attitude.

As the afternoon began to drag on, Jane was getting more and more nervous about the whole idea of trying to get Frank to agree to go with her. But, at least for now, she didn't have to think about that. After all, she had only made an appointment for herself, and that was just to tour the facility. What bothered her about that was what kind of facility were they talking about? Was it like an institution with patients and all? Or was it more like a resort where couples go to spend a weekend together getting to know each other better?

Jane decided that she would just have to drive over there and see for herself. She thought if she could just see the building, she would be able to tell just exactly what kind of thing she was getting herself into.

She jumped in her car and backed into the street. It was a quiet neighborhood. The kind you see in every town across the country. You could tell by looking at the houses that the people there were not rich folk, but they weren't hurting for money, either. The lawns were all kept neat and mowed. But they weren't very large yards. Most of the houses looked pretty much alike. Except for the occasional ranch style home, everyone had two stories, three to four bed rooms, and many had finished basements as well. Frank had never bothered to finish their basement. It was just one big open space with a staircase in the middle and a laundry area in one corner. There were half a dozen metal poles supporting the center beams for the main floor. But, other than that, it was empty.

No, the people in Jane's neighborhood were not particularly wealthy, but they were all comfortable. At least, until you opened the door. She knew of several neighbors who were having marital problems of their own. She didn't know the neighbors well enough to know just what their problems were, but she often heard them yelling at each other when she took a walk in the evening. Which she often did just to get away from Frank for a while.

Jane drove into the main part of town and looked for the building that housed Kathryn's Marriage Counseling Service. She was both confused and surprised to see that it was in a rather small building. In fact, there was a dress shop on one side and an optometrist's office on the other. Kathryn's place was the largest with several darkened windows on either side of the main entrance. It looked normal enough, but Jane couldn't figure out why they kept calling it a "facility." It looked more like a small office with, perhaps, several counseling offices inside. Kind of like a dentist's office might be.

She drove home even more perplexed than she was when she hung up the phone. "Oh, well," she thought to herself, "I guess I'll find out tomorrow." As she pulled into the driveway, she noticed Frank's car in the garage. She decided, then and there, not to say a word to him until after she had toured the place.

Frank was sitting in his favorite recliner reading the evening paper, just as he normally did. There was a bottle of his favorite beer (with maybe two sips gone from it) sitting on the end table next to him. Jane wondered if he was going to have another business meeting tonight. But she decided not to ask. After all, Frank wasn't very nice whenever he spoke to her, so she didn't usually try to start up any conversations.

The first words out of Frank's mouth when Jane greeted him was, "What's for supper?"

Jane had put a roast in the oven to slow-cook before she called Kathryn's. "We are having roast beef, mashed potatoes with gravy and peas," Jane replied as if there were nothing going on at all. She was doing her best not to say anything that would upset Frank since she wanted him in a good mood tomorrow. That's when she planned to break the news about the marriage counselor to him.

As it turned out, Frank did not have a meeting that night. So he and Jane just sat around the living room reading and watching a little television.

After the news, they decided to retire for the night. Even though Jane tried to make sure he noticed that she was wearing his favorite baby-doll nightie, he just didn't seem interested. At least not in having sex. As soon as his head hit the pillow, he turned away from Jane and pretended to fall asleep.

The next morning, when Jane awoke, Frank had already left for the office. Frank was an architect for a major home builder in town. He made a good living, though Jane always thought that he could have done better had he gone with another company that builds office buildings and strip malls instead. He was offered the position, but turned it down because it would have meant a great deal more traveling and Frank hated to fly. It wasn't a fear of flying, it was all the security put in place since Nine-Eleven.

Jane rolled herself out of the bed, threw on her house-coat and dragged herself to the kitchen to make a pot of coffee. While the coffee machine did its job, Jane went to the bathroom and took care of her morning ritual. She showered, put on some makeup (though she didn't normally wear much), and got herself dressed.

It wasn't until she was sitting at the kitchen table sipping her coffee that she remembered her ten o'clock appointment. Checking the clock on the wall, she realized that she only had fifteen minutes to get there. She took one last gulp of her coffee, grabbed her purse and car keys and headed out the door.

When she arrived, Jane was amazed to find a parking space right in front of the place. She gathered her things, locked the car, and walked to the front door. She took a deep breath before pulling the handle on the glass door to open it. When she stepped inside, she took a moment to look around. It was like any other doctor's office waiting room except that there was no one waiting in it. There was a wall at the back of the room directly opposite the door with an opening behind which sat what she assumed was the receptionist.

As Jane approached the window a nice looking twenty-something blonde asked, "Can I help you?"

"Uh, yes," Jane replied. "I have an appointment. Jane Walters?" She added, a little unsure she was in the right place.

"Oh, yes," replied the woman. "You're here for the tour, right?"

"I guess so," Jane said, letting her uneasiness show a bit.

"Have a seat. Mistress Kathryn will be right with you," the blonde behind the counter told her.

"Mistress Kathryn?," Jane thought to herself. "What kind of title was that for a doctor of psychiatry? Shouldn't she be called "Doctor" or something?"

Jane looked around. She chose a seat against the wall where she could see out the window just in case someone she knew went by. She was beginning to feel nervous again. She was just about to leave when a door

The Marriage Counselor

leading to the back opened and a nice looking woman in her late thirties entered. "Are you Jane?" the woman asked.

"Uh, yes," Jane replied. "That's me."

"My name is Kathryn," the woman said. "If you'll come with me, I'll show you what we do here. I think you are going to be impressed."

"Yes, Ma'am," Jane responded. "Are you the Kathryn who owns this place?"

"That's me, I like to give the tours to our new clients, myself," she said. "I want my clients to have confidence in me and my staff. I think personally showing prospective clients just what we do here is good for business. Besides, I do take a personal interest in all my clients. That's how I achieve such a high rate of success."

"I was wondering about that," Jane said as she followed the woman down the short corridor. "Just how do you achieve such a high success rate?" she asked emphasizing the word 'do.'

"You'll see," Kathryn replied with confidence. "Now, if you will just step into this room, I will be happy to answer all your questions." With that, Kathryn held the door open for Jane to enter the room.

"This is what we call the Installation Room," Kathryn explained as the door closed behind them. "This is where it all begins."

"Installation?" Jane asked inquisitively.

"Yes, dear. It's where we install the chastity belts on the men so we can control them," Kathryn explained. "Once we control their sexual organs, we can more easily convince them that they need to change their behavior."

"I see." Jane did not see, but she didn't want to sound stupid, so she just said she did. "And how do you get the men to agree to wear these chastity belts?"

"Oh, that's no problem," Kathryn explained. "Once we explain what will happen if they don't wear one, they are usually quite agreeable. You see, we strap them down and threaten to cut their cocks off. That's when they always choose the belt."

"I can understand that," Jane acknowledged, "but isn't that a bit drastic?"

"I was kidding, of course," she said, "we don't always do it that way. Actually," Kathryn continued, "you will be the one to convince your husband that he should wear it."

"I don't think I can convince Frank to wear a chastity belt," Jane said shaking her head.

"Don't worry, I'll help you with that," Kathryn said reassuringly. "Trust me, he'll wear it."

"You see, once we have their sexual organs under control," Kathryn explained, "we can make them do anything we want. All we have to do then is show them the error of their ways, and they will change almost immediately."

"Immediately?" Jane asked.

"Well, sometimes it takes a few sessions to achieve the desired behavior." Kathryn continued, "but they all come around eventually. Most of our clients only need one or two sessions to see the light, so to speak."

"I guess I can see why," Jane said. "But what if they don't stop doing whatever it is they have been doing to ruin the relationship?"

"Don't worry," Kathryn answered, "you have lots more to see. It will become clear very soon." With that, Kathryn led Jane out into the corridor and to an elevator. She pushed the down button and the doors hissed open. "After you," Kathryn gestured for Jane to step in.

"Where are we going now?" Jane asked.

"To the treatment room," Kathryn replied with a slight wink of her eye.

When the doors to the elevator opened again, Jane was awe struck. She couldn't believe what she was seeing. She rubbed her eyes as she stepped out of the elevator and looked all around the room again. "What is all this stuff?" she asked in amazement. "It looks like a medieval dungeon."

"This," Kathryn said proudly, "is the treatment room. Here, we can treat whatever ails your husband. If he is abusive, cheats on you, treats you badly, doesn't do enough around the house for you, whatever the problem, we can treat it."

"Oh, my!" exclaimed Jane in amazement. "You have a real dungeon. Isn't this illegal? How do you handle that?"

"It's not illegal. All this equipment is used to treat legitimate ailments. We don't keep them here against their will, or anything." Kathryn went on to explain, "All our clients agree to whatever treatment we deem is necessary. Besides, their wives all take an active role in rehabilitating their own husbands. That way, she knows just what to do if he slips back into his old ways at home. But don't worry, that very rarely happens."

"What do you mean that the wives take and active role?" Jane asks with a bit of skepticism.

"Well, we will teach you how to get your husband to do anything you want him to." Kathryn explained in more detail, "You will both be here together and you will be the one who actually teaches your husband to change his ways. It just wouldn't work any other way. You see," she continued, "once your husband has agreed to wear the chastity belt, we will hold the key here. If he wants to get it off, he will have to cooperate completely."

"I am beginning to understand," Jane said. "By making me the one who teaches him how to behave, he will always behave for me. Either that, or he suffers the consequences. Right?"

"Exactly!" Kathryn had a big grin on her face. "His graduation is when we turn the keys to his chastity belt over to you."

"So, he doesn't get released?" asked Jane.

"Not unless you release him," Kathryn said, "and you only need to do that when it suits you."

"Oh, this is going to be fun! But how do I get him to come here in the first place?" Jane wondered out loud.

"Let us worry about that," Kathryn said reassuringly. "We will contact him and get him to come in to our office. We will tell you when to be here to start his treatment. We know how to get him to come in. Don't you worry about that. In the mean time, you don't even have to mention a thing about any of this to him."

"That's a relief," Jane replied. "I was worried about telling him that we are going to go to a marriage counselor. He hates the idea."

"He may hate it," Kathryn said, "but he will do it. We will see to that. Shall we get on with the tour?"

Jane took one more look around the huge room. "All this stuff looks ominous. Don't the men hate their wives for this?"

"Not really," Kathryn said with a slight smile. "But I thought I would show you some of the equipment we will be using. By the time we are done treating your husband, you will be very familiar with what you will need most."

"Sounds good," Jane said with a renewed enthusiasm. "Where do we start?"

"Come this way," Kathryn said gesturing toward the right side of the huge room.

The first thing they came to was a large wooden table made of very sturdy oak. It had rings mounted at various points around the outside. It also pivoted at the center so that it could be tilted in either direction. That is, head up or head down. Jane was impressed with the table and Kathryn explained that it could be used for many types of treatments. It was sort of a universal exam table.

The next thing on the list was a set of chains hung from the ceiling about three feet apart. These were used to secure a man in a standing position for whipping, teasing, or disciplinary purposes. Jane thought it would be wonderful to see Frank hanging from those chains stark naked. "What do you mean by teasing? She asked.

"Again," Kathryn explained, "we will cover all that during his training. But it is one way for you to keep his attention on you, instead of on the porn he is probably used to watching on the Internet."

"I suspect he may be doing more than that," Jane replied.

Next on the tour was the electroshock therapy chair. "This is used to shock a man when he has the wrong reaction to certain sexual stimuli," Kathryn said. "It's really effective in masturbation deterrent therapy, too."

There were crosses of various styles, chairs, tables, benches and hooks in the wall. This place had everything. Everything a person could want in order to torture another person. There was even a video screen on one wall that practically filled the entire wall. "What's that for?" Jane asked.

"That's the video screen where we show erotic videos," explained Kathryn. "It works in conjunction with the electroshock therapy. And a few other things."

Kathryn even showed Jane several cabinets each filled with floggers, or whips, or paddles, or some things she didn't understand. There seemed to be a cabinet for everything you could imagine. There were even a few things she had never seen before.

There were a couple of rooms off the dungeon that each contained a sofa, a bed and a lounge chair. Each room also contained a chair with built-in restraints. Jane wondered what those rooms were used for. "You probably won't be using one of those rooms for your husbands therapy," Kathryn told her. "Those rooms are for cheaters and homophobes, mostly. Your husband isn't cheating on you, is he?"

"Uh, not that I know of," Jane replied. "But I suppose he could be. He does seem to have a quite a few evening meetings. Supposedly with prospective clients."

"Well, if he is, we will find out for you," Kathryn said reassuringly. "Everything always comes out in therapy, dear."

Jane thought about it for a moment and finally decided that if Kathryn guaranteed the results she was looking for, everything was going to be okay.

When the tour was complete, Kathryn took Jane to her office. "Have a seat," she said, handing some forms to Jane. "You need to fill these out so we can set up your husband's course of treatment."

Jane took the forms and began filling them out. They were mostly insurance forms and a page of health questions. There was one form that asked a lot of personal questions about their relationship, but Jane had expected that. She looked up from the paper work and asked, "How am I supposed to get Frank to come in for treatment?"

"Don't worry about that," Kathryn reassured her. "We will set it all up and let you know when to be here. You don't have to do a thing unless you want to. Just show up when we tell you and we will take care of the rest."

"You mean I don't have to convince Frank to come in?" Jane asked doubtingly.

"Oh, we will take care of that," Kathryn said. "We have our ways of getting reluctant husbands to come in for treatment. Trust me on that."

"Well, it all sounds so great," Jane began, "but just how much is all this going to cost?"

Kathryn leaned over and patted Jane's thigh, "Don't you worry about that, either," she said. "Your insurance should cover most of the costs. I work on a sliding scale. It won't cost you more than you can afford." She added, "but there is one expense the insurance won't cover," she said. "That's the cost of the chastity device. It's $200 and you can pay that at the front desk on your way out."

Once Jane had finished filling out the forms, Kathryn told her that they would be in touch with her when everything had been set up. She escorted Jane to the door and reassured her that everything would be just fine. Jane walked up to the woman at the reception window and paid for the chastity device.

Jane's mind was reeling from all she had just seen. However, she was now confident that whatever therapy Kathryn and her staff came up with would surely work and that Frank would end up being a much better husband than ever before. As she pulled into her driveway, Jane couldn't help but smile to herself as she thought about Frank wearing a chastity belt, possibly for the rest of his life. It made her happy. A feeling she had not had in years.

The rest of the day went like any other, except that Jane seemed to be in a particularly good mood. She and Frank ate dinner in front of the TV and when the news was over, they retired for the evening. Jane could hardly contain herself, but managed not to say a word to Frank about what she had done and seen that day. They both fell asleep, backs turned toward each other, just as they did any other night. To Frank, it was any other night. To Jane, it was a night filled with hopes and dreams of what was to come.

~ ~ ~

Chapter 2
SIGNING UP

Frank Walters was a good architect. He worked hard, every day, for his boss and his clients. But he was unhappy in his marriage. Frankly, he was bored to the point of wanting a divorce. It wasn't so much that he didn't love his wife, he was just tired of her. After all, they just didn't seem to have anything in common, any more.

The phone on Frank's desk rang. Thinking it might be his boss, Frank answered on the second ring. "Hello?"

The voice on the other end of the line responded, "Hello, Mister Walters?"

"Yes, this is he."

"This is Maggie Lawson. I got your name from a realtor friend of mine, June Alcott? She said that you design houses? Is that right?"

"Yes, I work for Bradly & Sons construction," Frank replied. "What can I do for you?"

"My husband and I are thinking of building a new house and we were wondering if we could meet with you to go over some possible designs?" Maggie asked.

"Certainly. I would be happy to take a look at your ideas and see what I can do to help," said Frank, hoping he might get a raise if he could bring in some more business himself. "Can you come by my office sometime?"

"Well, that's the problem," Maggie replied. "My husband and I really can't get away from work. I was hoping that you could stop by here so I can give you some drawings he and I have worked up."

Thinking that he might score extra points with Mr. Bradly if he could get these people started on a home before they talked with Mr. Bradly, Frank said, "Yeah, I could do that. Where do you work?"

I work for Dr. Andrews," Maggie replied. "It's the counseling center downtown next to Barbara's Boutique. Do you know it?"

"Yes, I know it. That's the one on Main St. Right?" Frank responded.

"Yes, that's the one," affirmed Maggie. "Can you stop by around five o'clock this evening?"

"Sure," said Frank. After work was great because it would show Mr. Bradly that he was willing to put in a little extra time to make a sale. "I'll be there."

"That's great," replied Maggie enthusiastically. "I'll be waiting for you. Good bye."

"Good bye," Frank said before hanging up the phone. He was getting a little excited now that he thought he might be able to bring in some business. Mr. Bradly had been after him to actively find some more clients. Business had been down because of the economy and Mr. Bradly was sure to give him a big bonus for this. He smiled to himself when he thought about it. Maybe he would get enough to pay for the divorce he had been contemplating.

When four-thirty finally rolled around, Frank grabbed his briefcase and headed out the door. His office was a small mobile building Mr. Bradly had set up for him. It was mobile because, in the past, when business was better, they would place it on a developer's lot when they were working on a subdivision. It was on the back lot of the Bradly Construction Company now, though.

On his way to his car Frank saw Mr. Bradly. He couldn't resist the opportunity to tell him about the new client he may have for him. "Hi, Chuck," he said when he got close enough to speak without yelling across the yard. "I've got some good news for you. I am going to see a prospective client, right now. They want to give me some drawings and let me draw up plans for a new house."

"That's great, Frank!" Mr. Bradly actually sounded pleased. "Don't forget to get them to sign an exclusivity agreement."

"I won't," replied Frank. "See you tomorrow."

"Yeah, I can't wait to see what your client wants." Mr. Bradly was having some financial difficulties. Home construction had been at an all-time low and he could certainly use the business.

Frank got into his car and started the engine. He was so happy as he drove down town, he actually sang along with the radio as he drove, something he hadn't done in years.

When he finally arrived at his destination, he parked right in front of the entrance. He noticed Jane's car was parked in front of the boutique. She was probably shopping for a new dress or something he thought as he got out of the car.

When he opened the door and stepped inside he was greeted by a young blonde woman sitting behind the window at the back of the room. "Hi, you must be Mr. Walters. I have been waiting for you. I'm Maggie," She continued.

"Hi. Yes, you can call me Frank," he said as he approached the window.

"Well, if you will step through that door on your left, I will meet you in the hall," Maggie said in the friendliest voice she could muster.

Frank looked to his left. There was an unmarked door with one of those fancy, lever-style doorknobs on it. "See you on the other side," he said as he turned to walk to the door. He pushed the handle down, pulled the door open and then stepped through the doorway into the corridor. Maggie was there to meet him as she said she would be.

Maggie lead Frank down the hallway to another door. She twisted the handle and pushed the door open. "I have those drawings I told you about in here," she began as she stepped through the doorway into the room beyond. "Come on in and I'll show them to you."

Frank followed her into the room. As the door closed behind him, two men grabbed his arms and pulled him backwards onto a large table. Before he knew what was happening, his wrists were bound to steel rings at the sides of the table. He struggled to get free, but soon realized the bindings were quite secure.

"What are you doing to me?" he shouted. "You'll never get away with this. I'll have you arrested for kidnapping!"

"Relax," Maggie said. "We aren't going to harm you, as long as you cooperate. There is someone who wants to talk with you, though."

She opened a door on the opposite side of the room from the one through which he had entered. Jane stepped into the room and closed the door behind her. "Fancy seeing you here," she said. "I hope you haven't been waiting long."

Frank was really angry now. He shouted at Jane, "What's going on here? What are you doing to me?"

"Just relax," Jane spoke in a soft, soothing tone. "I just want to talk to you for a minute. You never listen to me at home, so I thought this would be a good way to get your undivided attention. Do I have that, Frank?"

Taking a deep breath after realizing there was nothing he could do about his current situation. Frank finally responded, "Yes, Jane, you have my undivided attention. Now what's this all about?"

Jane stepped to the foot of the table where Frank was now restrained. "Honey, we are going to make our marriage better. You know we have had some problems. Well, now we are going to work them out."

Frank, still a bit angry, responded, "Release me and we can talk about this."

"No, Frank," Jane said in a soft, even tone. "I am going to talk and you are going to listen. When I am done, you can speak. Understand?"

The Marriage Counselor

Realizing the situation was clearly under Jane's control, he relinquished. "What's this all about," he asked in a more relaxed, civilized tone."

"Let me explain what's going to happen," Jane began. "We are going to undergo a little marriage counseling. It's a special program designed by Dr. Andrews. She has had an outstanding rate of success with her methods. So I decided that we should at least give it a try. I want you to think about something carefully," she continued. "I don't want you to answer, yet. I just want you to think about something for me while I tell you how I feel. Okay?"

"Okay, dear," Frank agreed, though he was more than a little annoyed. "What is it?"

"I want you to think very carefully about what life would be like for you," Jane began, "if we got divorced. First, I would take you for just about everything you have. You would have to pay me a large maintenance fee to maintain my current standard of living. I will get the house, and you will have to find an apartment because you won't be able to afford another house. At least not with our current mortgage, which you will have to pay."

Frank opened his mouth to speak, just then, a large hand covered his mouth and held his head firmly against the table. Frank struggled at first, then he remembered he was to wait and think about what Jane had just told him. He shut his mouth and looked at her in silence. The large hand removed itself from his face. He started thinking about it. At first he thought about what Jane had said and knew she was right. Then he thought about what it might be like suddenly living from paycheck to paycheck. He hadn't done that since he graduated from college. Finally he spoke, "Okay, so what did you have in mind?"

Jane looked around at the other people in the room, then she turned to Maggie and said, "Could we have a few minutes alone?"

"Of course," Maggie replied. "When you are ready, just push the red button on the wall by the door and we will return." With that she gestured to the two men who had been standing by Franks head. They all quickly exited the room, leaving Frank and Jane alone.

When the door closed, Jane moved beside the table. She leaned over and gave Frank a kiss on the cheek. She let her hand drift slowly down the front of his shirt toward the buckle of his belt. She stopped with her hand resting on his belt buckle, then said, "Sweetheart, you know that our marriage has not been as good as it could be, right?"

"Yes, dear," he murmured, resigning himself to his current condition. Besides, it was all Frank could think of to say, at the moment.

"Well," Jane continued, "I want to do something about that. I still love you and I know we can work this all out and improve our marriage. Don't you want to try?"

"Yes, dear," he confessed, "I love you, too. But things have been so bad between us for so long, I am afraid I was contemplating divorce."

"I thought as much," Jane continued. "In fact, I saw you looking at divorce attorney's in the yellow pages the other day. That's when I decided to give marriage counseling a try." Jane began to unfasten Frank's belt as she spoke. "I know that you haven't been getting as much sex as you would probably like." She pulled the tail from the buckle and laid it back out of the way. She did the same with the buckle. "Are you willing to give it a try if I promise to give you more sex than you ever thought you would get?"

Frank was getting a bit nervous. He didn't understand what was going on. "Yeah, I...I guess so," he replied. "Do you really mean that? About the sex, I mean."

With that, Jane unfastened his pants and began to pull the zipper down. "You won't mind if I give you a little sample right here and now?" she asked.

"Um, right now?" he asked with a slight tremor in his throat as he looked around the room.

"Yes dear," she replied with a twinkle in her eye. She stepped to the foot of the table again and tugged his pants, complete with underwear, down to his ankles.

"What are you doing?" Frank asked in disbelief. His manhood now completely exposed.

"I told you, sweetie," Jane responded with a smile. "I am going to give you a sample of what you can expect in the future. Don't you want me to?"

"Well, uh, sure. I guess so," Frank replied nervously.

"Good! Lay back and close your eyes," Jane told him. "I'll give you a sample of what you can expect in the future." With that, she took hold of Frank's cock and began gently stroking it. It began to grow in her hand. She smiled again and said, "See? Your cock wants some attention."

Frank only moaned something unintelligible and pushed his head back harder against the hard surface of the table. It was difficult trying to hold his head in position to see what Jane was doing, anyway.

Jane continued to stroke Frank's cock ever so slowly, while she recounted one of her favorite memories about their honeymoon. She reminded Frank of the first night when he carried her into the motel room to lay her gently on the bed. She reminded him how he had slowly undressed her removing one garment at a time. How he kissed each patch of newly exposed skin so softly and gently.

Frank's cock grew as hard as Jane had ever felt it before. She knew she was on the right track. Dr. Kathryn had been right. She told Jane that she should try this and, right now, it seemed to be working. Working even better than Jane ever thought it would. She continued her story, describing the entire evening in as much detail as she could remember and making up

The Marriage Counselor

what she couldn't. Then, just before she got to the point where Frank had filled her pussy full of his semen, she stopped stroking Frank's cock. She finished describing what they had done and how wonderful it all felt to her that night, but she didn't touch Frank again.

Frank was frantic. "Why did you stop? I was just about to cum," he announced with an urgency Jane had never heard before.

"I'm sorry, sweetie," she said. "I didn't want you to cum now. I am reserving that for later." She smiled at him as she stepped to the door and pressed the little red button to summon the others back into the room.

Frank squirmed. "Don't bring them back while I'm like this," he protested. "Pull my pants up first!"

Just then the door opened and Maggie and the two male aids walked into the room. "I see you have been busy," she said to Jane. "Is he ready?"

"I think so," Jane replied confidently. She turned toward Frank and asked sweetly, "Do you remember what I asked you to think about?"

Frank looked at her inquisitively and replied, "Yes?"

Just then Maggie held up a chastity belt and announced, "This is a chastity belt. It will prevent you from having any kind of sex, even masturbation, without Jane's express permission. Would you like to wear it or would you rather live the rest of your life as your wife described it earlier?"

Frank looked around the room. His cock was shriveling fast. He looked at Jane and asked, "Did you really mean what you said about more sex?"

Jane looked at him with loving eyes, "Of course, sweetie. More than you have ever imagined."

Frank thought about his choices then announced, "I want the chastity belt."

"Good," said Maggie. "Then we have some papers for you to sign. She signaled one of the men who unfastened his right wrist restraint. She placed a clipboard in his lap and handed him a pen. "Just sign and date this at the bottom, please."

She stepped back and waited for him to sign the form. Frank looked around as everyone else in the room stared back at him, waiting. The next move was his. Frank looked down at the form which was entitled Chastity Agreement. He looked once again at Jane who was smiling back at him as if to say, "It's okay, honey. Just sign the form."

Frank realized he had no choice. He looked at the form again, then hesitantly signed and dated it in the appropriate space. He handed the pen back to Maggie who took the clipboard and smiled. "Thank you," she said politely and headed for the door. On her way out, she handed the chastity belt she had been holding to Jane and said, "He's all yours, sweetie." And with that she left the room.

The belt came in two parts, the belt itself and a cock cage to keep him from getting an erection. Jane placed the belt snugly around Frank's waist and snapped it shut. Then she took a metal ring and put it over his cock. She pulled his balls through the ring and positioned it just right. Then she took the cage part and slipped it over Frank's fully deflated cock. She pushed it upward into the belt until she heard a soft 'click.' Lastly, she fitted a small lock into place. It locked the cock cage into the belt so that it could not be removed. She clicked the lock closed and said, "There! Now we can go home if you're ready."

Frank said, "Yes, I am ready, but you do have the keys to this thing, don't you?"

"No dear, I don't." Jane smiled as she spoke. "The keys remain here so you will not be late for our counseling sessions."

"I get the point," Frank said, resolving his situation in his head. "But how often will our sessions be?"

"That all depends on you, sweetie," Jane replied. "If you cooperate and attend your sessions with a willingness to learn, we may be done in a few short sessions. If you don't, there may be many sessions and it could take years. Understand?"

"I get the picture," he responded. "Can we get out of here, now?"

With that, one of the men released his left hand and Frank jumped off the bed and quickly pulled his pants up and fastened them. He straightened himself up, picked up the briefcase he had dropped when he was so rudely grabbed, and opened the door for Jane.

They drove home in separate cars since that's the way they arrived. All the way home, Frank thought of a thousand questions he wanted to ask, but didn't know where to begin. He also wondered what he had gotten himself into. Would Jane actually give him more sex than he had ever dreamed of? Was she actually capable of that? And exactly how was she going to accomplish that with his dick locked up in this contraption? He realized, Jane was the only one who could answer that question and he would just have to wait and see.

~ ~ ~

Chapter 3
FRANK'S FIRST LESSON

Jane and Frank drove home in separate cars. All the way home, Frank began to wonder what he had gotten himself into. Then he realized, none of this was his fault. It was Jane's idea to see this particular marriage counselor, not him. But there he was, wearing a locked chastity device with no way of taking it off himself. "But," he thought to himself, "just because he had this stupid device on, didn't mean he had to do everything Jane told him to. After all, he was still the man of the house. Wasn't he?"

When he pulled into the driveway, Jane was already in the house. He parked the car, grabbed his briefcase, and headed into the house. As he entered the kitchen, he saw Jane sitting at the table with a bottle of wine, already chilling in the ice bucket, and two glasses. "What are you doing?" he asked.

"I thought we could sit and talk while we enjoy a glass of wine before dinner, dear," Jane replied. "Don't you think we should talk about all this before we get started?"

"I thought we had already started," Frank said, "what with this chastity thing and all."

"Well," Jane began, "we could start with that and see where it leads us. Come on, have a seat and let's discuss all this. After all, I know you have a lot of questions."

Frank set his briefcase down on the counter and pulled out a chair. "This isn't going to hurt, is it?" he asked half-jokingly.

"No, of course not," Jane said. "I just thought we ought to set some ground rules so that we both understand our roles better. Kathryn told me it was a good idea for us to communicate more."

Frank sat down. "What do you mean, by our roles?" he asked.

"You know, as husband and wife," she replied.

"I still don't know what you mean." Frank retorted, "We have been married for fifteen years, don't we know our roles by now?"

"Well..." Jane began, not really knowing how to explain it all. "Our roles have...Well, changed, don't you think?"

"Changed?" Frank was not liking what he was hearing. "What do mean changed? I am still the master of this house and you're still my wife, aren't you?"

Jane thought for a second before answering him. "Well... Yes and no."

"Okay, you are really starting to irritate me," Frank responded. "What do you mean by 'yes and no'?" With that Frank popped the cork on the bottle of wine, figuring he could probably use a good drink the way this conversation was going. He poured Jane a glass, then himself.

Jane picked up her glass and took a large gulp, more as a stall tactic than anything else. "We have been married for fifteen years, right?"

"Yeah, I just said that," he replied showing his irritation a bit more.

"Well, are you totally happy with our marriage as it has been up until now?" she asked.

"Well, now that you mention it, there are some things that I would like to see change," he said, calming his tone to a more relaxed one. "What are you getting at?"

"Are you totally happy with our sex life?" Jane was getting braver as she sipped her wine.

"Now that you mention it," he began, "I suppose it could be better, but how is that going to happen when my cock is not available?"

"Don't fret about that," Jane's tone changed to reflect a cheerier attitude. "What would you say if I told you that it was going to get a whole lot better over the next few weeks?"

"I guess that would be nice," he conceded. "But how is it going to improve?"

"You'll see," Jane said with a slight grin appearing at the corners of her mouth. "We are going to be trying some new things and I promise you will enjoy them. Well, most of them, anyway."

"What kind of things?" Frank asked suspiciously.

Jane took a deep breath before answering Frank's question. "Remember that time, when we first got married, and you tied me to the bed using some of my silk scarves? Remember how hot we both got from that?"

"Of course I remember," he said, thinking back to those times when sex was really fun.

"If you will allow me to take control for a while, I'll show you how much better, and hotter, sex can be," Jane told him with all the confidence she could muster.

Frank finished what wine was left in his glass and refilled both their glasses as he thought about what Jane had said. "You mean, that if I let you be in control of our sex, you will make it better than it was back when we first got married?"

"That's what I am saying, sweetheart," she replied. "I promise you will enjoy this more than you ever have enjoyed sex before. You have my word on that."

Frank thought to himself for a moment then said, "Hmm. I guess we could try that. Will there be more sex than we have had recently, as well?"

"Of course," Jane replied, almost giggling. "There will definitely be more. So what do you say? Shall we try it?"

Frank didn't really have to think about it, but he pretended to. "Okay, I guess we could give it a try. But just how are we supposed to have sex with this chastity thing on my cock?"

"Let me worry about that, dear," she replied, "There are other ways to enjoy sex than you poking that thing in and out of me. Besides, I don't have the key, so you are pretty much stuck with the idea for now."

"Yeah," he began, "about that. Just what are we supposed to do about this thing, anyway?"

"Oh, don't you worry, I know how to give you a good time even with that thing in place." Jane explained, "Kathryn gave me some ideas that we can explore this weekend. It'll be fun!"

"Well, if you're that sure of yourself," Frank replied skeptically. "What do we do first?"

"If you're that anxious to get started, take off all your clothes," Jane replied in a matter of fact tone. She didn't really expect him to comply, she was testing him more than anything.

"What? You mean here? Now?" Frank sounded surprised, though he could feel his cock beginning to stir.

"Yes," Jane said in a matter of fact tone. "Here, and now!"

Frank felt a definite surge in the blood rushing to his cock. "Well," he began, "you really want me to get undressed right here in the kitchen?"

"Yes I do," Jane replied with a firmness she was unaccustomed to using in Frank's presence. "You agreed to let me take control for awhile. Now stand up and get naked."

Frank was actually getting excited. He stared at Jane while he slowly stood up and began removing his clothes. He started with his shoes, then his suit jacket, and then his shirt, pants and underwear. His cock was swelling. It now filled its cage completely and was beginning to get a little uncomfortable. "How's this?" he asked holding his arms out to present himself to Jane. "Aren't you going to strip, too?"

Jane chuckled at his question, "No, I ordered a pizza on the drive home and it should be here any minute. You want to go to the door naked? You want me to go to the door naked?"

"Well, no," he said. "That wouldn't do at all."

"Okay then, let's go to the living room and watch a movie or something," Jane suggested.

"Like this?" Frank asked incredulously. "I thought we were going to have some kind of sex right here in the kitchen. Aren't we?"

Jane stood up, grabbed the bottle of wine and her glass and headed for the door. "Nope. We'll get to that some other time. Take your socks off and join me." she said as she walked toward the living room. "That is, unless you want to sit out here alone and masturbate. Oh, wait. You can't." Jane chuckled to herself for that last remark.

"Uh, yeah, sure," Frank said, feeling a little uneasy about all this. He had never been naked while Jane was dressed. Well, not outside the bedroom, anyway. He removed his socks and followed Jane out of the room, through the dining room and into the living room.

Just as they arrived in the living room, the doorbell rang. Jane grabbed her purse and took out her wallet. She began searching for a twenty-dollar bill as she walked toward the door. "You might want to hide," she said as she reached for the door handle.

Frank panicked. He ran back into the dining room and stood in the corner out of site of the front door. His cock was attempting to get harder, but it was impossible in the confines of its metal cage. It was really starting to be uncomfortable. It was a very new feeling for him.

Jane paid the delivery boy and returned to the dining room. She set the pizza box on the table. "Grab a couple of paper plates and bring me one slice of pizza," she said to Frank as she returned to the living room. She sat down on the end of the couch and picked up the remote for the TV. "Get yourself one piece as well," she half yelled hoping Frank could hear her.

In a couple of minutes Frank returned with two paper plates. He handed one to Jane and sat down next to her on the couch.

"I told you to get yourself one piece," she said looking at the three slices on Frank's plate.

"I thought I wouldn't have to get up so often if I brought more than one," he replied.

"But I told you to get yourself one," she said, emphasizing the word 'one.'

"Yeah, but it's not a big deal," he replied.

"You didn't follow directions," Jane began. "From now on, pay attention to what I say and follow my directions to the letter. Understand?"

"Okay," Frank said not understanding what was going on. "What's the big deal?"

"The 'big deal' is that you didn't follow my instructions," she replied. "From now on you will do exactly as I say and you will address me as Ma'am or Mistress. Got it?" Her tone had turned stern.

"Yes, Ma'am," Frank replied a little bit confused. He had never heard Jane speak so confidently or seen her so dominant before. "Do you want me to take these back?"

"No, you can keep them," she replied, "but there will be consequences."

"Yes, Ma'am," was all Frank could think to say. "What are we going to watch?" he asked, trying to change the subject.

"I thought we would watch one of your favorite X-rated movies," she said.

"What? What X-rated movies?" Frank asked innocently.

"One of those you have hidden in the coat closet, dear," Jane replied knowingly.

"But..."

"But nothing! Get out your favorite one and put it in the DVD player," Jane ordered.

"Yes, Ma'am," Frank replied embarrassed that she even knew about those videos. He got up and walked to the closet. He took out the old briefcase that he had hidden the movies in and opened it. He removed his favorite movie and returned the briefcase to the shelf where he had originally hidden it. Then he opened the DVD case and removed the disc. Jane had turned the DVD player on and opened the drawer, so he placed the disc in the player and returned to his seat next to Jane.

Jane hit the play button and waited for the menu to pop up. When it finally did, she pressed the play button again and sat back as the title credits ran. She reached over and began to fondle Frank's balls as soon as the action started.

Frank squirmed in his seat as his cock tried it's best to burst through its confining cage. As it swelled it began to get a bit painful. In fact, after only a few minutes it became almost excruciatingly painful. He looked at Jane and said, "Could you please stop playing with me, this cage is making my cock really hurt?"

Jane smiled at him with a slight twinkle in her eye, "I told you there would be consequences. Besides, you'll get used to the pain. But I insist you keep your eyes on the movie."

That wasn't what Frank wanted to hear. In fact, the movie was making it impossible for him to lose his erection. Looking down at his poor cock, trapped in that metal cage, he figured that his cock was actually a good inch longer than the cage allowed. He was probably half an inch bigger in diameter as well. No wonder he was in such pain. He ventured to speak again, "Isn't there something we can do about this damned cage?"

To which Jane replied, "Honey, that cage is the only thing keeping me from filing for a divorce. Are you sure you want to take it off?"

Frank had to think that over. He didn't realize that Jane was that serious about their marriage that she might have divorced him if he hadn't agreed to all this. But wasn't there some other way to handle this than a cage for his cock? "Yes, dea... Um... I mean... Mistress."

Jane had placed her hand back on Frank's balls and she gave them a pretty good squeeze for his slip up. "That's right," she said, "remember who I am and that I am in control. At least as long as you are wearing that chastity belt I am."

"Yes, Mistress," Frank said humbly. Having been reminded of his situation and told that if he didn't cooperate Jane might just divorce him, Frank spent the rest of the movie thinking about just how serious Jane was. The last thing he wanted was an expensive divorce, and it had nothing to do with support payments or any of that crap. No, it was about the fact that he really did love Jane. He didn't want to lose her for all the money in the world. As he sat there thinking, he realized that he had not been all that good, as husbands go. He didn't pay much attention to her. He let her go about her own business, doing her own thing without a thought about his marriage. He thought about how they had gradually slipped apart and how much of it might have been his own fault.

Frank decided right then and there that things would be different. From that moment on, he would do whatever it took to make Jane happy. To regain all that they had lost over the last fifteen years. He was determined to make it up to her. To prove to her that he was serious about making their marriage a better one. Then he realized that he had completely lost interest in the movie and that his erection was completely gone. He was relieved.

Jane's hand was still resting in Frank's lap, her fingers still wrapped lightly around his balls. As the movie continued, she gave them a good squeeze and asked, "Where have you been? I noticed you lost your erection a long time ago. Don't you like this movie anymore?"

Frank looked at her, his eyes soft and loving, "Yes, Mistress, I do like the movie, but..."

"But what, dear?" Jane prompted him.

"But it's just that I realized how much I love you and I want our marriage to work as much, if not more, than you do. I love you and if it makes you happy, and will save our marriage, I will go to this marriage counselor for as long as it takes."

Jane smiled back at him. "You know, I think I agree with you. We both want our marriage to work and I can already see an improvement. I think this is all going to work out just fine."

Jane had an idea. If Frank was losing his interest in the movie, she would give him something he wouldn't lose interest in. "Be a dear," she said. "Get on your knees between my legs. And start licking my pussy."

Frank was surprised by her obvious command, but he had not licked her pussy, or any pussy for that matter, in a long time. In fact, he couldn't remember the last time he gave his wife head. "Yes, Ma'am," he replied as he slid off the couch and took up the position Jane had commanded.

Jane pulled her dress up and slipped her panties off. Then she slid forward so that her bottom was right at the edge of the couch, giving Frank complete access to her nether regions. As she did so, she almost wished she had shaved her genitals to give him better access. She had never actually done that, but she wanted to, for some reason. It seemed somehow... sexier, and it would give Frank easier access. He was always pulling her hair in an effort to get at her pink inner lips.

As Frank moved his head closer to her vagina, he used his fingers to spread open Jane's outer lips. He could see that she was already wet in anticipation of what he was about to do. He felt his own arousal crowding the cage that confined his cock so securely. His tongue slid out from between his lips to taste the sweet nectar that was beginning to flow from Jane's waiting pussy. It tasted just as he remembered it, though it had been a long time since he had the opportunity to taste it. He lapped at her inner lips for a few seconds and then searched out that little bud that always gave her such great orgasms. He flicked it up and down, then from side to side. He remembered how good she tastes and how much he enjoyed pleasing her with his tongue.

In a matter of minutes, Frank had Jane writhing on the couch trying to keep her pussy available even though she could not hold herself still. Frank's tongue felt fabulous and she could not remember the last time she had had orgasm that came from anything that didn't have a switch on it. She grabbed Frank's ears and pulled him hard against her. She wanted to push his head inside her hungry pussy, but settled for his tongue instead. Her orgasm swept over her like waves beating against a rocky shore. She pulled Frank tighter against her open pussy and came again, and again, and again. She lost count of the number of orgasms she had before she pushed Frank away, but she knew that, from that moment on, he was going to be eating her out a whole lot more.

She held Frank's head just inches from her still throbbing pussy until she had caught her breath again. Then she pushed him away and said breathlessly, "That was great! We are going to do a lot of that in the future."

With that, Jane told Frank to go upstairs to the bedroom and prepare a nice warm shower for the two of them. She joined him once she had removed her clothes and they both enjoyed washing each other like they had done years ago, before they drifted apart.

After their shower, Jane told Frank that she was tired and just wanted to cuddle until they fell asleep. Frank agreed, it had been a long day and he didn't know what they could do with his chastity belt in place, anyway. Jane put on a cute little baby-doll nighty and Frank put on his light blue pajamas.

They snuggled up against each other with Frank's arm wrapped around his wife. They had not fallen asleep like that in years. It felt good.

The two of them fell asleep dreaming of a better tomorrow.

~ ~ ~

Chapter 4
TREATMENT BEGINS

Jane woke Frank up early. It was Saturday and they were going for their first session at Kathryn's that afternoon and she wanted to make sure Frank was ready for it. She kissed him on the lips and said, "Wake up, sweetie. We have a lot to do this morning and we have to go to Kathryn's this afternoon."

Frank opened his eyes and squinted at the clock on the night stand. "It's only six o'clock," Frank said as he tried to wipe the sleep from his eyes. "Why so early?"

"Because, sweetie," Jane began, "you are going to make me breakfast in bed and I have lots of other chores that need to get done before we go to Kathryn's this afternoon. That's why."

Frank realized that he needed to get up to pee, anyway. His cock was trying to get hard and it was causing him a little bit of pain. "Yes, dear, I'm getting up," Frank said as he sat up and threw the covers back.

"What did you say?" Jane asked, sounding rather perturbed.

"What?" Frank was still not fully awake and his brain was a little foggy. Then it hit him, "Yes, Mistress. I'm sorry, I forgot." Then he climbed out of bed and headed for the bathroom to pee, brush his teeth and splash a little cold water over his face. "I'll be right back."

Frank had almost forgotten what the chastity belt meant when got to the toilet. But when he reached down to take hold of his cock to aim it properly, he remembered he could no longer do that. He would have to sit to pee until this contraption was removed. He turned around and sat on the seat to do his business. He thought about all that had happened and what he had agreed to at Kathryn's the evening before. "How did things ever get so bad?" he thought. "All I had to do was pay a little more attention to Jane and I wouldn't be sitting down to pee." The more he thought about it, the more he began to realize that this was really his own fault. God knows, Jane had been a great wife. She tried to get him to be more interested in sex, but he was just too preoccupied with his job and worrying about their finances to notice, much less be interested. "I guess I owe her this," he thought as he stood up and wiped the cock cage clean.

Frank finished his business in the bathroom and made the decision to try his best to make this thing work. When he was ready, he went back to the bedroom to find Jane, who was now sitting in bed making notes on a little notepad. He sat on the edge of the bed and announced his decision.

"That's great, sweetie," she responded, "but where is my breakfast?"

"Uh... Yes, Ma'am, what would you like?" Frank asked.

"That's better," Jane began. "I would like one egg, basted, two strips of bacon, a slice of buttered toast, orange juice and coffee."

"Yes, Ma'am," he answered like a true waiter. "Will that be all?"

"Yes," she said, "and you can fix yourself something as well. Oh, and before you go," She continued, "take off those ridiculous pajamas. You won't be needing them ever again."

"What?" Frank was taken aback. "You mean I have to fix breakfast naked?"

"Oh, you're not naked," Jane replied with a slight grin on her face. "You've got your chastity belt on."

"But..." Frank wasn't sure what to say in protest, but he knew he had to say something. "But what if someone sees me?"

"So what if they do?" Jane retorted, "You will do as I say even if I tell you to walk down the street naked. Understand?"

Frank was shocked at her response to his plea. He hung his head, realizing she was right. He would have to do whatever she asked or he would never get out of that infernal chastity belt. "Yes, Mistress," he said with a certain sadness in his voice. With that, he removed his pajamas and laid them on the foot of the bed. Then he left the room without a word.

Jane was proud of herself for having been able to get Frank to obey. She wasn't sure that she could maintain control over him all the time. But, for now, he was doing what she wanted. That was enough.

As he made his way to the kitchen, Frank was acutely aware of his lack of clothing. He watched carefully out of every window he passed along the way. He hoped that he would not see anyone. Well, he hoped no one would see him.

Jane spend the next few minutes writing down everything Frank had done that was wrong. He had forgotten to address her correctly several times and he questioned her order to cook breakfast in the nude. By the time Frank returned with a tray full of food, she had created quite a list of things she wanted to address with Frank, and with Kathryn when she got the chance.

"Here's your breakfast," Frank announced as he stepped into the bedroom. Where would you like me to put it, Ma'am?" he asked.

Jane sat up and pushed the bed covers to the foot of the bed revealing her very sheer baby-doll nightie she had worn to bed. "Just set it right here," she said patting the sheet next to her. "We can share the table this time." Then she scooted back so that she could rest against the headboard.

Frank set the table down where she had indicated and climbed onto the bed. Jane looked over the plate that was obviously hers. "You did a great job, sweetie," she announced. "The egg looks perfect."

"Thanks, Ma'am," Frank replied. He was proud of himself. He had never basted an egg before, though he had seen it done several times before. "I hope you like it," he added.

As the two began to eat their breakfast, Jane said, "There are some things... Well, rules we need to discuss while we're eating."

Frank replied, "Rules?"

"Yes, dear," she began, "Rules. I have some rules that you will follow as long as you are under my control. And I want you to pay attention and don't ask questions. These rules are clear enough. They need no explanation."

He could tell by the tone of her voice that she meant business. So Frank decided he needed to show some real respect. "Yes, Mistress," she said. "I am listening."

Jane looked at her list and took a deep breath. "First of all, you will never wear any clothes while you are at home unless I tell you otherwise. You will remove them when you come in the door and take them upstairs to the bedroom immediately."

"Yes, Ma'am," was Frank's only reply, though he did have questions, he kept them to himself.

"Secondly," Jane continued. "You will obey my every command without question. If I tell you to do something, you will do it and you will do it without complaint. Is that clear?"

"Yes, Mistress," was all Frank could say.

"Finally," Jane continued. "You have to trust me. You have to trust me completely so that you will do whatever I tell you to do without question. Is that understood?"

"Yes, Mistress," Frank replied. "May I ask one question?"

"Okay," Jane replied, "what is it?"

"Can I trust that you won't make me do anything that might get me arrested?" Frank asked.

"No," Jane said firmly. "If I want you to be arrested, then I will give you a task that will result in your arrest. Any more questions?"

"Uh..." Frank was getting nervous after that answer. "Uh... Just one?"

"Yes?" she asked, losing her patience. "What is it?"

Frank was getting more nervous with each passing second. "Uh, what happens if I don't obey you?"

"The answer is, you will find out the hard way, dear," Jane replied, sounding a bit annoyed.

"Yes, Ma'am," Frank replied as he began to worry about what that truly meant.

Since they had finished their breakfast, Jane ordered Frank to clear away the dishes and pour her another cup of coffee. "I'll come down stairs to drink it. Just set it on the kitchen table for me." With that she got herself out of bed and said, "I'm going to take a quick shower. I'll join you in the kitchen in a few minutes."

Frank acknowledged her and took the breakfast tray back down to the kitchen. He poured them both a second cup of coffee and sat down at the table to wait for Jane. He thought about the rules Jane had given him. He wondered just how far she intended to take this thing. Would she really give him an order to do something that might get him arrested? He thought he knew Jane, but this new woman who now occupied her body was beginning to scare him. Just how far would she push him if he didn't protest? If he protested, what kind of punishment was she liable to inflict on him? All these questions and more raced through his mind. He was nervous and, yes, afraid. He had no idea what Jane was capable of, much less, what it all meant for him.

When Jane arrived in the kitchen, Frank was just finishing his second cup of coffee. She ordered him to wash the breakfast dishes while she relaxed and read the morning paper.

Jane found all sorts of chores to keep Frank busy while she anxiously awaited the time to return to Kathryn's for their appointment. She was hoping that Kathryn would have some suggestions as to how to punish Frank when he was disobedient. That was about the only thing she had not discussed, yet. Jane didn't know if she would be able to keep up the dominant woman facade she had been using to keep Frank in line so far. She suspected that it would not always work.

Frank washed the dishes, dusted and vacuumed the living and dining rooms and even cleaned the master bath. But he was not particularly happy about doing it. Although, being naked was very erotic and he would often find his cock getting (well, trying to get) hard. The pain he felt when that happened was even erotic. Just knowing that Jane had complete control over his cock, and the fact that she had promised him more sex than he had ever dreamed of, was arousing to him. He was a bit concerned over her response when he asked if he could trust her not to get him arrested. That worried him. But, again, it was a little erotic when he stopped to think about it.

The morning finally passed and lunch had been eaten. Jane announced it was time for Frank to get dressed for their appointment at Kathryn's. He got dressed and they left the house and drove down town to Kathryn's place.

When they arrived, Frank was led to a tiny room where he was told to undress and wait for Jane to retrieve him.

Jane was taken to Kathryn's office. "Have a seat, Jane," Kathryn said gesturing toward one of the two guest chairs. "How is it going? With Frank, I mean."

Jane told her about the list she had made of all his failings so far. She indicated that she was concerned about maintaining discipline and that she was uncomfortable not knowing how to punish him. She also brought up the fact that she had promised him more sex than he had ever dreamed of, but was unsure just how to keep that promise.

Kathryn made a few notes on her own small pad and reassured Jane that, by the time today's session was over, Jane would have all her questions answered and that she would feel much more confident in handling her husband. She also promised Jane that by the end of the day, she would understand how giving Frank more sex would be more fun than she ever imagined it could be.

Jane was happy and felt reassured by Kathryn's own confidence in her. She followed Kathryn out of the office and down to the room where Frank was supposed to have disrobed. Kathryn pointed to the elevator at the end of the hall and said, "Just bring Frank to the dungeon. It's on the bottom floor." Then Kathryn headed off that way herself, leaving Jane standing outside the door to Franks dressing, or undressing, room.

Jane knocked on the door as she slowly opened it. "It's me," she said so as not to cause Frank any undue discomfort.

"Oh, good," Frank said as Jane stepped into the room. "I was afraid I had been forgotten. Is this where our session is to be. It's a bit small, don't you think?"

"No, dear," Jane replied, "we have to go downstairs for that."

"Like this?" he said gesturing to his nakedness.

"Yes, dear. Like that." She replied with a chuckle.

"But...Won't someone see me?" Frank was obviously nervous about being in a strange place completely naked.

"They might," Jane replied, "but it's okay." She took Frank by the hand and led him out of the room and down the hall to the elevator. There was no one in the hallway to see him. Together they stepped into the elevator and Jane pressed the "B" button.

When the door to the elevator finally opened again, Frank got his first view of the Treatment Room, or dungeon, as it was often called. He was afraid to leave the elevator and wanted to run back home and forget all this.

Jane tugged him out of the elevator just as Kathryn stepped up to greet them. She was wearing a black leather teddy, black stockings and high-heeled boots that laced up over her calves. Jane, a little startled by her outfit said, "You've changed clothes?"

Kathryn replied, "Not really, I just removed my dress. I wear this for every session and it's just easier to wear it under my street clothing. That's why I always wear long dresses."

"Oh," Jane replied, "I guess that makes since."

"Follow me, you two," Kathryn said as she took Frank's wrist in hand.

"Yes, Ma'am," Frank replied, unable to take his eyes off of Kathryn and her outfit. He had not noticed what a sexy woman Kathryn was when they met before. But then, he only saw her for a brief moment.

Frank was led over to an open area where he was immediately secured to two chains that dangled from the ceiling. His wrists were fastened in leather cuffs and his ankles were secured to rings in the floor. Before he knew what was happening, he was standing spread-eagle for all to see. There were two other women there that had grabbed his wrists and fastened them in place. He had met the short blonde woman before. Her name was Maggie, as he recalled. She was the one who had lured him into Kathryn's in the first place.

"This is Terri," Kathryn said, pointing to the taller, red-haired woman. "She will be helping us today. Maggie, you have met."

Offering her hand to the red-head, Jane said, "Hi, Terri, glad to meet you." Then she offered her hand to Maggie, "How are you today, Maggie?" she asked.

Kathryn nodded in Terri's direct and said, "Shall we get started?" With that, Terri picked up a remote control from a small table located several feet in front of Frank and aimed it at the large screen on the wall. The 100-inch TV came to life and displayed a video of two women on a bed. One of the women had her face buried in the crotch of the other.

Frank watched the screen carefully. He noticed that the two women in the video appeared to be the very women who had chained him up only moments ago. His cock began to respond, but was limited by the embarrassment he felt at being strung up the way he was in front of so many strange women. He wanted to ask if the women in the movie were Maggie and Terri, but dared not say a word in his present condition.

Kathryn stepped in front of Frank and smiled. "Would you like to have your cock set free for awhile?" she asked looking directly into Frank's eyes and dangling the keys to his chastity belt where he could clearly see them.

"Yes, Ma'am," was all he could say. After all, who was he to complain?

With that, Kathryn inserted the key into the small lock that held the cage in place and it popped open. She carefully removed the lock and the cock cage. Franks cock felt free at last, even though he was still wearing the belt.

Kathryn set the lock and cage on the small table and handed Jane a small, wooden paddle.

"What's this for?" Jane asked.

"That's for making sure Frank understands who is in charge," Kathryn replied. "I will teach you how to use it before you go home. For now, just watch Terri and Maggie. You can learn something from what they are doing."

Jane looked at the two women. They were both standing next to Frank, pressing their bodies against him. They were both wearing teddies and little else. They were fondling Frank. Each had one hand on his ass and the other was fondling his cock and balls. Frank's cock was as hard as Jane had ever seen it and he was already leaking pre-cum, of which the two women were making good use.

Jane walked over to get a better view. She noticed that neither of them was touching him very firmly. "Do you always use such a light touch? He likes me to stroke his cock firmly."

Terri replied, "We are not trying to get him off, we are only teasing him. If he gets too close to cumming, I'll tell you to hit his ass with that paddle. Okay?"

"Oh," Jane said, "I get it, you don't want him to cum. You just want him to be all aroused. Right?"

"Maggie replied to Jane's query, "That's the point. The more we tease him without allowing him to cum, the more compliant he will be for you. By having you paddle him if he gets too close," she continued, "he will begin to understand who is in charge."

"Do you allow him to cum when you're through?" Jane asked.

"That depends on you," Terri said. "Do you want him to cum or do you want to deny him an orgasm until such time as he has earned it?"

"Earned it?" Jane was obviously unclear about what Terri meant by that.

"Yes," Terri continued, "whenever you decide that he deserves an orgasm, you can allow him to have one. Otherwise, he will just have to wait. The more you tease him, the more obedient he will be. Get it?"

Jane thought about that for moment. Then replied, "Yes, I think I do. In other words, I don't just tease him at night when we go to bed, but I can tease him in other ways throughout the day and that will keep him wanting to earn an orgasm. Right?"

"Exactly!" Maggie affirmed. "The more aroused you keep him, the more obedient he will be."

"But how do I know when he has earned an orgasm?" Jane asked.

"That's entirely up to you," Terri began, "but understand, once he has an orgasm he will be more difficult to control. That's, normal. You will find ways to handle that, though."

"Okay, so I don't want him to have too many orgasms, right?" Jane confirmed.

"You're getting it," Maggie said. "Your job now, is to learn all you can about how to tease him and keep him sexually aroused as much of the time as possible."

"So, do I have to let him watch dirty movies whenever he wants, or what?" Jane asked.

"Don't worry about all that, right now," said Terri, "all you need to do now is learn how to handle his cock and keep him from cumming when you don't want him to. Just watch what we do, then do it yourself at home."

Jane watched as the two women continued to whisper in Frank's ear and gently fondle his cock and ass. It really wasn't long before the two women stepped back and told Jane to paddle him because he was getting too close. Jane stepped up beside Frank and drew the paddle back. She glanced over at Maggie who gave her an affirmative nod.

With that, Jane swung the paddle until it made a soft "smack" on Frank's exposed bottom.

"Oh, you can do it much harder than that," Terri complained.

"Yeah," Maggie agreed. "Give it to him good. Get rid of that hard-on of his so we can start over."

With that, Jane felt encouraged. She took a deep breath and drew the paddle back again. This time she really it fly, and it made a much louder "smack" as it hit its target.

"Ahhhhh..." Frank let out a loud yell, almost as loud as the sound of the paddle hitting his tender flesh. "Ooowwww!" he yelled when the paddle struck him a third time.

"Shut up, wimp, "Maggie shouted at him, "or the next one will be even harder!"

Frank bit his lip and let out a whimper when each of the next three blows landed. He was almost in tears when Jane stopped and the two women moved in beside him again. His erection was definitely gone.

Maggie looked at Jane and asked, "You want to try your hand at this for awhile, Jane?"

Jane handed her the paddle and said, "Yeah, I've got to learn it sometime." She took Maggie's place next to Frank, one hand on his ass and the other taking turns with Terri fondling his cock and balls. She leaned in close and whispered in Frank's ear, "How would you like me to suck your cock and rub some nice soothing lotion on your poor bottom tonight?"

Frank mumbled as best he could, "Yes, Mistress." he could feel her hands on his private parts and remembered just how gentle those hands could be. He also remembered his cock in Jane's warm, wet mouth. Jane was always so good at sucking his cock. He always had trouble holding back when she did. But as he recalled, she was good at knowing just when to stop so that she could mount him before he came, too. Watching the two women licking and sucking each other's pussies on the big screen in front of him, plus the feeling of his wife's hand on his cock, combined with the thoughts of what she was whispering in his ear, was getting to be too much, and soon, Frank felt his hot steamy cum building up inside. He was getting ready to shoot a huge load and he knew it.

Just then, the two women stopped touching him. Jane was no longer whispering in his ear. He was ready, but no one was helping him any longer. He felt his cock swell and his balls pumping, but his load only dribbled out of his cock. Try as he might, he could not make it shoot. He was frustrated to no end. He could hear the women laughing at him. He was being made fun of because his cum would not shoot out as it always had in the past.

Then he felt the paddle strike his ass again. It hurt. It stung badly. There was nothing he could do about it. His cum stopped dribbling out and his ass grew very sore very quickly. Jane was wielding the paddle again. She was laughing both at the fact that he couldn't cum hard and that his ass was turning a bright red very quickly.

Jane stopped after five blows and said, "I get it now. This is fun! And I get to torture him like this anytime I want!?"

"Any time," Kathryn interjected. "We will teach you other ways of teasing him and other ways of humiliating him, if you like that sort of thing."

"Humiliating him?" Jane responded with delight. "I love that part! I guess I can do this. Take control of him, I mean."

"Of course, you can," Kathryn said. "You can do anything you want and we will teach you how."

"Tell me," Jane asked, "Why didn't his cum shoot out as it normally does?"

"That's what we call a 'ruined' orgasm," Kathryn explained. "He doesn't shoot his cum, as you say, because you stopped stimulating him just in time. If you had stroked his cock just one or two more times, he would have shot his load out hard. But since you ruined it, he is still horny and will be able to continue this way as long as you like."

Jane took a look at Frank's punished bottom and said, "He's not used to this, yet. Maybe we should stop for now and I can do it more this weekend. Is that okay?"

"Of course it is, my dear," Kathryn reassured her. "We will give you some literature to read that will help you in learning other methods of teasing him and punishing him for any disobedience. You can take until Monday to learn what you can and to teach him who is in charge. Come Monday, we will see what the both of you have learned and decide if you need any further treatments." She walked over to the little table and picked up the cock cage used to keep Frank from doing anything Jane didn't want him to. She placed it back on Frank's cock and snapped the lock shut.

"That would be great!" Jane replied. "I promise to practice hard until Monday."

"I am sure you will do very well," said Kathryn. "I'll have Terri bring Frank's clothes down here so that he can get dressed. You know the way out, don't you?"

"Yes, Ma'am I do," Jane replied very sure of herself.

"Good," Kathryn replied, "Then I'll see you at seven PM, Monday." She held out the keys to Frank's chastity belt ad said, "You'll need these if you are going to try some of the methods I the literature I gave you."

As Jane took the keys she said, "Thanks! I will try some them as soon as we get home."

With that, Kathryn headed off to the elevator.

Jane and Maggie released Frank form his bonds and helped him to a nearby chair to wait for Terri to bring his clothes. "Well, Frank," Jane began, "do you think you can behave yourself at home now?"

"Yes, Mistress." Frank said a little breathlessly. "I will do whatever you ask, Mistress."

When Frank's clothes arrived, he dressed, and he and Jane returned to their car.

~ ~ ~

Chapter 5
A LESSON IN TEASING

Once they were seated in their respective seats in the car, with Frank behind the driver's seat, Jane said, "I want you to stop off at that sex shop on Ninth Street on the way home, dear."

"Yes, Mistress," Frank replied. "Can I ask for what?"

"Yes, of course," Jane said. "I want you to pick up a couple of things on the way home. Some things we will be needing." She was being particularly evasive because she wanted it to be a surprise to Frank.

Frank started the car and backed out of the parking space. It was only about a little after three so there was plenty of time left in the day. He could see that Jane had something special in mind, but he was afraid to ask what it might me. He simply drove to the sex shop without a word.

Once Frank had parked the car, right in front, as Jane had requested, Frank asked, "What did you want to get here, Mistress?"

Jane looked over at him ad smiled one of those wicked little smiles she used whenever she had a secret that Frank new nothing about. "I'm not going in with you. I want you to pick up a small wooden paddle, a pair of wrist cuffs that can be fastened together, some condoms, lubrication, and a butt-plug." She stifled a snicker when she said it.

"What?" Frank asked, almost in horror. "You want me to buy all that stuff by myself?"

"Of course, dear," Jane replied. "And I want you to pick everything out yourself. Can you remember all that?"

"Yes, Ma'am," Frank replied. "A paddle, cuffs, condoms, lube and a plug."

"Very good," Jane said. "Now go. And don't take too long. I want to get home and try some of these things out."

Yes, Ma'am," Frank replied as he opened the driver's door and stepped out of the car. He leaned down and said, "I'll be right back, Mistress." And with that he closed the door and walked into the shop.

It was not one of those little shops where everything was jammed in tightly together, and the aisles were really narrow. No, this place was well lighted and very spacious. Frank was embarrassed when he had to ask where to find the butt-plugs. He had found everything else, but those had eluded him.

The guy at the counter told him to look on the wall, one aisle over from where he was. Frank picked out the first small plug he saw and hurried over to pay for the items Jane had requested.

Once he was back outside, Frank opened the driver's door and handed Jane the bag of toys he had just purchased, then climbed into the seat and fastened his seat-belt.

Jane looked at the items in the bag and said, "Good job. Now let's go home."

Frank started the car and drove home. Once inside, Frank remembered to remove his clothing as soon as he stepped in the door.

Jane ordered Frank to take his clothes to the bedroom and then meet her back in the living room. She had been reading the information on teasing that Kathryn had given her in the car on the way home. There were a few things she wanted try immediately, but there were far too many for her try all out at once. So she chose a couple to get her started.

When Frank finally entered the room after putting his clothes away, he started to sit down on the couch next to his wife. "What do you think you're doing?" she asked, with a stern look on her face. "I didn't give you permission to sit. Did I?"

Frank sprang to his feet and said, "No, Mistress. May sit down, Ma'am?"

"No you may not," Jane replied abruptly. "You will stand in front of, and facing me, unless I give you permission to sit. And you will stand there without a word until you are spoken to."

Frank was taken aback by Jane's obvious no nonsense attitude. He immediately stood up and stepped around the coffee table in front of him and took a position directly in front of his wife. "How's this, Mistress?"

"You were in the Army. Stand at parade rest," she barked.

Spreading his feet part and placing his hands behind his back, Frank replied, "Yes, Ma'am. How's this, Ma'am?"

"Much better," Jane said in a more relaxed tone. "Now, present your arms to me so that I can put these cuffs on you."

Frank held his arms out in front of him angled downward so that Jane could place the restraints on his wrists. "Why do we need these?" he asked.

"Because I want to make sure you don't try any funny business when I remove your chastity cage," Jane replied. "You need to learn to let me know

The Marriage Counselor

when you are on the edge of orgasm before it's too late. Before you ejaculate."

"Yes, Ma'am," Frank said as Jane finished buckling the second cuff firmly on his wrist.

Next, Jane took the new butt-plug out of its wrapper and applied a liberal amount of lubrication to it. She held it out in Frank's direction. "Put this where it belongs," she said in a firm tone.

Frank understood her meaning and bent down and reached between his legs. He carefully pushed the plug into his anus as he had been instructed. He had bought a small one, but right now, it didn't feel very small to him. At first, it was rather uncomfortable, but he soon got used to it as his anus quit trying to expel the thing.

Jane stood up and moved to where she could reach the tiny lock on Frank's chastity device. She inserted the key and looked up at Frank. "If you don't do exactly as I tell you, I will never remove this again. Do I make myself clear?" she said sternly.

"Yes, Ma'am," he replied.

With that, Jane turned the key and removed the lock followed quickly by the cage that prevented Frank's cock from becoming fully erect. She sat back down on the couch and grabbed the bottle of lubrication Frank had just bought. "Hold out your hand," she said.

Frank proffered his right hand and Jane poured a liberal amount of the gooey liquid into his palm.

"Now, cover your cock completely with that and start stoking it slowly," she instructed. "That's it," she said as he did as she had told him. "Now don't cum, but let me know when are right on the edge. Understand?"

"Yes, Mistress," Frank replied humbly. He knew he was in no position to disobey his wife. He was just not sure if he could stop before ejaculating. He had never done that before and wasn't sure he knew exactly how to tell until it was too late. But he was getting very aroused by both his wife's attitude and the situation in general. He kind of enjoyed being told to masturbate for her, even though it was very humiliating. Yes, he was embarrassed. He had never masturbated in front of anyone before, least of all his wife. He couldn't take his eyes off of her as she watched his every move.

"That's it, Sweetie," she encouraged. "Keep going until you feel like you are going to cum. Then stop. If you cum, I will be forced to punish you. You know what that means, don't you?"

"Yes, Ma'am," he replied, trying not to lose his concentration. Frank was almost tempted to go ahead and cum, even though Jane had promised to punish him if he did. After all, he didn't know how long she would make him go before allowing him an orgasm, and he did sort of enjoy the paddling she had given him at Kathryn's.

As his orgasm drew near, Frank decided not to push it this first time and he stopped, saying, "I am ready to cum, Mistress."

With that, Jane told him he had done a good job and then, after a brief rest, she made him repeat the procedure. In fact, she made him do it three more times.

By the time he stopped the forth time, Jane went to the kitchen to fetch a bowl of ice cubes. She began stroking Frank's cock with one of them and, despite his complaints about how cold the ice was, Jane continued until his cock had shriveled enough for her to replace the cage of his chastity belt.

Once she had locked it back in place, she removed the cuffs around Frank's wrists and told him that he needed to wash the dishes before dinner.

Needless to say, Frank thought that maybe this last time he should gone ahead and cum. He didn't realize Jane was going to leave him in such a frustrated state as he was now in.

Later, Frank made dinner for the two of them and they spent the rest of the evening discussing their new relationship. Frank was concerned about how often he would be allowed to have an orgasm. Jane assured him that he would get relief more often, the better he behaved. She assured him he would not lack for sexual attention, as she had plans to give him sexual attention every day.

They talked about all sorts of things and Jane answered all of Frank's questions, some a little bit vaguely. But she did answer them. They finally went to bed and held each other all night long.

It was a Sunday, not unlike any other Sunday as far as Frank was concerned, except that it was the first Sunday in his life that he wore a chastity belt. Frank slept naked for, maybe, the second or third time in his life. Certainly the first time since his honeymoon. He awoke early because the cage that confined his cock was causing him a little pain. He had to pee and, as often was the case, he had gotten a morning hard-on. But this time, the cage prevented him from getting completely hard and his cock was hurting.

He wandered into the bathroom and sat down to relieve himself. "How long," he wondered, "am I going to have to sit down like a woman to pee?" The thought left his mind quickly when he realized that he would not be able to masturbate, either. Frank was used to getting up early on Sunday mornings so that he could watch a video and relieve his sexual frustrations before Jane got out of bed. That would now be impossible. But he was extremely frustrated from yesterday's teasing and he needed relief.

Frank decided to go downstairs to the kitchen and make some coffee. While he sat there waiting for the coffee to finish dripping, he thought about how things had already changed and wondered what other changes might be forthcoming. Actually, he had to admit to himself that he kind of liked Jane being in charge. He liked serving her, as long he was told to do it naked. He liked the idea of more sex, though he wasn't sure exactly what that would entail. It turned him on when Jane would order him around. He didn't understand why, but it did.

When the coffee was finally ready, Frank went to get himself a cup. He heard Jane coming down the stairs. Glancing at the clock he realized it was almost nine o'clock. He got out two cups and poured one for Jane as well as one for himself. He set the two cups down on the table just as Jane entered the kitchen.

"Good morning, Mistress," he said as Jane sat down in front of one of the cups. "Did you sleep well?" he added.

Jane, still half asleep, gave her husband half a smile and said, "Yes, thank you, I did." Then she picked up her cup and sipped at it for a moment. "Thanks for the coffee, too."

"Would you like some breakfast, Mistress," he asked, hoping she wouldn't.

"Not really," Jane answered. "Maybe a slice of toast... with cinnamon sugar, too, please."

"Yes, Ma'am," Frank replied as sweetly as he could. Then he headed over to the counter and got out two slices of bread. He looked over his shoulder and asked, "May I have one, too, please, Mistress?"

"Yeah, sure. Whatever you want," Jane replied not really paying any attention. She needed to drink some more coffee before she would be ready to think about anything.

"Thank you, Ma'am," Frank said politely. Then he dropped the two slices of bread into the toaster and pushed the lever down. He walked back over to the table and sat down. "May I speak candidly for a minute?" he asked in a soothing tone.

"Sure," Jane replied, "what is it?"

Frank took a sip of his coffee and said thoughtfully, "You know, I think I am going to like having you in charge. I hate to admit it, but I actually enjoyed it when you paddled me yesterday. I don't know why, but it was kind of erotic."

Still holding her cup in front of her face, Jane looked up at Frank and said, "Really? You enjoyed that?"

"Uh... Yes Mistress, I did," Frank admitted again.

"I was afraid I was hurting you," she said.

"Well... you were," Frank began, "but I liked it. I also liked giving you head, again. It has been so long since I did that, I wasn't sure I was doing it right... Until you came so hard."

"Yes, well, that was nice," Jane said with a smile. "I am planning on getting a lot more of that kind of thing in the future."

"I would like that, too," Frank replied.

Jane perked up. She had an idea. Sliding her chair back from the table and turning it toward Frank, she said, "Why not do it again right now?" It was more of a command than a question, and Frank sensed that.

"Yes, Mistress," he said as he slipped off his chair and knelt in front of her. Resting his hands on her knees he gently pushed them, and her robe, open to allow himself room to do what he had been instructed to do.

Jane slid forward on her chair to grant him better access to her pussy. "Now don't be in such a hurry to get me off this time," she said. Then added, "Take your time. I want this to last awhile."

As Frank leaned in he replied, "Yes, Mistress." Then he gently ran his tongue upward, spreading her lips as he went. She was not as wet as the last time, so he took his time sucking each inner labia into his mouth and tugging each one gently.

Jane leaned her head back and closed her eyes. She wanted to relax and enjoy Frank's tongue. She moaned her pleasure so Frank would know he was doing a good job.

Frank used his thumbs to pull Jane's inner labia apart and allow his tongue better access to her clit. He was more gentle with it this time, though. Instead of flicking it hard, he ran the flat of his tongue up and over it. Then he repeated the process while listening to Jane as she moaned her delight. He drove his tongue deeply into her, now wet, hole and lapped up all the juices he could get. Then he returned to his long, slow tonguing of her clit. Back and forth, up and down, he ran this tongue over that tiny little nub until Jane tugged at his hair, pressing his face hard against her. Then he dug his tongue into her hole as deeply as he could, one last time, before he started flicking her clit in an effort to bring her to the brink of orgasm.

In seconds, Jane was screaming, "Yes... Yes... Yes!" as Frank's tongue did its job and pushed her over the edge. She pulled him tighter against her crotch until she had at least seven orgasms. Then she released her grip and Frank slowed his pace and lapped up all the juices he could get.

When it seemed that Jane was finished, Frank stopped and sat back on his ankles. "Was that what you wanted, Mistress?" he asked with a smile on his face.

Breathlessly, Jane replied, "Yes... Yes, it was perfect. You are getting better. I can't wait to see how you do tonight." Frank was proud of himself. He had a right to be, but his job wasn't done. "Stand up," Jane said.

Frank got to his feet and stood between her legs, "Yes, Mistress?" he said.

Jane sat up and leaned forward. His caged cock was right in front of her face. She reached out and took his balls in her hand. She squeezed them gently, then hefted them as if weighing them as one would a bag of gold. "I have some reading to do and I am going to need you so that I can practice a few things while I do."

"Yes, Mistress," he replied.

"And fix me another piece of toast," she added.

Somewhere along the line the toaster had popped up while Frank was too busy to notice. "Yes, Mistress," he said, "I guess the first piece is cold by now." He turned around and stepped over to the counter and prepared two more slices of bread, after tossing the first two into the trash bin.

"I'll be in the living room reading," Jane said as she stood up from her chair. "Bring that to me along with a fresh cup of coffee as soon as it's ready."

"Yes, Mistress," Frank responded, "It will be ready in a minute, Ma'am."

Jane wandered through the dining room and into the living room where she plopped herself down in her favorite spot on the sofa. She picked up the pamphlets that Kathryn had given her and looked at the them. She decided to read the one on teasing first. Dropping the other one on the end table, she began to read. Jane found that the pamphlet had a great number of ideas that she could use to tease Frank and to keep him aroused, even on those days when he was at the office. She was particularly intrigued by the section that described several ways she could physically tease Frank's cock both, while he was in his cock cage, and out of it.

When Frank brought her breakfast to her, she told him to set it down on the end table. Without even looking up from the page she was reading, she ordered Frank to go upstairs and make the bed. Then he was to get all the dirty laundry from the hamper and bring it down and start a load in the washer. Frank did as he was told without question and that, in itself, made her grin a little. She ate her toast, sipped her coffee and continued reading her pamphlet.

When Jane finished reading the pamphlet, she called Frank into the room. She ordered him to make her a sandwich and iced tea for lunch. It was almost one o'clock and she had been reading and thinking about all the things she could have Frank do for her that she had lost track of time.

Frank went into the kitchen and prepared Jane's lunch. He served it to her with all the newly required respect. He knelt in front of her and offered the meal by holding out until she took it from his hands.

Jane finally finished the first of the two pamphlets and called Frank back into the room. She had him stand directly in front of her with his legs spread, facing the television. With his back to her, she had access to his bottom and, by reaching between his legs, his balls as well. She began by gently running her fingernails up and down over the tender skin of his buttocks. Then she let them run softly up his inner thighs. Finally, she let her nails rack gently over his balls.

"How does that feel," she asked.

Mistress Ivey

"Wonderful, Mistress," Frank answered. "Please don't stop."

"I have no intention of stopping just yet," she said as her nails ran from the top of his balls to the bottom, sending chills up his spine and through his caged cock. "I want you to get turned on so much that you will beg me to stop. Then, maybe, I will." Jane had a smirk on her face. She was almost sorry Frank couldn't see it. With one hand, she continued teasing his balls while the other teased his bottom.

After about ten minutes of this Frank's cock was getting so hard that the cage encasing his cock was beginning to be too much for him. "Mistress?" he begged, "Please stop teasing me this way. My cock hurts from being confined and it wants to get hard."

"So you like this?" she asked with obvious joy in her voice.

"Yes, Mistress, but..." Frank was getting desperate, "I can't take it much longer unless you release my cock from this damned cage."

"I'm sorry," Jane replied almost sarcastically, "but I am having too much fun making you squirm."

"Please, Mistress. Please stop. I can't take it anymore," Frank begged as earnestly as he could.

"I'll stop on one condition," Jane said.

"Yes, Mistress, anything. It hurts!" There was genuine pain in his voice this time.

Jane put her hands in her lap and told Frank to turn around and face her. What she wanted him to do, she wanted to tell him face to face. Then she told him to kneel at her feet.

Once Frank was in the correct position, she said, "I want you to go out to the back yard and collect all the clothespins still on the old clothesline I used to use. Bring them to me."

"But... Mistress?" Frank protested.

"No 'buts' about it. Go now!" There was a firmness in Jane's voice that made Frank realize she was serious and no amount of protesting on his part was going to change her mind.

Frank went through the kitchen to the back door. He looked carefully through the window to make sure no one would be able to see him, but the fence was too high to see if anyone was in one of the neighbor's yards. They call it a 'privacy' fence, but right now, it didn't look too private, in Frank's eyes anyway. He eased open the door and stepped out onto the back porch. He looked at the old clothesline. It seemed terribly far away, all the way in the back corner. He decided to go for it.

Running as fast he could, Frank made it to the clothesline. He started grabbing all the old weathered clothespins still hanging on the line. As soon as he grabbed the last one, he turned and ran back to the porch, only to find Jane standing just inside the door. It was locked. "Let me in, I got the clothespins like you asked."

The Marriage Counselor

Jane yelled from inside the house, "How many did you get?"

Frank, feeling more vulnerable by the second, looked down at the pegs in his hands. He counted as quickly as he could. "Eleven," he announced loudly so Jane could hear him.

"Okay," she said, "put five of them back on the clothesline and I'll let you in."

Frank let out a breath of exasperation. He looked over his shoulder, drew in a deep breath and took off back across the lawn toward the clothesline. He quickly fastened five of them back onto the line and returned to the porch. Jane was gone, but the door was unlocked, so he turned the handle and let himself back into the house.

He found Jane sitting on the couch, right where he had left her. He knelt down and held out his hands with the six pegs he had gotten from the back yard.

Reaching out to take the pegs from Frank's hands Jane said, "Thank you. Now wasn't that fun?"

"Yes, Mistress," he replied, though he was wondering just who had the most fun.

"Stand up," she told him.

He stood up with the obligatory, "Yes, Ma'am," and stood there waiting for Jane's next command.

"I really like this new arrangement," she said as she fastened one of the pegs to his ball sack. "Does that hurt?"

"Not really, Mistress," he answered.

"Good," she said. "I have more." And with that she leaned over and fastened three more pegs to his ball sack. "How about those?"

"They are uncomfortable, but they don't hurt," he replied.

Jane sat up in her seat and reached up and attached the remaining pegs to Frank's nipples. "How do those feel?" she asked.

"Those do hurt, but it's not unbearable," he replied.

"Good," Jane said, "just stand there for a few minutes. I want to see how long you can stand all those." In the meantime, Jane watched his cock carefully. She began telling Frank all the things she could do with him. She told him she was planning to bind him to the bed so she can tease his cock as much as she liked. She told him how she wanted to put some numbing cream on his cock and ride him until she had as many orgasms as she could stand while still denying him one.

Before long, Frank's cock expanded as much as his cock cage would allow. He began complaining about the pain it was causing him. Jane just started making fun of him and the fact that he had six pegs on him and all he could do was to complain about his cock.

After about ten minutes, Jane decided he had had enough. She removed the pegs and allowed his cock to shrink to the point where Frank could endure it. But every time he started to shrink too much, Jane would tell him some more things she planned to do with him which only made his cock swell again.

Jane spent over an hour making Frank's poor cock expand and contract over and over again. She was loving the power she just realized that she held over his erections, his pain, and him.

Finally, Jane gave poor Frank a break. She ordered him to go finish the laundry and not to return until it was all washed, dried and folded.

Frank spent the next two hours in the laundry room, but when he was finally finished, he brought the basket of clean clothes back into the living room for Jane's approval. She told him to put them away and then prepare to cook dinner.

When Frank returned, Jane told him that there were two steaks in the refrigerator that he was to cook for their dinner. She told him to make baked potatoes and some green beans to go with them. Meanwhile, Jane finished reading the pamphlets that Kathryn had given her.

When it was ready, Frank served dinner at the dining table and Jane complemented him on how well he had done. The steaks were cooked perfectly and the food was delicious.

When Frank had cleared, and washed the dinner dishes, Jane called him back into the living room. She praised him for the job he had done and told him to relax on the couch next to her. Jane, having never been out of the house that day, was still wearing her bathrobe. She let Frank fondle her breasts for a few minutes then she announced that they were going to watch the same movie they had watched before.

She picked up the remote and turned the television on. Then she clicked play on the DVD remote and the movie loaded up again. One last click of the play button and the movie started. Jane allowed Frank to fondle her breasts for a while until she noticed Frank's cock was not straining against its cage. So, she reached over and began fondling his balls.

It wasn't long before Frank was in obvious pain. Jane stopped the movie and invited Frank to go upstairs. She wanted a repeat of that mornings oral activity.

Frank followed her to the bedroom where Jane laid on her back, legs spread wide and her bathrobe spread out around her like angel wings.

Frank climbed up on the foot of the bed and buried his face in her crotch. He took his time, even though he was in a great deal of pain. He licked her outer labia. He licked her inner labia. Finally he began sticking his tongue as deeply into her hot, wet hole as far as he could. Her juices were just as sweet as they had been the first time he ever got to taste them. In spite of the intense pain his cock cage was causing him, Frank pressed on. He licked in and around every nook and cranny of Jane's sweet pussy until she was overwhelmed by her own desires. He continued to devour her sweetness until she had had several orgasms and was pushing his head away.

Jane was completely exhausted. She thanked Frank for the orgasms and laid back on her pillow. Frank climbed up the bed and laid next to her. "I love you, Mistress," he whispered in her ear.

"I love you, too, sweetheart," Jane replied. "Let's get some sleep now."

Frank agreed and they fell asleep in each other's arms for the second time in years.

~ ~ ~

Chapter 6
THE SHOPPING TRIP

Frank awoke to the infernal sound of the alarm clock that sat on his nightstand. He had already hit the snooze button twice, and now he had to get up. There was no time to waste. He had to get up, brush his teeth, pee, shower and shave. The usual morning routine. It was Monday and Frank had to find a way to tell Mr. Bradly he had not signed up that new client he said he was meeting on Friday. Thoughts raced through his head, lies, half-truths and the whole truth. But which one was he going to tell his boss? He couldn't tell him the truth, that it was all a rouse to get him into marriage counseling, and that he had been forced into wearing a chastity device. He thought about it while he was getting ready to leave for work. He thought about it in the car while driving to work. He prayed about it. He just could not come up with a good excuse why he hadn't signed on a new client.

As he pulled onto the lot and drove to the trailer he called his office, he noticed that Mr. Bradly's car wasn't in its usual spot. In fact, it wasn't anywhere on the lot. Mr. Bradly always got to work before Frank. In fact, Mr. Bradly had never been this late as long as Frank had worked for him. He even came in and made sure everyone knew what to do when he was sick. Frank thought his prayers had been answered. Maybe he wouldn't have to explain the lack of a new client if Mr. Bradly didn't show up.

Feeling relieved that he would not have to explain himself to Mr. Bradly, Frank's attitude changed, he was suddenly happy, again. But when he opened the door to his office, he discovered Mr. Bradly sitting in a chair waiting for him. His heart sank. He was suddenly terrified.

"There you are," Chuck said. "I new you wouldn't let me down. So how did it go with the new client? Did you sign them up?" Mr. Bradly seemed to be in an exceptionally good mood, but Frank thought that was because he was supposed to have signed a new client Friday, after work.

The Marriage Counselor

"Uh... I'm fine, Chuck," Frank stammered, trying to think of a way out of telling Mr. Bradly the truth. "I'm just fine. I didn't see your car outside, what happened?"

"Oh, I needed to get some work done on her so I had my mechanic drop me off. He'll bring her by when he's done with her," Chuck answered. "Say, how did it go with that new client last Friday?"

"Uh... Well," Frank searched for the right words to break the news to his boss, but nothing was coming to mind. "To be honest, Chuck, I didn't get it. The new client, I mean. I mean, she wasn't a prospective client as it turned out."

Chuck broke out in laughter, "So, you got roped in too, huh?"

"Wha... What do you mean?" Frank didn't understand. He had just given his boss bad news and he was laughing at him.

"I know why you went to that meeting," Chuck explained. "Remember last year when my wife and I were having all that trouble? Remember when I would sleep in my office just so I wouldn't have to go home? Then Sally made me go to a marriage counselor and all?"

Frank thought for moment, then said, "Oh yeah. I remember that. You guys got it all straightened out in only a couple of sessions as I recall."

"That's right, Frank," Chuck said. "Did you know it was the same counseling agency that you went to on Friday?"

"What?" Frank was confounded. How did his boss know where he had gone? "How did you know..."

"Because they called me before they called you, silly," Chuck replied. "They wanted to make sure you could get off work a little early for your first session."

"So you knew?" Frank asked in amazement. "You knew that I was going to a marriage counselor and that there was no client?"

"Right," Chuck replied. "So, tell me, how does it feel? I mean, is it giving you any trouble?"

"Is what giving me any trouble?" Frank was confused.

"You know," Chuck said. "The chastity belt. Is it giving you any trouble?"

Frank came to the sudden realization that his boss knew all about the treatments at Kathryn's. And that Chuck himself had had to wear a chastity belt just like his. "You know about that?" he asked, as if he hadn't just figured it out.

"Of course, Chuck replied. "I'm still wearing mine."

"What?" Frank was shocked to hear that Mr. Bradly, his boss, his friend, was wearing a chastity belt. "You're still wearing one? After what, fifteen months?"

Chuck laughed, "Yeah, you didn't think you were going to lose it just because you went to all the required sessions, did you?"

"Well, yeah, I did," Frank said feeling a little shocked and betrayed. "You mean I will have to keep this thing on indefinitely?"

"No. You won't have to wear it all the time," Chuck said. "I'm sure Jane will take it off when she wants to play with your dick or maybe even to give you a break, sometime."

"My God," Frank said as he sank deep into thought and his chair. "I never thought of that."

"Well," Chuck said in an attempt to console his friend, "you might just want to give it some thought. After all, Jane is in charge, now."

"That's true," he replied. "I guess things will be different for a lot longer than I thought."

"It ain't so bad," Chuck said patting his friend on the shoulder. "After all, things will be a whole lot better in the sex department. Isn't that worth something?"

Frank realized that he did enjoy the idea that he would be getting whole lot more sex. And he did kind of like Jane being in charge of everything. "I guess it is. Tell me, are things really as good as promised?"

"Yeah, buddy," Chuck replied, "they are." Chuck headed for the door, but just as he opened it, he turned back toward Frank and said, "Things could be a whole lot worse. Kathryn has asked me to build her a whole new facility and guess who is going to design it?" With that he stepped out and pulled the door shut behind him.

Frank suddenly realized that maybe, just maybe, this marriage counseling stuff wouldn't be so bad after all. A new commercial building meant a great deal more money for the company and possibly a raise for himself. After all, he would get to design it. He sat down at his desk and started thinking about how he might be moving up in the world.

Frank spent the rest of the day doing his job and thinking about Jane and what kinds of things she might do, sex-wise, to liven things up a bit. After all, she had promised him more sex than he had dreamed of. That was a pretty tall order in itself. Frank could really dream...

Jane woke up about eight-thirty. She showered and made the bed, drank a cup of coffee. Then she remembered that she had another pamphlet to read. She poured herself another cup and went into the living room to read. This pamphlet was titled 'Discipline & Punishment' and promised to teach her how to maintain control of her husband. That was something she definitely wanted to know more about. It was even thicker than the first pamphlet she read.

It took her about forty-five minutes to read it, the first time. She read it twice to be sure she understood the concepts the pamphlet contained. Then she took out her trusty note pad and scribbled a list of items she would

The Marriage Counselor

need to start out. A quick check on the Internet and she had all the information she needed.

She picked up her cell phone and typed in a message to Frank. She listed everything that she thought she would need and that she wanted him to purchase and hit the send button.

Frank picked up his cell phone to see who had sent him a message. He was shocked when he read what Jane had sent. It was a list of items that she wanted him to get before he went home from work. There were several types of lubricants, a realistic dildo, a set of training butt-plugs, whatever they were, a riding crop and another paddle. Frank was more than a little shocked. As he looked over the list he realized each item was a hyper-link to a web-site. He clicked on one of them and discovered the web-site was that sex shop on the East side of town. She had used the Internet to find these items, but instead of ordering them, she wanted him to actually go to the store and purchase them himself.

Frank had never been in that sex shop before last Saturday, or any other sex shop, for that matter. He was too embarrassed to set foot in a place like that. Besides, if he bought the kinds of things on Jane's list, they would think he was some kind of pervert or something. He didn't think he could actually do that. He thought maybe he could just order them himself and avoid all the embarrassment of actually having to go to the store.

Just then the phone rang. It was Jane. He pressed the button to answer the call and said, "Jane, are you nuts?"

Jane laughed through the phone and said, "No, I'm not nuts. I want you to go to the sex shop and purchase all those items before you come home tonight."

"I can't go in there," Frank protested, "They will think I am some kind of pervert! I was just in there Saturday. Going back now will look like I am addicted to kinky sex!"

"No it won't," she replied. "People buy that kind of stuff all the time. Sure, you'll be embarrassed, but I want that. I like knowing that you are humiliated while doing something just because I asked you to. It's not like I am asking you to walk down Main Street naked or anything."

"Yes, but..." Frank was getting nervous. "But I can't do it. I can't go in there in broad daylight. Somebody will see me. Somebody I know!"

"Of course, they will see you," Jane chuckled, "You can't buy anything without being seen. Just think, if someone you know is in the store, why are they there? Because they are buying sex stuff, too. That's why. And if they see you go in or come out, who cares?"

"I do!" Frank said into the phone. "I care. I don't want my reputation as an architect ruined because someone saw me going into that store."

"Don't be silly," she said trying to reason with him. "Just because you buy stuff at a sex shop doesn't mean your reputation as an architect is in any danger of being ruined. Hell, you want to see ruined? Wait until you see what I have planned for your next orgasm."

"What? Frank was getting even more nervous now. "What do mean? What are you talking about?"

"Just relax," Jane said trying to calm her husband down. "No one will think you're perverted or anything. Just go to the store and pick up the things on that list before you come home tonight. You can do that. And nobody cares what you do in your spare time, at home. Trust me."

"Yes, dear," Frank replied.

"Don't you mean 'Mistress', Frank?" she said sternly.

"Yes, Mistress." he said in compliance. "I'll get the stuff you ordered." there was a hint of defeat in his voice. "I'll see you around six, then."

"That's better," she conceded. "Don't you dare forget anything on that list. Bye, now." Jane clicked the button to end the call without waiting for Frank to say, "Good-bye."

Frank put down the phone and thought about what he had just agreed to do. "Was there nothing he wouldn't do for his wife?" he thought to himself. "What will she ask of me next? Will she make me walk down Main Street naked or what?"

At five o'clock, Frank packed up his briefcase and headed out to his car. He drove out to the East side of town to the sex shop he had passed so many times before. He pulled into the parking lot and looked around to see if there was anybody he knew hanging around. When he didn't see anyone, he got out of his car and hurried into the store. He was amazed at how brightly lit it was inside. He had thought it would be dimly lit and dirty, but this place was as clean as the local super market.

He looked around and realized that he would not be able to find everything on Jane's list by himself. There were just too many items in that place. He started toward the back where he could see a wall of what looked like dildos hanging on it. He no sooner got there than a young, attractive woman stepped up to him and said, "Can I help you find something?"

Frank turned a very bright shade of red. About the same shade as the hair of the woman who had just spoken to him. "Uh... Yeah, I guess so," he replied trying to hide his nervousness. He quickly pulled out his cell phone and recalled the message Jane had sent him.

"Oh," said the clerk, "You have a list?"

"Uh, yeah," he said, hoping she couldn't hear the sheer terror in his voice. "My wife sent it to me."

"Here," she said gently taking the phone from his hand. "Let me see. Okay, yeah, we have all this stuff." She started walking along the wall looking for the exact dildo on the list. Reaching up to the top row, she slid one fairly large realistic-looking dildo off its hook. She held it in front him and announced, "This is it."

Frank took the package from her and looked around for some way to hide it. The sales clerk reached behind him and grabbed a small shopping basket from a stack at the end of an aisle. "Here," she said, "try this," and she handed Frank the basket.

"Uh... Thanks," was all he could think of to say. He dropped the rather scary-looking phallus into the basket and followed the woman along the wall a little farther. She looked over one section carefully and finally grabbed a set of butt-plugs and handed them to Frank. He was beginning to become more relaxed since the clerk seemed to be very professional. Still, his list was far from complete. He looked over the set of three plugs and dropped them in the basket along with the dildo.

"Follow me," the woman said, "the crops and paddles are over there." She pointed in the general direction of one corner of the store.

Frank followed her like a puppy dog following a handful of treats. When they arrived at the display of riding crops, the clerk looked carefully at Frank's phone that was still in her hand. Then she reached over and took one of the crops out of the stand and said, "This looks like the one." She handed it to Frank.

Frank thought it looked pretty frightening, but it did look like the one on his phone. He took it from her and tried to fit it into the basket. It stuck out the back like a flag. He followed the clerk a few feet to the wall where there was a huge collection of paddles of all shapes and sizes. The woman said, "It's really hard to tell which one she wants. So many of them look alike and I can't tell what size this one is." She was staring at the tiny screen of Frank's phone in an attempt to ascertain exactly which paddle was pictured there. She held it in front of Frank and asked, "Can you tell?"

Frank squinted at the tiny screen, then looked at the paddles on the wall. "It looks like one of those," he said, pointing to a section of about ten or twelve paddles.

"Yeah, I can see that," the clerk acknowledged, "but I can't tell how big it is from this photo."

Frank realized that he was going to have to choose one himself. So many of the paddles had the same shape, though they were different sizes. His red ass and an angry look on Jane's face flashed before his eyes. He was sure that if he chose the wrong one she would make him pay for it, and not with cash either... With his ass! "I don't know...," Frank looked scared. "I guess that one will do the job." He had picked out a fairly large paddle knowing that if he got one too small, Jane would be furious with him. At least, that's what went through his mind.

The sales clerk reached up and pulled the paddle Frank had indicated off the rack and handed it to him. Frank was so afraid of getting the wrong one he asked the clerk, "Do you think she will be happy with this one?"

The poor woman looked at the fear in Frank's face. She placed her hand reassuringly on his shoulder and said, "I'm sure it will be fine." Then she guided him to a rack of lubrications near another corner of the store. "We should be able to find all these lubes on this rack," she said with a smile. Reaching for one of the bottles she added, "This is the anal lube your wife wanted." And she handed Frank the bottle.

"How do you know what my wife wants?" Franks asked nervously.

"Because..." the woman began, speaking slowly, "your wife sent you this list of things to buy?"

"Oh, yeah," Frank muttered, "that's right." He took the bottle of lubricant and dropped into his basket.

"Here's the silicone based lube she asked for..." the clerk said as she handed him another bottle. "And the water based lube..." she took another bottle from the rack and handed it to Frank. "And this is the numbing lube she wanted. There. You're done. That wasn't so bad. Was it?"

Frank felt a wave of relaxation flow over his entire body. He was done. Now all he had to do was pay for the stuff and he could leave. "Not so bad," Frank admitted with a half-smile.

The sales clerk led Frank back to the front of the store where she stepped behind the checkout counter. Frank set the basket of goods on the counter and she began to ring them up. "That's one hundred-eighteen dollars and forty-two cents," she announced after punching the 'Total' button.

Frank took his Visa card out of his wallet and handed it to the nice woman. "This should cover it," he said.

The sales clerk slid Frank's card through the slot on the card-reader and pointed to the keypad. "You need to enter your pin number, Sir."

Frank looked down and realized what the woman was trying to tell him. "Oh, yeah, sorry," he said as he began pressing the keys on the little number pad. "There you go," he said when he was finished.

The woman behind the counter tore off the slip of paper that was ejected from the machine and handed it, and his Visa card, to Frank. "And there you go," she said with a smile. "Come back and see us any time." She handed him the bag of goodies he had just purchased with the handle of the paddle and the floppy end of the riding crop sticking out the top.

Frank nodded in her direction with as much of a smile as he could work up, then headed out the door. He kept his head down so no one would recognize him as he hurried to his car. He placed the bag on the seat next to him, on top of his brief case. He looked at his watch and started the car. He estimated that he would arrive home just about six o'clock like he told Jane. All the way home he tried to forget about his shopping ordeal and hoped the paddle he picked out would be the right one.

~ ~ ~

Chapter 7
GRADUATION DAY

When Frank entered the front door, Jane was waiting for him on the sofa. "Did you get everything I asked for?" she said before he could even set his briefcase down.

"Yes, Mistress," he replied. "I wasn't sure about the paddle. I hope I got the right one." He handed her the bag of items from the sex shop.

Jane accepted the bag and immediately dumped the entire contents out onto the sofa next to her. One by one, she examined each item before slipping it back into the bag. When she came to the riding crop, she smacked the palm of her hand with it a couple of times and smiled. Then she dropped it into the bag as well. Finally, she picked up the paddle. She examined it carefully. She weighed it in her hand, then waved it around as if she were using it. "This paddle is bigger than I thought, but I guess it will work."

Frank sighed a huge sigh of relief. He was certain she would hate it and make him return it to the store right then and there.

Jane put the paddle back in the bag and said, "Put these in our room and I'll get the burgers and fries I bought for dinner. Frank took the bag and headed upstairs. "Oh, and don't bother getting undressed. We have to leave for Kathryn's as soon as we finish eating. But take off that tie," she added.

Frank took the bag from her hand and headed up the stairs. He was relieved that Jane had accepted the paddle he bought and that he didn't have to get undressed for dinner. He removed his tie and laid it on the bed alongside the bag from the sex shop.

When he returned to the living room, Jane was carefully unpacking the bag of burgers she had bought at a fast-food joint a few blocks away. "Sit right here," she said patting the cushion next to her. "We can eat, then we have to get to Kathryn's right away."

Frank took the seat next to his wife and she handed him a paper-wrapped burger and a cardboard container of fries. She had already set a drink on the end table for him. "I got you tea," she said. "I hope that's alright."

"That's fine," he replied. He really didn't care as long as it was wet.

They didn't talk much as they ate, but they both knew what was coming. Another session at Kathryn's. That meant pain for him and fun for her. Frank just hoped it wouldn't be too long a night. He was tired after working all day and didn't know if he could take too much of whatever Kathryn might have planned for them.

When they had finished their burgers, Frank balled up the wrappers and took the empty fry containers and stuffed them all back into the bag they came in. He headed off toward the kitchen to dispose of the evidence. When he returned, he opened the door for Jane and followed her out to his car. He opened the front passenger door and held it while Jane sat in her seat. After closing the door, he walked around to the driver's side and climbed in.

On the way to Kathryn's, Jane asked Frank how it felt to go to the sex shop and make the purchases she had picked out from their web-site. He admitted to his embarrassment, and she pressed him to elaborate. He explained how he thought he would just find everything himself and make the entire ordeal less humiliating, but the woman who helped him find everything had been very professional and she had helped him to relax. He even confessed that the paddle had been his choice because they all looked alike except for the size.

Jane laughed at his dilemma over the paddle. "I am just proud of you for overcoming your fears and doing exactly what I asked," she reassured him. "It shows me that you really want this thing to work."

Frank thought for moment then responded, "I do want it to work. I found out that Chuck went to Kathryn's last year when he and Sally were having difficulties. He told me that everything was great between them because of it."

"I didn't know that," she admitted. "I just saw an ad in the yellow pages and figured if they guaranteed success, we had nothing to lose. Right?"

"I guess you're right about that," Frank admitted. "What have we got to lose?"

Frank pulled the car into a parking space right in front of Kathryn's place. He turned off the engine and looked at Jane. She was looking back at him. "Ready?" she asked.

"Yes, Ma'am," he replied. "Let's go."

With that, he climbed out of the car and walked around to open the door for Jane. Once they got inside, they were met by Maggie. She told Jane that Kathryn wanted to see her for a minute in her office and that Frank was to go ahead and get undressed in the same room he did before.

Jane followed Maggie to Kathryn's office while Frank entered the dressing room and began to remove his clothes. That's when it hit him. He had not had an orgasm for more than a week, unless you count that dribble that he had the last time he was in Kathryn's dungeon, and he didn't. He hoped that things would be different tonight.

When she entered Kathryn's office, Kathryn was waiting for her. "How are you doing?" Kathryn asked gesturing for Jane to take a seat.

"Good," Jane replied as she eased into one of the chairs. "I've been good."

"Did you read those pamphlets I sent home with you?" Kathryn asked.

"Yes I did." Jane said proudly.

"Well, do you have any questions?" Kathryn asked.

"Well, not really a question," Jane began, "more of a fear."

"I'm here to help," Kathryn said, placing her elbows on the desk and leaning forward. "What seems to be the problem?"

Jane took a deep breath before answering her. "I am afraid of hurting Frank if I paddle him to hard and I have never used a riding crop or a cane before."

Kathryn smiled warmly and said, "Don't worry about that. That's why we're here tonight. You will not leave until you understand just how to use them without harming him. We will teach you how and when to use each one and you won't have to be afraid any more."

"Jane felt reassured by Kathryn's words. "Thank you," she said, "that makes me feel better about the whole thing."

"So, if there are no more questions," Kathryn said, pushing herself up from her desk, "shall we get started?"

"I'm ready," Jane replied as she stood up and followed Kathryn out of the office.

Frank was waiting for someone to get him and take him downstairs to the dungeon. The longer he waited the more nervous he became. Finally, Maggie opened the door and offered her hand, "Ready?" she asked.

Frank took her hand and responded, "Ready as I'll ever be." Maggie led him to the elevator and pressed the down button. Frank, even though Maggie had seen him naked before, was still self-conscious about it. He tried not to look in her direction.

As the elevator door slid open, Maggie said, "Here we are." And she gestured for Frank to enter first.

Frank stepped into the elevator followed by Maggie who pushed the 'B' button for the basement. "Shouldn't that be a 'D' for dungeon?" he said jokingly. It was his way of hiding his nervousness.

"You're not the first one to think of that." Maggie told him. "Maybe we can get it changed."

When the elevator doors opened again, Jane and Terri were both standing there waiting. Terri offered her hand to Frank and said, "Come with me."

Frank took her hand and dutifully followed her to a large wooden table. "Face the end of the table and lean over," she said. Then she took his arms, one at a time and fastened them to leather cuffs causing him to stretch just a bit to reach them. Then she put leather cuffs around his ankles and fastened those to the legs of the table. There he was, all spread and bound for whatever Kathryn and Jane, had in mind for him.

Frank couldn't see Jane or Kathryn. Terri was standing at the head of the table wearing a sheer, black teddy that really set her hair off. He could just make out her nipples through the thin material. His cock began to respond just a little. Not enough to cause him any pain, though.

Just then he heard Kathryn's voice. She was explaining to Jane how she could use their dinner table to bind him in the same manner at home. "God," he thought, "don't tell her that! All I need is for her to figure out how to make a dungeon out our dining room."

Then, the conversation changed. Frank really didn't like the way it was going now. Kathryn was using a riding crop to show Jane exactly where to strike his ass. She wasn't hitting him with it, but in his current position, he felt quite vulnerable.

Jane was asking questions about how hard she should hit him and what would happen if she accidentally hit him too hard or in the wrong place. He heard Kathryn say something about that wouldn't matter since the riding crop was very versatile and easy to use. That wasn't very reassuring to Frank. Kathryn explained the different ways Jane could use the riding crop, as well. It could be used like a cane if she allowed the shaft of the crop to strike across Frank's bottom. Or she could strike him with just the tip, or flapper, as it was called.

Then he heard the words he had been anticipating ever since he first heard Kathryn's voice behind him, "Go ahead and try it, Jane," she said. And then... Smack! Frank could feel a welt beginning to form. It extended from one cheek of his ass to the other in a nice straight line. The pain seemed to spread out from that line of impact as if it were a delayed reaction of his body to the sudden sharp pain the shaft of the crop had left.

"Very good," Kathryn's voice announced. "Get up close and see what that did. See it? See the initial point of impact and how the redness is spreading out from there?"

"Yeah, I do," Jane replied as if studying something intently. Frank knew just what that something was, too. His butt!

"Take a couple more swats until you get comfortable with it," Kathryn said.

"Okay," Jane said. That was quickly followed by three more smacks to Franks tender ass.

Frank did his best to remain silent. He was only successful until the last blow. It felt like his skin had been ripped open and he let out a "Yelp!"

Kathryn showed Jane how to use the flapper to create a single spot of pain by repeatedly striking the same spot with the tip of the crop. Jane was a fast learner and Frank's ass was a testament to that. Jane would start gently, but each stroke would be just little harder until she was really smacking Frank's ass hard. Then it would suddenly stop. After a short break, Jane would repeat the process on another part of Frank's bottom. By the time she was finished, Frank thought his butt was on fire.

But that was not the worst of it. Jane had to practice hitting Franks balls, too. At first, Jane was tapping them gently and it didn't even hurt, but then, suddenly, Jane came into her own and began to smack his balls with the flapper like an expert. And it DID hurt...Immensely! Frank let out a scream of pain that he was sure was heard by anyone passing by on the street outside.

Jane immediately quit and Frank heard her say, "Ooops. I guess that was too hard."

To which Kathryn replied, "Depends on what you want to accomplish. I'm sure you got his attention with that last one." Then Frank could swear he heard her giggle.

Next on the agenda was the cane. Frank had hoped they would skip that one since Jane had not asked him to buy one at the sex shop earlier. But his hopes were dashed when he heard Kathryn say, "Now you don't want to hit too hard with that. At least, until you know what he can really take."

Then he heard Jane say, "You mean, like this?"

Frank's ass tensed up and he felt the cane rip a slash across his butt that he was sure had drawn blood.

"Very good." Kathryn said. "You are getting the hang of this punishment thing, aren't you?"

To which Jane replied, "I thought that was the whole purpose of this session."

"Yes, in part," Kathryn said. "Now I want you to take this paddle and turn his entire bottom as red as that last stripe you just gave him." That made Frank cringe. He braced himself as best he could, knowing how hard Jane could hit his ass with the paddle. He couldn't help thinking that perhaps he had bought too big a paddle.

Just as Frank was certain she was going to hit his ass with the paddle, he heard Jane ask, "Should I start out easy, or just jump right in?"

To which Kathryn replied, "Any way you want to, sweetie. He's your husband. Let him know what awaits him if he disobeys you."

With that, Jane took a huge back swing and hit poor Frank's bottom as hard as she could. Frank heard the 'smack' and then instantly felt the pain. It shot through his whole body like someone had shocked him with an electrical charge. He screamed his discontent, but it did no good. The first blow was followed quickly be a second, and then a third. Frank was screaming, "Stop, stop, stop! I can't take any more."

To which Jane replied with a chuckle in her voice, "Sorry, dear, I just had to get all my years of frustration out. I hope you understand." And with that, she struck him three more times. His bottom was redder than Jane ever thought it could be. She looked at Kathryn and asked, "How was that?"

"Great!" Kathryn replied, "But I think we better stop there. He will bare those marks for several days, I'm afraid. I don't think he can take any more and there are still a few things I want to show you."

Franks bottom was truly on fire. He had never felt pain such as this before. There were tears streaming down his face. His bottom had never felt so sore. He hoped that that part of the session was truly over. He didn't ever want to feel anything like that again. He knew now that he would have to obey Jane or she would really give it to him.

"Here, Jane," Kathryn said as she handed something to the woman whose husband was still splayed out before them. "Rub some of this Tiger Balm on his balls and his anus."

"What?" Frank thought to himself. "What the hell was 'Tiger Balm'?" It sounded soothing and he hoped that it would feel good.

Jane took the little tin from Kathryn and scooped out a little bit of the salve with her fingertips. "Like this?" she asked as she began to massage Frank's balls with it.

"That's, right," Kathryn replied. "Now rub the excess over his anus between his cheeks."

Frank could feel Jane's fingers rake gently across his anus. Then the burning hit. "Argh!" was all that came out of his open mouth. It felt like his balls and his ass were just set on fire...Again! Well, in some new places as well. His balls began to feel the burn almost as quickly as his ass did. He looked into Terri's eyes and she could see the tears pouring out of his. He was begging her, with his eyes, to make it stop. To make the pain and burning go away. But Terri could do nothing to help him. She was only there to watch and make sure he wasn't harmed by anything Jane did. Tiger Balm, no matter how much it burned, would never actually harm him.

Frank couldn't see what, but Kathryn handed something else to Jane. "It's all lubricated so go ahead and insert it," she said.

The Marriage Counselor

Again, Frank had no idea what they were about to do to him, but he knew, somehow, he wasn't going to like it.

Then he felt something being pressed against his anus. Jane was pushing something hard, yet flexible into his poor abused ass. Was it a butt-plug? Or maybe a dildo? As the thing pushed its way passed his sphincter, he could tell it was not a butt-plug. It was, in fact, a dildo of a smallish size. But all Frank knew was that it hurt and he didn't like it one bit.

"Relax," Jane said leaning over his back to speak softly to him. But Frank couldn't relax. Not with this monster of a cock being rammed up his ass. The truth was, it was rather small as dildos go, but to Frank, it was huge. He had never had anything bigger than a doctor's finger, or perhaps a thermometer, inserted in there before and he just couldn't relax. It was much larger than the butt-plug he had bought a few days ago. That one was no bigger than his own finger.

Finally, Jane stopped pushing and Frank began to relax his sphincter. Then Jane was able to gently ease the rest of the dildo into his tender bottom. She leaned over Frank's back again and whispered, "Get used to it, buddy. I like doing this."

With that, the last of Frank's dignity flew out the window. There he was, strapped to a table while his wife fucked him with a fake cock and three other women watched. He was certainly glad none of his friends could see him, now. He would never be able to face them again.

When Frank was finally able to focus, and keep his sphincter relaxed, the dildo didn't feel so bad. Jane was gently guiding it in and out with smooth, even strokes. In fact, it was becoming quite erotic and Frank realized his cock was starting to get hard. Now he would have to deal with the pain of a hard-on on top of everything else.

After what seemed like an eternity, Jane slowly removed the dildo from his ass. It felt really good to have it out. His sphincter closed as the tip of the cock-shaped device slipped effortlessly out of his ass. Frank breathed a sigh of relief and collapsed, as much as possible in his predicament. He was exhausted.

Kathryn announced that the session was over. Frank let out a big sigh of relief, though he knew his pain would not stop. Terri released Frank's bonds one at a time and he was finally able to stand up straight. His muscles ached and his bottom, balls and anus were all still on fire, but he could relax now. It was over.

Kathryn told Terri to take Frank back to the dressing room and then to her office once he was fully dressed again. Terri guided Frank to the elevator and the two stepped through the opening and the doors closed behind them.

"You did very well." Kathryn said to Jane. "Do you still feel any fear or doubt about your ability to control Frank?"

"No, Ma'am," she replied. "I think I can handle him pretty well by myself, now."

"Good," Kathryn said. "Come with me to my office. I have something for you and Frank, when he gets there."

The two of them walked to the elevator and pressed the button to call it. A few minutes and a short elevator ride later and they were sitting in Kathryn's office waiting for Frank to finish dressing and join them.

"Jane?" Kathryn queried. "If there is ever anything you need, advice, another session for some reason, or whatever, just call me. I will be here to help you with anything."

"Thank you," Jane replied. "That's a big help. I know that there will be someone I can turn to should any problems arise."

When he was finally dressed, again, Frank headed out into the hallway to Kathryn's office. He stood outside the open door, waiting for permission to enter. Kathryn noticed him right away and invited him to join Jane and herself. "Have a seat, Frank." She said.

"I would rather stand, if you don't mind, Ma'am." Frank replied rubbing his still sore bottom.

"I can understand that," she chuckled. "But I have a few questions for you, if you don't mind."

"No, go right ahead," Frank said as he positioned himself right behind Jane.

"I guess the first question is," Kathryn began, "are you alright? Jane wasn't too hard on you, was she?"

"Well," Frank began, "I think I'm okay, but there were a few times there that I was afraid Jane was going to really hurt me. By the way, that Tiger stuff really burns. How long does that last, anyway?"

Kathryn chuckled, "It won't last forever. But how do you feel about Jane being in charge of your marriage, your life?"

"I think I am going to like it," Frank said. "I feel like we can reconnect. Kind of like we did when we first met. It's a whole new experience for me."

"Good," Kathryn said. "Do you feel the same way, Jane?"

"Actually, Kathryn," Jane began, "I think this will be very good for our marriage. Since this all began last week, I think Frank and I have formed a new understanding. A new way of doing things that will make us stronger... As a couple, I mean."

"Great! Then I have something for you," Kathryn said reaching into the top, right hand drawer of her desk. "It's your diploma. You have both done very well and I wanted to reward you. So, here you are." She reached across the desk and handed the diploma to Frank.

"Thank you," Jane said.

"Yeah, thanks," said Frank.

The Marriage Counselor

"Remember, if either of you ever have any questions, just call me." With that, she stood up and presented her hand to Jane.

Jane took Kathryn's hand and shook it briefly. Then it was Frank's turn.

"Have a good night and I hope I never have to see you back here again," Kathryn said as the couple walked out of the office and headed out through the lobby.

When they were back outside and settled in the car, Frank turned to Jane and said, "Mistress?"

"Yes, Frank," she replied.

"Please don't ever hit me that hard again."

Jane grinned. "Behave yourself and I won't."

"That's good enough for me," Frank replied as he put the car in gear and backed out of the parking space. "I promise to be good."

"That's all I ask, dear. That's all I ask..."

~ ~ ~

Chapter 8
A SPECIAL TEASING

As Frank pulled into the garage and put the car in park, Jane said, "It's still early. I want to play a game I think you will like."

"I don't know about any games, but I need something to drink," Frank replied. "I'm parched!"

"Then I guess we had better get inside," Jane replied. With that, they both exited the car and entered the house.

"Why don't you fix us something to drink while I get the game set up?" Jane announced as she laid her purse on the kitchen table. "We'll play in the living room."

"Yes, ma'am," Jack replied as he reached into the cabinet for a couple glasses. "Iced tea?" he asked.

"That will be great," Jane called out from the next room.

Jane had been planning this for some time later in the week, but she couldn't wait. It had taken her several hours to make the rules and set everything up and she was just in a hurry to try it out.

By the time Frank entered the room, Jane was setting up the checker board and placing the pieces in their proper places for the beginning of the game.

"What's all this?" Frank asked placing Jane's drink on the coffee table in front her. "I was hoping we were going to play some kind of sexual game."

"Oh, we are," Jane replied with a smile. "We are going to play a special teasing style of checkers."

"Teasing style?" Frank asked. "What's that?"

"Let me explain," Jane said as she finished placing the final playing piece on the board. "Each of the red pieces has a number on the bottom."

Frank reached for one of the checkers in front of him, but Jane stop him by placing her hand on top of his. "Don't look," she said. "Let me explain." Frank withdrew his hand and waited for Jane to continue.

The Marriage Counselor

"Okay," Jane continued, "each of the red checkers, your pieces, has a number on the bottom. I numbered them from one to twelve. Whenever I jump one of them and remove it from the board, I will show you the number."

"Okay," Frank said, listening intently. "Then what?"

"Well," Jane said, "each number corresponds to particular activity I have in this this list." She held up a piece of paper with writing on one side. "But you can't see the list just yet."

"Okay, what kind of activities?" He asked.

"You will just have to wait and see," Jane said. "If I take one of your kings, then we double whatever the activity for that checker is."

"Okay," Frank replied. Still not certain whether he was going to like this game or not.

"Before we begin, I will tell you that, should you win the game, I will grant you a full orgasm, but..." she paused for effect. "You will have to do it my way. That is, under my direction. Got it?"

"Sure," Frank replied, "but what happens if I lose the game?"

"If you lose," Jane began, "I get to give you a ruined orgasm. How about that? Either way, you get an orgasm." Jane had a big smile on her face. "What do you think?"

"I think I am getting screwed either way," Frank replied, "but what the heck, I like games. Let's play."

"Um..." Jane began, "You will need to be undressed for this."

"Frank looked at Jane and asked, "What about you?"

Oh, I don't need to get undressed," she explained. "There are no numbers under my checkers."

Frank stood up and carefully removed his clothing. Once he was naked, except for his chastity belt, of course, he asked, "What about this thing?"

Jane reached across the table and unlocked the cage on Frank's chastity belt and removed it. "There. How's that?" she asked. "Now no masturbating unless told to do so. Got it?" Jane raised one eyebrow to indicate that she was serious about that last remark.

"Yes, Ma'am," Frank replied. "Can we play now?"

"Okay," said Jane. "Red goes first."

With that, Frank stared at the board trying to decide on his opening move. He finally reached over and slid one of the red checkers to a new position. "There you go," he said, as he looked up at Jane to see what she thought of his first move.

This went on until after Frank had made his fourth move. Jane reached out and picked up one of her pieces and jumped the piece her husband had just moved. "Ah ha!" she said with glee as she picked up the piece she had just jumped and turned it over.

Mistress Ivey

She looked at the bottom of the checker and announced, "Three! Let's see what activity you have to perform for a three."

With that she picked up the piece of paper with her list of activities on it. She read it aloud. "You have to wear a clothespin on your right nipple until you take one of my pieces."

"I what?" Frank asked in surprise. "I have to wear a clip on my nipple until I jump one of your pieces?"

"On your right nipple," Jane added.

"Okay, okay," Frank replied as he let out a sigh.

With that, Jane reached down between her feet and retrieved a small paper bag she had placed there in hopes Frank would not see it until she was ready. She reached into the bag and drew out a single clothespin. Handing it to Frank, she said, "Here you go."

"You are really prepared, aren't you, Sweetie?" Frank said reaching for the clothespin.

He took the clip from jane and pinched a healthy amount of skin surrounding his right nipple. He carefully fitted the clip over the pinched skin and gently released it. "That's not so painful," he remarked.

Jane chuckled to herself knowing full well it would be more painful to remove the clip than it was to put it in place. "Your move," she said with a smile.

Frank looked at the board intently. He didn't want to lose another checker, nor did he want to lose the game. He had never played checkers with Jane before. In fact, he hadn't played since he was a kid. But, he used to be pretty good. Or so he thought. So, he planned his next move carefully.

Frank chose to move a piece that would protect two others from the possibility of being jumped. "There," he said, "your turn."

Jane chose to move one of her checkers into an advantageous spot in hopes of forcing Frank to leave himself open at some time in the future.

The game played on until Jane's plan worked. Frank was forced to make a move that left one of his pieces exposed.

Jane made the jump and, after lifting the piece from the board, announced, "Seven!"

"What do I have to do for a seven?" Frank asked, realizing that he was still wearing the original clip on his right nipple. It was beginning to hurt a bit. "Does this mean I can remove this thing?" he asked, pointing to the clip on his nipple.

"No, silly," Jane replied. "Remember? You have to wear that until you jump one of my pieces."

"Oh, yeah. Right," he replied. "So, what do I have to do now?"

The Marriage Counselor

Jane looked at the activities list again and replied, "According to this, a number seven means I get to snap your balls with a rubber band three times… Each."

"Each!?" Frank was a little surprised at that. "You mean I have to let you snap my balls six times with a rubber band?"

That's right, Dear," Jane said reaching into the bag of items she kept hidden from Frank. With drawing her hand, she said, "Here we are. Now step over here where I can get at them and let's get this over with."

Frank slowly stood up and stepped around the end of the coffee table. He spread his legs slightly, placed his hands on his hips and said through gritted teeth, "Okay. Go ahead." He closed his eyes tightly as if that would block the pain, or something. It didn't.

Jane snapped the rubber band four times fairly gently. She didn't know how it would effect Frank, or just how hard she could do it without really hurting him, too much.

Frank commented, "that's not so bad."

So, for the last two snaps, Jane really pulled the rubber band back tight. When it snapped Frank's left ball, he winced in pain, let a short yelp, and almost doubled over. But that was nothing compared to how his right ball hurt when Jane repeated the process on that one.

As the game progressed, Frank had to wear clothespins on his left nipple, several on his scrotum, and had to suck on a dildo for two minutes as well.

When Jane finally made her final move, jumped Frank's last checker, a king, she explained that he still had to perform the last activity, and at double what it called for. The last checker had the number nine on the bottom and Jane read off the activity. "You have to wear a clothespin on the head of your penis for two minutes," she said. "That's double the one minute called for."

Jack picked up one of the clothespins now lying beside the checker board and carefully attached it in the proper place.

"Okay," Frank announced. "That one hurts!"

"Oh, you can take it, "Jane replied. It won't kill you or do any permanent damage." She chuckled to herself because she never thought that would be the last activity, nor that it would end up being doubled. She actually felt sorry for Frank, for a moment.

When Frank's two minutes were up, and Jane told him he could take the clip off his cock, Frank breathed a sigh of relief as he carefully removed it. He tossed the clip onto the coffee table next to all the other toys he had to use during the evening.

"So, Frank said, "what now? I lost, so I guess you get to ruin my orgasm, huh?"

"Well, yes, I do," Jane replied. "But I think we should retire to the bedroom for that. Don't you?"

"That sounds good," Frank said. "On the bed, perhaps?"

Jane agreed. Once the two of them were on the bed, and Franks hands were bound to the headboard so he couldn't interfere with Jane's plans. She placed a blindfold over his eyes. Grabbing a bottle of lubrication, she climbed up on the bed and sat down between Frank's legs. That way, she could hold his legs in place with her own while she teased Frank's cock for as long as she liked.

Jane spent over twenty minutes just toying with Frank's cock and balls. Keeping him hard the entire time. She asked him to tell her what it was he fantasized about when he was looking at all those pictures and videos online.

Frank told her about his favorite fantasy. All the while, Jane toyed with his cock and balls.

When she finally tired of playing with him, Jane began to seriously stroke him, bringing him right to the brink of orgasm. Once she was sure he was about to shot his load all over himself, she stopped.

She didn't touch his cock again. She simply watched and laughed as his cock twitched and jerked in an attempt to shoot his cum all over himself. But, alas, Jane had stopped just in time, and Frank's cum began to dribble out of the end of his frustrated penis. She watched as the tiny streams of cum slowly ceased oozing out of Frank's cock onto his tummy.

"Well," Jane said. "How was that? Do feel as if you have been relieved of all your cummies?"

"Frank was still as horny as he was when Jane began her toying with his cock. "No, Ma'am, I don't. I am still horny. It's not fair! How did you do that?"

"That, my dear, Frank, was a ruined orgasm," she explained. I expect you will be having many of those in the future. Get used to it." She smiled and climbed off the bed. She pulled the blindfold from Frank's eyes and quickly placed a small bag of ice on his cock and balls.

"Hey! That's cold!" Frank complained. "Let me loose, please?"

"I will, Jane replied, just as soon as I can get your cage back on you."

~ ~ ~

Chapter 9
HAPPILY, EVER-AFTER

Saturday morning... Frank thought it would never arrive. He had been promised a fun day, whatever that meant, and he wanted to get an early start on it. He sprang out of bed at eight-thirty, showered and all that other morning stuff and was already carrying Jane's breakfast tray up the stairs. All before nine o'clock.

"Wake up, Mistress," he said softly as he stepped through the door to the master bedroom. "I have your breakfast for you."

Jane was already awake. Well, half awake, anyway. She had been laying there pondering whether or not to actually crawl out of bed or just sleep the day away. She sat up and looked at the tray Frank held in his hands. "Is that for me?" She asked rubbing the sleep from one eye.

"Yes, Mistress," Frank said, holding the tray lower so she could see what he had made her. "One egg, basted the way you like, bacon, toast, juice and coffee. Everything just for you." The smile on his face just wouldn't go away. He was promised sexual release this weekend and he wasn't going to waste a second of it.

Frank set the tray down across Jane's lap. "I hope you like it, Mistress."

Jane studied the contents of the tray for a moment, then looked up at Frank, "It looks great, sweetie. Thanks."

Frank sat down on the edge of the bed and asked, "Is there anything else I can do for you, Mistress?"

"Yes, there is. Run me a bath and use that new bubble bath I bought the other day," Jane said after swallowing a bite of egg. "I'll be in there as soon I finish this."

"Yes, Mistress," Frank replied as he got up from the bed and headed off toward the bathroom.

While Frank was gone, Jane thought about her plans for the weekend. All week she had been promising Frank that she had something special planned and she meant to keep her promise. After all, the only sex he has had since their graduation from marriage counseling was to orally bring her to orgasm every night. Poor Frank had not received any relief. She had been teasing him in various ways all week. Once she made him put a butt-plug in his ass before driving home from work. She sent him text messages and voice mails telling him all kinds of fantasies. She even talked to him a couple times telling him to fondle himself during meetings with clients. All of which were designed to keep poor Frank as aroused as possible. Yes, Jane had plans for Frank this weekend and she fully intended to carry out those plans.

When she had finished her breakfast, Jane set the tray on the nightstand and climbed out of bed. She stripped off her nightie and proceeded into the bathroom where Frank was waiting.

"Your bath is ready, Mistress," Frank announced as Jane entered the room. "I hope I got the temperature right."

Jane sat down on the toilet to pee. She looked at Frank and smiled. "First things first," she said. "Why don't you go ahead and get in?"

"What? You want me in the tub, too?" Frank was both shocked and aroused by the thought of taking a bath with his wife.

"Yeah, go ahead and get in," she affirmed. "I'll be right there."

Frank stood up and stepped into the huge garden tub. He looked back at Jane just to make sure he heard her correctly. She didn't say a word, so he lowered himself into the hot, steamy water covered in white, fragrant bubbles. "This really feels great, Mistress." he said as he leaned back against the end of the tub. "I can see why you like taking baths so much. You know," Frank said, "I can't remember the last time I took a bath."

"You should try it more often," Jane replied. "They can really be relaxing." She stood up and wiped herself, flushed the toilet, and joined Frank in the tub. "You know," Jane said thoughtfully, "this tub has always had room for two, but this is only the first time we have both been in it together."

"This is the first time I've been in it at all," Frank replied. "I always used the shower."

"From now on," Jane began, "we are going to take a Saturday morning bath together. That will be our discussion time. As long as we are in the tub together, we can both talk freely about anything on our minds. Including our relationship. There won't be consequences for anything you say while we are both here. Sound good?"

Frank looked at her for a second and asked, "You mean that I can complain about something and you won't get upset or punish me, or anything like that?"

"That's right," she said. "No retaliation, no consequences."

The Marriage Counselor

"So, if I have a complaint about the way you are running things, I can just say it here and you won't mind?" Frank was not entirely convinced.

"That's right, dear," Jane affirmed. "You can say anything you want. Is there something you want to say?"

Frank looked up at the corner of the wall where it meets the ceiling and thought for a second. He was still pondering what he had just been told. "Yes, there is something I want to say," he began. "You have never given me any indication of when I might be able to get some relief. I mean, when I might be able to actually cum."

"No, I haven't," Jane replied. "I figured that was totally up to me and you really have nothing to say about it."

"Yes," Frank complained. "But I was hoping that you could give me an idea of when that might be so that I would have something to look forward to."

Jane thought about it for a moment, then replied, "I see your point. I will try to come up with some kind of game you can play that will give you a chance at an orgasm. But they still may be few and far between."

"That would be great!" Frank said. "Anything that would give me hope."

"I'll come up with something this weekend," she promised. "And when I do, I'll let you know."

"That's all I ask," he said. "I just need some kind of 'something' to keep me going."

The two spent the next two hours sitting in the tub talking. They talked about their new relationship and what each of them was hoping it would do for them, as a couple. They talked about Frank's job. About what Jane truly expected of Frank, what Frank expected from Jane, and on and on.

When they finally ran out of things to talk about, they decided to get out and dry off. Frank dried Jane's body and she got dressed while he dried his own.

Frank was ordered to do a few chores until lunchtime. Jane sat around watching Frank do all of his chores in the nude. She liked being dressed while Frank was naked. It gave her a feeling of power over him. She liked that feeling. She didn't want to be mean and cruel to Frank, she loved him. No, that wasn't it at all. She just liked the fact that he would now be pulling his own weight around the house and that she could play sexual games with him and at his expense. The new relationship seemed just the thing they needed to bring them back together. Jane was happy that they were a couple, again.

After lunch, Jane decided it was time for Frank to be teased. She bound him to the four corners of the bed so that she would have full access to his privates and so that he would not be able to touch himself. Kathryn had told her that she should never leave his hands free when she removed the cage from his cock. So she was going to make sure that never happened. Then she applied a blindfold (a sleep mask, really) she had obtained at her local drug store. She didn't want him seeing what she was doing while she teased him.

Once he was in position, and blindfolded, Jane could do anything she wanted to poor Frank, and he knew it. When Jane produced the key to Frank's cock cage, he was thrilled. It would be the first time his cock had been free of that damned cage since that first night they went to Kathryn's, just over a week ago.

Jane spent the next few minutes gathering a few things that she would need before climbing on the bed. She sat between Frank's knees so that she could reach everything with ease. The first thing she did was unlock the tiny padlock that kept his cock cage in place. She carefully removed the cage, which wasn't easy since Frank's cock had begun swelling the moment she ordered him to lay on the bed. But she was even prepared for that. She had a small plastic bag filled with ice-cubes ready to shrink his cock at a moments notice.

"Sweetie?" Jane began, "I have devised a game that you can play that will allow you to have a few orgasms from time to time."

"Really?" Frank said excitedly. "What is it?"

Jane reached down and took hold of Frank's cock in hopes that she could tell if he liked the game she was about to describe to him. If it got harder, he liked it. If not, or if it got softer, she would know he didn't.

"You will draw one card from a deck and the card you draw will determine one of several possibilities."

"Okay," Frank said. "I'm listening."

"If you draw a numbered card, two through ten, you have to wait that many days to draw another card. If you draw a face card of any kind, Jack, Queen or King, you get a ruined orgasm, like the one you had a Kathryn's last week. If you draw an Ace, you get to have a stifled orgasm where I hold your cum back and it doesn't get to shoot out. Now," she continued, "if you draw one of the two Jokers in the deck, you get to have a full orgasm. But there is a stipulation."

"A Stipulation?" Frank asked bewildered.

"Yes," Jane explained. "You see, one of the Jokers is colored but the other is black and white. If you draw the colored one I will bring you to orgasm any way I want. But, rest assured, it will be a full, unfettered, orgasm."

"What happens if I draw the black and white Joker," Frank asked suspiciously.

"Well," Jane continued, "you will have to masturbate for that one."

"What?" he asked incredulously. "You mean I will have to get myself off?"

"Yes," she replied, "but you will have to do it in the way I instruct you to do it."

Frank thought about it for a minute and finally replied, "Okay, I guess that will work."

"Look at it this way," Jane explained, "you will get to have at least two orgasms each time you go through the deck."

"Wait a minute," he said. "You mean I don't draw from the entire deck each time?"

"Of course, not, sweetie," she explained. "You will draw from the same deck until the you have gone through the entire thing, naturally."

"Wait a minute..." Frank said, doing the math in his head. "You are telling me that out of about two-hundred-thirty-four days I will only get one orgasm by you and one I have to produce myself?"

"Don't be ridiculous, Sweetie," she answered. "I didn't do the math, but that means eighteen orgasms in under eight months. Right? So, that's more than two orgasms a month. Right?"

"Well," Frank conceded, thinking about what she just said, "I guess that will do. You are the one in charge and if you say that's how it's gonna be, then I guess that's how it's gonna be. But Mistress? I don't think it will be quite enough orgasms. Ten to twelve full orgasms a year?"

Frank's cock, in spite of his protests, had grown decidedly harder. Jane knew that he liked the idea of having his orgasms controlled with the chance he could draw a lucky card every now and then. She decided to get down to business.

Jane picked up the bottle of lubrication she had laid out and poured a liberal amount onto her hand. She carefully, and very gently, spread it onto Frank's hard cock. She let his cock rest on her fingers which curled around the shaft so delicately. She began to slowly stroke up and down the full length of the shaft applying as little pressure as she could. Frank's cock would twitch, ever so slightly, as her fingers slid softly over, and off, the sensitive head. As she continued to stroke his cock in this manner, Jane started relating one of Frank's all time favorite fantasies. She spoke softly and erotically. She wanted Frank to fully enjoy what she was doing to him, but not to have any orgasm from it.

After about thirty minutes of this kind of treatment, Frank began to beg for an orgasm. Well, truthfully, he was begging Jane to grip his cock tighter because he realized that, no matter how good she was making his cock feel, he wouldn't be able to cum without more stimulation. He wanted to cum so badly he could scream.

Jane only laughed at his pleas for more, and she stopped touching him altogether, just to see what would happen. It didn't take long for Frank to start begging her to touch him again. As terribly frustrating as it had been before, not being touched at all was worse. He couldn't stand not being touched at all.

When Jane had heard enough of Frank's begging, she took hold of his cock and gave it five good, rapid strokes. Then she quickly released it again. "How's that?" she kidded.

"That's great!" Frank replied breathlessly, "Do more of that!"

So Jane repeated the five rapid strokes and again released his cock. "Want more?" she asked as if she didn't know the answer.

"Yes, please," Frank begged. "More! I want more!"

So Jane gave him more. She would give him the same five strokes, letting go of him for ten seconds or so, just to listen to him beg. Then she would do it again, over, and over, and over again. Jane teased Frank with her intermittent stroking for more than thirty minutes. She taunted him continuously saying things like, "Do you like that? Huh? Frank? Do you like it when I stroke you and don't let you cum?"

It was driving Frank mad. He didn't want it to stop, but it he wanted it to end all the same. What he really wanted was to feel his cock throb and spasm as it shot out a huge load of his hot cum. But Jane would not permit that. Oh no. She wanted him to suffer. She loved his pleas for release and his begging her not to stop each time she would stroke him for a few seconds. She loved the joy of his, "yes, yes, yes's" and the anguish of his, "don't stop, please don't stop's" as she continued to tease and torment him.

Finally, Jane decided that she was getting tired and stiff from sitting in the same position for so long. She decided to release Frank from his bondage and have him make some lunch for the two of them. So, she iced down Frank's cock until it would fit easily into its little cage. She replaced the cage and locked it. She hid the key in a safe place, then untied Frank's restraints and let him up.

"Now," she said, "I am not through with you, yet. Go and make us something to eat and we will continue this later."

Frank wasn't sure what she meant by, "continue this later." Was she simply going to tease him some more? Or was she going to allow him the orgasm he so desperately wanted? Either way, he figured he would enjoy it. So he said, "Yes, Mistress," and stumbled off toward the kitchen.

After lunch, Jane called Frank back into the bedroom where she had something special planned for him. She had purchased an item from the sex shop herself that Frank knew nothing about. It was called a 'Venus for Men' and it promised to be quite enjoyable for the both of them.

When Frank arrived in the bedroom, Jane bound him to the bed as she had done before. She applied the blindfold again so Frank couldn't see what she was doing. She retrieved the machine from her closet shelf where she had hidden it. It took her several minutes to get it all set up, while Frank tried to figure out what she was doing. All she would tell him was that he was going to experience something truly wonderful. Something he had never had before.

Once everything was set up, Jane put some silicone lubricant onto the rubber lining of the tube. Then she took a moment to stroke Frank's cock ad make sure it was hard.

"Are you ready?" she asked.

Frank assured her that he was ready for whatever she might have planed. But he wasn't ready for the Venus machine. He just didn't know what he was in for.

Setting the controls to provide a very, very slow stroking action, Jane turned the machine on. "What's that?" Frank asked nervously when he heard the quiet whisper of the Venus' pump.

That's a surprise, Sweetie," Jane said reassuringly. "It won't hurt. I promise you will like it." With that, she lowered the plastic tube down over the tip of Frank's cock until the rubber lining grabbed it and suck his penis inside.

"Oooohhh!" Said Frank. "That feels really nice!"

"I told you, you would like it," Jane teased. "Now just relax and enjoy it for a while." With that, Jane left the room.

Frank relaxed on the bed and relished the truly wonderful feeling, the gentle pumping his penis was getting from the mysterious machine. He loved how it seemed to hug his cock with every stroke. How it seemed to suck his cock into it and glide gently back off with each stroke.

After about twenty minutes of this, Frank began to realize what was happening to him. His cocked was being stroked, almost sucked, at such a slow rate that he might not be able to ejaculate from it. It felt terrific, but it was just not quite enough. If it would speed up, even just a little bit, he might be able to cum. But as it were, he knew it was just as bad as what Jane had been doing with her hand. It was stoking him, but no firm enough, or fast enough, to allow him to ejaculate.

He started to beg, again. "Please. Please! Please make me cum. I can't take this. I need to cum. Oh, please Mistress!? Let me cum!"

But Jane was not even in the room. She had gone down to the living room to watch a little television. There was a movie she had been wanting to see and this was her chance to watch it without interruption. It would only last about two hours, and she thought it be just long enough to drive Frank crazy. She was right.

When her movie finally ended, Jane went to the bedroom to see how Frank was doing. He was still begging and squirming in an attempt to make that infernal machine give him an orgasm. He had long ago figured out that Jane had left the room, but, still, he begged the machine to grant him his wish for an orgasm.

Jane laughed when she realized what Frank was doing. "Frank, Sweetie. The machine can't hear you. Besides, it doesn't care how much you beg and plead, it will never take pity on you and give you that orgasm you are begging for. Only I can do that."

Frank was surprised to learn his wife had returned to the bedroom. "Oh. Please, Mistress, please let me cum," he begged.

Jane reached over and switched off the machine. The tube engulfing Frank's penis slowed to a stop and she removed it from his penis altogether. "There, now. Does that feel better?" she said teasingly."

"No Ma'am. I wanted to cum. That would make me feel better!" Frank complained.

"Well," Jane replied, "maybe we can do something about that after dinner."

Once Jane had released Frank from his restraints, she ordered him to go into the kitchen and make dinner for the two of them. "I think some spaghetti would be nice," she said.

"Yes, Mistress," Frank said as he slowly stood up and rambled off to the kitchen.

It took Frank about forty-five minutes to prepare dinner. They sat down at the dining room table to eat the spaghetti and meatballs with a side of garlic bread that Frank had made for their dinner. Jane commented what a good job he was doing with his chores and his cooking.

When they had finished eating, Jane pulled out a brand new deck of playing cards she had hidden in the pocket of her skirt, and laid them on the table in front of Frank. "Shuffle those," she said in a firm tone.

Frank picked up the deck and flipped through them. They had pictures of men and women in various sexual positions. "Where did you get these?" he asked as he began to shuffle the deck.

"The same place you got this," Jane said as she produced the riding crop Frank had bought at her request. "And if you don't do what I tell you to, from now on, I will be using this to encourage you. Get my meaning?" With that, she laid the crop on top of the table in front of her.

"Yes Mistress," Frank replied staring at the crop. "I completely understand." He shuffled the deck twice more and laid them back in the exact same spot where Jane had first placed them. "Interesting cards, by the way," he commented.

"I thought you would like them," she replied with a slight grin. "Now pick one."

Frank didn't realize he was going to have to draw a card that very day, so he hesitated for a few seconds. He reached, tentatively toward the deck of cards in front of him. "Any card, or the top one?" he asked.

"It's up to you," she replied. "Just take one or wait until tomorrow."

Frank carefully slid the top card from the deck. He looked at it. "May as well have waited," he said with disappointment. Turning the card face up on the table he added, "A deuce."

"Well then, you can try again on Monday," she said excitedly. "Now you have something to look forward to, and... There is one less deuce in the deck.

Go wash these dishes and meet me in the bedroom, I have a whole lot more planned for you tonight."

# # #

End...

The Marriage Counselor
(Part 2)

CONTENTS

1	Bridge Club	1
2	A Visit to Kathryn's	5
3	Fran's Training	12
4	The Belting	19
5	The Cow Stall	24
6	Frank's Humiliation	34
7	Revelations	42
8	Pain or Pleasure	48
9	No Barber Needed	57
10	Game Time	65

Chapter 1
BRIDGE CLUB

"Two hearts," said Jane, hoping her partner understood her bid.

"Pass," said Myra laying her cards on the table face down in front of her.

"I bid... Three, no trump," Fran said, hoping Jane had what she bid.

"You got it," said Barb. She picked up her pencil and scribbled the winning bid on the score pad.

Laying down her first card in the center of the table, Fran complained, "You know? I caught Jack jerking off the other day. Apparently, he has been doing it a lot and I didn't even know."

"I think Simon has been doing the same thing," Barb piped up. "I was looking at his history on the computer the other day, and he has been to a lot of porn sites. But I don't really care. He doesn't bother me for sex, so I just leave him alone."

Myra laid a card down and announced, "Bert leaves me alone and I leave him alone. I did notice that he has been reading a lot online though. I just never bothered to see what he was reading. Maybe I should."

"Well, in Jack's case," Fran said, "apparently he has been doing it at least once a day. It really bothers me. I mean, I like sex. Why isn't he just asking me for it instead of jerking off?"

"I don't know about Jack," Jane replied, "but I won't ever have that problem with Frank. I took him to that marriage counselor down town."

"Kathryn's?" Myra interjected.

"Yeah, that's the one," she replied smiling at Myra. "Anyway, Frank is now my dutiful husband who will do absolutely anything I tell him to. And the sex is great!"

Fran looked at Jane and in a hushed, serious tone, asked, "Do you think they could do anything about Jack's problem?"

"Oh, I am sure they can!" Jane said emphatically. "I am convinced they can fix just about any problem you have with a man." She smiled to herself, knowing how Kathryn works. "If you want, I can give you the number and you check them out yourself."

"That would be great," Fran replied, "if you really think they can help."

"Trust me," Jane said placing her hand on top of Fran's to reassure her. "They can fix Jack's problem with jerking off."

"Are they really that good," asked Barb.

"You have no idea," Jane said looking Barb directly in the eye. "They are that good!"

"That's the game, girls," Barb announced. "Jane and Fran won this time."

"I think we should call it a day," said Myra as she stood up and stretched. "I have to stop by the store and get something to make for Bert's dinner it's after four now."

"Wow," Barb added. "I didn't realize it was so late. I better get going, too." She turned to Jane and said, "Thanks for hosting again this week, Jane. Maybe next week I can host again."

"No problem," Jane said, "I kind of like hosting here. I don't have to drive home."

"I'll stay and help you clean up," Fran offered. "I want to talk to you about this counseling thing, anyway."

As Myra and Barb gathered their things, Jane said her good-byes and ushered them out the door. She turned around and said to Fran, "Fran, I know Kathryn can help you because, and don't mention this to anyone, the first thing she does is to put a chastity belt on your husband."

"Really?" Fran replied in shock. "They really do that?"

"Yep," Jane replied, "They really do that. She turned Frank into the perfect husband in less than a week."

"But isn't that a bit drastic?" Fran asked.

"Listen, if you are having any kind of problem with Jack, Kathryn will solve it. She's absolutely wonderful. I wouldn't recommend her if I didn't believe she could help you. You know that."

"Yeah, it just seems like such a drastic measure," Fran repeated as she folded another chair. "But if you say it can help, then I guess I could check them out."

Picking up the glasses from the game table, Jane said, "Just make yourself an appointment and go in and talk with Kathryn. Once you talk to her by yourself, I think you'll understand."

"You mean I should make an appointment for myself?" Fran asked inquisitively. "Don't Jack and I have to go together?"

"You don't need to worry about Jack," Jane explained. "If you go by yourself for the first visit, Kathryn and her staff will take care of everything else for you. Just relax. It won't hurt to go talk to her, will it?"

"No," Fran said thoughtfully. "I guess not."

"Then it's settled," Jane confirmed. "Call her right now and make an appointment for yourself. Sometime when Jack will be at work."

"Okay, if you insist," Fran relented, taking her cell phone out of her purse. "What's the number?"

Jane gave Fran the number and went into the kitchen to wash the few dishes that she and her friends had used during their card game. She wanted to give Fran the chance to make her appointment in privacy.

A few minutes later, Fran came into the kitchen. "Well," she began, "I made an appointment for tomorrow afternoon. Are you happy?"

"Yes," Jane said trying not to sound arrogant. "I am. And you will be, too. I promise. Just you wait and see."

"I have to admit, Jane," Fran replied, "I am a bit nervous about this. Even if I like it, how am I ever going to get Jack to go?"

"Trust me, Fran," Jane reassured her, "everything will be just fine."

"Well," said Fran, "I really hope so. Listen, Jane, I really have to get going. Jack will be home soon and he's going to want dinner, so I had better get moving."

Jane looked around as she rinsed another plate and set it in the dishwasher. "I'll see you soon. Just don't worry, everything is going to be just fine. Wait and see."

"You seem awfully sure of that," Fran said as she opened the front door. "If it doesn't go well, I'll have to come gunning for you. I'll see you later." With that, Fran stepped out onto Jane's front porch and gathered herself together before walking the short distance to her car.

All the way home, Fran thought about what Jane had said about Kathryn's Counseling being the right place for her to go. She was particularly intrigued about the fact that Jane said Frank wore a chastity belt. She had never heard of anyone actually using such a device. Hell, she didn't even know they made such things for men. She thought they were something out of the middle ages that men put on their wives when they went off to war. Just to keep them from being raped, or unfaithful... Or something. She had no idea that there was something like that for men. She wondered what they looked like. Her imagination ran wild as she envisioned all sorts of contraptions that might be used to keep a man in chastity.

When Fran arrived home she realized that Jack was already there. When she got into the house she looked for him, but he wasn't in the kitchen or the living room. She headed up the stairs to the bedroom area and discovered Jack was in the master bathroom. She started to turn the knob and walk in on him, but she found it locked.

"Jack?" she yelled through the door. "Are you in there?"

"Uh... Yes dear," Jack responded, but he sounded nervous. "I'll be out in a minute, honey."

"Are you jerking off again?" Fran asked, certain that he was.

"No! I'm not," came the reply from the other side of the door. "I'm, uh, just finishing up on the toilet. I'll be right out."

Fran knew what he was doing. Jack never locked the bathroom door. It must be because she had walked in on him the other day. He wasn't shy about using the toilet any other time. In fact, he usually left the door wide open. That's how he had gotten caught yesterday.

When Jack finally opened the door and stepped out into the bedroom, Fran went in and checked the hamper for evidence. Sure enough, there was a freshly 'soiled' washcloth with what looked like cum on it, laying right on top. She didn't say anything about it. She just figured that she would wait to see what this Kathryn person would advise her to do. But it was all she could do to keep her mouth shut and not confront Jack about it.

The evening passed uneventfully. Fran cooked a simple meal of tacos and nachos. She didn't even want to do that much for Jack, the way she was feeling. She barely even spoke to him that evening and she suspected that he knew why, even though he made no effort to mention it himself.

Later, when Jack had been asleep for about an hour, Fran decided to find his porn stash. She knew, at least some of it had to be in the bathroom, somewhere. She began taking everything out of the linen closet, one shelf at a time. She found nothing there. Then she started with the drawers and cabinets under the sinks. Bingo! She found three porn magazines, featuring large-breasted women, in a small box under Jack's sink.

Now she had the evidence she needed. If this Kathryn's Counseling didn't have a better suggestion, she was going to do something herself. She had no idea what that something was. But she would figure that out later. For now, she simply left the magazines sitting on the counter between the sinks where Jack was sure to see them.

Fran went to bed. She was angry. Too angry to fall asleep. The last time she looked it was after one o'clock in the morning and she figured she could sleep in since Jack would, most likely, not want to wake her once he saw the magazines laying out.

~ ~ ~

Chapter 2
A VISIT TO KATHRYN'S

When Fran awoke, Jack had already gone to work. He owns a Toyota dealership and normally leaves for work around eight. Fran looked at the alarm clock on the nightstand. It read 9:14am and she was glad Jack was gone. She climbed out of their king-sized bed and, rubbing the sleep out of her eyes, and wandered into the bathroom. Jack had not bothered to move the magazines. They were right where she had left them.

Fran decided to take a nice long, hot bubble bath. Other than doing a little vacuuming, she had nothing to do until her appointment at Kathryn's Counseling Service. She wanted to relax. She ran herself a tub of water with her favorite bubble bath and climbed in. She had had trouble sleeping after finding those magazines of Jack's and soon fell asleep in the tub.

When Fran awoke, the water was getting cold so she knew she had been asleep for quite a while. She climbed out of the tub, dried herself off and went to the bedroom to get dressed. By the time she made it to the kitchen it was almost eleven o'clock. She decided to fix herself some lunch. She had a ham sandwich with some Swiss cheese, mustard and mayo. She also fixed herself a large glass of iced-tea.

She found the newspaper laying on the end table in the living room, right next to where Jack always sits to read it while he drinks his morning coffee. She decided to read a little while she ate. There wasn't much in the news that interested her so she decided to take a look at Jack's magazines to see what he found so erotic.

Fran ran up the stairs to fetch them. When she got back, she settled back on the couch and laid two of the magazines on the cushion next her and started looking at the third one. She was shocked at what she saw when she started flipping through the pages. It wasn't exactly the kind of magazine she thought it was. In fact, Fran was quite shocked at what she saw. There were photos of women in all different sorts of bondage. Some were bound to tables, some to chairs and even some were suspended above the floor by the very ropes that bound them. Some of the photos showed these women being tortured. At least, that's what it looked like. There were nipple clamps, clips on vaginal parts, and even electrodes attached to some box. She didn't understand it all, but she knew it wasn't anything she had done before. Was Jack really into all this stuff?

She put the magazine down and picked up another one. This one featured women dressed in leather or latex and high heels carrying riding crops and things. It wasn't only women who were bound in this one. Men, too, were bound in all sorts of ways. They had clips and clothespins all over their bodies, including their dicks and balls. Now Fran was really shocked. Did Jack have fantasies about tying up and torturing women, or was he the one who wanted to be tortured? It was all very confusing to her.

When she put that magazine down, she noticed it was after twelve-thirty. She stuffed the magazines into her large purse and headed out the door. She had to get down town for her appointment at Kathryn's.

Fran pulled her Prius into a parking space in front of the boutique that sits right next door to Kathryn's, even though there were two open spaces right in front of the counseling service. Fran was a little embarrassed about parking right in front of a marriage counseling service. Someone might recognize her car and she didn't want to have to answer a lot of questions. Since she was a few minutes early, Fran nervously looked at some of the things in the window of the boutique as if she might be going in there. Then, when she could see no one she knew, she walked quickly to the door of Kathryn's and slipped inside, hoping no one had seen her.

She walked straight back to the receptionist and announced her arrival. "I'm Francis Jacobs. I have an appointment."

"Yes Mrs. Jacobs," the woman behind the counter replied, "Mistress Kathryn is waiting for you. Just step through that door on your left and I will show you to her office."

Fran walked over to the door and opened it. "Come on in," said the blonde woman who had just been sitting behind the counter. "My name is Maggie. If you'll follow me, Mistress Kathryn's office is back this way." The woman turned around and headed deeper into the building. They turned a corner and stopped at the first door on he left. "Mistress? You're one o'clock appointment is here."

"Come on in," said the black-haired woman behind the desk as she stood up to greet Fran. "I am Kathryn, and you must be Francis."

"Yes, but please, call me Fran," Fran said offering her hand.

Kathryn reached over the desk and shook Fran's hand. "Are you nervous, Fran?"

"A little," she admitted as she sat in the nearest guest chair.

"Relax, I don't bite," Kathryn told her as she returned to her seat and scooted close to the desk. "Can I ask you how you heard about us?"

"My best friend told me," Fran explained. "Jane Walters?"

"Oh, yes," Kathryn said with a smile. "I remember her. How is she doing?"

"Well," Fran replied. "Pretty good, I guess. Jane says that Frank is much more attentive to her needs since they came to you. Whatever that means."

"Good," Kathryn replied. "It's always nice to hear that."

Kathryn folded her hands in front of her and leaned forward on her elbows. "So," she paused for a second, "what can I do for you?"

Fran dug into her purse and brought out the three magazines she had found in her bathroom. Tossing them onto the center of Kathryn's desk she said, "I have caught my husband masturbating to these a couple times. I think he has been doing it for some time now. I don't know what to do about it."

"How are things in the bedroom between you two?" Kathryn asked probing for information.

"Not good," Fran admitted. "Not good at all. We have only been having sex once a month or so for the last six or eight months."

"I see," Kathryn said as she started thumbing through one of the magazines. "And you think he has lost interest in you as a wife, or do you think he is looking for something more?"

"What do you mean?" Fran had a puzzled look on her face.

Kathryn held the magazine up for a second and then said, "Something like this."

"Oh..." Fran thought for a second before continuing. "You mean, like bondage and stuff?"

"Yes, like bondage and stuff."

"I don't know," Fran began as if in thought. "He has never said a word to me about liking anything like that."

"Of course not," Kathryn explained. "He's probably too embarrassed to say anything to you. I take it you two have never experimented with bondage or anything?"

"Well, no. I mean, Jack tied my wrists to the headboard once with some silk scarves. But that was years ago," Fran confessed.

"I see," Kathryn responded as if deep in thought. She put the magazines down and stacked them neatly in the middle of the desk. Looking up at Fran, she said, "I think I can help you. Did you notice that all three of these magazines," she patted them with one hand, "deal with bondage and two of them with male bondage in particular?"

"Yes," Fran answered. "I did notice that. But I don't know what that means."

"Well," Kathryn explained. "It looks like those are the two he has used the most, judging from the finger smudges on the pages."

"What can I do about it?"

"Why don't we take a little tour of our treatment room and I'll show you what you can do about it," Kathryn said getting up from her chair. "Follow me." And with that she headed for the door. She opened it and motioned for Fran to step though first. "We are heading for that elevator at the end of the hall," she said pointing down the hallway.

When the pair reached the end of the hall, Kathryn pushed the down button to call the elevator. "The treatment room is downstairs." she informed Fran.

"Okay," said Fran.

When the elevator door opened, the two stepped inside. Kathryn turned toward Fran and said, "Now I don't want you to be shocked by what you are about to see, so let me warn you. The treatment room has all sorts of bondage gear, not unlike what you saw in those magazines. I don't want you to be frightened, or anything. Okay?"

"Yeah, I guess so," Fran answered wondering why they needed that kind of equipment in a marriage counseling office.

Just then the doors opened again and Fran just stood there looking at the strange equipment with eyes the size of golf balls. "What is all this stuff for?" she asked in a amazement.

"I told you," Kathryn replied. "This is the treatment room." She took Fran by the hand and lead her out of the elevator. "We will be using some of this equipment to make Jack's dreams come true. Only... More than he ever thought possible."

"I don't get it," Fran said still looking around at the all the dungeon equipment. "How is all this supposed to help Jack with his masturbation problem?"

"I'll explain all that later," Kathryn began, "for now, I want to assure you that we have everything you will need to make Jack obey you. That's the first step in his rehabilitation. Once we have him under your control, we will teach him how bad masturbation can really be."

"Okay..." Fran's voice trailed off and up. "Exactly how does this work?"

"Let's go back to my office and I'll explain everything to you." With that, the pair stepped back into the elevator and Kathryn pushed the button for the first floor.

"You see, Fran," Kathryn began, "the first thing we have to do is put a stop to his masturbation. Then we have to train him to obey you so that he will be more compliant. Finally," she continued, "we teach him that masturbating is only to be done when you allow it."

The Marriage Counselor

The elevator doors opened again and the two ladies stepped out and headed along the hallway until they reached Kathryn's office. "You mean that we have to use all that equipment down there?" Fran asked.

The two women entered Kathryn's office and sat back in their respective seats.

Kathryn pulled her chair back up to the desk and said, "Not ALL of that equipment. Just enough to accomplish our goals."

Fran looked a little bewildered, but didn't say a word.

"Let me explain the plan I have for Jack," Kathryn said filling the void. First I said we have to stop his masturbating. We will use a chastity belt to accomplish that. He won't be able to masturbate while he is wearing it."

"Oh, I remember Jane saying something about a chastity belt," Fran said with a touch of excitement in her voice. "But I thought those were only for women."

"No, dear," Kathryn explained. "They make them for men as well. Once we have stopped Jack from masturbating, we can begin to train him to obey you. He needs to learn that if he wants any kind of sex, he will have to do everything you tell him, or he simply won't get any. He won't even be able to satisfy himself."

"But I don't know the first thing about any of this stuff." There were tears welling up in Fran's eyes.

"Relax, Fran." Kathryn reassured her. "I will teach you everything you need to know. The first thing you need to know is that you will be in charge of Jack from now on. He will have to obey you or he gets no sex what so ever."

Fran wiped the tears from her eyes and asked, "You will? Teach me, I mean."

"Yes, sweetie," she began. "Don't worry. I won't let you fail. I will be right there with you during all the training. You don't have to do this alone. We are not one of those counselors who sits you down and tells you what you need to do, then sends you home to do it all on your own. We will teach you everything before turning you loose on poor Jack. Okay?"

Kathryn reached across the desk and took Fran's hand and gently squeezed it reassuringly. "Let me explain something you need to know. You will come in for your appointments at least an hour before Jack is due to come in. That way we can give you some training before he gets here. You won't have to do anything you are not comfortable doing."

"That sounds great," she replied. "but do I have to tell him he has to come in for an appointment? Because he will probably throw a fit if I do."

"We will take care of all that," Kathryn assured her. "We will find a way to get him here so we can put the chastity belt on him. Everyone worries about that, but, I assure you, we have never failed to get the results we want. He will cooperate once we explain it all to him."

Fran was still worried. How was she ever going to explain all this to Jack? "How will you get him in here?" she asked.

Kathryn leaned toward her across the desk and said softly, "We will trick him. Just don't mention that you were ever here. You'll see. It will be fine."

Kathryn reached into the top drawer of her desk and produced some papers. "Here," she said as she handed them to Fran, "fill these out and we will take care of everything. Of course, you will need to pay for the chastity device itself. You can pay Maggie on your way out."

"So..." Fran questioned, "My insurance covers this?"

"We work with most insurance companies," Kathryn replied. "If they won't, I work on a sliding scale, but don't worry about that now. Your only expense should be the two-hundred dollars for the chastity device."

"Okay," Fran said. "Do I just fill these out here or what?"

"That will be fine. You can just give them to Maggie on your way out." Kathryn stood up from her seat and stepped out from behind her desk. "I have some things to attend to. You can stay in here until you are finished. Can you find your way out?"

"Oh, yes," Fran replied. "I think so."

"Okay then." Kathryn patted Fran on the shoulder and headed out of the room. "I'll see you tomorrow."

Fran filled out the forms, including the one describing Jack's problem with masturbation, and where he worked and the usual personal stuff. Then she gathered herself together and headed for the front desk where she found Maggie, the receptionist, waiting for her.

"All finished?" Maggie asked when Fran stepped into the room.

"Yep," Fran replied, "all done."

"I'll take those," Maggie said holding out her hand.

"Oh, yeah, here." Fran said handing the papers to her. "How much do I owe you for that chastity thingy?"

Maggie chuckled at Fran's obvious lack of savvy. "Yes, Ma'am. It's two-hundred dollars. We take all major credit cards and checks. How did you want to pay for that?"

Fran reached into her bag and found her wallet. She pulled out a credit card. Handing it to Maggie she said, "This aught to do it."

Maggie took the card and slid it through the little device sitting next to her computer. When the device printed a receipt, Maggie handed it to Fran and said, "Sign that and you're all done."

Fran picked up a pen from Maggie's desk and signed the slip of paper. She handed it back to the receptionist.

Maggie handed Fran her copy along with her credit card. Then she picked up a large pamphlet and handed that to Fran as well.

"What's this?" Fran asked.

"That's something you need to study before your next visit." Maggie replied. "And you should be here by four o'clock tomorrow. Okay?"

"Four? That will be perfect." Fran looked at the cover on the pamphlet. "So this is my homework, then?" she asked.

"I guess you could look at it like that," Maggie replied. "See you tomorrow?"

Fran stuffed everything into her bag and said, "Yes, tomorrow." Then she headed out of the office and got in her car. All the way home she tried to imagine what Jack would look like in a chastity belt. When she realized that she didn't even know what one looked like, she decided she would do some research on her computer as soon as she got home.

The minute Fran entered the house, she hung her bag on one of the hooks on the coat rack by the door and headed strait for her computer. She typed 'male chastity belt' into her favorite search engine hit 'Enter.' A list of websites dealing with male chastity belts appeared on the screen and she scanned the list for one that sounded interesting.

After about twenty minutes she shut the computer down and fixed herself a glass of iced-tea. She went back to her purse and dug out the Pamphlet that Maggie had given her and sat down in her favorite chair. She looked at the cover. It read 'Controlling Your Man' and there was a photo of a man kneeling in front a woman.

She opened it up and started reading. It was all about learning to be in charge. It said that she needed to be strong and to find it within herself to have the courage to take control. She read the entire pamphlet. Then she though about what she had read. Could she do something like that? Did she have what it takes? What would she do if Jack didn't want her to be in charge? She had a lot of questions, most of them about herself and her abilities to control her husband.

When Jack got home from work, Fran fixed their dinner and was careful not to say a word to him about Kathryn's or anything she had learned that day. Jack didn't mention the magazines which had disappeared from the bathroom, and neither did Fran. The evening dragged by, but Jack finally went to bed. That's when Fran went back on the Internet to see what she could find about women being in charge of their marriage and what they did to get it that way.

She found lots of information, but most of it talked (and showed pictures) about women called 'Mistresses' who were always beating their husbands with paddles, riding crops and such. She didn't know if she could do that kind of thing, but Kathryn had promised to help her, so she was willing to give it a try.

Fran went to bed around midnight dreaming of the kinds of things she had seen while doing her research.

~ ~ ~

Chapter 3
FRAN'S TRAINING

When Jane awoke, she could smell fresh coffee. She dragged herself out of bed and went to the bathroom for her morning ritual. When she was done, she followed the smell of coffee downstairs to the kitchen.

Frank was just finishing up frying some eggs and said, "Have a seat. I just poured your coffee and your egg is just about ready."

Jane loved the new order of things, Frank waiting on her hand and foot, making breakfast every day, and doing everything else she wanted him to do. "Thanks, sweetie," she said. "I am hungry."

"Here you go," Frank said as he set a plate with an egg and toast on it in front of her. He sat down in the chair next to her. "I hope you like it, Ma'am."

"They look good, sweetie."

Frank reached out and took the top card off the deck of cards that was sitting in the middle of the table. "Damn!" he said throwing the card down on the table. "I got an Ace."

"What's wrong with that?" Jane asked.

"I was hoping for a Joker," he complained. "I want a full orgasm today, Ma'am."

"Well, look at it on the bright side. You still get to have an orgasm."

"Yeah, but you know it's not the same."

"Of course, it's not the same. That's the whole point. How about I give it to you before you go to work? Would you like that?" Jane asked with a smirk on her face.

"Actually," Frank replied, "that would be great, Ma'am. Would you really do that for me? Or are you just playing with my desire to cum, again?"

"No, I'm not kidding," she assured him. "Stand up."

"Yes, Ma'am," Frank responded as he got to his feet and faced in his wife's direction.

Jane knelt down on one knee in front of him and, using the key she now keeps around her neck, unlocked the cage portion of Frank's chastity belt. She carefully removed the cage allowing Frank's cock to dangle freely.

After setting the cage on the table, she leaned forward and wrapped her warm mouth around his slowly expanding cock.

Frank stood still, not wanting to disturb Jane while she was making him feel so good. He made a few deep groaning noises as Jane began to move her head back and forth sliding gently over the surface of his cock. Her mouth felt so good to him. Her hand gripped him between his body and her mouth and it, too, was gliding back and forth along the full length of his shaft as she sucked him.

It might not have seemed like it, but Jane was monitoring Frank's every little twitch as she moved back and forth. She watched his face, his stomach, and listened to his moans and groans for any sign of an impending orgasm.

Frank could feel her fingers sliding over the sensitive skin at the tip of his cock and it was driving him crazy. It was fantastic. He wanted this blowjob to last forever, but his body disagreed with him. It wanted to reach that point of no return and shoot a load of hot, white cum down Jane's throat. It wanted to pump every last drop of cum that had been building up in his body for the last six weeks into her warm wet mouth.

Not wanting this to happen too quickly, Jane took her time. She would let Frank get close to an orgasm then she would pull away and say something like, "Is this what you like?" or perhaps, "Does this feel good or do you want me to stop?" It was driving Frank mad. He knew why she was stopping every now and then. She was trying to drive him crazy. She wanted to make him suffer for as long as she possibly could. But right then, frank just wanted to cum. Yeah, it felt good, but he hadn't had an orgasm in over six weeks. He wanted to cum!

Jane wasn't about to make this a quickie. She knew exactly what she was doing, and what it was doing to Frank. Every time she stopped sucking on him, he would be forced to back off of his orgasm. He would have to start the build up all over again. Frank might hate it, but Jane loved every sweet, torturous second of it. She wanted to make Frank suffer before she gave him any kind of relief. What Frank didn't know, was that a stifled orgasm wouldn't be any relief for him.

Jane kept on coaxing his ejaculate to the very edge of what she knew her husband could stand. After she felt he had suffered enough, Jane gave him what he wanted. She noticed the expression on Frank's face and felt the tightening of his balls just before he would explode into a full-force, full-blown orgasm. She pulled her mouth off of his ready cock and squeezed her hand very tightly around its base. She held on tightly while his body, his cock, jerked and pumped as hard as it could.

Frank let out a loud grown as he realized that his cum was not going to be ejected from his body as it normally was. No, in fact, it was not being ejected at all. His body was doing its best to pump everything out hard, but Jane's tight grip on his cock was holding it back. Nothing was coming out. Nothing...

Jane held on until long after the cock in her hand stopped twitching. When she finally released it, a small amount of white liquid dribbled out onto her hand. She waited until she was sure that she had all that was going to drip out, then offered her hand to Frank who was expected to clean it up with his tongue.

Frank, now almost exhausted, carefully licked Jane's hand clean. He slumped down into his chair and sighed.

"What's the matter, sweetie?" Jane asked grinning at him. "Didn't you enjoy that?"

"Yes," Frank began breathlessly, "it was wonderful. Thank you, Ma'am."

"Too bad I couldn't let you have a full orgasm," Jane said as she sat back in her chair, "but those are the rules of the game."

Fran looked at the clock. It was almost time for her to go. She had to be at Kathryn's by four. She wasn't sure what she should wear. After all, she was going to be learning how to control Jack and she didn't exactly know what that would entail. She decided just to wear the jeans she had on with a t-shirt that said "Sweet Thing" on the front. She checked herself out in the full-length mirror and was pleased with her reflection. She ran downstairs, grabbed her bag and headed on out to her car.

When she arrived at Kathryn's, Fran parked in front of the boutique again. She was still a bit shy about leaving her car in front of a marriage counselor's office. "Besides," she thought to herself, "it might not be good for Jack's business if people thought they were having marital difficulties." She stepped out of her car and headed on into Kathryn's without even looking around to see who might be watching her.

Maggie greeted Fran as she came in through the door. "I have been waiting for you," she said. "Did you do your homework?"

"Yes," Fran began, "I did more than that, too. I went on the Internet to see what I could learn there, but everything I found seemed too severe. I mean, compared to what your pamphlet said."

"Right," Maggie replied. "You won't find much on the Internet that isn't aimed at men's fantasies. At least not when it comes to this sort of thing."

"Mistress Kathryn will explain it all to you," Maggie reassured her. "Follow me to the treatment room. Mistress is waiting for you there."

"Oh, am I late?"

"Not at all, Mrs. Jacobs," Maggie assured her. "She is just setting things up for your session."

"Oh, that's good," Fran replied, "I didn't think I was late. At least, I was hoping I wasn't."

When they reached the elevator, Maggie said, "You can go on down. Mistress is waiting for you. I have to get back to the front desk and take care of something."

Fran entered the elevator and pushed the down button. When the doors opened again, Kathryn was standing there waiting for her. Kathryn was wearing her usual black leather teddy with black stockings and high-heeled patent-leather boots. "Hi," she said, "are you ready for your training session?"

"Yes I am." Fran was feeling a little more confident this time and she was ready for anything. "You look like all those women in Jack's magazines and on the Internet."

"Yes, well, this is what I wear when I am using the dungeon equipment," she explained. "It's what the men expect to see and I like to reinforce their fantasies by dressing the part. I used to wear 'normal' clothing, but I get a much better response from the men when I dress like this."

"That makes sense," Fran said remembering what the pamphlet had said about men's fantasies. "By dressing up, you are feeding his fantasies. That was in the pamphlet. Right?"

"Yes it was," Kathryn replied. "I'm glad to see you read it. Let me show you some of the equipment you will be using in Jack's training. Follow me." Kathryn headed off toward the right side of the large room, and Fran followed her.

"Now don't be afraid to ask me anything," Kathryn said as she stopped next to a low bench with straps and some odd-looking equipment around it. "We are going to cover a lot of ground and I don't want you getting confused. So if don't understand something, ask me to explain it."

"Yes, Ma'am," Fran replied.

"This is what we call the 'Cow Stall' because it is used to milk a man's cock," Kathryn explained gesturing toward the bench and all the equipment surrounding it. "You will be using it on Jack."

"I see," Fran replied. "How does it work?"

"Jack will be placed on his knees right here," Kathryn began pointing to the straps on the bench. Then she picked up a long silver object with some straps attached. It looked like a huge cigar tin like the ones that some cigars come in. "His cock goes into this tube and the straps hold it in place," she said handing it to Fran for her inspection.

Fran examined the object for a few seconds then slid two fingers into the soft lining of the tube and asked, "Like this?"

"Exactly," Kathryn said. Then she reached over to the machine attached to one end of the bench and grabbed a long tube. This attaches to the end of the tube and creates a suction that is controlled by that machine. It all works together to give Jack one orgasm after another in order to drain him of all his semen."

"I see," said Fran, looking at the machine. "I assume all these knobs control things like the speed and the pressure?"

"You catch on quick," Kathryn replied. "That's exactly what they do. And that," Kathryn gestured toward a small video monitor, "displays a continuous video of men being fellated to orgasm."

"So, you show him dirty movies to keep him aroused while the machine does its job. Right?"

"Again, you are correct," Kathryn replied. "However, you will also be describing some of the things that you might do to him sexually as well."

"Sort of a double whammy," Fran said.

"That's right," Kathryn said. "The whole point of this is to make him so drained he won't want to cum again for a while. Follow me over here."

Kathryn walked across the room to a large wooden cross. "This is where you will be working today. We will teach you how to use a few different items for discipline."

The first thing Fran saw was a full-sized naked mannequin strapped facing the cross. She pointed to it and said, "That looks so real!"

"It's a life-like silicone doll. Go ahead and touch it," Kathryn said.

Fran walked up behind the doll and reached out. She tentatively touched the realistic-looking skin of the mannequin. "Oh, my," she exclaimed, "That really does feel like skin!"

"That's to make your practice feel more real," Kathryn replied.

Fran was running her hands up and down the doll's back and bottom. She peered around the doll and said, "Is it complete?" then she reached her hand around to its front crotch and took hold of what felt like an erect penis. "My God, it is! How much does something like this cost?"

"They are about $2,000," Kathryn explained. "I can tell you where you can get one, if you like."

"No, that's fine. I don't think I need it. But it's really nice," Fran said as she stood up straight and turned back to face Kathryn.

Kathryn picked up a paddle from a nearby table and offered it to Fran. "I am pretty certain you know what that's for."

"Yes, Ma'am, I do," Fran replied.

"So show me," Kathryn said, "on the doll."

Fran took the paddle from her hand and positioned herself to the left of the doll. She raised the paddle up and then brought it down hard. A loud 'smack' resonated throughout the huge room. "How's that she exclaimed," with a proud smile on her face.

"That was pretty good," Kathryn said walking over to stand behind Fran. "But try it this way." She took hold of Fran's wrist and brought it, and the paddle, back level with the doll's bottom. Then she said, "from here."

"Okay," Fran replied as she swung the paddle at the doll's ass again. This time the paddle landed squarely on the doll's bottom, hitting both cheeks equally hard.

"That's better," Kathryn said encouragingly. "Keep doing it like that. It's much more effective when you get a good back swing and hit it squarely."

Fran took five more swats at the dolls ass before Kathryn stopped her. "Now try it with this," she said offering her a riding crop.

Fran swapped implements with Kathryn and took a hard swing at the doll's bottom again. The crop landed exactly where it was intended. Kathryn said, "Excellent. If that were a real person, I would show you what kind of mark that blow would have left. It's different than the paddle. If you hit too hard with the crop, you can actually cause damage. You are doing it right, just not so hard this time. Try again."

Fran hit the dummy one more time, but not as hard as the first time.

"Good job!" Kathryn told her. "Give me that and I'll show another way to use the crop. One that is less painful but more for correction when he needs it.

Fran handed the crop to Kathryn and stepped back out of the way. Kathryn began to hit the doll in several different places. First on the bottom, then on the shoulder, and finally on the inner thigh. Five quick smacks with the tip of the crop on each spot. "That's how you do it," Kathryn said handing the crop back to Fran. "Nice and easy. You don't have to hit hard. I like to hit five times in each spot. Now you try it."

Fran took the crop and stepped back up to the doll. She repeated what Kathryn had done almost exactly. "How's that?" she announced proudly.

"Perfect!" Kathryn replied. "You're a natural. Now let's go up to my office so we can talk about your husband for a few minutes before he gets here." She took the crop from Fran's hand and laid it on the table from whence it came.

"Alright," Kathryn began, "there is one more thing you need to see. She picked up the chastity belt that she had lain out for just this reason. She held it up and carefully unlocked the cage from the back ring and then unlocked the back ring from the belt. "You see," she began, "there are three parts to the belt. The first is the belt itself. It is easy enough to install. You wrap it around Jack's waist and pull it snug. You don't want to get it too tight. Just tight enough that he can't slip out of it. See how it fastens here?" She pointed to the latch where the belt can be adjusted for different sizes by slipping the lock down over one of the studs.

Fran looked at the mechanism carefully. "So, you just press down here to lock it?"

"That's right," Kathryn responded. "Once it's locked, and you have placed this ring around his cock and balls, this part slips up into the belt until it clicks in place. The ring can't be removed without unlocking the belt. See," she tugged on the ring to demonstrate how secure it was.

"I get it," Fran said as she examined the belt and ring assembly. "I suppose then that you slip this part over his cock and lock it to the ring with that tiny padlock. Right?"

"Exactly," Kathryn said patting Fran on the back. "Think you can handle it?"

"I'm ready," Fran bragged, "just show me the guy to put it on." She smiled knowing exactly who that guy was.

The two of them strolled back to the elevator and rode it back upstairs.

"How do I get Jack to come in?" Fran asked on the ride up.

"Maggie has already taken care of that. She got Jack to personally bring a car here for me to test drive. He'll be here about five o'clock."

"That was cleaver," Fran remarked, "so I don't have to do a thing?"

"Nope," Kathryn replied. "It's all been taken care of. But we need to talk about how you are going to convince Jack to wear a chastity belt."

The elevator doors opened and Kathryn led Fran back to her office. They sat down in their respective chairs and made themselves comfortable.

"About Jack," Kathryn began, "I think he might actually be open to wearing the chastity belt without a great deal of fuss."

"Really," Fran asked curiously. "why do you think that?"

"Those magazines," Kathryn explained. "He seems to be into bondage and chastity belts are a form of bondage. I just think we should give him a chance to accept it before we 'force' it on him."

"Do you really think he might accept it?" Fran asked.

"Yes, I do," said Kathryn and here's what I want you to do..."

Kathryn told Fran how to approach the subject with Jack. She told her that if he wasn't receptive, she was to ask for help and Maggie, along with a couple of other staff members would put it on him and then give him another chance to agree to keep it on. She told Fran that, one way or another, Jack was going to go home tonight wearing a chastity belt.

By the time they had finished talking, it was time for Jack to arrive.

~ ~ ~

Chapter 4
THE BELTING

Kathryn pressed the button on her intercom and said, "Maggie? Has Mr. Jacobs arrived?"

There was a short delay then the intercom box made a brief squelching sound and Maggie's voice came back over the box. "I thank he just pulled up outside. Do you want me to bring him to your office?"

Kathryn pressed the button again and said, "Yes, just bring him here and stand by." She released the button and looked at Fran. "Are you ready for this?"

Fran looked a little scared. She drew in a deep breath and replied, "Yes, I'm ready."

Fran moved to the chair furthest from the door so Jack wouldn't see her until the door was closed. A few minutes later, Maggie knocked on the door. "Dr. Andrews? Mr. Jacobs is here."

"Show him in, please, Maggie," Kathryn replied.

Maggie opened the door and gestured for Jack to go in. When she closed the door behind him, he noticed Fran sitting in the corner.

"What are you doing here," he asked looking at Fran.

"I asked her here," Kathryn replied as she stood up and offered to shake his hand. "I'm Dr. Andrews, but most people just call me Kathryn."

Looking in her direction, Jack took her hand. He mumbled, "Happy to meet you," while he looked back at Fran with a puzzled expression.

"Have a seat, Mr. Jacobs," Kathryn said, "and I'll explain."

They both sat down and, leaning forward on her elbows, Kathryn said, "Your wife has expressed some concern over your... Masturbatory habits. We think that we have a solution to your problem and would like to discuss it with you."

"I don't really see it as a problem," Jack explained. "The fact is, Francis and I have not been having sex regularly and in order to keep our marriage together, I have been taking matters into my own hands, so to speak. It's not like I am cheating on her or anything."

"Mr. Jacobs," Kathryn began, "I don't think your wife is concerned about you cheating on her. That's not the issue, here. Francis enjoys sex every bit as much you do, but then you go off and take care of your own needs, that makes her feel ignored, unloved, and useless. No, the issue isn't that you might be cheating on her, it's those magazines of yours."

"Yes, well..." Jack was nervous now. Embarrassed, as well. He had been put on the spot about the magazines Fran found. How was he going to explain those away? "I...er...My tastes have changed a bit and I was embarrassed to talk with Fran about it."

"You mean," Kathryn reiterated, "you just couldn't talk with the only person in the world who is close enough to you, to maybe, do something about it? Is that what you're saying, Mr. Jacobs?"

"Well... Yes, I guess I am," Jack stuttered. "I didn't want her to think I was some kind of pervert or something."

"It's alright, Mr. Jacobs," Kathryn said, trying to reassure him. "Correct me if I am wrong, but what I think you are saying is that you would like to spice up your sex-life with a little bondage. Am I correct?"

"Yes, Ma'am," Jack said meekly as he hung his head. "Sort of."

"Sort of?" Kathryn asked. "Can you be more specific?"

"I would like to try some bondage, but I don't want to tie her up..." Jack's voice trailed off. It was just too weird and kinky to say out load. He just knew that Fran would never understand. She would just think he was sick and perverted.

"You mean," Kathryn led him on, "you want Fran to tie you up. Is that it?"

"Yes, Ma'am," he murmured, his head hanging, afraid to look directly at her. He could feel Fran's eyes burning into his brain as if she had x-ray vision and was trying to determine exactly where, in his brain, the problem was.

"I'll tell you what," Kathryn said in a resolute tone. "I am going to leave the two of you here for a few minutes and I want you to use that time to discuss all this. I want the two of you to be honest with each other. When I get back, we will see if we can't resolve all these pent up feelings you both seem to have. Okay, Mr. Jacobs?"

"Okay," he responded hesitantly.

"Okay, Fran?" she said turning to look at Fran.

"Yes, Ma'am," Fran said thinking that Kathryn really had a way of getting men to listen to her.

"Now, Fran," she said with a wink. "Remember what we talked about. Okay?"

"Yes, Ma'am," she responded knowing that Kathryn had just done all the hard work for her. "I'll remember."

Kathryn stood up and stepped around her desk as she made her way to the door. Jack was shocked. He had not paid any attention to Kathryn when he first walked in because he was too surprised by his wife's presence to notice anything else. But now he could clearly see how Kathryn was dressed. He almost got a hard-on watching her walk around the desk. All of a sudden, it dawned on him. This woman was a Mistress. The same kind he always fantasized about. The kind he wished Fran was, but he never could get up the nerve to talk about it with Fran.

When they first met, Fran was such a sweet, innocent girl. The kind every young man dreams of. But now that his tastes had turned more toward women like... Like Kathryn, he just couldn't imagine that his wife of ten years, that sweet innocent woman, would ever entertain the idea of becoming his Mistress. Not his sweet Fran. But maybe he was wrong.

"Jack?" Fran said, trying to snap him back to reality. She put her hand on his shoulder and gently shook it a little. "Jack?" she said again a little louder this time.

"Wha..." Jack started to reply. "Uh, yes dear?" he was still trying to shake the image of Kathryn standing over him with a riding crop in her hand shouting orders at him.

"Jack, we are supposed to be talking about our problems," Fran said, still trying to snap him out it, (whatever 'it' was).

"I'm sorry, dear. You're right," Jack said coming back to reality. "What was the question?"

Exasperated, Fran decided to take advantage of Jack's lack of inattention. "The question was, do you really want me to become your Mistress?"

Jack new he had missed something because he could not remember any such question, but just in case, he decided to answer it anyway. "Yes, dear. I am ashamed to admit it, but that's exactly what I want."

Fran, thought for a moment. She didn't even realize that her hesitation was making Jack more nervous than ever. "I guess we could try that, if you really want to."

Jack looked up. There was genuine surprise in his eyes, along with some joy. "I would love that very much," he said almost before he realized what he was saying, and well before he knew just what he was getting himself into.

"Okay," Fran said, but I have only one thing to ask before I agree to do anything else."

"Anything for you, Fran," he said eagerly, and with compassion in his voice. "I will do whatever you want."

"Okay," she began, "then you won't mind wearing a chastity belt for me? I mean, we wouldn't want you masturbating without my permission now. Would we?"

"We wouldn't want that, no," Jack replied. "I mean, yes, I will do it. Just for you, my sweet."

With that, Fran pushed the intercom button on Kathryn's desk and said, "He agreed!" rather excitedly. Jack didn't know what hit him. He suddenly felt like taking it back, but it was too late for that now. He had already confessed to Fran what all his fantasies were about and she had accepted them. In fact, she had agreed to try it out. He had agreed to... To what? Wear a chastity belt? He didn't think they were done talking, yet. Shouldn't they discuss what kind of chastity belt, when he would and would not wear it and that kind of stuff?

Just then Kathryn burst into the room alone and slapped a piece of paper down on the desk in front of Jack. "Sign it!" She said in no uncertain terms. "Sign it and you can go home."

Jack looked at the piece of paper, "What is it?" he asked.

"It's your agreement to wear a chastity belt, silly," Kathryn responded. "You did agree to wear one. Didn't you?"

"Uh... Yes, I guess I did," he admitted. "But how did you know that?"

"Because, silly, why do you think we brought you in here?" Kathryn said mockingly, "To sell me a car?"

"Well, to be honest..." Jack started to say when he was cut off by Kathryn.

"Just sign the agreement so we can all go home," she said impatiently.

Jack picked up the pen that Kathryn was holding out to him and, after giving the paper the once over, signed it."

Kathryn snatched up the paper and turned toward Fran and said, "Maggie will take you to the installation room." She turned back toward Jack and said, "You can go home just as soon as your chastity belt has been installed."

With that, she turned around and walked out of the room.

Maggie, who had been waiting just outside Kathryn's office, stepped in and said, "Now if you will follow me..."

Fran stood up and tugged on the back of her husband's suit coat in an effort help him up from his chair. "Follow her," she said firmly. She was proud of herself for being so strong.

It gave her confidence to hear Jack's reply when he said, "Yes, Ma'am."

Maggie led them down the hall to another room. There were two men waiting inside the room as Jack stepped in. He looked at the two men and at the wooden table with four leather restraints, one at each corner, and he got scared.

Maggie closed the door behind them and remained outside the room. The two men just stood there silently.

"Okay," asked Jack, "what do we do now?"

"You're gonna drop your pants, and I'm gonna put this thing on you," Fran said as she picked up the chastity belt that was on a metal instrument tray.

"What about them?" Jack asked nodding his head toward the two men.

"They're just here to make sure you don't back out," Fran said with a wicked smile. "Now, drop'em, cowboy."

Jack turned his back to the two men and said, "Please understand, honey," he explained, "I am doing this because I love you."

"I know, dear," she replied. "Drop your drawers and hold your shirt up out of the way."

Jack did as he was told and Fran wrapped the belt around his waist snapping the lock shut in the front just like Kathryn had taught her. Then she pulled Jack's penis and his balls carefully through the back ring until the ring rested tightly against his body. She pushed the latch on the ring up into the belt lock until she heard it click into place. Then she looked up at Jack and said, "This it it. Once I lock this last piece into place there will be no more jerking off."

Jack looked down at his loving wife and responded, "I'm ready."

Fran fitted the metal cage over his cock and slid it onto the back ring. Finally, she inserted the lock through the tiny hole and clicked it closed.

Standing up to face Jack directly, she announced, "Now you are mine. You can pull your pants up now, too." With a smile on her face she walked to the door and put her hand on the knob. "Hurry up, dear, I am hungry and I want to go out to eat tonight."

Jack pulled his pants up and stuffed his shirt into them as he fastened them. "We're going out?"

"Yes, dear," Fran said. "We are going to Antonia's for dinner."

"We are?" he asked.

"We are," Fran answered. "And by the way, I don't have the keys to that belt. Kathryn does."

Jack stopped tucking his shirt into his pants and looked directly at Fran. "What do you mean, Kathryn has them?"

"Don't sound so shocked," Fran said. "I will get them as soon as you graduate from your training."

"Training?" he said, his voice trembling just a touch.

"Yes," she responded. "Training."

Seeing that Jack was almost ready, Fran opened the door and said, "Come on, I'm hungry." And she stepped out into the hallway. She stopped and turned back toward Jack, "Coming?"

~ ~ ~

Chapter 5
THE COW STALL

Jane was sipping her morning coffee and reading the paper as she did most mornings these days when the phone rang. "Hello?" She said into her cell phone.

"Jane?" Came the voice from the tiny speaker. "Jane is that you? This is Fran."

"Oh, hi Fran," she replied. "What's going on?"

"I had to call and thank you," Fran said.

"Thank me? For what?"

"For sending me to Kathryn's. That's what!" Fran said excitedly.

"So you went?" Jane asked. "What did you think?"

"She's got to be the best marriage counselor I have ever heard of!" Fran could hardly contain herself as she spoke to her best friend.

"Well, I agree. But it's only been a couple of days. What could she have done in that time?"

"She got Jack to wear a chastity belt, that's what!" Fran continued

"That's great!" Jane replied, but you know, you are just getting started. Right?"

"Oh, yeah. We have another appointment tonight to start his training." Fran still couldn't contain her enthusiasm. "You should see what he is going to have to do tonight."

"Oh, and what is that?" Jane asked.

"Jack is going to be put into a milking machine!"

"Really?" Now Jane was getting excited. "That should be fun."

"I just think this is all going to be great." Fran said, trying to calm down. "But I was wondering... Last night I just wore a pair of jeans and a t-shirt. Do you have any better suggestions?"

"Not really. Not for training." Jane explained. "Training can be rather strenuous. You need to be dressed for comfort."

"I know that, but I just felt a little out of place. I mean, you've seen how Kathryn dresses. Right?"

"Oh yes. I have seen her outfit." Jane replied.

"Should I wear something like that or not?" Fran asked.

"Only if you really want to. I never did. I just wore my regular street clothes. Of course," Jane went on, "I dress differently now. You've seen my new wardrobe. At least part of it."

"You mean those short skirts?" Fran asked inquisitively.

"Yes, I've gone to wearing short skirts and dresses, stockings instead of pantyhose, and lots of high-heels." Jane explained.

"Why the new wardrobe?" Fran asked, feeling a little puzzled.

"Because, my dear Fran," Jane explained, "I am dressing to keep Frank aroused as much as I can. He gets all turned on when I wear that stuff."

"So that was all a part of your training, then?" Fran asked.

"Well, in a way," Jane replied. "You see, it will be your job to find ways of keeping Jack turned on as much as you possibly can. I chose to wear skimpy outfits because Frank just loves them. What you do may be something else. Something altogether different."

"Oh," Fran said, "I guess I haven't had that part of the training yet."

"Don't worry," Jane said reassuringly. "Kathryn will teach you all about it very soon. It's all a part of the wives training. You'll see."

"Okay, well thanks," Fran said.

"Listen sweetie," Jane said, "I have to go. Frank has a meeting this morning at ten and it's almost that now. I have to send him some text messages while he is in that meeting, so I better go now."

"Oh, okay," Fran said a little bewildered. "I'll talk with you later then?"

"Yeah sure," Jane replied. "But I have to say 'bye' for now."

"Okay, bye," Fran said. Then she hung up her phone and thought for a moment. "Why would Jane be calling Frank when she knew he had a meeting? That doesn't even make sense."

Fran began thinking about her life with Jack and how things were when they first got married. It had been ten years and Jack had never complained about not getting enough sex. At least, not to her. She had to admit that their sex life and had dropped off drastically over the years, but everyone's does. Don't they? She felt bad that Jack had started looking to porn for what he wasn't getting at home. She felt as if she had let him down by not keeping up with the sex like she had before.

There she was, approaching menopause, and they had never had any children. The day she found out that she was more or less sterile, was the day things started going downhill. Who could blame her? She had always wanted at least two kids, but when she found out she couldn't have any, she lost interest in sex. There seemed to be no point in it. She had never given a thought to how Jack might feel about it.

Fran decided that she had wasted enough time. She was going to make their sex lives better. Kathryn was going to teach her how to keep Jack from masturbating, but she needed to take the initiative and find out what Jack was wanting. She picked up her PC laptop and sat down at the dining table. She brought up her favorite search engine and typed in 'bondage' to see if that would help. It didn't. Not really, so she tried 'male bondage' and found a plethora of web sites all about men who enjoy being bound. It was an eye-opener!

One of the web sites Fran looked at mentioned something about female led relationships, so she tried searching for that. Bingo! Here was all the information she needed to prepare for what Kathryn would be teaching her. She didn't want to go into it like a complete idiot. She spent the rest of the afternoon studying web sites about male chastity, FLR's, and looking at bondage sites. It wasn't that she was particularly interested in the whole bondage thing, but Jack apparently was. So that made it important. However, it was quickly becoming a lot more than just bondage. Most of the photos showed men being whipped, paddled, or flogged. And a great many of those included some kind cock and ball torture as well. The more she studied them the more she began to wonder if it was the bondage Jack liked or some of the other activities in the photos.

When it was time to leave for Kathryn's, Fran shut her PC down and headed out the door. There were a million questions whirling around in her head.

When she arrived, Maggie led her back to Kathryn's office. "Hi," Kathryn said with a smile. "Are you ready for your big night?"

"My big night?" Fran asked a bit puzzled.

"Yes," Kathryn replied, "your big night. This is the first time you will be taking full charge of Jack and teaching him not to masturbate. You will also be showing him what happens when he doesn't do exactly what you want him to do."

"About that," Fran began. "I have some questions for you. I have been doing some research online about male chastity, FLR's, bondage and cock and ball torture. I have a lot of questions for you about all of it."

Fran and Kathryn talked for the entire hour about all the things that Fran had mentioned and more. Kathryn explained everything to her until she was confident that Fran could take control and do everything necessary to make her marriage to Jack become everything she and Jack wanted it to be.

When Maggie's voice came over the intercom announcing Jack's arrival, Kathryn asked Fran, "Well, are you ready for his first training session?"

"Yes, Ma'am," Fran replied, "I think I am."

The two of them left Kathryn's office and Kathryn headed on down to the treatment room while Fran went to collect her husband at the front desk.

"There you are," Jack said as soon as he saw his wife. "They told me you were already here."

"Hi, honey," Fran replied, "I had to come in to get some personal counseling from Kathryn before your appointment. Shall we go?"

"Yeah, sure," Jack said following his wife down the hallway. "Where are we going?" he asked when he noticed they were not heading in the direction of Kathryn's office.

"First, we are going to the dressing room," Fran said as she stopped next to an unmarked door. "Then we will go to the treatment room." She opened the door and held it open while Jack entered the room.

"Hey," Jack exclaimed as soon as he had stepped inside. "This is the same room where you talked me into wearing this chastity belt."

"That's right, honey," Fran explained. "It's called the dressing room because men are not allowed in the treatment room while dressed. Well, unless they work here."

"You mean I have to get undressed?" Jack asked not really believing what he had just heard.

"Yes, honey," Fran explained, "because if you don't, there are guys who will do it for you."

"Um...I see," he relented. And he began removing his clothes. "Where is the treatment room?"

"It's downstairs," she replied. "I'll take you there as soon as you're ready." Fran was giggling to herself. Jack wasn't bad looking, but like many men approaching their forties, he was beginning to show his age, around the middle anyway.

Once Jack was naked, except for his chastity belt, Fran lead him down the hall to the elevator. Once inside and after the doors closed, Fran said, "I think you are going to like the treatment room. You won't believe all the equipment Mistress Kathryn has down here."

"Mistress Kathryn?" Jack asked.

"Yes, dear," Fran replied. "And you had better address her that way or you will regret it."

"I see," Jack said thoughtfully. "If you say so."

"And you had better start addressing me with the same respect you show her."

"Does that mean I have to call you 'Mistress Fran'?" he asked.

"Well, Mistress or Ma'am will do."

"Yes, Ma'am," he said softly.

The elevator came to a halt and the doors slid open. Jack took one look around the room and was both shocked (and a little excited) by what he saw.

Maggie, dressed in a sexy, shear, black nylon teddy, approached the couple as they stepped out of the elevator. "Are you ready to begin your training?" she asked Jack.

"I think so, Ma'am" replied Jack swallowing hard.

"And how are you doing this evening," she asked Fran with a smile.

"Oh, I'm just great," she replied as she looked around. "Where's Mistress Kathryn?"

"She's right over here," Maggie replied leading the couple around the outside edge of the room. Maggie led them to a large wooden table designed to hold a 'victim' in place during whatever torment they were put through. Jack looked at the table wearily while trying not to appear nervous.

"Hi, Jack," Kathryn said as the couple approached her position. "How are you doing this evening?"

Jack was nervous and it showed. "I'm just fine," he replied with a slight detectable quiver in his voice. "What's going to happen here?" He nodded his head toward the table.

"What's going to happen here," Kathryn replied with a chuckle, "is you! Climb up and lay down on your back."

Jack climbed up on the table as he said, "Yes, Ma'am."

Maggie quickly fastened his wrists and ankles into the leather cuffs already attached to the table. Then she placed a blindfold over his eyes and said, "He's ready, Mistress."

"Thank you, Maggie," Kathryn said as she motioned for Fran to stand beside her.

"Now," she told Jack, "you have been masturbating behind your wife's back. Haven't you, Jack?"

"Yes, Mistress," he replied, more nervous than ever.

"Fran," Kathryn began, "I want you to take this key and unlock his penis cage and remove it."

Fran took the key from Kathryn and did as she had requested. "There," she said, "he's free."

"Now," Kathryn instructed her, "put on a pair of those surgical gloves and pour some of this lubrication on them."

Fran worked her hands into the gloves as directed and then poured a liberal amount of the thick lubrication into one hand. "How's this?" she asked holding out the hand with the fresh puddle of lube in it.

"That will be just fine," Kathryn replied. "Now I want you to fondle Jack's cock smearing the lubrication all over it. Work it in well."

"Like this?" Fran asked as her hands began to fondle and stroke her husband's cock.

"Exactly like that," Kathryn replied. "When he gets hard enough, I want you to start stroking his cock nice and slow while I talk to him. If you notice any indication that he might be on the verge of cumming, I want you to stop and let go of his cock completely. We don't want him to cum until we are ready. Now, do we?"

"No Ma'am," Fran replied. "That would not be good at this point."

"Very good," Kathryn said. "It sounds like you have been doing some homework."

"Yes, Ma'am," Fran said. "I didn't want to come here unprepared. As I understand it, we are going to get him all worked up and then deny him an orgasm. Right?"

"Absolutely correct," Kathryn said, praising her knowledge of what was going to happen. "In fact, you are going to do it several times during the next thirty minutes or so. Just keep him on the edge for now."

Fran looked up at Kathryn and asked, "Are we going to use that other thing you showed me the other day?"

"Of course," Kathryn replied, "we wouldn't want him going home without having been punished for his misdeeds would we?"

Jack couldn't see a thing, but the blackness was filled with visions of the two women standing by his side. Kathryn watching as Fran stroked his cock, teasing it with the skill of a professional. He knew he was getting near the point of no return and tried his best to hold back as long as he could. But just when he thought he couldn't hold off one more second, Fran let go of his cock completely.

"Good job," Kathryn praised Fran for her excellent timing. "I think you are a natural at this."

"Not really," Fran replied, "I just know my husband."

Jack could feel his need for ejaculation surging from deep inside, but nothing happened. He wanted so badly to feel that all too familiar surge from his balls and his groin that signaled the release of his sperm into the world. But it didn't come. And, apparently, neither would he.

Kathryn leaned down close to his ear and softly began teasing him verbally. "What's the matter, big boy, nothing happening down there?" she taunted.

"No, Mistress," Jack replied with a grimace.

Kathryn continued to tease and taunt poor Jack while his wife, stroked his hard cock until he was ready to shoot his load again. She repeated the procedure many times. Every time she stopped, Fran would laugh as he struggled to complete what she had started and Kathryn continued to taunt him continuously.

After what seemed like hours to Jack, Kathryn put a halt to the entire activity. "Okay," she said to Maggie, "you can let him up, now. Bring him to the stall."

Mistress Ivey

"Yes, Mistress," Maggie replied as she began releasing Jack's ankles.

"Let's go get ready," Kathryn said motioning for Fran to follow her.

"Yes, Ma'am," Fran said as she walked behind the woman in the leather teddy while removing the gloves from her hands. "Is this where I get to use the riding crop on him?"

"If that's what you want to use," Kathryn replied. "But we have paddles, too. If you would prefer something like that."

"No," Fran replied, "I have been wanting to try out the crop. I think it's really neat."

"Okay by me," Kathryn said as she picked up the metal tube of the cow stall. "Here, put some lubrication inside the entrance to this," she said indicating where the lube was to go. "Get plenty of it here and it will slip on him much easier when the time comes."

Fran picked up a bottle of lubrication that was sitting on the table next to the machine and squirted some around the opening of the silicone lining in the metal tube. "Is that enough?" she asked showing it to Kathryn.

"That will be just fine," Kathryn told her.

About that time, Maggie approached, guiding the still blindfolded Jack. She led him to the side of the bench and told him to get on his hands and knees on it. Jack felt his way onto the padded bench and Maggie proceeded to fasten the leather straps in place to hold his knees and elbows in place.

Standing behind him, Kathryn guided Fran through the procedure of placing his cock into the milking device. His cock slipped easily into the silicone lined metal sleeve. Then Fran turned it on. There was a low humming sound from the machine itself, but other than that, it was very quiet.

Jack could feel the device begin to pulsate as it began to rhythmically work on his, already tired, cock. It was a strangely erotic sensation to have one's cock massaged by a strange machine. It felt quite good and he was sure he was going to be allowed to ejaculate. After all, Fran wasn't doing this herself, so she couldn't possibly make it stop in time, once he reached the edge of orgasm.

Fran looked at Kathryn as if waiting for a signal. "Go ahead," Kathryn told her, "let him have it."

"This for all those times when you masturbated instead of coming to me for sexual pleasure," Fran said as she raised her riding crop back, poised to strike Jack's exposed bottom. Then she let him have it alright. Fran brought the crop down swiftly making a loud smacking sound as it landed straight across both cheeks evenly. She paused for a few seconds to give the red stripe (where she had just struck his bottom) more time to fully form. Then she let him have it again. Then a third stripe was laid across his ass that matched the first two.

Jack let out a very surprised yelp with the first blow and two more with the next two blows. Fran switched to hitting him with the flapper at the tip of the crop. She would pick one spot and hit it repeatedly harder and harder in rapid succession until, with as much strength as she could muster, the final blow landed. Jack's ass was rapidly turning a very bright red.

Fran repeated the process in several different spots until she felt vindicated for all the times Jack masturbated without her knowledge.

Besides having a very sore bottom (which aroused him considerably) Jack began to realize that he was about to cum. In seconds, he was blowing his load into this contraption, whatever it was, attached to his cock. But just as suddenly, he realized this contraption was not going to stop. It continued to suck and pump his cock relentlessly. He thought he would never stop cumming. When he finally did stop cumming, the machine kept on sucking and pumping, sucking and pumping, as if it would never quit. Which, of course, it wouldn't.

Fran watched as all of his ejaculate was sucked through a clear tube and deposited into a small jar. She asked Kathryn, "What do we do with that?" pointing at the jar.

"He will have to drink it, of course," Kathryn replied with a slight grin on her face. "But he isn't done, yet," she added. "He has another twenty to thirty minutes to go."

Fran laughed out loud thinking about Jack drinking his own cum. After all, she thought, she had had to swallow his cum many times in the past. Now it was his turn to find out how unpleasant she found it.

Fran went back to smacking Jack's ass with the riding crop, but a bit more gently this time. "Why does he need to stay hooked up to that thing that long?" she finally asked Kathryn.

"Because he needs to be completely drained before we lock him back up," Kathryn replied.

"You mean he can cum again?" Fran asked having never seen Jack cum more than once a night.

"He isn't getting out of that thing until he has cum at least three times," Kathryn responded. "More if we have time.'

"Wow!" Fran said surprised, "I didn't know he could do that."

"Neither did he, I'll wager," Kathryn said placing her hand gently on Fran's shoulder.

Jack thought he was going to die by the time he had cum two more times, but Kathryn decided they had time to see if he could do it just one more time before they let him loose. He did.

Kathryn switched the machine off and told Fran to remove the tube from his cock and give it a few minutes before replacing his cock cage.

Once the cage was secured back in place, Jack's blindfold was removed and the straps holding him in place were released. Jack carefully got to his feet and took a deep breath. He wondered if he looked as exhausted as he felt. "Can we go home now?" he asked Fran.

"Not just yet," Kathryn interjected. "You have to drink this first." She held up the little jar containing his ejaculate.

"But..." Jack began to protest. "Do I really have to?" He looked at Fran with big puppy-dog eyes, but Fran wasn't paying any attention.

"Yes, you do," she replied in a firm tone. "the sooner you do, the sooner we can get something to eat. So hurry up. I'm hungry!"

Jack took the jar from Kathryn's hand and looked at for several moments. He seemed to be deciding whether or not he really wanted to do this. He felt a sharp pain shoot through his already sore bottom. "Ouch!" he said.

"Drink it!" Fran said in no uncertain terms. "Or I'll smack your ass with this riding crop again!"

Jack put the jar to his lips and hesitated for just a second before tipping head back and allowing the entire amount of his own ejaculate to spill into his waiting mouth. He swallowed hard. For a second he thought he was going to throw up, but the feeling passed without incident. "I hope I never have to do that again," he said wiping his mouth with the back of his hand.

"We will see about that," Fran said.

"Can we leave now?" he asked.

"Maybe," she replied, "if you think you can address me properly."

"I... I'm sorry," he began. "Please Mistress, may we go home now? I am exhausted and I don't think I can take any more tonight."

Fran looked at Kathryn. Kathryn nodded in the affirmative and said, "I think he has learned enough for one night. You gave him a pretty good walloping there."

Looking at Jack's sore ass, Fran replied proudly, "I guess I did. Didn't I?"

"Yes, you did," Kathryn said as she escorted the couple to the elevator. "I'll see you in a couple of days, then. Just make an appointment with Maggie."

"Thanks," Fran replied as they stepped into the elevator. "We will do that."

Fran returned Jack to the dressing room where he was happy to have his clothes back on. After leaving Kathryn's in separate cars, they met up at their favorite Italian restaurant where they decided to share a pizza.

While they are waiting for their order to arrive, Jack downed his first beer as if he were dying of thirst.

"Wow," Fran commented, "you sure went through that in a hurry."

"I know," Jack explained in a whisper, "cumming four times while strapped to a machine that just won't quit makes you kind of thirsty."

"And sore, too. I'll bet," Fran added.

The Marriage Counselor

"Yeah," Jack admitted, "that, too."

All during their dinner, Jack and Fran discussed how the night went, how Jack felt about it, and what Fran had planned for their future. She assured Jack that if she ever caught him looking at porn again, she would make him regret it. Of course, Jack swore he would never do it again. Fran was glad to hear that because it always made her feel a little bit inadequate.

When they had finished eating they returned home. They were both pretty tired, and went straight to bed.

After a few minutes of laying in bed, Jack spoke up, "You know," he began, "I think I am going to like you being in charge. It's kind of... a relief to know that I don't have be responsible for everything any more. And it gives me time to do more things for you."

"I'm glad," Fran said. "But if you don't start addressing me properly, you may never cum again."

"Yes, Mistress," Frank replied before they both fell asleep.

~ ~ ~

Chapter 6
FRANK'S HUMILIATION

It was a typical morning at the Walters' house. Frank had Jane's breakfast prepared and the table set before Jane even got downstairs. He hadn't started it until he heard her get up and start her morning ritual, so he knew she would be down soon.

"Good morning," he said when Jane entered the kitchen. "Did you sleep well, Mistress?"

"Good morning," she replied. "Yes, I did. Did you have a good night?"

Frank thought about the hard-ons that had woke him up, but decided not to mention it to Jane. "Yes, Mistress. I slept pretty well... All things considered." He didn't know why he had added that last comment, but he knew Jane would pick up on it.

"Having some 'nighttime' difficulties with your chastity belt are you?" Jane asked him, as if she didn't know. She took her first sip of coffee of the day, but managed to keep her eyes on her husband's face where she could detect a hint of embarrassment. She liked it when Frank was embarrassed.

"Yes, Mistress," he confessed. "It woke me up several times." Frank took a big gulp from his cup and set the cup down firmly. He reached across the table and placed his hand on the stack of cards from which he had to draw every morning. "May I?" he asked.

Jane swallowed the bit of egg and toast she was chewing and nodded in the affirmative, then asked, "Sure, don't you want to shuffle them first?"

Frank had to think for a moment. That was always a choice, but he never knew if it were better to shuffle or not. In his mind, he knew the odds would always be the same, whether he shuffled the remaining cards or not, but he always had trouble making that decision. "I think not, this morning," he finally decided. He slid the top card off of the deck and looked at it. "Woo-hoo!" he shouted as he slammed the card down onto the table face up. "I got one!"

Jane looked at the black and white Joker laying in front of her. She half suspected that Frank had cheated and stacked the deck whenever he didn't want to shuffle them, but it really didn't matter to her either way. After all, there were only two Jokers in the deck and he pulled the other one last week. Now he would have to wait until he had exhausted the rest of the deck before he would get another chance for a full orgasm. "That's great, sweetie," she replied, trying to show at least some enthusiasm. "Of course, you realize that you can only have that orgasm if you masturbate the way I tell you to. Right?"

"Yes, Ma'am," he said, sounding a little bit dejected. But, an orgasm was an orgasm, even if he did have to do it himself. "Can I do it right now?" he asked.

An evil thought suddenly ran through Jane's head. "No, sweetie, I'll tell you when you can do it."

"I was afraid you would say that," he responded, trying not to show is disappointment. He knew Jane was planning something that would take all the fun out it for him. She was good at that.

Meanwhile, at the Jacob's house, Fran was just waking up. Jack was already gone. He liked to get to work first since he owned the place. He liked setting a good example for his people.

Fran dragged herself out of bed and went straight into the bathroom. She did her morning ritual, used the toilet, washed her face and hands, brushed her teeth. She happened to glance over at the bathtub. She paused for only a moment, then decided to take herself a nice leisurely bath. After all, she didn't have anything to do until the weekly bridge game at one. She thought it was strange that they called it a 'bridge game' because they usually ended up playing hearts, spades, or even poker, instead of bridge. She thought to herself, "Where was the game supposed to be, today?" Then she remembered it was going to be at Claire's.

Fran slipped into the steamy water of the tub. It felt good. She hadn't taken a bath just to relax in quite a while. She leaned back and closed her eyes. Thoughts of what life might be like if she really took control of Jack like Jane had taken control of Frank. Frank seemed to do everything Jane wanted him to, even if it embarrassed him. She thought how nice it would be to be able to humiliate her own husband for having ignored her in the bedroom in favor of his porn and self-gratification. It made her angry every time she thought about it. But at least he wasn't cheating on her like Claire's husband. She wondered if Claire even knew about that. She had never said anything, but then, why would she? It wasn't anybody else's business.

When Fran woke up, she realized she had slept for over half and hour. But it felt really good. And now she felt more like herself than she had in a long time. She decided she would have to do that more often. She climbed out of the tub and dried herself off, then strolled into the bedroom to get dressed.

Once downstairs, she made herself a pot of coffee and grabbed a couple of yesterday's doughnuts and sat down at her computer to do some more research. She came across the term 'tease and denial' while surfing some male chastity sites and decided to find out what that was really all about. By the time she had finished she realized that she was almost late for the bridge game with the girls. It was just about the only time she could relax and talk about other people's problems so hers would not seem so bad. She shut down the PC and headed out for Clair's house.

When she pulled up outside Claire's house, it appeared she was the last to arrive, which was good because she didn't plan on staying too long. She wanted to get home and do a little more research. She was beginning to enjoy learning about things she could do with her new-found power.

Once Fran was inside and had greeted everyone properly, she found a comfortable place to sit in the living room with the other girls. Claire had a game room in her basement, where they usually played poker instead of bridge. Fran liked poker, even if she wasn't very good at it. They never played for real money, they each started out with a hundred dollars in chips and if they lost all their chips, they had to serve the drinks for those still playing. Fran wasn't in the mood to serve drinks today, so she figured as soon as she ran out of chips she would head home and do some more research.

There were several conversations going on between the girls in the room as everyone was trying to catch up on the latest gossip, but Fran didn't feel much like talking. She was too distracted. Jane stood up and asked for everyone's attention. She said she had an announcement to make.

Once she had everyone's attention, Jane said, "I am going to bring Frank over to join us today. As you know, Frank is now my chastity boy. He has to do anything I tell him to do. Today, I am going to test his obedience. I need to know, would anyone object if I make him strip naked and give us all a little show?"

There were a lot of comments, giggling, and joking around, but no objections. Jane excused herself so that she could call Frank and give him his instructions. When she returned from the kitchen, where she had made the call, everyone was already going down to the basement to play poker.

There was a total of six women at Claire's that day. They all sat around the large game table that even sported a green felt playing surface with eight cup holders and eight trays in which to store your winnings, if any. Claire's husband, Zack, had bought it for him and the guys to play poker on and Claire never objected because it was perfect for her and the girls, too.

The Marriage Counselor

Once everyone was seated, Claire handed out a starting pile of chips to each woman and placed a deck of cards in the center of the table. Each player drew a card to see who would be the first dealer. Briana drew a seven. Jane got a nine. Myra picked up a Queen. Claire drew a four. Barbara got an Ace and Fran a three. Claire handed the deck to Barb and said, "Looks like you get to start us off, Barb."

"I hate being the dealer," Barb said taking the cards from Claire and retrieving the rest from the other girls. I always lose when I deal."

"Good," said Myra. "That gives me a better chance of winning this hand then."

Brie piped up then, "I always win when I deal. That's because I stack the deck while I'm shuffling." Then she giggled and everyone else laughed at her joke as well. It seems Brie is usually the first to drop out when she loses all her chips.

Everyone tossed a dollar chip into the center of the table for their ante. Barb shuffled the deck and then dealt five cards to each player.

Myra placed three cards face down and said, "I bid three, no trump." and giggled and so did everyone else. "We tell the guys we're playing bridge, I just thought we should pretend so Frank won't know the difference."

Everyone laughed out loud at that one. It was true, they never did tell their husbands that they actually played poker at some of these gatherings.

After only a couple of hands the doorbell rang. Jane quickly laid her hand face down on the table and announced, "I fold. I'll get the door, it's probably Frank. I'll get him all set up. You girls just keep playing until I'm ready." With that she stood up and headed for the stairs.

When Jane got to the door she could see Frank standing on the porch looking nervous. She opened the door and let him in. "Okay," Frank said, "I told Chuck I had a meeting with Kathryn to discuss the design for her new offices so he wouldn't expect me back for awhile. Why are we at here?"

"The girls and I are having our weekly card game here today," Jane explained. "Since you drew that Joker this morning I thought I would give you a chance to have that orgasm."

"What?" he exclaimed. "You mean you want me to masturbate here? I can't do that."

"Well, sweetie," Jane explained calmly, "It's either here or not at all. The deal was, I get to say how and when you get your orgasm. Remember?"

"Yes," he replied with a sigh, "I remember. But I didn't know it would include doing it in someone else's home."

"Don't worry about that," Jane said trying to hide her own amusement at his obvious embarrassment. "You don't know the half of it. I want you to masturbate in front of all my friends."

"You what?" Frank whispered in protest. "You want me to do it in front of your friends? I can't. I just can't do that."

"Oh yes you can," she said. "You will do it or you will miss your chance, and it's going to be several months before you get to start the deck over again. Think about it. It's now, or be prepared to wait another three or four, maybe even five, months."

Frank thought about it. He started to speak, then thought about it some more. He let out a huge sigh, and said, "I guess I have no choice. Okay, what do you want me to do?"

"Good," Jane replied as she walked over to the spot where she had left her bag. She reached in and pulled out a small wooden paddle Frank had never seen before. "Come with me."

"What's that for?" he asked.

"Incentive," was all she said as she headed down the stairs to the basement.

Frank followed her, but he was extremely nervous. He had never even masturbated in front of Jane before. This was the first time since they started their chastity card game that he had even drawn the black and white Joker. It would have been bad enough to masturbate in front of Jane, but now? "Oh God!" he thought to himself, "What have I gotten myself into?"

As Jane reached the bottom of the stairs, she told the girls sitting around the poker table to finish their hand because, as she put it, "Frank has something he wants to show you."

Frank had never felt so nervous in his life. But what he could not understand was, why his cock was beginning to swell. Was he actually turned on by the prospect of masturbating in public like this, or was it just having to get undressed in front of so many good looking women? He wasn't sure he liked the feelings he was having.

Jane held the paddle in both hands as if she were getting ready to use it. She turned to Frank and said, "Okay, sweetie, get naked."

Frank didn't know if it was what she said, the way she said it, or just the way she was holding that new paddle, but something was making his cock swell even more. "Yes, Ma'am," he answered. Then he began to slowly, timidly, remove his clothing.

The girls all folded, leaving Fran to collect the ante with whatever was in her hand, and turned to watch Frank undress. Frank could feel every eye in the place on him. Not that he wasn't nervous enough already.

When Frank was finally down to just his boxer shorts and his chastity belt he hesitated for just a moment. He looked down and realized the top of his black and silver chastity belt could be seen above the waistband of his shorts. He thought how he should have joined that gym his boss recommended a few months ago. He was getting a bit of a middle-aged spread. Nothing serious, but enough to make him keep his t-shirt on at the beach. He placed his thumbs just inside the waistband of his shorts and quickly pushed them down to his ankles. "At least I can still reach my ankles," he thought.

All the girls started screaming, laughing, and making cat-calls as he stepped out of his shorts and laid them atop his other clothes on a nearby chair. It was the most embarrassed he had ever been. The most humiliated. But then he remembered why he was there and his level of humiliation went through the roof. He turned a bright shade of red and let his hands cover his caged manhood as it tried to squeeze it's way out of its tiny prison.

He was further embarrassed by the shouts of "come on Frank, let us see what you got there" and "hey buddy, move those hands!" He couldn't tell who was saying what, partially because they all seemed to be yelling things at him, and partially because he didn't want to make eye contact with any of them. He just stood there until he felt the sting of Jane's little paddle as it struck his ass for the first time. But he got the point and moved his hands to his sides.

Jane produced the tiny key she kept on a chain around her neck and stepped in front of Frank. She bent down and unlocked the cage and removed it, with some effort, since his cock was so swollen.

Jane stepped back to the table and took her seat. She looked directly at Frank and said, "Okay, Frank, show us what you can do."

All the other women started yelling and screaming again encouraging Frank to do something. His cock was growing harder and straighter by the second. Frank slowly moved his right hand back around to his cock. He began slowly stroking it nervously. "You can do better than that," Jane chided. "Come on, we don't have all day."

Frank closed his eyes and sped up his stroking. He tried to imagine all those women sitting there in front of him were naked in hopes it would help him. It wasn't working. His embarrassment was getting in the way.

After several minutes of intense stroking, Jane motioned for silence. Then she asked Frank, "Is this going to work? Or are you too embarrassed to cum?"

Frank took the opportunity to stop stroking his cock and answered, "I don't think I can do this."

"Okay," Jane said. "Let's try something different." With that she stood up and walked over to where Frank was standing. She had him turn around so that his back was toward the poker table. Then she had him bend over and place his hands on the seat of the chair where his clothes were lain. "Now stay there!" she ordered.

Jane turned back toward the other women and asked, "Anyone want a take a crack at this?" She was holding the paddle out offering it to anyone who might want to use it on poor Frank's exposed bottom.

Myra practically jumped out of her seat. "I would," she shouted with enthusiasm. She took the paddle from Jane's hand and got into position behind and to the side of Frank's bare bottom. She drew back and, without hesitation, she let herself go. Thwack! The paddle landed perfectly across both cheeks of Frank's reddening ass. She took two more whacks at it while Frank did his best to stand still, in spite of the pain that was shooting through his bottom.

Myra turned toward the other girls and said, "That's fun! Anyone else want to try?"

They all wanted a turn. So one by one, they took turns smacking Frank's poor bottom. By the time they had all taken a turn, including Jane, Frank's bottom was a bright red with some crooked purple streaks running through it.

Jane helped him straighten up and face the girls again. "Shall we try this again, or would you rather continue the paddling?"

Frank's cock was strangely as hard as Jane had ever seen it. "I'll try it again," Frank said meekly. With that he carefully took hold of his manhood and began stroking it again. This time, closing his eyes and imagining a room full of naked women was working. Well, they weren't naked. He imagined them wearing all sorts of Mistress-style costumes. Perhaps that was the problem the first time. Naked women didn't arouse him as much as dominant women wearing leather teddies, and stockings. He was far more excited by the new images.

After only a few hundred strokes, Frank reached the point of no return. But before he could expel any of the hot, white orgasmic fluid, Jane grabbed an empty glass off the table and placed it over his cock. Frank was forced to release his cock because the glass was in his way and instead of his cum shooting powerfully from the end of his hard penis, it began to dribble out into the glass.

"Damn it!" he said as the women all began clapping and cheering.

"Awe, did I ruin it for you?" Jane asked sarcastically.

"Yes, Mistress," he replied, feeling almost cheated. "Yes, you did."

When the commotion died down, Jane held the glass up for everyone to see. Then she handed it to Frank and said, with an evil smile, "Dink it down, sweetie."

Frank looked shocked. Jane had never required him to drink his own cum before. But, then, she had never made him cum in front of a crowd before either. He slowly took the glass from Jane and looked down into it as if looking at the last drop of water remaining in his canteen while deep in the desert. He didn't want to drink it, but Jane had ordered him to do it. He took a deep breath and tipped the glass up all the way. The white liquid ran down the inside of the glass and into his mouth. He then lifted the glass up

The Marriage Counselor

for all to see and swallowed hard. It didn't taste as bad as he thought it would. But it wasn't ever going to be his favorite drink, either.

Jane took the glass from his hand and told him he could get dressed. The girls all began talking about what they had just witnessed, but they paid no further attention to Frank. When he was fully dressed, Jane ordered him to go back to work and not mention this to anyone. Frank had no intention of telling anyone about this ordeal. No one! But he really didn't want to go back to work. He could still taste his own cum in his mouth and he just wanted to run home and down a large glass of whiskey.

Frank exited as fast his feet would carry him and drove directly to work. He had a suspicion that Jane would check up on him just to make sure he did as he was told. Sure enough, when Frank got back to his office trailer, the phone on his desk was ringing. It was Jane. The poker party had just broken up and she was calling to make sure he had gone back to work as she had ordered.

As soon as he hung up the phone, Chuck (Frank's boss) knocked on the door and then stepped inside. "Hey," Chuck sounded excited. "I hear you got your first taste of your own cum, today. Congratulations!" Obviously, Jane had called Mr. Bradly while he was on his way back to work. Now Frank was feeling totally humiliated.

"I don't want to talk about it," Frank replied with a deep, no nonsense voice.

Mr. Bradly slapped him on the back and replied, "I'm sure you don't, son. But I tell you what I'm gonna do. It's almost five o'clock, so what do you say we go down to that new bar on Stevens Street and I'll buy you a drink?"

Frank looked at Chuck and thought that he was probably the only guy in town who would understand what he was going through, so he accepted his offer of a free drink and the two of them headed for the bar. It had been a long time since Chuck had taken him out for drinks anyway. Frank figured he owed him one.

~ ~ ~

Chapter 7
REVELATIONS

Thursday morning... Fran woke up in the middle of a dream. She had been dreaming about what happened at the last Bridge Club meeting. Only, in this dream, it was Jack who was masturbating for the girls. She had been beating him with a riding crop while he stroked his own cock. She woke up before he squirted his cum all over the place, but then, she really didn't know if he would.

She rubbed the sleep out of her eyes and looked at the clock. It was seven-fifteen. Jack was downstairs in the kitchen. She could hear him rustling around. He was probably fixing himself some breakfast.

Fran crawled out of bed and headed for the bathroom. When she had completed her morning ritual, she stumbled down to the kitchen. Jack was gone. He had left her most of a pot of coffee, though. She poured herself a cup and sat down to enjoy it... And to wake up. As she sat there staring at the wall, she couldn't get the image of Frank masturbating for the girls out of her mind. And that dream she had about Jack. Maybe she should make him do that. It might just teach him a lesson about masturbating too much. Then she remembered that they had another session with Kathryn scheduled that night.

Fran poured herself another cup of coffee and went to do some more research. "That's funny," she thought. "I know I turned the computer off yesterday." She realized that at some point, Jack must have used it. He was always forgetting to shut it down. She opened the browser and then had a thought. She hit the "History" button. There it was. As big as day. Jack had been visiting porn sites again. At least he couldn't masturbate. Not with his chastity belt on, anyway.

She clicked on one of the more recent links in the history list. When the page opened, it was filled with images of the typical Mistress type women whipping and tormenting naked, bound men. She examined several of the

The Marriage Counselor

photos closely. In some, the man's cock and balls were covered in clothespins. There were others in which his balls were all tied up with twine. But in almost every picture it appeared that these men had been, or were being, whipped with some kind of flogger or single tail whip. Fran was shocked, but also aroused. She began looking at more and more of the pictures. Men, in various forms of bondage, were all being tortured in some way.

Fran was surprised at herself for being so turned on by the images on her computer screen. Or maybe, it wasn't the images on the computer at all. Maybe it was Fran thinking about doing those things to Jack that was actually turning her on. And to think, Jack was obviously turned on by this kind of thing, too.

Then it hit her. Jack had purposely left this in his history so that she would find it. It was his way of telling her that he would enjoy this kind of treatment. It was like a light went on in her head. How could she have missed this before. Jack wanted to be bound and tortured. He wanted Fran to be in charge of him, sexually anyway.

Having just had this new revelation, Fran knew what she needed to do. She rushed up the stairs to her bedroom and got dressed. She had a plan, and she knew Kathryn would be proud of her for thinking of all this on her own. But just to be sure, she decided to give Kathryn a call.

Fran explained to Kathryn everything she had discovered that morning. Then she asked, "Do you think it was a message to me? I mean," she continued, "he always clears his history."

"It could be," Kathryn said into the receiver. "At least you know he likes that kind of thing. So what are you planning to do?"

"I was going to run out to the hardware store and pick up some rope and things to use for bondage," she replied, not able to hide her excitement. "And then I thought I would go to that adult sex shop in town and see what they have."

"That's a good idea," Kathryn replied. "If you can, find some leather wrist and ankle cuffs. That will make things easier. You have an appointment this evening. Don't you?"

"Yes, Ma'am," Fran said. "Six o'clock."

"Good," Kathryn replied, "Don't say a word to Jack about your discovery or what you plan to do about it."

"Okay," Fran said. "I won't tell him a thing."

"I have something special to teach you tonight and I think you're going to like it," said Kathryn.

"Great! I can't wait. See you tonight." Fran hung up the phone and headed for her car.

She drove to the nearest hardware store and went inside. It didn't take her but a minute to find the rope section. She put several sizes of prepackaged rope in her cart along with some screw-in hooks and screw-eyes she found. She grabbed several double-ended clips, too. Then she looked around for anything else she thought she might need. She grabbed a box of latex gloves and headed for the checkout.

Once she had paid for the items, she put them on the floor of the car behind her seat, then drove off to the sex shop.

Fran was not in the least bit concerned, or embarrassed, by going into a sex shop. After all, everyone has sex, or should have, anyway. The place was practically empty. She saw only one other customer who was, apparently, searching through a stack of discounted porno movies.

"Can I help you?" Fran turned around to see a cute, but short, sales girl standing behind her.

"Yes," Fran answered, "Yes you can. I just found out that my husband wants me to become his Mistress. That's with a capital "M" if you know what I mean."

"Okay," she girl began. "I'm Lisa. Why don't you tell me what you need and I'll help you find it."

Fran looked at the five-foot-two young woman for a second, trying to determine if she would even know what a Mistress was. Then she said, "Okay, I need everything, but I don't know where to begin."

"All right then," Lisa said thoughtfully. "How about bondage equipment? Will you be needing anything like that?"

"Oh, definitely!" Fran replied with a hint of excitement. "I'll need some cuffs for his wrists and ankles, some vibrators, dildos, lubes, and I will definitely need to see some whips and stuff like that."

Lisa looked up at her in surprise. She wasn't used to customers being so openly excited about buying sex toys. They usually act quite demure when asking for certain kinds of things. "Let's start with the cuffs."

"Okay," Fran replied, eager to get started. She followed Lisa to where the bondage equipment was displayed. There were maybe, twenty different styles to choose from. "Do you have any good leather ones?" she asked, not finding just what she wanted.

"Yes, we do," Lisa replied. "We have some that are locally made if you are interested. They're a really good quality."

"That would be great," Fran said. "Where are they?"

"They're in the back," Lisa informed her, "I'll get them." And with that the sales girl scooted off toward the stockroom door.

She returned a few minutes later with two pairs of cuffs in hand. "These are the best leather cuffs we have," she said handing Fran the wrist cuffs. "They are handmade by a guy here in town. We sell them on consignment for him. They are kind of expensive, though. Thirty-five dollars a pair."

"These are really great!" Fran said looking the cuffs over carefully. "So it's seventy bucks for wrists and ankles?"

"Yep. We have cheaper ones, but these will last you forever. And they're very strong, too." Lisa replied.

"I'll take them," Fran said decisively. She picked up a small shopping basket and dropped the cuffs into it. Then she held it out toward Lisa who dropped the ankle cuffs in as well.

Fran spent the better part of an hour shopping for sex toys to use in her new adventure into the world of BDSM and female dominance. She bought all kinds of things. There were lubricants, vibrators, dildos, butt-plugs, clips and clamps of all kinds. She even picked out an electroshock device and a few attachments to go with it. Then she finally came to the aisle with the whips, floggers, paddles and other implements of pain.

"I have to admit," Fran confessed, "I don't really know how to use all of these things, but I have a great teacher."

"Well," Lisa began, "you can always come back once you find out what you really like."

"Oh, I think I know what I want," Fran said. "I just need your help in choosing the right ones. Like floggers. I don't know what the differences are."

"Well," the sales girl explained, "the ones with a lot of tails are heavier and hit with a thud. They don't cause much pain, but you can hit a person a bunch of times before they start to really feel it. The ones with only a few tails are lighter in weight and sting a lot more."

"Oh, that helps," Fran said as he reached out for one with fewer tails. She picked it up and weighed in her hand. Then she swung it a couple times as if hitting an invisible man. "So, this one would sting more than one of those?" she asked pointing to some of the heavier ones.

"That's right," Lisa said, "it's lighter and easier to use, too."

Fran picked up a couple more and tried them out, but eventually settled on the first one. It had about twelve tails and was very easy to swing. Then she looked at the riding crops and picked up one of the longer ones. It felt good in her hand. Sort of like the one Kathryn had let her use. "I'll take this, too," she said handing it to the sales girl.

Next, she picked up a cane. "What do these do?" she asked.

"Those can cause a LOT of pain," Lisa told her.

"Then I don't think I need one," Fran admitted. "I don't want to hurt him or anything. I do need a paddle though. My friend had one the other day. It was... Like this!" She said picking up a small wooden paddle like Jane had used on Frank at the Bridge Club meeting.

"Those actually hurt more than the bigger ones," Lisa told her. "Have you tried a wooden hair brush?"

"No, I haven't," Fran answered showing her curiosity. She looked very closely at the short girl who had been so helpful. "Are you into all this stuff?"

45

The girl blushed for a moment. Then she perked up and said, "Yes. My boyfriend and I have been trying to find a group we can play with. But there aren't any in the area."

"You mean people get together and do this for fun?" Fran said curiously.

"Oh yeah. A lot of people do. Just not around this town apparently," Lisa said.

"I didn't know that," Fran confessed. "Maybe we can change that. I'm really getting into it and it sounds like fun."

Fran looked over her basket of toys and thought for moment. She was trying to make sure she had everything she needed. "Do you have any leather teddies or corsets or anything like that?" she asked Lisa.

"Well," Lisa explained, "we don't carry anything like that, but I can put you in touch with a guy who custom designs that kind of stuff. It's the same guy who makes the cuffs."

"That would be great," Fran said. "I don't really have anything like that to wear."

"Oh," Lisa said, "Try that boutique down town. They don't have leather, but they have a large number of teddies and garter belts and the like. I think they have regular corsets, too."

"Thanks. I'll check them out," Fran said. "I guess that's it for today."

Lisa took Fran to the front counter for checkout. In all, it cost Fran $463 and change.

Fran rushed home so that she could look at all the new stuff she had just bought. She went straight to the bedroom and dumped her bags out on the bed. She sorted everything into categories. Vibrators in one place, dildos in another, her flogger, crop and paddle in another. One whole pile was for anal toys in which she had a special interest. She even bought a strap-on device so that she could have some real fun.

Fran took everything out its packaging and laid each item out carefully. When she had everything unwrapped and laid neatly on the bed, it dawned on her that she had no idea where she was going to store it all. Then she remembered the large leather bag Jack used to use when he traveled. She ran to the closet and looked on the top shelf. There it was. Just sitting there waiting for her to fill it with all her new toys.

She dragged it down and set it on the bed. "It will be perfect," she thought. It had lots of little pockets to put things in. Fran organized all the things she had bought and they fit nicely. She wondered what else she could get since there was actually room left over. But then she remembered that she needed something to wear that would really turn Jack on. She quickly closed the bag and put it back on the shelf where she found it.

Fran jumped back into her car and drove to the boutique next to Kathryn's Counseling Service. When she got inside she looked around for the 'sexy' stuff. She found a rack of teddies, and picked out several she liked. She got a red one, two black ones, and a white one. Then she bought a black, lace-up corset. Finally she picked out some garter belts and a couple of regular garters for her legs. Then she bought several pairs of stockings.

Once she was satisfied that she had everything she needed, Fran paid for her purchases and drove home to put them away. She didn't want Jack to see anything she had bought until she could surprise him with it. Fran had a plan, but she needed time to prepare.

The only thing Fran had left to do was to set up the "dungeon" she had planned for their basement. She checked the time. It was still early enough for her to start work on the dungeon. She fixed herself a sandwich and Pepsi and headed down the steps. Jack had never finished off the basement. It was still a plain concrete floor and the joists for the ceiling above were still exposed. It was a ten-foot ceiling, but Fran was not afraid to use the ladder to install hooks and things. She was quite the tom-boy as a child. She could even use certain power tools. All she needed was a drill to make pilot holes for the hooks.

Fran mounted two hooks about four feet apart so that she could fasten ropes to them. The idea was to attach Jack's wrists to the ropes and then pull them taught, effectively immobilizing him like the photos she had seen on the computer. She also took one of Jack's sawhorses and put some screw-eyes where she thought she might need them. She intended to fasten him bent over the top so she could tease, torment and whip or paddle him.

Fran was getting more excited by the minute as she worked setting everything up the way she wanted it. She even decided to use the step ladder to bind Jack to as well. She placed a folding chair in one corner, and a wooden bench they used to use on the patio before they bought the new patio furniture. She found some old foam pads and placed them on the bench to make it more comfortable. She also found a big over-stuffed chair that belonged to her father before he died. She decided it would make a great throne for her to sit on when she wanted Jack to kiss her feet and the like. Yes, the chair would be perfect. So she dragged it into another corner and looked around at her new dungeon.

When she looked at all she had accomplished, she was proud of herself, with good reason. By the time Fran finished setting up her dungeon, there was just enough time to grab a bite to eat and go to her appointment at Kathryn's.

~ ~ ~

Chapter 8
PAIN OR PLEASURE?

Fran arrived at Kathryn's just in time for her appointment. This time she was brave enough to park right in front. When she got inside, Maggie greeted her and said, "She's ready for you. Go on back to her office." So Fran opened the door that lead into the office area of the building and strolled proudly back to Kathryn's office.

She found Kathryn sitting at her desk going over some paperwork. Kathryn looked up and smiled. "There you are. How're you doing this evening?"

"I'm just great!" Fran was beaming. She was proud of what she had done, setting up her own dungeon and all. She couldn't wait to tell Kathryn all about it. "Let me tell you what I did today," she added.

"Oh?" Kathryn replied in a curious tone. "And what was that?"

"I discovered that Jack had been looking at porn sites on the web again," Fran explained. "But I don't think he was doing it just for the pleasure of it." She paused for a second, and then continued, "I think he wanted me to see what it is that he likes. You see," she explained, "Jack always deletes his history on the PC, but this morning he didn't. Since he obviously can't masturbate, I figured he wanted me to see what kinds of things he really likes. Sexually, that is."

Kathryn had heard all this before, but didn't want to interrupt Fran's obvious excitement. "Okay," Kathryn said not sure where this was leading. "Go on."

"Well, anyway, he had been looking at a lot of sites... I think you call them 'Femdom' sites?" she continued to explain. "Anyway, it was one of those where all the women were mistresses and the men were bound and tormented, and tortured. Not in a bad way, you know, like flogging and stuff."

"Yes, I see," Kathryn said, still not sure what Fran was getting at.

The Marriage Counselor

"I figured that if he left those sites in his history for me to see, then I know what it is he wants from me. Right?" Fran was certain that she had gotten her point across.

"Oh," Kathryn smiled as she was starting to see what Fran was all excited about. "So you think Jack was giving you hints?"

"Right!" Fran continued. "But that's not the best part. I took the hint and built a dungeon in our basement. I also bought a whole bunch of toys and stuff to use on him."

"I see," Kathryn said, suddenly realizing what all the excitement was about. "And you don't mind doing all this for him?"

"Mind?" Fran asked, as if she had been insulted. "No, I don't mind. I love the idea! The more research I did, the more I realized how much fun this mistress thing can be. I just need your help with one thing... I don't really know how to use a flogger, but I bought one anyway."

"We can take care of that," Kathryn assured her. "In fact, I have an idea. How would you feel about pulling one over on Jack by making him think you didn't get his hint? That you are angry with him for going to those porn sites?"

Fran replied, "I don't get it. Why would I want to do that?"

"So you can punish him for it?" Kathryn explained. "You can use a flogger or we can tease the hell out of his cock until he is really frustrated."

"Oh, now I get it," Fran said as the little light above her head went on. "Then I can surprise him with our new dungeon later. Right?"

"Exactly!" Kathryn was glad that Fran finally got the point. "So," Kathryn said as she stood up from her seat behind the desk, "Shall we go see how well you can use a flogger?"

"You mean on the dummy, again?" she asked.

"Yes, Jack won't be here for another forty-five minutes anyway," Kathryn said, starting toward the door. "You do want to get some practice in before he arrives, don't you?"

"Yes, Ma'am," Fran replied following the counselor out the door.

When the two arrived in the dungeon, Kathryn set the life-like doll on a spanking bench. "I think this is the best place to practice your flogging techniques," Kathryn said. "It puts the doll in just the right position for you. Do you have a spanking bench in your dungeon, Fran?" she asked.

"No, Ma'am," Fran replied, "but now I am thinking of having Jack build me one."

"That's excellent," Kathryn said encouragingly. "I think making Jack build some equipment for you to use on him is a great idea. It will give him something to look forward to and maybe arouse him as well."

"Thanks," Fran replied, picking out a flogger from the cabinet on the wall. "This one is about the same size as the one I bought," she announced holding it up for Kathryn to see.

"Then let's use it," Kathryn said. "but before you try to hit anything with it let me give you some idea of how floggers differ, and how each is used."

"Okay," Fran replied handing the flogger she had chosen to Kathryn.

"Look here," Kathryn began, holding the ends of the tails out. "The width of the tails varies. The narrower the tails, the more sting they can cause."

"I see," Fran remarked looking at the ends of the tails carefully.

"Secondly," Kathryn continued, "is the number of tails. The more tails the less sting, or more thud they produce."

"That makes sense," Fran indicated that she was paying attention.

"Finally," Kathryn concluded, "the thicker the leather used, the more sting they will cause. Thinner leather is usually cheaper, as well."

"Okay, I got it," Fran said confidently. "So... How do I hit with it?"

"First of all," Kathryn began, "you have to be careful not to let the tails wrap around his body. When that happens, the tails begin to travel faster and they can leave some pretty nasty welts where you don't want them."

"Oh," said Fran. "so I should make the end of the tails hit his butt and not the center of the tails?"

"Exactly!" Kathryn confirmed. "Let's see how you do." Kathryn took Fran by the shoulders and placed her in the proper position, slightly behind and to the side of the doll's posterior. "Now, swing the flogger with your whole arm. Do it in a way that feels natural."

Fran swung the flogger from over her shoulder and it smacked the doll on top of its butt. "Like that?" she asked.

"No, not like that," Kathryn said. She stepped over to Fran and took her hand and made a motion slowly swinging the flogger from side to side. "Like this."

"Oh, I get it now," Fran said. "More of a side swing instead of straight down."

"Right," Kathryn said. "Just swing it nice and easy at first, until you get the hang of it."

Fran swung the flogger so that the tails hit the doll's bottom square on. "Like that?" she asked.

"Like that," Kathryn replied reassuringly. "Now keep doing it until you are comfortable hitting harder. Always swing your arm and not your body. That way you will produce exactly the same swing every time. It makes it easier to hit your target in the same place as well."

Fran took several swings and then began to increase the speed of each swing. When she started hitting a little harder, Kathryn stopped her.

"You are beginning to use your body." Kathryn corrected her stance so that she did not have to lean so much. "There, try it now. And remember, don't move your body, only your arm. Got it?"

"Yes, Ma'am," Fran said as she took careful aim once again. She swung the flogger several more times and each blow landed exactly where she aimed it. "How was that?"

"Perfect," Kathryn replied. "See how using only your arm gives you better control?"

"Yeah, and I won't get so tired," Fran replied. "It's not as much exercise."

"Right," Kathryn said, "and you don't have to wear yourself out so fast. Why don't you practice for a while until it's time for Jack to arrive. You can try some back-handed swings too, if you like. Just remember to swing with your arm, not your body."

"Okay," Fran said enthusiastically, "that will be fun."

Kathryn sat down on a nearby bench and watched as Fran practiced flogging the doll. She noted how Fran seemed to be really getting into all this. Not just the flogging, but taking control of her husband and controlling his behavior. If this truly is something that Jack enjoys, then they should both be very happy after tonight's session.

Kathryn intended to teach Fran how to tease Jack's cock without allowing him to ejaculate unless SHE wanted him to. Of course, now she would have to include flogging as well as teasing in the lesson. But if Fran was right about Jack wanting her to find those web sites, then this might just be the last session for them both.

When Kathryn was convinced that Fran had practiced enough, she told her to leave the flogger out and join her upstairs while they wait for Jack to arrive. It would be about fifteen minutes and she figured Fran could use a little rest before the session with Jack.

The two went back to Kathryn's office to wait for Jack and talk a little bit about how Fran intended to handle things at home. She wanted to be sure that Fran had a good grasp of everything before she turned them loose on the world.

When they had both settled into their respective chairs, Kathryn leaned on her elbows and asked, "So, tell me, what are you going to do if Jack decides he doesn't like you being his mistress?"

"Well," Fran began to explain her plan, "I don't really think that makes much difference. I mean, he started this thing and I really think I am going to enjoy it. So I wasn't going to give him a choice in the matter."

"Very good," Kathryn said. "I was hoping you would feel that way. But what if he decides not to do something you tell him to do, like... Oh I don't know... Say... He refuses to vacuum the carpet?"

"I will march his ass to the dungeon and paddle him, I guess," Fran replied.

"Really?" Kathryn said curiously. "And what if he won't go?"

"Oh, I see what you're getting at," Fran answered. "As long as he is wearing that chastity belt, I guess it will be easy to coax him to do what I ask. If he refuses, he will get nothing until he changes his mind. Then I will punish him."

"Very good," Kathryn said with a sigh of relief. "I was hoping you would say something like that. First you use your power over his orgasms, then you reprimand him for his misdeeds."

Just then Maggie came on over the intercom. "Mistress Kathryn? Mr. Jacobs is here."

Kathryn pressed the button on her intercom box and said, "Send him to my office, please, Maggie."

Kathryn stood up and told Fran that she was going to go ahead and get a few things ready for their session and that she could bring Jack down as soon as he was ready. Then she left the office while Fran waited for Jack to arrive.

When Jack found Kathryn's office he stuck his head inside and said, "Does anyone know where the ladies room is?" Then he chuckled out loud.

Fran turned around in her seat and saw Jack standing there. "Sure," she replied, "let me show you." Then she stood up and escorted Jack to the changing room. She pushed the door open and said, "You know the drill, knock when you are ready."

"You aren't going in with me this time?" He asked.

"Nope," Fran replied, "you're a big boy. You can handle it by yourself." She was trying to show an air of disinterest. She wanted Jack to think she was upset about something.

"What's the matter, baby?" Jack asked realizing that Fran was not being as friendly and loving as usual.

"Nothing," Fran replied in that way she had of saying things when there really was something upsetting her.

"Okay," Jack replied knowing that he might just be in trouble. Fran always acted like this whenever he had done something that she expected him to know all about, even when he had no clue. But he secretly did know. It was the web sites he'd been to and failed to hide on the PC. He was afraid his little plan of showing her what he really wanted had backfired on him. He hesitated a few seconds, waiting for Fran to say something, but when she didn't, he went on into the dressing room and removed his clothing.

When Jack opened the door again, Fran was standing in the middle of the hall. He peered out, looking both ways to make sure they were alone, then stepped out and closed the door behind him. Without saying a word, Fran grabbed his wrist and led him down the hall to the elevator. When she pressed the button, Jack asked, "Are you upset with me?" He was really starting to worry. Fran usually didn't act this way in public. She always waited until they got home.

"No, dear," Fran answered in that tone that let Jack know that, indeed, he was in trouble.

The ride down in the elevator was a silent one. Jack was afraid to speak for fear he would dig himself in deeper. But Fran just wanted him to feel that way so he would be more compliant. The truth is, it worked out fine for the both of them.

When the elevator doors opened again, Fran took Jack by the wrist again and led him to the spanking bench where she had practiced her flogging only minutes ago. The life-like doll that she had so skillfully beaten was now gone and Kathryn was standing there ready to fasten poor, unsuspecting, Jack in its place.

"There you are, Fran," Kathryn said, speaking only to her, further increasing Jack's trepidation about the evenings session. "Are you ready for this?"

"Yep," Fran said with confidence. "I'm all set." Jack noticed how her disposition sounded much better when she talked with Kathryn. Not at all like when she talked to him.

"Good," Kathryn replied. "Before we proceed, why don't you remove his cage. That way we won't have to do it later." She handed the key to Fran who bent down in front her husband and opened the lock to his cock cage and gently removed it. His cock dangled in front of him making no attempt at getting hard. Jack was too afraid for that at the moment.

Fran handed the key back to Kathryn and placed Jack's cock cage on a small table that was sitting next to the spanking bench.

She looked at Jack and patted the top of the bench. "Bend over this," she said without showing any emotion.

Jack stepped up to the end of the bench and leaned forward. Kathryn took his left hand and placed it into the leather cuff on the side of the bench, then she fastened it in place. Then she stepped around to the other side and did the same with his right wrist.

Mean while, Fran nudged his feet apart and fastened leather straps to his ankles so that his legs would remain spread during his upcoming ordeal. Then she stepped back and picked up the flogger she had used earlier on the practice doll.

Kathryn moved over to the regular bench and sat down to watch the show while Fran moved up to where Jack's head was resting on the padded top of the spanking bench. She whispered in his ear, "You forgot to clear your history on the browser. This is for going to all those porn sites."

Jack tried to object, but he knew it would do not good, and then again, this is what he wanted. Wasn't it? He knew he was about to find out.

Fran stepped back into position, and poised herself to make the first blow. "Ready?" she asked.

Jack began to protest, but before he could get the first word out, Fran smacked his exposed ass with the flogger. "Ouch!" was all that came out of his mouth.

"Oh, good," Fran said, "you liked it." And with that she began smacking him over and over in the same exact spot. She set up a steady rhythm and continued until she had hit Jack's bottom at least twenty or more times. When she stopped, she heard Jack breath a sigh of relief. "Oh, don't get comfortable," she said, "I'm just getting warmed up."

With that, Fran stepped to the other side of the bench and began striking his bottom again, using backhand strokes this time. "Smack! Smack! Smack!" The sound of Fran's flogger was all Jack could hear. He flinched each time he felt it hit his exposed ass. He could feel the heat and the pain spreading throughout his bottom, but he also felt something strange... His cock was getting rock hard from the experience. It had wedged itself between his abdomen and the cushion of the spanking bench. It was getting quite uncomfortable.

When Fran felt that she had made her point with Jack, she stopped flogging him and walked up to whisper in his ear again. "Get the point?" she asked.

"Yes, Ma'am," he answered meekly.

Without changing her position, Fran reached out and slapped his bottom hard with her right hand. "That's 'Mistress' to you buddy boy."

Jack quickly corrected himself, "Yes, Mistress. I understand. No more porn sites."

"Very good," Fran said patting Jack's bottom in a more soothing manner. "How would you like me to give you a reward for learning your lesson so well?"

"Yes, Mistress. Anything you want," he replied, hoping she meant what she said.

Kathryn approached the spanking bench and leaned down to look at Jack's cock. She motioned for Fran to do the same. "See that?" she asked in a whisper. "You were right about what he wanted."

Fran and Kathryn quickly released Jack's bonds and Kathryn led them both to a St. Augustine's cross that was nearby. They refastened Jack's wrists and ankles so that he was facing outward. Then Kathryn placed a blindfold over his eyes so that he wouldn't be able to see who or what anyone was going to do to him next.

Fran asked Kathryn, "What do I do now?"

Kathryn handed her a little black stick with an ostrich feather sticking out of one end. "Tease his cock with this for a while, then I'll give you something else to use."

Fran took the ostrich feather and began stroking Jack's whole body at first, then she concentrated her efforts directly on his cock which was standing up as hard and proud as Fran had ever seen it. Fran took her time. She ran the feather over and around his balls, up between his thighs and up and down the underside of his cock.

It didn't take long before Jack was arching his back and moaning in an attempt to increase the sensations the feather was giving him. It did no good. The feather was just too soft to create the sensations he needed to get off. He was getting extremely frustrated. The more he squirmed, the more fun Fran had teasing him. It was win-win for Fran, but Jack didn't feel like a winner. All he wanted was to release his cum like a fountain, one squirt after another, but Fran wasn't giving him what he needed for that. All he was doing was dripping a lot pre-cum.

Fran was beginning to really love the feather teasing. She loved the way Jack squirmed around trying to get more sensation out of it. It was actually turning her on to make him squirm so much.

Kathryn tapped Fran on the shoulder and held out a bottle of lubrication. Fran handed her the feather and took the bottle. Kathryn leaned in close to Fran's ear and whispered, "I'll tell you when to stop so you don't have any accidents."

Fran whispered, "Thanks, Ma'am," back to her as she poured some of the thick liquid into her hand.

Fran stepped up close to Jack so she could look directly at his face as she gently took his cock in her hand and smeared the heavy lubricant all over it. She started slowly, and gently, stroking the full length of his cock as she started to whisper, "How does that feel? Is that better than that old feather?" Fran was talking in a little girl tone of voice. The kind that makes her sound so innocent. She wanted to taunt him. To tease him. To make him so turned on that he would be ready to explode at any moment.

Her plan was working. Jack began to moan and groan and writhe against her body. She had him right where she wanted him. When it seemed like Jack might be getting too close to ejaculating for comfort, she stopped touching his cock while she taunted him some more. She said things like, "What's the matter, baby? Did you want me to keep going? Do you really want to cum and end all this wonderful pleasure I'm giving you?"

It was driving Jack totally out of his mind. Time and time again he would reach the edge of orgasm only to be denied the release he so desperately wanted. No, needed. At least that's what he thought.

But Fran was having nothing to do with any orgasms on his part. No, she wanted to make him truly suffer. She was enjoying listening to his pleas and making him squirm. She had no intention of allowing him to squirt his cum all over her. No, not this night. After all, this is what he wanted. Or at least, it was what she wanted, even if he didn't. If she was going to expend all that energy spanking, paddling and whipping him, Jack was just going to have put up with a little tease and denial on her part.

Fran was truly loving Jack's torment. She never expected that teasing Jack like this could be so much fun. She had plans to make him lick her to several orgasms once they got home, but as for him? Nothing to night!

Finally, Kathryn stepped in and signaled Fran to stop. It was time to release Jack and go up to her office for some talk about how the couple felt about what they had experienced that night.

Kathryn handed Fran a cold-pack and waited for Jack's cock to lose its tumescence. Then his cock was carefully re-inserted into its cage and the lock was fastened back in place. Kathryn told the couple to get Jack dressed and join her in her office. She went on ahead since Jack was still secured to the cross. She left Fran to release him.

When the couple was finally able to join Kathryn in her office, Kathryn asked each of them what they felt about the new relationship they had formed, and if there were any special concerns either of them had about what had just happened.

Jack, of course, wanted to know when he would be allowed to cum since he had not done so in several days. Kathryn smiled at him and said, "That is entirely up to your new Mistress."

Jack looked at Fran and asked, "Well? Mistress? When can I cum again?"

Fran looked at Kathryn and smiled. Then she looked at Jack and said, "It all depends on how well you behave. Do everything I tell you to do and you will be rewarded. How's that?"

Jack wasn't sure if that really answered his question, but he was afraid he had already pushed his luck, so he said, "I'll do whatever you want, Mistress."

Kathryn stood up and said, "I have a surprise for you both." She handed Jack a piece of paper with a gold seal at the bottom. "That's your diploma," she said. "It means that you don't have to come back here any more."

"Thank you, Ma'am," Jack replied as he took the paper from her.

Then she turned toward Francis. Holding out a gold necklace with two small keys dangling from it she said, "And this is for you. May you use it wisely."

Fran recognized the keys. She reached out and took them in her hand saying, "Thank you so much for all your help. I can't thank you enough. But now, we have to get home so I can show Jack that surprise we talked about earlier."

"Oh, yes," Kathryn smiled as she spoke, "I am sure Jack will love it."

With that, the two, said goodbye to Kathryn and walked out to their respective cars for the drive home.

~ ~ ~

Chapter 9
NO BARBER NEEDED

Fran woke up and rubbed the sleep out of her eyes as she did every morning. But this was a special morning. It was Sunday. Sunday is Jack's day off. The only day of the week when the two of them can spend some quality time together. And Fran knew just what kind of 'quality' she wanted to fill that time. Yes, Fran had a plan...

The first thing she did was to prepare herself for the day ahead. She went to the bathroom and performed her morning ritual. Then she took a nice hot bath. She used her favorite bath salts to make her skin really soft and help her relax. As she soaked in the huge tub, she carefully planned the whole day. It was the third day since their graduation from Kathryn's Counseling and Jack had not yet seen what she had done in the basement. She was going to surprise him.

She went to her closet to pick out just the right outfit. She chose a black teddy with bright red trim, black stay-up stockings, black elastic garters with a little red bow on each, and a pair of bright red high-heeled shoes. She admired herself in the full-length mirror and decided Jack would melt when he saw her like this. Finally, she put on a black t-shirt that read, "Sexy Bitch" on the front and a pair of blue-jeans. Now, only her shoes were visible, but that was okay, she had worn high-heels with jeans before. Jack wouldn't suspect a thing. Fran went downstairs to make herself some breakfast.

Since this wasn't just any Sunday, Fran decided to make it special for Jack, as well. She would start things off right by making Jack breakfast in bed. She didn't want to wake him up too early, so she fixed herself some coffee and a couple of toaster pastries. Then she went to fetch the Sunday paper so she could read while she sipped her coffee.

When nine-thirty rolled around, Fran decided it was time to start making Jack's breakfast. She cooked him two eggs over-easy, three strips of bacon, two pieces of toast with butter and jelly, orange juice, and, of course, coffee. It was almost ten o'clock when Fran carried the tray of food up the stairs to the bedroom and placed it on the nightstand next to Jack's side of the bed. Sitting on the edge of the bed, Fran leaned down and whispered softly in Jack's ear in order to wake him gently.

As Jack opened his eyes, he could see his wife sitting next to him on the bed. "Wha... What's going on?" he asked rubbing his eyes to clear away the sleep.

"I've brought you your favorite breakfast, dear," Fran explained. "I thought it was the least I could do for you on your only day off."

"What?" he said, still not fully awake.

"I made you breakfast in bed," Fran reiterated. "Now sit up so I can serve it to you." Her voice had changed. She was losing patience with him.

Jack was getting suspicious. Fran hadn't made him breakfast in bed since... Well, since their honeymoon. He thought she must want something. And it must be expensive, or she wouldn't be trying this hard to butter him up. He scooted himself up against the headboard so that he could get a better view of the room. Yep, there was a tray full of his favorite breakfast food all right.

Fran picked up the tray and placed it across his lap. "There you go, dear," she said as she stood up from the bed. "When you're finished, you can take a bath and relax for a while. I'll be back in a few minutes to clear away your breakfast dishes. You just relax and eat." With that she turned and walked out of the room.

Jack was confused. Why all this attention all of a sudden? What did she want? Did she wreck the car or something? He finally decided that she would tell him in her own good time and he may as well take advantage of her generous nature as long as it lasts.

Jack did as Fran had instructed. He finished his breakfast and went to the bathroom to brush his teeth, etc., before taking a well-deserved shower. Jack didn't take baths as a general rule, he liked the feel of the tiny jets of hot water streaming over his body. So he showered instead.

Once he felt relaxed enough, he got out of the shower and dried himself off, got dressed, and went downstairs to find out what was up with Fran. "Okay," he said as he entered the living room where Fran was sitting, reading the Sunday Times and sipping a cup of coffee. "What's up? Why all the loving attention, all of a sudden?"

"Can't a woman show a little appreciation for her husband once in a while?" she replied.

"Nope, not when it's been three whole days since we were at Kathryn's and she gave you the key to this damned chastity belt, she can't," Jack retorted. "I thought things were going to be different around here since we went to that counseling and all. What happened?"

The Marriage Counselor

"Sweetheart," Fran said trying not to give anything away just yet, "I promise you that things will be different from now on, but I just needed some time to think about it. That's all."

"What do you mean?" Jack was getting a little agitated. He knew something was up and he wanted answers. "What's to think about? Either we are going to start this new relationship or not."

"Calm down, dear," Fran said softly as she turned the page in the paper she was reading. "Don't be in such a rush. The fact is, I have some plans for today that will clear everything all up for you. I promise," she continued, "you will get everything you want and more."

Jack settled down and resigned himself to waiting until such time as Fran was ready to tell him what was going on. She was always so vague about things that it sometimes irritated him. He picked up the sports section of the paper that Fran had so graciously laid in his favorite chair and sat down to read. "Okay, as long as you promise I won't have to wait another day."

"You won't dear," Fran said without so much as batting an eye. "I promise."

After a few minutes, without even looking up from her paper, Fran spoke in a soft, even tone, "Take your clothes off, Jack." It was said almost as a matter of fact, rather than an order. But she expected Jack to obey, just the same.

Jack looked up over the top of the paper he was reading. He couldn't be sure, but he thought his wife had just told him to strip. Maybe it was just wishful thinking on his part. He went back to reading about his favorite team.

Fran pushed her newspaper down into her lap, crushing it so that it made that special kind of noise that newspapers make when being crumpled. With her best commanding voice she said firmly, "I told you to take your clothes off. Why are you just sitting there?"

Jack was startled by Fran's sudden change in character. He didn't know how to react. She sounded serious, but then why was this coming out of the blue? He looked at Fran who was now buried in her paper again, and seemed oblivious to him. Then he decided he had better play along. "Yes, Ma'am," he said as he stood up and started to unfasten his belt.

"That's Mistress to you!" Fran said firmly without even looking up from the page.

Now Jack was starting to see what was going on. Fran had, indeed, kept her promise. "Yes, Mistress," he replied, practically jumping for joy inside. He quickly removed every stitch of clothing he was wearing and laid them on his chair. "What else can I do for you, Mistress," he asked.

"You can stand there until I give you another order," Fran said nonchalantly, as she kept on reading her paper.

"Yes, Mistress," he replied. He could feel his cock beginning to stir already, and he had only been told to stand in place. He was amazed at how good he felt after having been a little angry when he thought Fran was never going to take control.

Ten minutes passed before Fran finally folded her paper up and set it on the end table next to her. Jack had been standing in front of his chair facing her ever since she had given him the order. She ordered him to come and stand in front of her so that she could inspect him and his chastity belt.

Jack moved quickly. He stood at parade rest with his hands in the middle of his back. It was how he had always dreamed his Mistress would require him to stand while awaiting orders.

Fran stood up and slowly walked around him. She didn't touch him, she just looked him over closely, hoping to make him a little nervous and maybe even aroused. It worked. By the time she had made one trip around him, Jack's cock was already starting to fill its tiny cage. She smiled to herself, proud that her plan was working. She made a second trip around her, now stoic, husband. This time she let the back of her hand brush against his body as she walked. She brushed across his bottom and allowed her hand to pause for a moment between his cheeks. When she came back in front of him, She took his balls gently in her hand and hefted them as if testing their size and weight. Then she stepped back and looked him up and down one more time, giving Jack time to feel more on display than he already did.

Stepping back another pace, Fran commanded him, "Go get a towel and fill a large bowl with very hot water. Bring them to me in the basement. I'll be waiting for you there."

"Yes, Mistress," Jack said trying to contain his excitement. Then he rushed off to the kitchen to fetch the required items.

Fran went to the basement, now her dungeon, stripped off her t-shirt and jeans and sat down in her father's old chair. It was a winged, high backed, Victorian chair worth quite a lot. That's the only reason they hadn't sold it with the rest of his things after he died. The seat was kind of hard, but it looked rather regal. It was covered in red velvet with gold trim. "Mistress Fran" thought it made an excellent throne on which she could sit and be waited on. Anyway, that's how she intended to use it. Fran picked up the riding crop she had laid out earlier and crossed her legs to complete the picture. Then she waited for Jack to come down the stairs.

A moment later Fran heard Jack open the door to the basement and start down the stairs. She watched as his nearly naked body slowly appeared, feet first, followed by the rest of him as he descended the steps. When he reached the bottom, and turned to face her, Jack stopped in his tracks. He couldn't believe what he saw. His wife/Mistress sitting on what looked like a throne, ropes and hooks and other paraphernalia all around

The Marriage Counselor

the room. It didn't look like the basement he remembered. It looked like... Well, it looked like a dungeon.

"You can put that stuff on the end of that bench," Fran said. "Then come over here and kneel on this carpet. She nodded in the direction of a small rectangular piece of carpet that she had placed directly in front of her chair so that her feet wouldn't have to touch the cold concrete. She also figured it was large enough for Jack to kneel on without destroying his knees.

Jack set the bowl of water and the towel down on the bench and quickly scrambled over to kneel in front of his new Mistress. "How may I serve you, Mistress?" Jack asked as he knelt down and hung his head as if to bow.

Fran reached over to the table next to her chair and grabbed the leather cuffs she had purchased at the sex shop. She tossed them down in front of Jack and said, "Put those on your wrists and ankles."

"Yes, Mistress," was Jack's only reply as he reached for the cuffs.

As soon as Jack had all four cuffs secured in place, Fran ordered to him lay down on the bench with his legs on either side of it. As soon as he was in position, Fran stood up and gave Jack his first full view of her new outfit. His cock immediately tried to free itself by bursting through its cage. Which only caused poor Jack significant pain.

Fran fastened his ankles to the legs of the bench with two double-ended clips and then attached his wrists in the same manner to screw-eyes at the head of the bench. Fran produced a can of shaving cream and a razor that she had kept hidden by her chair, and placed them on the bench between Jack's thighs. She then placed a blindfold that she had purchased at a local pharmacy over his eyes so that his other senses would be heightened. After setting the bowl of hot water on the floor next to her, Fran straddled the bench and sat between her husband's knees with her legs over the top of his to keep them from moving too much.

Taking the key that she now wore around her neck, Fran opened the lock to Jack's cock cage and tugged it off. Finally, she released the lock that held the base ring to the belt and removed that as well. Fran squirted a good amount of shaving cream all over Jack's groin area and carefully rubbed it in so that everything was covered. Then she began to remove all the hair around his cock and balls with the razor. It took her several minutes and she was proud that she never even nicked him once.

When she had finished, Fran washed all the remaining shaving cream off and dried the area with her towel.

Before she removed the restraints holding Jack in place, Fran gave his cock a few strokes to be sure it was awake enough for what she had planned next.

She released the clips that held him in position and, without removing his blindfold, she led him to the place where she had ropes dangling from the ceiling. She fastened his wrist cuffs to the ropes and pulled the ropes taught so that Jack's arms were stretched over his head. Then she tied off the ends to keep him that way. Next, she got the home-made spreader bar she had created from a three-foot piece of wood she found and several screw-eyes she had bought at the hardware store. She used the double clips to fasten his ankle cuffs to the two screw-eyes furthest apart.

Now Jack was truly at her mercy. Next Fran attached a pair of nipple clips to Jack's nipples and tugged on them to make sure they were secure. Jack winced when she did that. Now Fran was ready. She started walking round Jack letting the tip of her riding crop slid over his body. She even flicked the nipple clips to make sure she had Jack's full attention. Finally, she positioned herself behind and to the left of him.

She landed one firm blow with the riding crop right across his bottom. Jack twitched when she did, but he kept his mouth shut. "Okay," Fran began, "Here are my rules. First and foremost, you will obey me at all times." She smacked his ass again, a little harder this time. "Got that?"

"Yes, Mistress," Jack said hoping to avoid any more pain than necessary.

"Two," Fran continued, "Every day when you get home from work, you will go directly to the bedroom and strip. You are not allowed to wear any clothing in the house unless I tell you otherwise." She struck his bottom again. "Got it?"

Again, Jack answered in the affirmative, "Yes, Mistress."

"And three," Fran continued, "you will build, or buy, me a spanking bench like the one you were on at Kathryn's last time." Again, she smacked his ass, this time very hard.

"I got it, Mistress," Jack replied again, "I will order one this afternoon."

"Good, see that you do," she replied before striking him one more time for good measure.

Fran walked over to where she had left her bag of toys and fished out some lubrication and her strap-on dildo. She stepped into the harness and pulled it up in position, then pulled the straps tight. She marveled at the way it hung on her like a real cock. She flipped it up a couple of times just to watch it flop around. Then she stepped up behind Jack and asked, "remember all those times when you wanted to have anal sex with me, and I always said, 'No'?" She poured a good amount of lube into her hand.

"Yes, Mistress," Jack replied a little curious as to what brought that up.

"Well, I've changed my mind." With that she pressed her hand between the cheeks of Jack's bottom and across his anus smearing the lubrication all around.

The Marriage Counselor

"Yes, Mistress," Jack said, suddenly realizing that this was not what he had in mind at the time.

Fran poured some lube onto the dildo that now dangled delightfully in front of her. "Get ready," she said as she eased the tip against Jack's anus. "This is going to hurt you more than it does me." With that, Fran grabbed Jack's hips and pushed until the tip of the dildo popped inside. Then she allowed him to get used to it for a moment, then she pushed it harder and it eased on in until her hips were pressing against his ass cheeks.

"You are no longer the only 'fucker' in the house," she whispered in his ear. Then she started to pull back again. "Now there are two of us. And you can only fuck when, where and what I tell you to." Fran felt her true power finally coming through. She liked fucking Jack's ass and she wasn't going to quit until she was sure he got the point as well.

Fran managed to plunge her toy into Jack's bottom for over ten minutes before she tired out. Then she withdrew it and removed it. She set it aside for Jack to clean when she was done with him. They had been in the basement now for over an hour, but there was one more thing she wanted to do before she released Jack.

Fran released the nipple clips and Jack almost jumped out of his skin. Then she unfastened the spreader bar and untied the ropes that held his arms in place. She left the cuffs in place as sort of a reminder that she was still in charge and that she could bind him to something else if he didn't do as she demanded. She pulled off the blindfold and then sat on her throne. Pointing at the floor directly at her feet, she said, "park it right here. I have another job for you."

Jack knelt down in front of Fran, right between her outstretched legs. He waited for her to give him a command.

Fran reached down and unsnapped the crotch of her teddy exposing her pussy to Jack's gaze. "You want some of the that?" she asked.

Jack said, "Yes, Mistress, I want to please you, if I may."

Fran liked the sound of that so she ordered Jack to bring her to orgasm using only his mouth. Jack leaned forward, bracing himself on her thighs, and began to lap at her swollen, wet pussy. He tasted the lust that she had felt when she was using him and it turned him on. His tongue dug deeply into her hot moist hole and would then flick up and over her hard clit.

Jack's tongue felt so good. Fran had not had oral sex in over a year. She had almost forgotten how good a man's tongue could feel as it licked and probed her inner reaches. After only a short time, and because she had not had an orgasm for a long time, she soon found herself in the throws of one orgasm after another. She gripped Jack's head and held it tightly between her legs in an effort to increase the pleasure he was now giving her.

After what must have been a dozen orgasms in quick succession, Fran finally pushed Jack away. She was exhausted. She had not had that many orgasms in a row since before she was married. She felt good. She knew now that life would definitely be more exciting, especially in the sex department.

Once Fran had recovered, she made Jack stand again so that she could replace his cock cage. But one look at Jack's hard cock, told her that she was going to need some ice before she would be able to accomplish that. She made Jack run up to the kitchen and fetch a bag of ice. Then she made him hold it in place until his cock had shriveled enough to replace the missing items of his chastity belt. Once she had locked him back up, she told Jack that he was going to take her out to lunch and then he was going to treat her to a bath.

"Yeah, that sounded good," she thought to herself, " A bath and a nap."

~ ~ ~

Chapter 10
GAME TIME

When Fran awoke from her nap, Jack was on the computer looking up dungeon furniture. After all, he had promised to order Fran a spanking bench for their dungeon. And he said he would do it today. Fran had fallen asleep on the couch after they got back from lunch and now she was thirsty.

"Jack!" she yelled, not knowing where he was.

"Yes, Mistress?" Jack answered from his desk behind the couch.

"Oh, there you are," she said a little bit surprised to find him so close. Get me a glass of iced tea."

"Right away, Mistress," Jack said as he got up from his seat and headed toward the kitchen. He was still not comfortable being naked anywhere except the bathroom, and possibly the bedroom. Well, the bedroom was only embarrassing when Fran was there fully dressed. Which was most of the time.

Fran had stripped back down to her sexy clothes again once they got back from the restaurant. She was beginning to feel quite comfortable wearing so little in front of Jack. She knew it always turned him on, and that was a turn-on for her. She was beginning to love teasing him at every opportunity. And that just brought something to mind she had prepared for Jack, but hadn't told him about, yet.

When Jack returned from the kitchen with her tea, Fran told him to take a seat on the floor in front of her. He sat down cross-legged and folded his hands in his lap. "What do you need, Mistress?" he asked.

Fran took a sip from her iced-tea and set it on the end table. Then she opened the drawer and pulled out a small bag. She poured the contents into her hand. There were three dice, one red, one green, and one white. She held them out for Jack to see. "These are going to be your life, so to speak," she told him.

"Oh?" Jack looked puzzled.

"We are going to start playing a little game," she said. "Let me explain how it works."

"Yes, Mistress, I'm listening," Jack replied.

"You will roll all three dice each morning," Fran explained. "The number shown on the green die will determine how long your teasing session will last that night."

"How is that going to work?" Jack asked, still a little puzzled.

"We will multiply the number shown on the die by five," Fran continued. "So if you roll a six you get a maximum of thirty minutes of whatever kind of teasing I choose to give you. A one will get you only five minutes,"

"Yes, Mistress, I see," he said beginning to like this game.

"The red die," she said, "will determine how many swats you get."

"Swats?" Jack asked.

"Yes. Swats with whatever implement I choose to use on you," she explained. "Again, we will multiply the number shown on the die by five."

"Ouch!" Jack replied. "I know that's gonna hurt."

"Maybe," Fran said, "depending on your conduct that day."

"So... What's the white on for?" Jack asked.

"The white will be used to determine when and if you get an orgasm, and what type of orgasm you will get."

"Huh?" Jack replied.

"Let me explain," Fran went on. "If the number on the white die matches the number on the green die, you get a ruined orgasm. Again, I will determine how you get it. That is, whether you will masturbate, or if I will give it to you. Understand?"

"Yes, Mistress," he replied again.

"Now," Fran continued, "if the white die matches the number on the red die, you get a stifled orgasm. That means you can cum, but your semen will be stopped before it can come out."

"Okay," Jack said, not really sure what that meant since it had never been done to him. "But when do I get a normal orgasm, Mistress?"

"In order to be granted a full orgasm," She started, "the white die must match both the other dice. In other words, you must throw triples. All three dice must have the same number."

"Yes, Mistress," Jack said again. "I'll bet that doesn't happen very often."

"No, it won't," Fran admitted. "But that's the point. I don't want you to have too many full orgasms, so I designed the game to limit them to only a few."

"Mistress?" he asked.

"Yes, Jack?" she replied.

The Marriage Counselor

"Mistress, are you aware that the odds of rolling the same number are only six in 216 rolls?" Jack queried.

"Six?" Fran repeated. "that sounds like too many. We'll just see how it works out."

"Too many, Mistress?" Jack said thinking that was not enough. "I was hoping for, maybe, one a week?"

Fran laughed. "There's no way you're getting a full orgasm every week. Just be glad you'll be able to have about two a month. Remember, I can always change the rules."

"Yes, Mistress," Jack said feeling a little depressed. "I guess fourteen orgasms in seven months will be fine."

"So..." Fran asked, "Would you like to start today, or do you want to wait until tomorrow to get started?"

"If it's all the same to you, Mistress," Jack said, "I would like to start today."

"Here you go," she said handing the dice to Jack. "Roll away."

Jack took the dice and cleared a spot on the end table. He shook the dice as if he were playing craps, which in a way, he was. He let all three dice roll out of his hand onto the end table. He balled up his fists and scrunched up his face as if he could will the dice to land a certain way. He watched intently as each die came to rest.

Fran called out as each one stopped, "green is six; red is two, and white is..." the white die was spinning rapidly and had not yet come to rest. "The white die is... Awe... It's a four. Sorry, no orgasm for you today."

Jack stared at the three dice as if he could change them in some way. "Yes, Mistress," he repeated, "No orgasm for me today."

"Look at it on the bright side," Fran touted, "You get thirty minutes of teasing and only ten smacks with my paddle."

"Your paddle, Mistress?" he asked,

"Yes," Fran replied gleefully, "I haven't used it yet and I am anxious to try it out."

"Yes, Mistress," he replied.

"We can wait until after dinner," Fran remarked. "After all, don't you have a spanking bench to order this afternoon?'

"Yes, Mistress," Jack said as he got to his feet and strolled back the computer and sat down. He resumed his Internet search for the perfect spanking bench like Mistress had ordered him to do.

Fran decided to watch a movie before dinner and so she went into the TV room. It was really a spare bedroom that they had converted in order to keep the TV out of the living room. It was the only bedroom on the main level of the house, so it worked out perfectly.

When Fran's movie was over, she returned to the living room to find Jack sitting on the couch reading the paper. He looked up as she reached the center of the room and announced, "I found the perfect spanking bench, Mistress. It's almost exactly like the one Mistress Kathryn has in her dungeon. I bookmarked the site so you can see if there is anything else you might want from them."

"Thank you, sweetie," Fran replied. "Maybe I'll take a look tomorrow while you're at work. I'm getting hungry. What about you?"

"Yes, Mistress. Do you want me to order a pizza? It is Sunday," He reminded her. They always have pizza on Sunday because it's Jack's only day off and it gives Fran the day off from cooking.

"Yes," Fran replied. "Go ahead and order it." She suddenly had a thought. She would make Jack pay for the pizza. That should show him that she means business. After all, she was planning on humiliating him along with everything else she had planned to do.

When the doorbell rang, about thirty minutes later, Fran yelled to Jack from the other room, "Will you take care of that, sweetie? I can't go to the door dressed like this."

Jack new that this must be a test and she would make it an order if he didn't go ahead and do it. But still, he was naked, except for his chastity belt and wrist and ankle cuffs. Jack grabbed the twenty dollars he had laid out when he ordered the pizza, not expecting to be the one to answer the door to pay for it. He stood behind the door and opened it just a crack. Enough to see who was there but not enough to let them in.

The voice from outside said, "Pizza delivery for Jacobs."

Jack pushed the twenty out from behind the door and waited for the boy to take it. Then, peering around the door enough to see, he held out his hand for the pizza. Once he felt it in his hand, he said," Keep the change," as he moved the door open just enough to get the pizza through. Then he quickly slammed it shut and breathed a sigh of relief.

"Mistress?" he yelled toward the TV room. "The pizza is here." He had never been so embarrassed in all his life. He was certain he would accidentally expose himself to some unsuspecting kid who just wanted to deliver a pizza, and not get a show along with it. But it was over now, and Jack felt a little safer. He hoped that, in the future, Fran would handle all deliveries.

When they had eaten their fill and sat a few minutes waiting for their food to digest, Fran said, "Well, it's time. Get your butt down in that dungeon."

Jack was turned on by the way she spoke to him and immediately replied, "Yes, Mistress." Then he jumped up and walked toward the

The Marriage Counselor

basement door. Fran followed him down the steps into her new dungeon. She couldn't wait to show it off to some of the girls, Jane especially. But for now, she had a butt to paddle and a cock to tease.

Jack just realized that he was still wearing his leather bondage cuffs. "Oh my God," he thought to himself. "I just stuck my hand out the door with my wrist cuff still on it." His face turned about the same color as he imagined his butt was soon going be.

The first thing Fran did was to remove the cage that kept Jack's cock from getting erect.

"Since we don't have a spanking bench, yet," Fran began, "why don't you just lean across the bench with your hands on one side and your ass on the other?" It was a rhetorical question like many others she figured she would be asking Jack in the future.

"Yes, Mistress," Jack said as he assumed the position she had indicated.

Fran opened her bag of toys and rummaged through it until she found her new paddle. She looked at Jack and asked, "Want a blindfold?"

"Yes, Mistress, please?" He replied.

She grabbed the blindfold while she was there and handed it to Jack. "Here, put it on yourself," she said as she stepped behind him to get in the perfect position. "Now, how many was it again? Thirty?"

"No, Mistress!" Jack relied in a panic. "Only ten. I get thirty minutes of teasing. Remember?"

Fran knew, she just wanted to scare poor Jack a little. "You count them," she said as she prepared to deliver the first blow. She raised her arm up and brought the paddle down hard on the left cheek of Jack's exposed ass.

The paddle landed with a loud "Smack!" to which Jack responded just as loudly, "ONE, Mistress."

The first blow was followed in a few seconds by a second loud smack on his right butt-cheek. To which Jack responded, "TWO, Mistress."

There were four more blows to each cheek and Jack counted every one. When Fran finished, she rubbed his sore bottom for a moment and then helped him to his feet. His bottom looked like a ripe apple, it was so red.

Fran reattached his cuffs to the ceiling ropes and the spreader bar. Then she removed the cage that confined his cock. Once she was done, she stepped back to look at what she had done. He looked so vulnerable and he really had no idea what he was in for. "Are you ready for your thirty minutes of teasing?" Fran asked.

"Yes, Mistress," Jack answered.

Fran set up a small TV tray, the kind meant for eating TV dinners, next to where Jack was standing. She placed everything she thought she would need on the tray and prepared to start Jack's next ordeal. First she stepped up close behind him and rubbed his back and bottom with her bare hands.

Her objective was to get his cock hard before she ever touched it. She whispered in his ear things that she new would turn him on. She reached around his body every now and then to see if he was ready for the next phase of his treatment.

When his cock was nice and hard, Fran picked up a pair of surgical gloves and put them on. Then she added some lubrication to one hand and began to spread it all over Jack's waiting cock. Her hand barely touched him once the lube had been spread over the entire surface. She stroked him and teased him. She taunted him about some of the things she had planned for his future. Things like humiliating him in front of some of the girls in the Bridge Club. Or making him drink his own cum from now on. She told him about some of the torments she was planning, like binding his cock and balls with twine and making him drag a weight around the house all day.

Fran filled his head with all kinds of erotic images as she gently stroked his manhood. Each time she thought he might be getting close to having and orgasm, she would stop touching his cock and she would move to fondling his ass with the hand that was clear of lubrication. It felt a little strange to her to rub his body with a rubber glove on her hand, and she was sure it felt erotic to Jack as well. At one point, about half way through his allotted thirty minutes, she picked up a hand full of clothespins and proceeded to install them on his nipples and his balls. The pain, while intense, was lessened by the pleasure his cock was feeling every time Fran would stroke it.

By the time his time was up, Jack was ready to rip apart the house like the Incredible Hulk. He wanted to squirt his cum so badly he thought he would explode if he was denied the opportunity. But denied he was.

Fran began removing the clothespins, one by one, until they were all off. Then she patted Jack's still sore bottom and said, "That's it Jackie my boy. You're done."

Jack didn't feel done. In fact he felt like he had been as close to done as he could ever get, but wasn't allowed to finish. Which was, in point of fact, what Fran had planned all along.

Fran placed a bag of ice against Jack's cock and held it in place until it had shrunk enough to get his cage back on.

Once Jack's cock was securely locked back in its cage, Fran released all of Jack's bindings and told him to follow her up to the bedroom. She was tired and was going to give him a chance to show her how talented his tongue could be before they went to sleep for the night. Jack was still as turned on as he could ever remember being, so he jumped at the chance to give his wonderful wife and Mistress anything she desired.

# # #

End...

The Marriage Counselor
(Part 3)

CONTENTS

	Acknowledgments	i
1	The Bistro	1
2	A Swat In Time	9
3	Mall Shopping	17
4	Jim's Fashion Show	27
5	Party Planning	35
6	Not All Milk Comes from Cows	44
7	The Web-Tease	52
8	The Party	61
9	Briana's Game	69
10	Epilogue	78
	About the Author	81
	Other Books	82

Chapter 1
THE BISTRO

"What do you call four blondes walking down the street?" James asked the waiter who had just dropped off the menus.

"Um, I don't know, sir," the waiter replied trying his best to get back to his other customers.

"A wind tunnel," James said laughing at his own joke.

The waiter said. "Very funny, sir," and scurried off toward the kitchen.

"You do know that your wife is a blonde, don't you, Jim?" Fran said opening up her menu. "I mean, really?"

"Awe, lighten up Fran," James replied, "It was just a joke."

Briana studied her menu pretending not to pay any attention to what was going on around her. "Brie?" Fran said to Briana, "I don't know how you put up with this constant humiliation."

"Oh, I just try to ignore him," Brie replied. "I figure, if I ignore him, maybe he'll go away." Then she gave Fran one of her famous quickie smiles that only served to tell Fran that she didn't want to talk about it.

"Like I said, Fran," Jim began, "lighten up. It's only a joke. Brie can take a joke. Can't you, honey?"

Briana gave Jim one of her quickie smiles too, but didn't say a word. She had been down this road with him many times, but he just can't seem to quit. Jim has always been this way. Even when they first got married, he would make fun of her in public, tell off-color jokes, sometimes about her, when he thought she couldn't hear him. She just finally gave up. "Jim's just an ass, sometimes," she thought to herself. "There's no way in hell that's ever gonna change." But inside, all of Jim's jokes hurt. They really hurt. Yeah, she was blonde, but that didn't give him the right to tell every blonde joke he ever heard right in front her. But what was she to do? That was Jim.

Fran changed the subject, realizing that it was hard for Brie to talk about it, especially in front of Jim. "How's everything at school, Jim?" she asked.

"Not so bad," he replied, "I think I have a pretty bright bunch of students this year. At least, they seem a lot smarter than last years kids."

"Really?" Fran continued to press the subject, not wanting it to return to Jim's insensitivity to Briana. "I thought all kids that age were pretty much the same from one year to the next."

"Normally they are," Jim replied, "but for some odd reason, these kids are well ahead most classes I get. Maybe it's that new Freshman class science teacher they hired last year. Maybe the kids in his class actually learned something."

"Will wonders never cease?" Fran added.

Brie sat quietly as Fran and Jim talked about whatever Fran could think of until the waiter came back to take their order. Then Jim had to leave. He had only dropped by to leave Brie the car since the bistro was so close to the high school. But he couldn't stay, he had another class in fifteen minutes.

As soon as Jim had left, Fran reached across the table and placed her hand on top of Brie's. "Sweetie?" she began, "You can't let Jim go on humiliating you like that all the time. You have got to do something about it."

The two girls placed their orders and waited until the waiter had left their vicinity before continuing their conversation. "To be honest, Fran," Briana said hanging her head. "I don't know what to do. Jim has always been like this and it's getting to the point where I don't want to be seen in public with him anymore."

Fran could see the tears welling up in Briana's eyes. She knew that living with someone who constantly humiliated you could not be easy. "Brie?" Fran said in an attempt to console the woman who had been her friend for over ten years, now. "I think you need some help."

"I don't need a shrink," Brie responded. "He's the one who needs to see a shrink."

"I wasn't talking about a psychiatrist, Brie," Fran said still attempting to console her friend. "I was talking about a marriage counselor."

"What good would that do?" Brie asked with a frown on her face.

"I know this counselor who helped both me and Jane," Fran explained. "She's really, really good, and I think you should have a talk with her."

"I could never do that," Brie complained. "Besides, how would I ever get Jim to go? He's the one who needs the help."

"Well, I don't agree," Fran said shaking her head. "I think you both need help and if anyone can help you with this it's Kathryn."

"Kathryn? Who's Kathryn?" Brie asked.

"She's only the best damned marriage counselor you'll ever find," Fran replied. "If you don't believe me, just call Jane. You trust her, don't you?"

"Oh, Fran," Brie sobbed, "you know I trust you. It's not that. I just don't know if I could do something like that."

"Why don't we talk it over with Jane?" Fran coaxed. "After all, she has been your best friend for longer than I have known you. Maybe she will have some idea of what you can do." Fran knew what Brie needed, but if Jane could just convince Brie, then everything would work out.

Brie wiped her eyes with her napkin and looked up at Fran. "You really think Jane could help?"

"It won't hurt to talk it over with her," Fran replied cheerfully. "Besides, you know she has seen the problem."

"Yeah, I know," Brie said as she regained her composure. "I think that's why Jane hates James."

Just then the waiter showed up with their orders. A BLT for Fran and a Club sandwich for Brie. He placed their plates on the table in front of them and asked if they needed anything else. "Just a refill on our tea," Fran said.

"Yes, ma'am," the waiter replied before scurrying off to the drink station.

Fran leaned across the table toward her friend and whispered, "Remember when Jane brought her husband to our card game and made him masturbate for us?"

"Yeah," Brie whispered back with a chuckle. "I couldn't believe she could get him to do that."

"She had been to Kathryn's counseling and Kathryn taught her to take control of Frank like that," Fran whispered again.

"Really?" Brie said, shocked that Jane had even been to a marriage counselor. "I didn't know they had been to see a marriage counselor."

"I went there, too," Fran confessed. "It's the best thing I ever did. Jack has stopped his bad habits and our sex-life has never been better."

"I didn't know you guys were having problems," Brie admitted. "When did all this happen?"

"It was a couple of months ago," Fran replied, "but what's important is that you get some help for your problem with Jim."

"Yeah, I guess maybe you're right," Brie admitted. "Maybe I do need help. But I'm still not so sure about a marriage counselor."

"Do what I did," Fran urged, "make yourself an appointment and go talk with Kathryn. If you aren't convinced that she can help, then you don't have to drag Jim into it. He won't even have to know you went to see her. How's that sound?"

"I guess I could do that," Brie conceded. "Does she offer a free consultation?"

"Don't worry," Fran assured her, "you won't be charged a thing if you don't want her service. But believe me, by the time you walk out of there, you are gonna know she can help you. I think you should call Jane and talk with her before you do anything. If she can't convince you that it's the right thing to do, then no one can."

Brie agreed to call Jane and talk with her about James and his problem. After all, Jane was her best friend and if she thought this Kathryn person could help, then, maybe she would give her a try.

The two women finished their lunch and said their goodbyes. Brie drove home with a little more hope for the future than she had when she left the house to go shopping with Fran. She made up her mind to call Jane and see what she had to say. Somehow, she knew Jane would be all for her doing something to stop Jim's constant humiliation of her.

Once inside, Briana became a little more unsure of herself. But she knew she could confide in Jane, no matter what her problems were. Jane had always been there for her, no matter what. So she sat down in her favorite spot on the couch and pressed the speed dial for Jane on her cell phone.

"Hi, Brie!" Jane said when she saw who was calling. "How's it going?"

"Jane," Brie began, "I've got a problem and Fran said I should call you about it."

"Sure, sweetie," Jane said with concern in her voice, "what's the problem?"

"Well..." Brie hesitated for a moment. "You know how Jim is always telling those horrible jokes and embarrassing me all the time?"

"Yeah," Jane replied. "You know I have always hated him for that, right?"

"Yeah, well," Brie continued, "I've been talking with Fran and she said I should ask you about something."

"What's that?" Jane asked.

"She said I should go to this marriage counselor and see if she can help," Brie said a little unsure of herself.

"Kathryn's?" asked Jane.

"Yeah," Brie replied. "What do you think? She said you took Frank there and she helped you to work everything out."

"She did more than that," Jane confided. "That woman is a miracle worker! She not only helped me with my marriage, but I'm a whole lot more confident about everything in my life now. Haven't you noticed?"

"Actually," Brie said, "I have. I thought you seemed to be a lot more assertive than you ever were in the past. But I just chalked it up to some motivational book you read or something."

"Nope," Jane replied with a chuckle. "It was all Kathryn's doing. If Fran suggested you go see her, I heartily agree. Just go in and talk with the woman. You'll see. Before you know it, Jim will be putty in your hands. He won't be embarrassing you any more, that's for sure."

"You really think I should go?" Brie asked, needing some reassurance.

"Definitely! Just make yourself an appointment and talk to her. If you decide it's something you want to do, and I think you will, then Kathryn will make arrangements for Jim to be brought in."

"What do you mean?" Brie asked, sounding a bit confused. "You make it sound as if he will be arrested or something."

"No," Jane chuckled, "Kathryn will take care of getting him into her office. You won't even have to tell him."

"Really?" Brie perked up a bit. "I won't have to convince Jim to go with me?"

"Not at all," Jane replied. "Just make yourself an appointment and talk with her. I think you will be surprised."

Okay," Brie agreed, "I'll do it right now."

"That's my girl," Jane said. "Call her right now. Do you have the number?"

"Yes," she replied, "Fran gave it to me."

"Good," Jane said, "Call her right now."

"I will," Brie confirmed. "I'll talk to you later."

"Okay, bye," Jane said as she hung up the phone.

Brie dug through her purse to find the napkin that Fran had written Kathryn's number on. Then she called Kathryn's Counseling Service to make an appointment.

She was in luck. Kathryn had a cancellation and she was able to get in to see her at three. That meant she would have time to get home before Jim. He usually got home between four-thirty and five depending on whether or not he had papers to grade.

Brie grabbed her bag and headed out the door. It was already two-forty-five. She had just enough time to get there.

She pulled into a parking space across the street from Kathryn's and practically ran across to the front door. Once inside, she walked straight back to the receptionist's window and introduced herself.

"Hi," she said breathlessly, "I'm Briana Galloway. I am here for an appointment."

"Yes, you are and you certainly got here fast," replied the woman from behind the counter. "I'm Maggie. I'll tell Dr. Andrews that you're here. Just have a seat, it will only be a minute."

Brie sat in the closest chair she could find. She no sooner picked up a Modern Psychology magazine than Maggie stuck her head through the door and said, "She's ready for you now. If you'll just follow me."

Brie put the magazine back on the table next to her and stood up. She took a second to straighten her clothes before following Maggie through the door and down the hall.

"Here we are," Maggie said as she stopped outside Kathryn's office. She gestured for Brie to go on in.

"Thank you," Brie said as she stepped through the doorway.

"Hi, I'm Dr. Andrews," Kathryn said extending her hand toward Brie. "Come on in and have seat."

Brie shook her hand and said, "I'm Brie." Then she sat down in the nearest chair in front of Kathryn's desk.

Kathryn walked around her desk and took her seat. "What can I do for you today?" Kathryn asked, getting right down to business.

"I'm not really sure," Brie confessed. "I have a problem, well, my husband has a problem. Ever since we first got married, he always embarrasses me."

"And just how does he do that?" Kathryn asked with sincere interest.

"He tells blonde jokes and stuff like that right in front of me. Just today he told a waiter a blonde joke right in front of me and one of my best friends," Brie admitted. "It's not just blonde jokes. He tells perfect strangers humiliating things about me all the time. It's like he doesn't care."

"I see," Kathryn said thoughtfully. "And have you discussed this with him?"

"Yes," Brie said defending herself. "Many times, but he just doesn't get it. He doesn't seem to understand that it hurts me, inside."

"I understand," Kathryn tried to console Brie. She could see the tears welling up in Brie's eyes and she knew the woman was at her wits end. "You obviously love him. Do you think he loves you, too?"

"Oh, yeah," Brie replied defending Jim's honor, or what there was of it. "It's just that he is so insensitive. It's like he doesn't care how I feel."

"Okay," Kathryn replied, "and what do you think I can do to help you?"

"I don't honestly know if you can," Brie confessed, "but I didn't know where else to go. My two best friends told me that you could help."

"I think I can, Brie," Kathryn said. I just need to know if you are going to be willing to do whatever it takes to make this behavior of your husband's stop."

"I'll do whatever it takes, Doctor," Brie started sobbing for the second time that day. "I just don't know what that is."

"Well, I have some ideas that I think will help, but you have to be willing to work hard and learn how to control, not only yourself, but your husband as well." Kathryn sounded reassuring. "Do you think you can do that, if I help you?"

"I will try anything," Brie admitted wiping the tears from her eyes.

"I don't want you to just try," Kathryn said as she leaned on her elbows on the desk. "I want to know that you have it within you to do whatever I tell you to do in order to take control of yourself and your husband. Can you promise me that you'll do that?"

Brie drew a deep breath and tried to regain her composure. "I promise to do my best if you'll help me."

"Okay, then," Kathryn replied. "I will help you. But I promise you, it won't be easy."

"Yes, ma'am." Brie said, "I won't let you down."

"Let me tell you what you are in for," Kathryn began. "First of all, we are going to have to get your husband to agree to wear a chastity belt and to depend on you for sexual release."

"A chastity belt?" Brie seemed confused. "You mean, like the thing Jane's husband Jack wears?"

"Yes, if you mean Jack Walters," Kathryn replied. "But I don't think that's going to be the hard part. You say you have friends who are willing to help you? Women who I have already helped?"

"Yes," Brie assured her, "my two best friends who sent me here will help me. I'm sure. Jane is one of them."

"Good. The first thing you need to do is to learn how to be more assertive," Kathryn explained. "If they can help you with that, so much the better. I can teach you the mechanics, but I can't hold your hand when you are not here. So I am counting on you to be strong. Can you do that?"

"Yes, ma'am," Brie said wiping the tears from her eyes. "I can do that."

"Good, now let's go take a look at the treatment room and I'll explain how we do things here," Kathryn said as she stood up and and gestured for Brie to do the same. "Follow me, the treatment room is down stairs."

As they headed down the hallway to the elevator, Kathryn explained that what she was about to see might be a little shocking. But she assured her that it was necessary for her husband's treatment.

They entered the waiting elevator and rode it to the lower level. When the elevator doors opened again and Brie got her first look at Kathryn's dungeon, she had no idea what she was looking at. "What is all this stuff?" she asked.

"This is our treatment room," Kathryn explained. "This is where you and James will learn what a Female Led Relationship is all about. You will learn how to control him and he will learn to obey you. By that I mean, he will learn that when he embarrasses you in public, he will not only have to go without ex for awhile, he may also be punished by you."

Looking around the room, Brie asked, "What kind of punishment are we talking about?"

Kathryn placed her hand on Brie's shoulder and, in a reassuring tone, said, "Physical punishment. Like you might give a disobedient child, only more attuned to Jim, as an adult."

"Oh, you mean like spanking?" Brie asked.

"Well," Kathryn replied, like that, only mush more severe. Something that will make Jim understand that you mean business."

"Oh, I see," Brie said.

7

After a twenty-minute tour of the facilities, Brie finally understood what was about to happen. She was going to have to teach James how it feels to be humiliated. Kathryn would help her, James' insurance would pay for it, all except the chastity device, and she would have to develop her dominant side. She understood why Kathryn had been so hesitant to agree to take her on. She had never been very assertive and now, in spite of herself, she was going to have to learn to be in charge. Not just of herself, but of James as well.

She had to fill out some paperwork and pay the $200 fee for the chastity belt that would soon be installed on her husband, but with the prospect of Jim never humiliating her again, she would do whatever it took.

She made another appointment with Maggie for the following day and Maggie gave her a pamphlet about how to control your husband. Brie promised to study it before she returned.

Brie drove home happier than she could ever remember being. Fran and Jane were right. Dr. Andrews could solve her problem with Jim. She was positive that things would work out just fine.

~ ~ ~

Chapter 2
A SWAT IN TIME

The following morning, Briana got up and made breakfast for James. They didn't really talk much, but Brie did try to tell him that all his jokes, especially the ones about blondes, made her feel embarrassed and less confident in herself.

James' only comment, when Brie confronted him was, "Oh, Brie, you know I don't mean anything by them."

To which Brie replied, "But I don't think you understand how they affect me."

On his way out the door, Jim said, "Sure I do, honey. Just don't take it personally." Which only reinforced her belief that he would never change without Kathryn's help.

Once he was gone, Brie called Jane for some moral support. She was almost in tears again so Jane told her she would be right over. Jane had no intention of letting her best friend go through all this alone. "Besides," she thought, "Brie has never had much of a strong personality."

Brie cleared away the breakfast dishes and waited for Jane to arrive. When Jane finally pulled up outside, she saw Fran get out of the car with her.

Jane didn't even bother to knock, she simply opened the door and walked in. "Brie, we are here to help you," she said as Fran closed the door behind them.

"Come on in and sit down," Brie said. "I'll get you some coffee."

"That would be good," Jane said. "I'm sure we could all use a strong cup of coffee right now."

Fran and Jane sat together on the couch leaving one of the two chairs facing them open for Brie when she came back. It wasn't so much of a comfort thing as it was a strategic placement. They both wanted Brie to sit where they could face her directly. She needed support, and they were there to give it to her.

When Brie returned from the kitchen with a small tray of coffee cups and a pot, she set it down on the coffee table in front of the couch. Jane grabbed the pot and poured each of them a cup. Jane drank hers black but both Fran and Brie needed sugar and creamer.

"Okay," Jane began, "we all know why we're here. You did say you talked to Kathryn. Right?"

"Yes," Brie replied, "I saw her yesterday and she said she can help me. She gave me this pamphlet, but I haven't had time to read it, yet."

"Great!" Fran said. "That should at least be some comfort. Kathryn said she could help. If she said she could help, then she will. Trust me."

"Trust us," Jane said agreeing with her friend. "You know that we will do whatever you need, as well."

"That's why I called you, Jane," Brie began. "I don't know if I can be strong enough to take charge like Kathryn says I need to do. It scares me."

"I know," Jane said comforting her friend. "But I know you. Probably better than anyone, and I know you can do this. Why don't we study the pamphlet together. Fran and I can tell you how you need to approach this whole thing."

"Yeah," Fran piped up, "I didn't think I could do it either. I was scared, but you know what? Kathryn made it easy. She will make easy for you, too."

"That's right," Jane said confidently, "and we will help you too. Let's start by going through this pamphlet together."

The three women worked their way through the pamphlet one paragraph at a time. They made Briana practice using her "commanding" voice and helped her to understand why she needed to take control of Jim. They explained how Jim had been bossy and pushed her around a lot, but in a nice way. His intentions might be good, but he was just insensitive and needed to be brought down a peg or two. They instructed her on how to ask him to do things for her without having to say "please" and "thank you" every time. They told her that she needn't be afraid of Jim because once he was wearing a chastity belt, he would be much easier to handle. Brie didn't really understand exactly why that was, but she accepted it as fact since both her best friends assured her it would be that way.

By the time Jane and Fran left, it was almost noon. Brie was hungry and not nearly so frightened as she was before they came. Now she thought she would be able to do whatever Kathryn asked of her without having to question why about everything. She fixed herself some lunch and curled up on the couch with a book to pass the time.

The book wasn't working. She decided she needed to practice being in charge. Brie stood in her bedroom in front of her full-length mirror. For the longest time, she simply stared at her reflection. She was a good-looking blonde woman in her late thirties. She still had a great figure, and no wrinkles on her face. The longer she stood there, the more she realized that she was a very attractive woman. Her courage grew the longer she stared at herself.

Finally, she began giving orders. Not to herself, but to Jim. She imagined Jim kneeling at her feet, naked. She would order him to do this or that in the best, most commanding voice she could muster. She didn't shout. She didn't yell. She practiced giving orders for over an hour. Then, when she was satisfied that she could do it properly, she smiled. Suddenly the woman in the mirror wasn't the meek, mild woman she had been for so much of her life. No, not any more. Now she was a woman in charge. She would show Kathryn that she could handle Jim.

When the time came for Brie's appointment at Kathryn's, she was ready. She parked right out front and strolled confidently in through the front door. Her pace didn't slow or falter as she walked straight back to the receptionist's station.

"Maggie, I'm here for my appointment," she stated with all the confidence of a general announcing victory over the enemy.

Maggie looked up at the woman standing before her. She was wearing a pink pair of sweat pants with white trim, a white leotard, and a matching sweat suit jacket with a hood, and white high-heeled sandals. At first, Maggie looked around for someone else. She thought this could not be the woman who had just spoken so confidently. That woman would surely have been dressed in fatigues. "Yes, Ma'am," she replied as she pressed the button on her intercom box. "Ms. Galloway is here Mistress," she said still looking at Briana.

"Send her back, Maggie," came the reply from the tiny box.

Maggie asked Brie, "Do you remember how to get to Mistress Kathryn's office?"

Brie, still as confident as the second she strode through the door, answered, "I know where it is, the first hallway to the right, first door on the left." Without another word, Brie headed for Kathryn's office. Maggie was still in shock over the change she saw in Brie.

The door to Kathryn's office was open so Brie simply strode into the office and plopped herself down in one of the chairs across from Kathryn and said, "I'm here, and I'm ready to learn."

Kathryn detected an air of confidence in Brie that she had not seen before. Leaning back in her chair, Kathryn remarked, "Well, aren't you the confident one today. To what do we owe this change in your attitude?"

"I had a long talk with my two best friends this morning. I am tired of being the 'dumb blonde'," Brie said, in no uncertain terms. "I am NOT dumb."

"Well," Kathryn began, "I have to admit, I see a big change in you." Kathryn understood that having confidence when surrounded by close friends who support you is very different than displaying that same confidence to your husband. But not wanting to deflate Brie's ego, she kept her thoughts to herself. Who knows? She just might be able to bring it off.

"Thank you," Brie said. "I appreciate the support."

"Shall we get started on today's lesson?" Kathryn asked standing up from her chair.

"I'm as ready as I will ever be, "Brie replied. "Where are we going?"

"To the treatment room," Kathryn said. "You have a lot to learn and not much time to learn it."

Brie followed Kathryn as they entered the elevator at the end of the hall. They talked about James and what Brie would be called upon to do in order to get him into a chastity belt and then to maintain control of Jim after that. Brie practiced the entire hour with the riding crop and paddle using the lifelike silicone doll that Kathryn kept in the treatment room for just such a purpose.

When it was almost time for James to arrive, they returned to Kathryn's office. Brie was going to wait for Jim in the dressing room where he would be forced into his chastity belt. It was her job to convince him to agree to continue wearing it. So, when Maggie called over the intercom to announce Jim's arrival, Brie went to the dressing room before Maggie escorted Jim to Kathryn's office.

When Maggie arrived at Kathryn's office, with Jim in tow, she knocked on the office door. "Dr. Andrews?" she began, "Mr. Galloway is here as you requested."

Kathryn opened her door and greeted Jim, "Come on in, Mr. Galloway. I am sorry to have to bring you down here under these circumstances."

"Yes," Jim replied, "you said something about a problem with one of my students?"

Kathryn motioned for him to sit down as she returned to her own chair. "Yes, indeed," Kathryn began, "I think perhaps we need to talk for a minute first."

"Okay," Jim replied, puzzled about exactly why he had been brought into a marriage counselor's office for a problem with a student. "But aren't these kinds of things confidential?"

"Oh, it is," Kathryn replied, "it's very confidential. You see, the problem isn't really with one your students. It's with your wife."

"What?" Jim asked a bit startled. "What about my wife?"

"Well, it seems she has been having some difficulty coping with..." Kathryn paused as if in thought. "With a particular problem and I thought she could use your help."

"Really?" Jim asked. "And just what is this 'problem' she is having so much trouble with?"

"It's not easy to explain," Kathryn said. "Perhaps it would be better if I just showed you. Come with me, please." She stood up and walked to the door. She held it open for Jim as he stepped out into the hallway. "She's just down here." Kathryn pointed down the hall to the next room to the left.

When the pair reached the dressing room, Kathryn took hold of the door handle. She hesitated for a moment. Looking at Jim she said, "Briana is in here, I am going to leave you two alone for a few minutes. Brie will explain the problem she is having." Then she opened the door.

Brie was standing on the far side of the room. As he stepped through the door, Jim asked, "Brie? What's the matter?"

But just as the door closed behind him, two men grabbed his arms and pulled him onto a padded table. He fought, but they were way too strong for him to fend off. They quickly fastened his wrists with padded leather cuffs that were attached to the table above his head.

"What's going on?" Jim shouted. "What the hell are you doing?" But by the time he could say anything else he was securely fastened in place.

Briana stepped up beside the table and explained, "Jim? Sweetheart? I can't take any more of your humiliating jokes and comments when we are in public."

"What?" Jim replied angrily. "You mean all this is because you don't like my jokes? What's the matter with you, Brie?"

"Honey," Brie said calmly. "You might not think that it's a serious matter, but I have put up with your constant humiliation for years, and I am tired of it. It's going to stop. And it's going to stop NOW!"

Jim could tell that Brie was indeed upset. In fact, he had not seen her this upset in his whole life. He started to protest, again, but decided since he was in no position to do much of anything, he might as well hear her out. "Okay, dear," he conceded. "I can see you are seriously upset about this. So what do you want from me? What can I do to make things better?"

Jim was finally calming down and Brie thought he might actually agree to her demands without putting up much of a fight. So, she explained to him how all his joking around, especially the blonde jokes, made her feel. How every time they went anywhere in public, he would humiliate her. She also explained that she wasn't going to take it anymore. Then she broke the news to him. The only way he could begin to make it up to her was to wear a chastity belt and begin listening to her a lot more. He would have to do everything she wanted him to do and that he would be punished if he embarrassed again in any way.

"Not only no," Jim replied, "but HELL NO!" Obviously, Jim did not fully realize the seriousness of the position he was in.

"One way or another," Brie explained, "you will NOT leave here tonight without a chastity belt in place. If these guys," she nodded her head toward the men standing by the head of the table to which Jim was securely strapped, "have to forcibly put it on you, they will."

Jim looked up at the two men. Then he looked at his wife. Then he finally spoke. "Okay," he said in a more compliant tone, "what do I have to do?"

"Well," Brie explained, "the first thing you need to do is sign this agreement." She held up a copy of the chastity agreement. "Once you sign this, we will put your chastity belt on and you will be released."

"But I don't want to wear a chastity belt," Jim complained.

"That's irrelevant," Brie said bluntly. "The fact is, you are going to wear one. Like it or not. You might as well agree to it and save yourself all the pain of being coerced."

"Coerced?" Jim asked. "What do you mean 'coerced'? It sounds to me like I am being 'forced' not coerced."

"I mean coerced," Brie replied. "What does it sound like I mean?"

"Well then," Jim said resolutely, "I guess you'll just have to coerce me."

Brie leaned over her husband and whispered in his ear, "Sweetheart, I know this seems to be an extreme measure, but I love you. I don't want to leave you. However, if you don't agree to this, I am afraid our marriage is over. I just can't take it anymore."

Jim looked up at her. He was in shock. He had no idea that Brie felt that way. "Honey," he began calmly, "I didn't know it really bothered you that much." he paused for moment, reflecting on what Brie and just told him. Then, he said softly, "If this is that important to you, please, put me in chastity. I don't want to lose you, and I will do whatever it takes to keep you and to make our marriage something we can be proud of."

"If that's the way you want it," Brie said as she nodded to the gentlemen standing at the head of the table where James was strapped down.

The two men stepped on either side of James and began removing his clothing. They started with his pants and, in spite of his protests, Jim's pants and underwear were soon off. His ankles were then strapped down in the same way his wrists were. His shoes and socks were removed and then, one arm at a time was released in order to remove the rest of his clothing.

Once he was naked, Brie gave him one more chance to sign the agreement. But, since he had agreed to do whatever Brie felt was necessary, he said, "I will sign it, but not until you explain what it is you are going to do to me."

"Then," Brie asked, "shall we proceed as if you have refused?"

"Yes. I wouldn't want anyone to think I agreed to this too easily."

Whit that, brie signaled the men to proceed.

The Marriage Counselor

The two men released Jim's wrist cuffs from the table and fastened them behind his back. They also released the ankle cuffs from the table leaving them in place around his ankles. They pulled James off the table and out into the hallway.

From there, it was a short trip, with Jim kicking and screaming, to the elevator. Once inside, he calmed down, realizing there was nothing he could do. When the elevator door slid open again, Jim was hauled across the floor to an X-shaped wooden structure to which all four of his cuffs were quickly attached.

The two men left the room and returned to the elevator. Jim was left all by himself, strapped facing a cross, to think about his situation.

Ten minutes later, though it felt much longer, Jim heard the elevator doors open again. He heard Brie talking as she approached his position. "Brie?" he asked. "Is that you?"

"Yes, it's me," Brie responded. "And Kathryn, and Maggie, too."

On her way to Jim, Brie picked up a paddle that Kathryn had left out from her earlier practice session. She stepped up right behind James and made sure he could see the paddle in her hand. "I'll give you one more chance to sign that agreement," she said slapping her hand with the paddle. Kathryn was really proud of the way Briana was not being intimidated by her husband. She showed every bit as much confidence as she had when she first walked into the place that evening.

"Do you really think you can intimidate me into signing that agreement," Jim asked.

"Nope," Brie replied matter of factually, "I was hoping I would get to beat you into submission, but the choice is yours."

"You wouldn't dare," Jim said defiantly.

Briana didn't say another word. She stepped back and gave Jim's exposed bottom one hard smack after another. He screamed in both pain and protest, but Brie kept right on hitting his ass over and over again.

Jim started yelling, "Stop!" and "I'll sign it, I'll sign it!" by the tenth blow, but that didn't stop Briana. She continued hitting his bottom until she had given him a full twenty smacks.

Finally, Brie stopped and asked, "Ready to sign?"

"Yes, please," Jim said breathlessly. "I'll sign it. I'll wear the damned chastity belt. Just please, don't hit me again. My ass can't take it."

"Just so you know," Brie explained, "if you still don't want to continue, by signing the agreement, I will let you go. Both from any more pressure to sign and from our marriage. Is that clear?"

"I understand," Jim responded. "I'll do anything to save our marriage."

"That's what I wanted to hear," Brie said joyfully, setting her paddle down on the nearby table. Maggie grabbed the clipboard that contained the chastity agreement and stepped behind the cross, in front of Jim. Brie unfastened Jim's right hand so he could sign the form.

Once the form was signed, the three women worked together and managed to get James turned around on the cross so that the chastity belt could be installed. Kathryn showed Brie how the belt worked and how she can remove the cage without having to remove the entire belt. Once Brie was satisfied that she understood how the whole thing worked, Kathryn and Maggie left the treatment room and went back upstairs.

Brie took a few minutes to explain to Jim that if he didn't do exactly as she instructed, he would be punished, and that if he told one more of his humiliating jokes she would make him regret it. Jim said he understood so Brie let him loose and escorted him back up to the dressing room so that he could dress and they could go home.

~ ~ ~

Chapter 3
MALL SHOPPING

It was Saturday morning and Briana woke up early. She was excited about what she had planned for the day and wanted to get an early start. She had thought about making Jim cook breakfast, but remembered what a lousy cook he was, and decided against it. However, a bath sounded good. She decided to make her own breakfast and then, later, Jim could draw her a nice hot bath.

Brie put the coffee on and put a couple of pieces of bread in the toaster. She got out the butter and the cinnamon-sugar, a plate and a cup for the coffee. No sooner had the toast popped up when Jim came into the kitchen. The smell of the coffee brewing had wafted its way up to the bedroom and woke him up.

"Morning," Jim said as he stumbled into the room. "Is the coffee ready?"

"It will be in a few minutes," Brie replied. "If you want some toast, I'll put in a couple of slices for you."

"No thanks," Jim said, "just the coffee I think."

Brie sat down and started to butter her toast. "You might want to eat something. I have plans for the day," she informed him, "and you are a part of those plans."

"I was going to mow the lawn this afternoon," Jim explained, "but I won't mind putting that off for a day."

"Well," Brie began, "when you finish your breakfast, I want you to prepare a nice hot bubble bath for me. Today, you belong to me."

"Ooo," Jim said, "that sounds interesting. Can I join you in the tub?"

"No, not this time," Brie said smiling to herself. "I have other plans for you."

The coffee pot stopped gurgling and Jim got himself a cup out of the cupboard. He grabbed the pot and poured Brie a cup before filling his own.

He put the pot back onto the drip machine and sat down at the table. "What kind of plans do you have for me, today?" he asked after blowing the steam off his coffee.

"Well," Brie began as if deep in thought, "For starters we are going to the mall to find you some things to wear."

"New clothes?" Jim asked excitedly. "I love getting new clothes."

"Good," responded Brie, "because I am going to want you to try them on so that we are sure they fit."

"I know what size I wear," he retorted, "I've worn the same size for the last seven or eight years." Jim was proud of his physique. It wasn't perfect, but thanks to the free exercise equipment at the high school he used twice a week, he had a right to be proud.

"I'm sure you do, dear," Brie replied, "but I wasn't asking, I am requiring it."

"Oh," Jim replied rather meekly, "if you require it, then I guess I have no choice."

"Right," Brie replied, "and I do require it."

James remained silent for a while as Brie finished eating her toast. Then he suddenly piped up, "What do you call two blondes in a hot-tub?"

"I don't care," Brie said raising one eyebrow at Jim.

"Oh yeah," Jim said, "I'm sorry. I forgot. This is going to be tougher than I thought."

"You'll get used to it," Brie told him. "You know I can't let that go, don't you?'

"What do you mean?" Jim asked.

"You will have to be punished for that," Brie said calmly. "Go upstairs and get my hairbrush out of the bathroom."

"What?" Jim asked wondering why she would want that now.

"You heard me," Brie said raising her eyebrow again. "Now go, or I'll double your punishment."

"Yes, Ma'am," Jim responded as he stood up and headed for the bedroom.

Brie smiled again. James had listened to what she told him last night before they went to bed. He remembered how to address her, and that she very well could punish him in just about any way she wanted. The worst way was cutting him off from sex of any kind.

As James was walking up the steps, he thought about the changes that Briana was making in their relationship. He wasn't sure he was going to like them all, but he kind of liked the part where she could order him around. He didn't fully understand it, but for some reason it kind of turned him on. He knew she was going to use the hairbrush on his ass, but his cock was still swelling inside its tiny cage. He didn't have to understand it, he just wanted to enjoy the feeling.

The Marriage Counselor

When Jim returned to the kitchen, Brie's toast was gone and she was just finishing up her first cup of coffee. She held out her hand and motioned with her fingers for him to hand her the brush. He did, and she turned her chair away from the table and patted her thigh, "Lay across here," was all she said.

Jim looked at her lap, then at Brie's face, then back at her lap. "Yes, Ma'am," he replied and stepped forward so that he could do as he had been directed. He pulled down his night shorts and leaned down to lay across Brie's lovely legs.

"This is the first of what will, most likely, be many spankings," Brie said gently rubbing Jim's bottom in preparation for what was to come.

"I hope it won't be many," Jim said, "I am going to do my best to behave and control my tongue."

"Good," Brie replied, "I hope you do. Now count for me." She raised the brush high in the air and picked the exact spot on her husband's butt that she intended to hit.

"Yes, Ma'am," He replied. There was a loud 'smack' as the hairbrush found its mark. "OUCH! One, Ma'am."

Brie raised the brush again and brought it down on the other cheek this time. Smack!

"TWO, Ma'am," he shouted trying to control himself. He began to squirm a bit because his growing cock was beginning to fill its cage and he needed to get it into a better position.

"Stop squirming," Brie said just before the hairbrush landed again. Smack!

"THREE, Ma'am," Jim, still shouting the numbers instead of expressing his pain in other words that end up bringing even more pain. Smack! "FOUR, Ma'am."

Pushing James from her lap, Brie said, "The next time, it will be ten."

Jim landed on his side on the hard floor. "Yes, Ma'am," he managed to say as he picked himself up and pulled his shorts back into place.

"Now go," Brie commanded, "fix me a nice hot bath. Oh, and take off those stupid night clothes you wear. I never want to see those again."

Jim gave a slight bow, which did not go unnoticed by Brie, and said, "Yes, Ma'am." then he hurried out of the room.

When Brie arrived in the master bath, Jim was sitting naked on the side of the tub testing the water with his left hand. There was a nice layer of white bubbles covering the entire surface of the water. It looked very inviting.

Brie untied the belt of her robe and let it slip off her shoulders. She caught it in her left hand and held it out for Jim to take.

"You were naked under that robe?" Jim asked, surprised.

"Yep, and had you not started to tell that blonde joke," she said acting aloof, "you would have found that out in the kitchen."

"Wow!" Jim replied. "I guess I should hold me tongue next time."

"By the way," Brie said as she stepped into the tub, "there is a pair of pink lace panties in the top drawer of my dresser. Get them and bring them here."

"Yes, Ma'am," Jim replied as he stood up and headed for the bedroom. When he got to the dresser he opened the top drawer and found the panties Brie had asked him to bring her. He picked them up and returned to the bathroom. "Here you are, Ma'am," he said holding them out for her approval.

"Yes," Brie replied, "that's the pair. Put 'em on."

"What?" Jim said, startled that she would ask him to do that.

"You heard me," Brie responded. "I said, 'put – them – on!'"

"Yes. Mistress," he replied as he prepared to step into the tiny pink panties. It was the first time he had actually called her by that title, but somehow, it seemed like the right time. He stretched the panties open and stepped into them. He carefully pulled them up making sure they did not catch on his cock cage, then slid the waistband up over his bottom. They were snug, but they fit, sort of.

"Very nice," Brie commented. "Now turn around slowly so that I can see them."

Jim did as he was directed, all the while, feeling the embarrassment at standing before his wife in a pair of her pink panties. He didn't say a word. But he didn't have to, Brie could see the humiliation on his face and it was exactly what she wanted. She also made a note to herself that her panties were just a bit tight on him.

"You will wear those all day," she said. "Understand?"

"But, Mis..." he started to say when Brie interrupted him mid-sentence.

"But nothing!" She said, cutting him off short. "You will wear those until I tell you to take them off. Do – you – understand?" She said it slowly to impress upon him just how serious she was.

"Yes, Mistress," Jim replied softly. "Until you tell me to take them off." Jim could feel his cock growing with each passing second. Was it the panties, or the way Briana was speaking to him? He wasn't sure, but he liked the way his cock was reacting all the same.

Brie made Jim stand in front of the full-length mirror until she had finished her bath. Then she told him to get dressed and not to remove the panties or put a pair of his own on over them. Then she got out of the tub and dried herself off and got dressed. They were going to the mall, and she intended to buy him several new outfits. She smiled to herself about that. It was going to be fun.

Before they left the house, Brie gave Jim some instructions. He was to drive anytime they went anywhere together. He was to open all doors for her and, when shopping, he would carry her purse and any purchases, as well as walk two steps behind her. Brie had read the pamphlet Kathryn gave her and listened to what Jane and Fran had told her. She was determined to make James her personal slave. And she would find ways to humiliate James as he had humiliated her for years.

All the way to the mall, James wondered what Brie had meant when she said she wanted to buy him some new outfits. Normally, he would do his own clothes shopping. But he figured he would find out soon enough.

When they arrived, Jim parked the car as close to one of the entrances as he could. He opened his door and stepped out. He stretched as he waited for Brie to get out of the car too. Then he suddenly remembered, he was supposed to open the door for her. He hurried around the back of the car and opened the other door to let Brie out. "Sorry, Mistress," he said apologetically.

Brie ignored his comment and gave him a raised eyebrow look. He knew what that meant, but didn't bother to say anything for fear of getting into more trouble. He did, however, remember to carry her purse and walk two paces behind her. She resisted the impulse to look back to be sure. Brie thought he was behaving like a good little slave should.

Once inside, Brie led him directly to a little lingerie shop she knew of. She could have just as easily gone to Penny's or Sears, but she liked the idea of dragging Jim into a shop that was strictly for women. After all, she wasn't shopping for herself. She was shopping for Jim.

Jim felt embarrassed just walking into the place. He had no idea Brie intended to purchase clothing for him in a place like that. While Jim was looking around to make sure no one he knew saw him in there, Brie stopped to look at a rack of cute little baby-doll nighties. Jim almost ran into her.

Just then, a nice-looking sales girl, about twenty years old, Jim guessed, walked up to Brie and asked if there was anything she could help her with. Jim knew his wife. Or, at least he thought he did. She never wanted any help when she was shopping for clothes. Then it suddenly hit him. Jim remembered this girl as having been one of his students about four or five years ago. He hoped she wouldn't recognize him.

"Yes," Brie responded to the sales girl, "My husband needs a couple of these to sleep in."

The sales girl looked at Jim and chuckled to herself. Then it seemed a little light came on in her head. "I remember you," she said excitedly. "You were my science teacher when I was a Sophomore. How are you Mr. Galloway?"

James turned a bright shade of red as he said, "I'm fine."

Then she turned toward Brie and said, "I'm sorry, Ma'am. Did you say 'he' needs them?"

James was flabbergasted! He turned all shades of red and he tried not to look like he was not paying attention to what his wife or the sales girl were talking about. But when Brie said, "That's right, isn't it dear?" he couldn't fake it anymore.

"Uh..." Jim tried to think of something to say, but he was totally at a lose for words.

"Isn't that right, dear?" Brie repeated a little louder. "You need a few of these to sleep in. Right?"

Jim was still too humiliated to speak so he just nodded his head in the affirmative.

"What size does he wear?" the sales clerk asked without batting an eye. Though she had a bit of a smirk on her face as if she were trying hold back a laugh.

Brie selected a pink see-though nightie from the rack and held it up against Jim's chest. Looking at the sales girl she asked, "This is a medium. What do you think? Is it big enough? Or should we try a large?"

"I can't really tell," replied the sales clerk.

"Well," Brie explained, "he is wearing a pair of my panties now, and they are a size four, but I think they're just a bit snug. So maybe a six?"

"Okay," the sales girl said, "the medium should work, then."

"Great!" Brie replied turning back toward the rack of nighties. "Let me see... He will need one in black, one in red, the pink one we already have and... I think a white one, too. Don't you think?" She took each one off the rack and handed them to the sales girl. Then she repeated her last question directly at Jim, "What do you think?"

Jim looked at Brie, then at the sales girl who was holding the entire collection up for him to see. "Um... I guess so," was all he could manage to say.

"Good," said Brie. Looking at the sales girl she said, "Now we need some teddies, too. Probably large in those. He is taller than me."

"They're right over here" the girl replied walking toward another rack.

Brie took Jim by the wrist and pulled him in the direction the sales girl went. "You pick out the colors you want, dear," she said to Jim once they arrived at the rack of teddies.

"Um... Yes, Ma'am," Jim replied turning an even brighter shade of red than he already was. "I'll take the same colors as the night gowns," he said to no one in particular.

"That was easy," Brie said turning the rack to find the larges. She selected four matching colored teddies and handed them to the sales woman. "Now," she said to the sales woman, "Do you have any of those school-girl uniforms? The ones with the short plaid skirts?"

The Marriage Counselor

"Oh, yes," the woman responded. "They're over in the back corner. Let me set these things on the counter and I'll meet you there."

Brie had more surprises for her husband up her sleeve. She led him to the rack along the back wall and started looking through the selection of plaid skirts she found there. A few seconds later the sales girl returned. "What size do you think he needs for one of these?" Brie asked.

"I have no idea," she replied. "What does his waist measure? We could determine it that way."

Brie looked at Jim, "Well? What's your waist measure?"

Jim looked down at his waist, then replied, "thirty-two."

The sales girl grabbed a tape measure and one of the skirts. She measured the waist band and said, "This is a twenty-eight. Let's try this one," she said as she pulled a larger skirt from the rack. Measuring the waist of that one she said, "Here you go. That measures thirty-two inches." She handed the skirt to Brie who then asked for a white blouse to go with it. The sales woman reached up to the top rack and grabbed a white blouse. "This one should fit." She handed it to Brie. Brie held it up and studied it for a few seconds. Then she turned to Jim and handed the blouse and skirt to him.

"Here," she said. "Go try those on. And come out here because I want to see how they fit."

Jim was taken totally by surprise over being told to try them on, but even more humiliated thinking about having to come out of the dressing room with them on. "I... I... I don't..." he tried to stammer out a compliant but eventually conceded. "Yes, Ma'am." He took the items from his wife and asked the sales lady where the changing rooms were located. After she pointed them out to him, James headed off in their direction.

"Do you have matching ties for those skirts?" she asked the woman as they both watched Jim walking toward the dressing rooms.

"Yes, we do," she replied. "I'll get you one." Then she walked slowly toward a collection of plaid ties on a special rack, without taking her eyes off of Jim until he disappeared into the dressing room area.

When Jim entered the dressing rooms there were two other ladies using the full-length mirrors. They stared at him as he selected an unoccupied dressing room and stepped inside. He pulled the curtain closed and, for a moment, just stood there unable to believe where he was. It was humiliating enough just to have to go in there, but he also had to go back out once he put on these clothes. He wasn't sure he could go through with it. But he thought about the consequences of NOT doing it. Brie would probably blister his poor bottom, not to mention she might withhold sex of any kind for a month. So he decided he had no other choice.

As Jim removed his pants and shirt, he noticed that his cock was, again, growing to fill the tiny space available in its cage. Again, he wasn't sure if it was the thought of having to wear the blouse and short skirt Brie had picked out for him, or if it was the thought that he had to wear it out into the main part of the store. One thing was becoming clear. He apparently enjoyed being humiliated. Even though it was embarrassing, he enjoyed it. "How was that possible?" he wondered to himself.

When James was finally dressed, he slowly, cautiously, crept out of the back into the main part of the store. He saw Brie standing by another rack toward the front of the store. "Uh... I'm here," he said in order to get her attention.

"Oh, good," Brie said cheerfully. "Come here and let me see how you look."

Jim was afraid she would make him do that. She just wanted to increase his humiliation as much as she could. "Yes, Ma'am," he replied as he slowly walked in her direction.

When he finally arrived, Brie looked at him. She straightened his collar, checked the fit of the skirt around his waist, and said, "Perfect! We'll take them." Then she thought for second and added, "We'll take two if you have them."

The sales woman said, "I'm sure we do." And with that she went to find another set."

Brie said, "While you were in the dressing room I picked out some stockings for you. You'll love them, they have little bows on them and they come up just above your knees. Oh, I got you some panties, too."

Jim was almost at his breaking point, but he managed to keep his embarrassment to himself. Although, he was positive it showed on his face. "May I change back now, Mistress" he whispered to Brie.

"Sure," she said, "but we have one more stop to make before we can go home. You are going to need some proper shoes."

Jim thought about how embarrassing shoe-shopping would be after having just tried on a skirt in public. But, at least he didn't have to wear the skirt to do it. That would have been impossible! He headed back to the dressing room to change back into his normal clothes.

When Jim was finally dressed, and returned to Brie, he found her standing at the checkout counter. The sales woman took the blouse and skirt Jim had in his hand and folded them and placed them into one of the bags where she had already put their other purchases. She turned to Jim and said, "That will be two -hundred and seventy-three dollars and eighty-seven cents. How would you like to pay for that?"

Jim looked at Brie for a second. She nodded, indicating that he should pay for the purchases. He reached for his wallet and pulled out a credit card and handed it to the sales woman. She ran it through her machine and handed it back to him with a receipt. "There you go. Just sign that and you're all set," she said.

Jim signed the receipt and pushed it across the counter toward the sales girl. She picked it up and said, "Enjoy your new outfits." She said it with a smile. As soon as Jim and Brie walked through the door, the sales girl broke out in a full laugh she could no longer contain.

Brie led Jim to a shoe store a couple of doors down from the lingerie store they had just come from. She picked up a black patent pump and a high-heeled shoe with what Jim estimated to be a four-inch heel. She walked up to a young man about nineteen years old and said, "I need these," handing the kid the high-heel shoe, "in black, red and white, if you have them. Then I need this one, too. All in his size." She indicated Jim with her thumb as she said it.

The kid looked at Jim. Then looked at his feet and said, "I'll have to measure him first, but they look like they're pretty small so I'll bet we have everything you want. Have a seat over there and I'll measure your foot," he said looking directly at Jim.

Jim sat down in one of the chairs the boy had indicated and removed his right shoe. The kid pulled one of those stools with the ramp in front up to him and took Jim's leg by the ankle. He measured his foot and said, "Do you normally wear a size eight and a half?"

Jim replied, "Yes, I do."

"Okay, the boy said as he got up from the stool. Let me go in the back and see what I can find." then he disappeared through a small doorway into what appeared to be a store room.

Jim turned to Brie and asked, "Why are you doing this to me?"

Brie looked directly into Jim's eyes and answered, "I told you. It's to make up for all those years of humiliation I went through because of you. Payback, dear. Payback."

"Yes, Ma'am," Jim said looking down at his feet. "I'm sorry for putting you through all that."

Though he sounded genuinely sorry, Brie replied, "Don't bother apologizing. It's too late for that now. I am going to have fun getting even with you for it."

"Yes, Ma'am," was all he could say.

They sat in silence for a few minutes, waiting for the salesman to return with some shoes for Jim to try on. Jim wasn't looking forward to that, but he had to do whatever Brie wanted. No matter what.

When the salesman returned, he had four shoe boxes in his arms. "If these fit," he said as he set them on the floor next to his stool, "then we had everything you wanted." He sat down on the stool and motioned for Jim to raise his foot again. He opened one of the boxes and pulled out a black patent leather pump. He put a shoehorn in the heel and slipped it on Jim.

"How does that feel?" he asked.

"Embarrassing," Jim replied. Then he put his foot on the floor and pressed down in order to put a little weight on his foot. "It feels pretty good," he said.

"Stand up and walk around a little," Brie told him.

Jim complied, but only took one step, putting his full weight on the foot with the new shoe. "It feels pretty good," he repeated. Then he sat back down. He really didn't want anyone to see him trying on a woman's shoe. He wished they had sat nearer the back of the store, instead up front.

"Let's try one of the heels, then," the salesman suggested.

Jim sat back down and removed the pump. He handed it to the kid who placed it carefully back into the box from which it came. Then the boy opened another box and pulled out a bright red high-heeled shoe. Jim raised his foot and slipped it into the shoe as the boy helped him get it on.

"How is that one?" the kid asked.

"Stand up, dear," Brie said, not waiting for him to try and get out of it.

"Yes, Ma'am," Jim replied as he rose from his seat. He took one step again as he had done the last time and sat back down.

"Well?" Brie asked, "how are those?"

"They feel... Strange." he replied. "But they don't hurt, or anything like that."

"Good," Brie said looking at the salesman. "We'll take them all." And with that, she stood up and headed for the sales counter.

Jim quickly removed the shoe and replaced it with his own. Then he followed Brie to the counter. The salesman repackaged the shoe and gathered the four boxes in his arms and headed for the counter, himself. He set the boxes on the counter and began to ring them up. "The pumps are almost never on sale, except at the end of the school year, but the others are on sale. The pumps are twenty-nine ninety-five and the heels are regularly sixty-nine ninety-five, but they're twenty percent off this week," he said as he rang them up on the cash register.

"Your total is two-hundred-fifty-three dollars and seventy-nine cents plus tax. That comes to..." he paused for the register to give him a total. "Two-hundred-seventy-one dollars and fifty-six cents." When he looked up, Jim was holding out a credit card for him.

The boy took the card and ran it through the register. He put the shoes into two bags and handed the card and the receipt to Jim when he had finished. Jim signed the receipt and handed it back to the clerk.

"Have a nice day," the clerk said as Brie and Jim walked out of the store.

~ ~ ~

Chapter 4
JIM'S FASHION SHOW

As soon as Brie and Jim walked into the house, they went straight to their bedroom to put away all the things they had purchased at the mall. The nighties and the teddies were all hung in the closet. The panties and stockings were put in Jim's top drawer in place of his regular underwear, and the shoes were removed from their boxes and placed neatly in a row on the floor of Jim's closet.

Brie looked at Jim and with one raised eyebrow, she said, "Get undressed. All but those ridiculous panties. I want you to keep them on... For now."

"Yes, Mistress," Jim replied as he began to undress.

"I'll be in the kitchen," Brie said as she left the room. She went downstairs to make them some lunch. "I'm going to have to get that man some cooking lessons," she thought to herself. "After all, if he is going to be mine to do with as I please, then he damn well better learn to cook."

Brie made them a couple of sandwiches and tried to think of something she could do to further humiliate James. She was having a lot of fun at his expense, but considering all the humiliation she had put up with over the years, she felt he deserved it.

When Jim finally joined Brie in the kitchen, he found her sitting at the table eating her sandwich and drinking a glass of iced tea. Without even looking up at him, Brie said, "I put yours down there. From now on you will eat your meals while sitting on the floor. In fact, you will not be allowed to sit on any furniture until such time as I decide you have earned the privilege."

"You mean I can't sit at the table or on the couch, or anything?" he asked in disbelief.

"Until I decide otherwise, yes," Brie answered without even looking in his direction.

"What about the bed?" he asked. "Will I be allowed to sleep in the bed, or do I have to sleep on the floor, too?"

"You will be allowed to sleep in the bed, as long as you behave yourself," she explained, "but if you don't obey me, then you'll spend your nights on the floor, or in the guest room. It all depends on your behavior." She was proud of herself for coming up with that last bit. It gave her more leeway, should he displease her.

"But..." Jim began to protest. "Yes, Mistress," he decided it was better to concede than to risk sleeping on the floor or even in the guest room.

Brie's cell phone rang. When she picked it up and looked to see who was calling, she was surprised to see Fran's photo on the screen. She pressed the 'Answer' button. "Hi, Fran. How's it going?"

"I was just about to ask you the same thing," Fran replied. "I know you had that meeting at Kathryn's last night and I was wondering how it went."

"Great!" replied, Brie. "I had no trouble convincing Jim to wear the chastity belt, and I spent the morning shopping with him. I made him try on a school-girl outfit in the store, and some nice woman's shoes, too."

"I'll bet he was totally humiliated," Fran said laughing. "I wish I could have been there to see it."

Jim was listening to every word the two women were saying because Brie had put Fran on speaker so she wouldn't have to hold the phone while she was eating. He couldn't believe his wife was telling her friend all about his humiliating morning.

"Hey," Brie said suddenly coming up with what she thought would be a great way to humiliate Jim even more, "why don't you come over this afternoon and we can have some fun at Jim's expense?"

"That sounds like a great idea," Fran replied. "Give me time to eat some lunch and I'd be delighted!"

"See you in about an hour then?" Brie asked.

"Oh, it won't take me that long," Fran replied. "Give me about thirty minutes."

"Okay," Brie said excitedly. "See you then. Bye."

"Bye," Fran said as Brie clicked her phone off.

"How about that?" Brie said looking down at her husband who was sitting next to her on the floor. "You can give us a fashion show," she said, grinning like a Cheshire cat. "Won't that be fun, dear?"

"Oh, please, Mistress," he begged, "don't let anyone see me like this. At least let me get dressed."

"I'm sorry, baby," Brie said making a phony sad face, "but I think over the years, you have earned this. Besides, this is just the beginning, sweetie. I have big plans for you."

Feeling quite sorry for himself, Jim replied, "Yes, Mistress. Whatever you say."

When the couple had finished eating their lunch, Brie ordered Jim to wash and dry the dishes by hand and return them to the cupboard. "When you have finished that," she said, "come join me in the living room."

"Yes, Mistress," Was Jim's only reply. He was beginning to get nervous about having to wear only a pair of Brie's pink panties in front of one of her friends. Nervous, yes, but the more he thought about it, the more it began to arouse him. He couldn't really understand why it did, but his cock kept pressing uncomfortably against the inside of its cage. When he finished his chore, Jim joined Brie in the living room.

He no sooner walked into the room than the doorbell rang.

"Get that, will you?" Brie said expecting Jim to protest.

"If you insist, Mistress," was Jim's reply. He hoped she would change her mind and let him hide in the bedroom or something instead. But she didn't.

"That will be Fran. And don't embarrass me with any of your stupid jokes." It was her way of letting him know that she wasn't going to let him out of this.

Jim walked to the door and looked through the tiny peephole. "Oh God!" he thought. Fran wasn't alone. He slowly opened the door trying to stand behind it as if that would prevent the two women from seeing him when they came in. "Come in," Jim said as he opened the door a little wider.

Fran had brought Jane with her. She knew that Jane would want to be a part of this since she and Brie were such close friends. "Hi, Brie," Fran said as she stepped through the door. "Look who decided to join us."

Brie saw Jane coming through the door and she stood up immediately. "Jane! Fran!" Brie almost shouted with her excitement. "I am so glad you could make it. Jim, say hello to my friends and get them some tea to drink."

Both women turned around to get their first good look at Jim since he had hidden behind the door as they entered, but had since closed it. Jim was so embarrassed being dressed only in a chastity belt and his wife's panties, he could barely speak. "Good afternoon," he mumbled trying to hide his crotch with his hands. Then he scurried off to the kitchen as fast as he could go.

"I'm afraid he is a little shy," Brie explained. "It's his first time. You understand."

"Yes, Brie," said Jane, "and we are both proud of you. You have obviously made great progress since we last talked."

"Yes, you have," agreed Fran. "I can't believe you put him in a pair of pink panties. That's a nice touch!"

Brie giggled, "It just came to me this morning when I got up. I think he looks so cute." she said that last part loud enough that she hoped Jim would hear it. "Here, join me on the couch. I'm going to have Jim give us a little fashion show to show you what I made him buy this morning."

"That sounds like fun," Fran said as she stepped around the coffee table and sat next to Brie. Jane sat at the other end of the couch and asked, "When does the show start?" She placed her hand firmly on Brie's thigh and added, "I really am proud of you, Brie. You've taken his abuse long enough. It's time you got some payback."

"Thanks, Jane," Brie replied. "I don't think I could have done it without the both of you."

"Hey," Fran spoke up, "what are friends for? We both love you and it's nice to see Jim not telling jokes all the time."

"I told him I would punish him severely if he ever told another blonde joke," Brie said, "I just hope he paid attention, because I don't really want to punish him. Besides, I'm having so much fun humiliating him!"

About that time, Jim reentered the room carrying a tray with three tall glasses of iced tea and a pitcher full for refills. He set the tray down on the coffee table and handed Jane and Fran each a glass. Then he picked up Brie's half empty glass and replaced it with a fresh one. "I thought you could use a fresh drink, Mistress," he said.

"Thank you, James," Brie said as if talking to her butler or something. "I want you to go upstairs and lay out your new black teddy, your white nightie, your school-girl outfit, a pair of white stockings, and any pair of your new panties that you like. Then tell me as soon as you have finished."

"Yes, Mistress," he replied his face already starting to turn red. Then he turned and quickly disappeared up the stairs.

"Wow," remarked Jane. "He sure is a different guy today than he was the last time we saw him."

"He sure is," Fran agreed. "I am still trying to figure out how you accomplished so much so quickly."

"To be honest," Brie replied, "I'm really not sure myself. He hasn't really given me any trouble at all since we left Kathryn's last night."

"Maybe he secretly likes being humiliated," Jane said thoughtfully.

"Maybe," Brie admitted. "It would make sense. I guess I will have to push his limits and see what happens."

"That's a good idea," Fran remarked. "What made you think of that?"

"It was something Kathryn talked to me about before Jim came in last night," Brie replied. "I guess she was right. She said it could happen."

Jim came back down the stairs and announced, "Mistress, I have done as you asked."

"Very good, James," she replied. "Now I want you to go back and put on the nightie and a pair of matching shoes. And you better hurry."

"Yes, Mistress," Jim replied as he hurried back up the stairs.

"This ought to be good," Jane said to the other women. "I can't wait to make fun of him when comes back down."

"Me either," Fran added. "I think he really deserves this."

"This really is fun," Brie said. "I can't believe I never did this before. I mean, taking control like this. It's fun."

The ladies each took another sip of tea when they heard Jim on the stairs. He seemed to be having trouble walking in his new high-heeled shoes. They all laughed as Jim struggled to keep from falling down the steps. When he finally reached the bottom, he stood up straight and walked slowly into the middle of the room facing them.

"Well, aren't you the little doll?" Jane said trying to increase Jim's embarrassment.

"Turn around for us," Fran said, "so we can see the back."

Brie nodded, indicating that Jim should do as her friends asked.

Jim walked in a tiny circle to give the girls a good view of him. When he finally stopped, facing them once again, Fran pointed at his crotch and announced, "It looks like his cock is trying to force it's way out of the cage."

"You're right, Fran," Jane affirmed. "Look at how tight his cage is. His cock is bulging out all over."

Brie reaffirmed what her friends were saying, "You're right, girls," she said, "his cock is trying to become hard. What's the matter, Jimmy, does showing off for my friends turn you on?" she asked in her best mocking tone.

"Are you getting turned on by all this?" Jane asked him.

Jim hung his head in shame and responded, "Yes, Ma'am," as his face turned as red as a beet.

"Look at that, would you?" Jane said taunting Jim again. "His tiny little weenie is trying to grow all big so we don't make fun of it."

They all laughed. All except Jim, of course, who was turning even redder, if that were possible.

"Okay," Brie said as she finally caught her breath again, "you can go put on the teddy now. Don't forget the matching shoes."

"Yes, Mistress," Jim replied as he walked as carefully as he could back toward the staircase.

"I can't believe he is having so much trouble walking in a simple pair of high-heels," Fran remarked. "Wiggle that ass, you sissy!" she yelled in his direction. Jim tried to ignore her as he climbed the steps back up to his bedroom.

"I just hope no one else hears about this," he thought to himself. He had never been so humiliated in all his life. And the girls making fun of him didn't help a bit, either.

The women continued laughing and joking about poor James and his obvious aroused condition until they heard him coming back down the stairs. He did a little better navigating the steps this time. He was getting better.

James walked to the center of the room again and then slowly made a turn like he had done before. He wasn't going to wait for them to tell him to do it. He wanted to get this over with as quickly as he could.

The women continued to make insulting and humiliating comments about they way James looked and in particular, how they could still see, even through the thin material of the black teddy, how his cock was straining for release from its confinement.

Finally, Brie told Jim to go back and change into his school-girl outfit. He was to wear the stockings and the panties he had laid out and the black pumps, too.

Brie spent a little time explaining to the girls why she had made him purchase this particular outfit. She planned to make him wear it out in public sometime. But she needed to get him into a wig and some makeup, first.

When Jim came back down the stairs, he had no trouble navigating them in the pumps. So his decent was bit more graceful. He did his usual routine and stopped once he was facing the women again.

Jane leaned forward in her seat and said, "Turn around and face the other way for us." Jim turned his back toward the couch and stood there waiting for another order. "Now, Jane continued, "keep your back straight and lean forward placing your hands on your thighs."

When he did as Jane had requested, the girls got a good look at his panties as his skirt rode up high. "Look at that, girls," Fran said giggling, "Jim has on a pair of black panties. You know what that means... He wants someone to see them."

Brie laughed and then added, "He wants to get fucked is what."

Jane cracked up over that one. "Too bad we aren't at my house," she said, "I would use my strap-on on him." All the women laughed again.

"Okay, Jimmy boy," Brie said as Jim stood up straight, "Take those panties off right now and bend over again, for us."

As Jim bent down pushing his panties to his ankles, the woman hurled another barrage of humiliating insults and jokes at him. It continued right through his removal of the panties and his second bending at the waist. They joked about his hairy ass, and legs. They made him turn toward them and hold his skirt up so they see his cock as it strained to escape confinement in its tiny cage. They even made Jim wiggle from side to side with his legs spread wide so they could make fun of the way his balls dangled between them.

The Marriage Counselor

Then Brie got a brilliant idea. "Come over here," she said pointing to the spot right in front of her." Jim moved to stand with his feet on either side of hers. "Now lift up your skirt, sissy-boy," she said.

Reaching for his balls, Brie grabbed them and squeezed them tightly. "How do those tiny little balls of yours feel now, sissy-boy? Huh?"

It was all Jim could do to keep from crying out in pain as Brie tightened her grip on his tender nuts. "They hurt, Mistress," he replied gritting his teeth in pain.

"Good, Brie said as she slowly released her grip. "Don't you forget it. I'm in charge and you will do what I tell you, or I will rip these things off with my bare hands. Do you understand?"

"Yes, Mistress," Jim said with a sigh of relief as Brie's grip loosened.

"Now," she began, "Let each of these women squeeze your balls so you can tell me which one of us has the tightest grip."

"Yes, Mistress," he replied as he stepped first in front of Fran.

"My, but these are particularly small," Fran commented as she took hold of Jim's balls. "How's this feel, she said as she squeezed them tightly?"

"That hurts, Ma'am," Jim replied with an obvious grimace.

Fran let go of Jim's balls and said, "Don't you forget it, either, you sissy."

Next, Jim took the two steps necessary to position himself in front of Jane. He feared Jane most of all. She had never liked him and he never really understood why. But he just knew she would show him no mercy.

Jane wrapped her fingers slowly around Jim's balls and began to tighten her grip, second by second. Finally, she said with gritted teeth, "How's that feel you little sissy?"

"It hurts, Ma'am. It really hurts." It was all Jim could do to keep from screaming out in pain. He was right, Jane did squeeze the hardest. He knew she would. But was it because she was the strongest or because she hated him so much? He never knew with Jane.

When Jane finally release him, Jim almost fell to his knees from the pain. "I guess we know who he fears the most, now. Don't we?" Jane said.

It was time for the party to break up. Jane wanted to get home before Frank did, because she had something new she wanted to try out with him. Fran wasn't expecting Jack home for a while, but she wanted to plan something for him to do when he got home. Well, the fact is, all this playing with Jim had made her more than a little aroused and she wanted to make Jack give her some good old fashioned orgasms before he took her out for dinner.

As for Brie, she was planning on getting in a few orgasms herself. As it turns out, she was finding all this humiliating of her husband was making her rather horny too. Since Kathryn had not given her the keys to Jim's chastity belt, she was going to have settle for oral sex, for the time being.

The women said their good-byes and Jane and Fran drove home. Brie thought the afternoon was well spent and she had even learned something about what turns Jim on.

~ ~ ~

Chapter 5
PARTY PLANNING

Sunday morning, Brie thought the alarm clock was going off and tried three times to stop it before she realized it was her cell phone.

"Hello?" Brie said groggily as she wiped the sleep out of one eye and attempted to see the time on her alarm clock.

"Brie? It's Fran," the voice on the phone said. "I'm sorry if I woke you, but I wanted to invite you to come to my house this morning for some brunch. Jane is going to be here and there is something I wanted to show you both.

"Uh... Sure," Brie was doing her best to wake up, but so far, she was having no luck. "Who is this again?"

"Brie! Wake up," Fran said loudly in an effort to gain her full attention. "It's Fran."

"Oh, sure, Fran," Brie was starting to comprehend the voice coming from her cell phone. "What did you say?"

"I said," Fran repeated, "I want you and Jane to come over for some brunch. There is something I want to show you."

"Oh. Okay," Brie was beginning to put things together. "When?"

"Can you be here by ten?" Fran asked.

"Uh... What time is it now?" Brie still couldn't see the alarm clock clearly.

"It's almost nine o'clock." Fran was starting to get a little frustrated.

Again, Brie tried to clear her eyes. "Yeah, I can be there. I just need to take a quick shower and get some breakfast."

"No, Brie," Fran corrected, "it's a brunch. I have food here. You don't need breakfast."

"Oh... Right," Brie responded. "Sure, I can make it. I'll see you in an hour. Okay?"

Great, Brie," Fran said with a sigh of relief that Brie finally understood her. "See you in an hour. Bye."

Brie didn't bother to say goodbye. She just clicked the end button and laid her phone back on the nightstand next to the alarm clock. She rubbed both eyes this time and focused on the clock. Eight-fifty-two it said on the read out. She crawled out of bed and headed for the bathroom. Jim was still asleep. It had been a strenuous night. Jack had managed to give her twenty some odd orgasms with his tongue, fingers and her favorite vibrator. She had never had so many in one night in her life and she was exhausted. A shower would give her back some energy. Or, at least she hoped it would.

Brie took her time in the shower. The hot water beating down her back felt really good. She felt as if she could stay there all day, but she also wondered what was so important that Fran had called her and invited her to a brunch on such short notice. Fran had never been a very impulsive woman. Brie was getting more and more curious the more she thought about it.

When she had finished her shower, Brie got dressed and started out the door when she realized that Jim was still in bed. She shut the door and found her pad of sticky notes. She wrote Jim a note that simply read, "Jim, pick out a pair of panties to wear for the day, then start cleaning the house. Sweep and mop the kitchen and bathrooms, vacuum the carpets, wash the dishes, and start the laundry that's in the upstairs hamper. I'll be back soon, so you had better be working when I get home." She placed it on the mirror in the bathroom where he would be sure to see it. Then she left for Fran's.

When Brie pulled into Fran's driveway, she saw that Jane's car was there already. She parked the car and went to the front door. Fran met her at the door and welcomed her inside.

Jane was sitting on the sofa with a plate of fruit on her lap. "How are you, Jane?" she asked as she entered the room.

"I'm fine," Jane replied, "I have just been trying to figure out why we are here so early on a Sunday morning. Fran wouldn't tell me until you arrived."

"Help yourself to some fruit," Fran offered, "there are some bagels and stuff, too, if you want them."

Brie looked at the dinning table. There were several kinds of fresh fruit, a couple of styles of bagels, and even some fresh lox and cream cheese all laid out neatly. But the thing she was most happy to see was a pot of coffee with an empty cup just waiting for her, right in front of the pot. She grabbed the cup and began pouring coffee into it. "Thanks," said Brie as she finished pouring the coffee, "I believe I will. I am famished." She picked up a plate and filled it with fresh pineapple, some strawberries, a few melon chunks and a bagel. She spread some cream cheese on the bagel and found herself a spot on the sofa to sit.

"What's this all about?" Brie asked as she prepared to take a bite out of a large strawberry.

Fran was sitting in an overstuffed lounge chair across the room from the sofa. She leaned forward on her elbows and spoke softly, "You both have been to Kathryn's, right?"

Both Jane and Brie replied at the same time, "Yes?"

"I'm still going to her. Why?" Brie asked.

"I know you guys are gonna think that I am going overboard," Fran explained, "but I am really getting into all this stuff."

"What are you talking about?" Jane complained. "Come on, out with it. What have you done, now?"

Fran drew in a deep breath and said, "I have built a dungeon."

"You what?" Jane asked incredulously.

"A dungeon?" Brie asked. "You do you mean, like Kathryn's?"

"Yes," Fran began excitedly, "well, not exactly like Kathryn's, but I have some fun equipment!"

"Well," Jane asked, "where is it? We want to see it."

"Yeah," Brie agreed with Jane, "where is it? How did you ever find enough room for a dungeon?"

Fran was excited that her friends seemed to like the idea. She was so afraid they would think she had gone out of her mind. "It's in the basement," she replied. "Want to see it?"

"Of course, we want to see it," Jane replied. "I, for one, am not leaving until I do. What about you, Brie?"

"Oh, I definitely want to see it," Brie said as she stuck another strawberry in her mouth.

"Follow me," Fran said getting up from her seat.

Brie set her plate on the coffee table along side Jane's plate. The two stood up and followed Fran to the basement. As they descended the stairs, the first thing they saw was the large, antique chair Fran had set up as her "throne." She had added some expensive looking drapery behind it to hide the concrete walls and give it a more regal appearance.

"Wow!" exclaimed Jane as she stepped down from the last stair. "Where did you get all this stuff?"

Fran was smiling. She was proud of herself and the girls seemed impressed. "Most of it Jack ordered online, but some of it, like the ceiling chains and stuff, I built myself."

"Wow..." Fran said as she walked around looking at all the equipment. She ran her hand across the padded leather top of the spanking bench and remarked, "this is really nice. It's just like Kathryn's, only smaller."

"Well," Fran answered, "hers is the only other dungeon I've ever really seen."

"Oh," Brie replied, "I really like it. I didn't mean to infer you copied it or anything."

"Well," Fran admitted, "I sort of did." Gesturing toward one large wall she added, "Over here, I'm going to have Jack mount some cabinets like Kathryn has to store all the little stuff."

"I just think it's fantastic, Fran," Jane said looking at the large cross that leaned against one wall. "I really envy you, now."

"Well..." Fran began timidly, "I was kind of hoping you guys would want to get together and have a little dungeon party here, sometime."

"That would be great!" Jane said excitedly.

"You mean, like with our husbands and everything?" Brie asked a little unsure of herself.

"Yeah," said Fran, "it would be fun. We could play with them and humiliate them and... Well, do whatever we want to them."

"I don't know if Jim would want to do anything like that. I mean, with other people around," Brie said naively.

"Brie..." Fran started to explain, "It's not up to Jim. It's up to you. If you want to do it, or if you think it would be fun, then he has to do whatever you tell him to do."

"Yeah, Brie," Jane chimed in, "besides, we don't have to tell them. Just bring them with us. That's all."

Brie thought about it for moment, then said, "I guess you're right. Jim has to do what I tell him to do. Doesn't he?"

"Right!" confirmed Fran.

"Now you've got it," Added Jane. "Don't let him dictate what you want him to do. You're in charge now. Besides, we could really humiliate him good. After all, we have all had to put up with his stupid jokes ever since you two got together. Maybe now we can all get even. What do you say? Dungeon party, everyone?"

"Okay," Brie conceded, "I'm in."

"When do you want to have it?" Fran asked. "Sunday is the only day Jack doesn't work."

"Well, then," Jane replied, "how about next Saturday night? That way we can all still sleep in the next day."

The girls returned to the living room to plan their party. They spent about an hour planning everything out. Fran told her friends that she was planning a special surprise to humiliate Jim, but she wouldn't tell them what it was.

By the time Brie got home, it was almost one o'clock. Jim was in the living room vacuuming the carpet in a pair of white panties. He didn't hear Brie come in the door and she reached out and smacked his bottom with her hand. He jumped, partly because she startled him and partly because he didn't know who it was at first, and he didn't want to get caught running around in a pair of woman's panties.

Brie wished she had the key to Jim's chastity belt because she wanted to use him in ways that just were not possible with his cock locked away like that. But she did manage to use him for some oral pleasure a few times during the day. And that made her feel much better about not being able to let him out of his cage, so to speak.

After the other girls left, Fran went upstairs to wake Jack. He had slept long enough even though she had teased him and made him give her well over a dozen orgasms with his tongue alone the night before.

Once he was up, she allowed him to take a shower and clean himself up before ordering him to clean up the mess left by the girls in the living room and dining room. Then she allowed him to eat something himself. She recommended he eat some fruit because he would need the energy. Fran had plans for Jack. She was feeling a bit horny after planning the party with her friends.

"I'll be waiting in the dungeon when you get through eating," she told him.

"Yes, Mistress," Jack replied, "I won't be long."

Fran was really enjoying all the power she now wielded over Jack and fully intended to make the most of it. She intended to make the most of his only day off from the dealership, too. She went down to the basement to prepare for Jack, whenever he might get there.

As Fran searched through her bag of toys, she decided that Jack needed to get those cabinets put up soon. It seemed she always had trouble finding what she wanted in the bag. Finally, she fond everything she needed for the afternoon's festivities. She laid them out on a small TV tray so they would be handy. Finally, she dropped the wrist and ankle cuffs on the small carpet in front of her "throne." Then she sat down to wait for Jack.

Fran didn't have to wait long before Jack came down the steps to the dungeon. When he saw his wife sitting in her big chair, waiting for him, he hurriedly positioned himself on the little carpet in front of her and knelt down. He bowed his head and said, "How may a serve you, Mistress?"

"Put on those cuffs," Fran said calmly.

"Yes, Mistress," was his only reply as he picked up the wrist cuffs and began fastening them in place. When he had finished that, he sat down so that he could reach his ankles and place a cuff on each of them. Then he returned to the kneeling position and said, "Ready, Mistress."

Fran stretched out her hand with the three dice used to determine whether he gets an orgasm or not. "Here," she said, "you haven't rolled these yet, today. You may as well do it now."

Taking the dice from Fran, he said, "Thank you, Mistress." Then he shook the dice and rolled them on the carpet in front of him. The green die landed on five, the red die was a one, and the white die ended up on three.

"Let's see..." Fran said leaning over to get a good look at the dice. I owe you twenty-five minutes of teasing, five swats with my paddle, and well... nothing for the white one."

"Yes, Mistress," Jack acknowledged.

"Go lay down on your back on the bench," Fran told him. "We'll get your teasing out of the way first."

As he got to his feet, Jack replied, "Yes, Mistress." Then he laid on his back on the padded bench as instructed.

Fran secured his hands to the eye-screw at the top of the bench and his ankles to the legs so that his knees were separated by the bench itself. She placed a blindfold over his eyes and then unlocked and removed the little cage that kept his cock inaccessible. Finally, she asked if he was comfortable. He answered in the affirmative, so she was ready to begin.

She put on one of the rubber gloves she had laid out and scooped up some numbing cream from the container on the TV try. She smeared a liberal amount on Jack's cock fondling it all over to make sure it was well covered and that his cock was nice and hard. Then she stripped off the glove and tossed it into the trash. She picked up and unwrapped a condom, then carefully rolled it down the length of Jack's cock.

Now that that was taken care of, Fran wanted to give the numbing cream some time to do its job. She removed her pants and panties and positioned herself at the head of the bench. She slowly lowered herself down over Jack's face and ordered him to bring her to orgasm.

Jack stuck out his tongue as far as it would go and waited for Fran's lovely labia to reach it. Once it did, he began by slowly lapping at the outer labia until his tongue snaked its way between them. Then he worked on spreading her inner labia until his warm tongue found the sweet entrance to her wet, dripping pussy. He lapped it briefly before searching out her tiny clit. He found it and began to swirl his tongue all around it, teasing and tempting it to come out from under the tiny hood that kept him from giving it the attention it deserved.

Jack's tongue teased, lapped at, and pressed firmly against her clit as it quickly emerged from its hiding place. Fran's constant moans, groans and guttural sounds told him he was doing something right. Every now and then he would stop a moment to lap up the sweet juices flowing from deep inside her love hole. He could tell that she was nearing her first orgasm and that knowledge only served to encourage him to work that much harder.

Fran felt her first orgasm growing deep inside her womb as it pushed its way to the surface and spread throughout her body like waves hitting a rocky shore. One after another the waves crashed over the rocks sending her mind to a place of perfect harmony. A place where only pleasure existed and anything that might concern her about her everyday life simply vanished. Her mind was filled only with thoughts of how good Jack's tongue felt as he kept on tormenting her swollen clitoris.

Fran ground her pussy harder and harder into Jack's face as her second and third orgasms washed over her one after the other. Each sending her back to that place of ultimate pleasure, again and again.

When she could take no more, she stood up, pulling her sweet pussy away from Jack's eager mouth and tongue. Then she positioned herself, one leg on either side of the bench about even with Jack's waist and lowered herself down until she was close enough to guide his cock into her with one hand. She slowly lowered herself down until she was sitting comfortably on Jack's groin.

"How does that feel?" Fran asked Jack, knowing full well that he couldn't feel himself inside her.

"Great, Mistress," Jack replied, "except that I can't feel my cock at all."

"Well," Fran continued, "you can feel me on top of you and you know your cock is buried deep inside me. Don't you?" It was really more of a rhetorical question but Jack answered anyway.

"Yes, Mistress," he said, "I can feel you on top of me and I know my cock must be buried deep."

Fran began playing with Jack's nipples. She rubbed them rapidly with the tips of her fingers allowing the fingernails to just barely scrape across his skin. "How does that feel?" she asked.

"I love it, Mistress," Jack replied.

Fran began to slowly move her body up and down on Jack's cock as she pinched his nipples between her thumb and forefinger. She moved just a little faster with each little bounce. The faster she moved, the closer to another orgasm she came and the harder she pinched his nipples. Jack was initially turned on by her nipple play, and the harder she squeezed them, the more turned on he became. He wasn't the type of guy who was into pain, it was the knowledge that the harder Fran pinched him the closer she was to having another orgasm. That meant she was taking her pleasure from him and there was nothing he could do about it.

Suddenly, Jack felt Fran slam her body down against him and start grinding her pussy against his pubic bone. She was pinching his nipples unbearably hard, but he knew she had reached another orgasm. Though his cock could feel nothing, Jack was as turned on as Fran at this point and the pain she was causing his nipples didn't matter one bit. He endured the pain because he knew it was only because his wife was feeling extreme pleasure.

As her orgasm began to subside, Fran released Jack's nipples then leaned forward and took each one into her mouth and briefly suckled it, flicking her tongue back and forth over them to sooth the pain she knew she had caused.

After resting for a bit, Fran finally lifted herself off of Jack's still swollen member and stood up. She stepped to one side of the bench and carefully removed the condom covering Jack's numb cock. She tossed it into the trash and grabbed a small towel. She wiped his cock clean so that all traces of the numbing cream had been removed. Of course, she knew his cock would remain numb for some time after that, but she had gotten what she wanted from it and the fact that it would remain numb didn't bother her.

She unfastened Jack's restraints and lead him over to the new cross he had bought for their dungeon. She fastened his cuffs to the arms of the cross so that he was spread out facing the cross. Then she picked up her favorite paddle and stepped beside her husband. "Now, I believe I owe you five swats," she whispered in his ear.

Jack knew exactly what she meant, the red die had landed on 'one' and that meant five swats with the paddle. He braced himself and answered, "Yes, Mistress."

Fran stepped into position and began. "Smack!"

"One, Mistress," Jack yelled as the paddle created a reddening spot on both cheeks of his ass.

"Smack!" again the paddle struck.

"Two, Mistress," he yelled through gritted teeth, trying to keep his voice down to hide the pain."

"Smack!" the third blow landed in exactly the same place as the previous two.

"Three, Mistress," he replied as the pain in his bottom increased exponentially.

"Smack!" again the paddle struck his now, very red, bottom.

"Four, Mistress," Jack shouted in real pain this time.

"Smack!" again the paddle struck his bottom in the same spot, only harder this time.

"Five, Mistress," he shouted for, he hoped, was the last time.

Jack felt Fran's hand gently stroking his burning skin. It felt good. Soothing. Then it suddenly began to feel very cool. Fran had added some kind of lotion or other, hopefully designed to help sooth his pain.

"You may put your panties back on," Fran said as she unfastened each of his restraints. "Also, take off the cuffs and place them in front of you on the carpet."

Fran went back to her throne and sat down, waiting for Jack to comply.

Jack retrieved the panties he had chosen to wear that day from the floor beside the bench and stepped into them. He pulled them up over his sore bottom and then removed his cuffs. Kneeling in front of Fran on the carpet provided for that purpose, Jack laid the set of four cuffs on the floor in front of him. "How may I serve you, Mistress," he asked.

"How does your bottom feel?" Fran asked him.

At that very moment Jack realized that his bottom was beginning to warm up, in fact, it was getting down right hot. Burning, one might say. "It's beginning to burn, Mistress," Jack reported.

"Good," Fran replied with a slight grin spreading over her face. "I put some eucalyptus cream on it to sooth it."

Jack knew what that meant. She didn't put it there to sooth anything. She put it there to make his ass burn so that he would be reminded of the paddling she had given him for some time to come. His cock was quickly shrinking because of it.

Fran ordered Jack to stand up and she replaced the tiny cage that kept his cock in check and locked it in place. "There you go," she said feeling proud of herself. "You can go and order our pizza now. "I'll tease your cock some more after the numbness wears off."

~ ~ ~

Chapter 6
NOT ALL MILK COMES FROM COWS

"I packed you a little something special in your lunch today, sweetheart," Brie said as Jim was headed out the door. "And don't forget, we have an appointment at Kathryn's at five o'clock."

Jim looked back over his shoulder, "Yeah, maybe I can finally get this belt off," he said.

"Yeah, maybe," Brie replied knowing full well Jim wasn't going to get rid of it that easily.

Brie went back inside and fixed herself a cup of coffee. She chuckled to herself, proud of the little trick she was playing on Jim. He had no idea what that 'something special' was she had packed in with his lunch. He was in for a real surprise. But he would find out soon enough.

The rest of the day was pretty boring except for the phone call from Jim at eleven, his lunch time.

"Hi, Jim," Brie said into the phone. "I take it you are calling about that little surprise I packed in your lunch today?"

"Yes, I am," replied Jim, though he didn't sound very happy. "Exactly what am I supposed to do with this thing?"

"You are supposed to lubricate it really good and shove it up your butt," she said as if he didn't know.

"And why would I do that?" he asked.

"Because you love me and you want to make me happy," Brie said. "You do want to make me happy, don't you?"

"Yes, dear," Jim answered, "I want to make you happy, but I don't see what that has to do with a butt-plug."

"Well," she explained, "if you don't wear it as my note directed, I'll have to paddle you."

"Oh," Jim said, pausing a moment to think. "I see. So, how long do I have to wear it?"

The Marriage Counselor

"Until you get off work today," Brie replied knowing he was going to go through with it.

"You mean I have to wear this for four periods?" he asked rhetorically.

"No," Brie replied, "you can take a paddling instead. I would love to administer it for you."

"Yes, Ma'am," he resigned himself to doing as he was told.

"That's better," she said. "Bye now." and she hung up without waiting for her husband to say his goodbye. It made her feel more confident knowing that he would comply with her wishes.

Brie decided to do some research on her own while waiting for her appointment with Kathryn. After all, Kathryn did tell her that it would be a good idea. She said Brie had a lot to learn and that the Internet had a great deal of information about how to humiliate a man. Especially sexually. So Brie spent the entire afternoon reading up on male sexual humiliation.

She ran across one particular method that intrigued her. It was called 'web-teases'. She had never heard of such a thing so she did a search for them. She found a web page devoted to them and read a few of them to familiarize herself with what they were and how they worked. They all seemed to be designed for men to do by themselves, but Brie came up with her own idea about that. She would make Jim do one while she watched and made sure he didn't cheat. She decided to ask Kathryn about them during her session that afternoon.

When four o'clock rolled around, Brie found herself strolling into Kathryn's full of confidence... And questions.

"Hi, Maggie," she said as she stepped up to receptionist's window. "How are you doing today?"

"Very well, thank you," Maggie replied. "You can go on back. Mistress Kathryn will be with you in a few minutes."

"Okay, thanks," Brie said as she opened the door to the back-office area. When she got to Kathryn's office she went in and sat down in her usual chair. She started looking at the diplomas mounted on the wall. There was a bachelor's degree from the University of Illinois, in Urbana. A Master's degree from the same place. And a PhD from Yale University in New York. There was also a license to practice from the state as well. On another wall was a photo of Kathryn and her staff. Maggie and another woman on Kathryn's right and two men who looked like the guys who made sure Jim put on the chastity belt on her left. The caption under the photo read, "Our Family."

Out of curiosity, Brie looked around for other photos, but Kathryn's desk didn't have any. Brie thought that was strange.

Just then, Kathryn entered the room. "Hello, Briana," she said, startling her.

"Oh, hi Kathryn," Brie said feeling nervous at having been caught looking around. "I was just checking out your diplomas and stuff."

"It's quite alright," Kathryn assured her, "that's what they're there for."

"If you don't mind my asking," Brie queried, "why are there no photos of your family here?"

"I don't mind your asking," Kathryn explained, "but that's my family up there in that photo," she pointed at the photo on the wall that Brie had examined earlier.

"You mean your staff is your family?" she asked.

"No, I mean my family is also my staff," Kathryn explained cryptically. "You see, Maggie and Terri are my female slaves and Harrison and Tony are my male slaves. We've been together, at least in part, for over six years now."

"Oh wow," Brie said a little unsure how to deal with that bit of information. "So you have four slaves?"

"Well, I don't think of them as slaves," Kathryn replied, "but it's the easiest way to explain our relationship. I think of them as my family."

"Oh, I see," Brie said as if she understood. She didn't, but she felt uneasy talking about it. "So what are we going to do today?"

"I planned on talking about how you plan to use humiliation on your husband," Kathryn began. "I don't think you should be using it for revenge. That could get ugly. But there are a great number of things you can do that would be fun for you and embarrassing for him. Did you do that research I suggested?"

"Yes, Ma'am," Brie replied, glad the subject had changed. "I found out a lot. There were several places that had lists of things, but I don't think I could do that 'cuckold' thing. I'm pretty sure it would ruin our marriage."

"You are probably right about that," Kathryn agreed. "If in doubt, stay away from anything that even sounds like it might be risky. Now, bi-sexual activity for James might not be a bad way to go. After all, it's one of the most humiliating things you can make him do. But I don't think either of you are ready for that, yet."

"It sort of turns me on thinking about it, though," Brie admitted. "But I wouldn't know how to go about finding a partner for that."

"To start with, you don't have to," Kathryn explained. "You could make him suck a dildo or, better yet, a strap-on dildo."

"I have made him dress up in woman's clothing." Brie announced, letting her pride show. "I took him to the mall and made him purchase it all for himself."

"That's really terrific," Kathryn exclaimed. "That's the kind of thing I was going to suggest for you. I think it would be perfect for Jim. Then you could use a strap-on to make his humiliation complete."

The Marriage Counselor

"Oh, I hadn't thought of that," Brie exclaimed. "He would just die if I made him do something like that. Thanks for the idea!"

"That's what I am here for," Kathryn said with a smile. She always enjoyed it when her clients began thinking for themselves.

Brie and Kathryn spent a few more minutes discussing various methods of humiliating Jim before going down to the treatment room for some hands-on experience. Kathryn intended to teach Briana how to milk Jim's prostate and she wanted to show her how to do it using the life-size doll. It wouldn't be quite the same as the real thing, which was why Jim was coming in later. Brie would be able to practice on him while Kathryn was there to make sure she was doing it right. But for now, the doll would give Brie a way to learn the mechanics of it.

When it was finally time for James to arrive, Brie went back upstairs to wait for him. She no sooner got to Maggie's office, then Jim came through the front door. Brie escorted him to the dressing room where he was to get undressed before his session.

"Before you get undressed," Brie said curiously, "are you still wearing your butt-plug?"

"No," Jim admitted, "I took it out in the men's room before I left the school. I didn't want to sit down with it in."

"Then what did you do with it?" Brie asked.

"It's in my briefcase," he replied. "I washed it off when I took it out."

"Well, hurry up and get undressed," Brie commanded. "You are wasting my time."

"Yes, Ma'am," Jim responded, realizing that Brie was not in a good mood. Perhaps he shouldn't have removed the plug until she could verify that he had actually warn it. Now he was getting worried that he would be punished for it.

Once Jim removed the remainder of his clothing, Brie led him down the hall to the elevator. Once inside, Brie scolded him for having removed the butt-plug before she told him to. All he could do, was apologize and hope that his punishment wouldn't be too severe.

When the door to the elevator opened again, A red-headed woman greeted them. "Hi, I'm Terri. I will be helping you and Mistress Kathryn this evening."

Terri was dressed in a black, lacy teddy that didn't really conceal much of what she had beneath it. Jim felt his cock swell in its tiny cage. In fact, it was getting quite uncomfortable. The problem was, Jim couldn't keep his eyes off of Terri.

Jim was led to a bench where he was strapped down on his hands (well, his elbows) and knees. His legs were spread wide and he was forced to bend down far enough for his elbows to be strapped to the middle of the bench.

"Don't we need to remove his cage for this?" asked Brie.

"No we don't," replied Kathryn. "Terri, show Briana how we milk a man without having to remove his cage."

"Yes, Mistress," the cute red-head answered. "Here, Brie, put one of these gloves on your right hand." She handed Brie a rubber glove from the nearby tool stand she and Kathryn had been preparing when Brie first arrived.

Brie worked her hand into the glove and pulled it down tightly. "Now what?" she asked.

"Now we put a little bit of this lubrication on your glove," Terri responded as she squeezed the tube of lubricant so that a small amount was expelled onto Brie's gloved hand. "Now smear that around and into your husband's anus. Push your fingers in to get it all lubed up."

"Like this?" Briana asked as she did as Terri instructed.

"Exactly," Terri said. "Now push your index finger in up to the second knuckle." She held up her finger and pointed to the correct knuckle.

James was feeling very humiliated. He had never felt anyone put their fingers into his ass before, other than a doctor. In fact, the butt-plug Brie had him insert earlier that afternoon, was the only time he could remember ever having anything in his ass. It wasn't entirely unpleasant, though.

"Now," Terri continued, "you should be able to feel his prostate gland. The doll you did this with doesn't have one, but if you feel around for it you'll find it. It feels about the size of a walnut and should be right at the tip of your finger."

"Yes," Brie said excitedly, "I can feel it. That's neat!" She had a big grin on her face as she stood there wiggling her finger back and forth over Jim's prostate.

"Massage it with your finger," Terri said, "work it in circles if you can. Try to get a second finger in. Then you can rub back and forth with one finger on each side of it."

"Oh, yes," Brie announced, "I can feel it. It's kind of... squishy. So, I just rub back and forth for a while? Then what happens?"

"Well," Terri began, "we will see. If all goes well, Jim will feel his cum seeping out of this cock and you will have successfully milked his cum out without him getting to enjoy an orgasm."

"That just sounds so cool," Brie replied.

Terri set a small stainless steel dish beneath Jim's cock. "This will catch anything that you manage to get out," she said. "If you bend down a little you can watch it."

Brie bent down a little and looked at the dish. After a few more minutes of massaging Jim's cock, a small amount of clear liquid dripped into the bowl. "Look!" Brie said full of excitement. "Something is happening."

"Yes," replied Terri, "that's what we normally call 'pre-cum'. It's clear and is used to feed the sperm and lubricate the penis so it can more easily enter the vagina. But keep it up. You're getting there."

Terri was standing directly in front of Jim and his eyes were level with her pussy. He could see the outline of it through the thin material of her teddy. He could also tell that she shaved her pussy and it was turning him on more than he wanted it to. His cock was swelling but the cage surrounding his cock wouldn't let it get hard. It was causing a great deal of pain, by this time.

Kathryn handed Terri a strap-on dildo and said, "Here, give him something do while Brie milks him."

Terri took the strap-on and stepped into the leg openings. She pulled it up into position and tightened the straps. "Suck on this, little man," she said pushing the dildo into Jim's face. Jim tried not to open his mouth at first, but realizing the position he was in, he finally relented. He opened his mouth and Terri pushed the tip in. She kept pushing until Jim gagged, then withdrew a little so that he could breath. "Work it," she ordered, pushing it back in again. "Suck that cock."

Jim thought he was humiliated before, but now... pretending to suck a cock? That was not only new, but extremely embarrassing. Did she have to keep calling him 'little man'? It was so demeaning.

Brie kept working her fingers back and forth over Jim's prostate like Terri had instructed. The discomfort Jim felt in his groin was growing. After a few more minutes, he felt as if his reproductive system was exploding from the inside. His cum began to dribble out into the bowl below his cock.

"Look!" Brie exclaimed, "I did it! I did it!" her voice was full of joy and excitement at her accomplishment.

"Very good!" Kathryn said patting Brie on the shoulder. "You sure did. And you can stop now."

"Look, Terri!" Brie added, I did it!"

Terri pulled her dildo out of Jim's mouth and stepped to his side to look at the bowl. "You sure did."

Brie was proud of herself and Jim was feeling used.

"Here," Terri said as she removed the strap-on she had been wearing, "try this." She handed it to Brie.

Kathryn helped Brie get the dildo strapped on correctly and pulled the straps tight. "Put some lube on the dildo and fuck his ass," she said.

Brie grabbed the tube of lubricant and squeezed some out onto the dildo. She was still wearing the rubber glove so she used it to smear the lube all over the dildo. Then she stepped up behind her husband who was still strapped to the bench and guided the tip carefully against his anus.

"Now, push!" Terri said as she walked back in front of Jim, giving him something to look at. She placed her hands on his shoulders to hold him steady as Brie pushed forward hard, as the head of the dildo forced its way passed the tight ring of muscle that was Jim's virgin anus.

Jim tried to resist, but with Terri holding his shoulders and Brie pushing hard against his tight little opening, his ass gave way. He felt every inch of the fake cock as it slid deeper and deeper into his bottom. He thought it was going to hurt like hell, but, to his surprise, it actually felt kind of good. He felt filled. Even the butt-plug didn't fill his ass like this thing. He could tell his anus was being stretched beyond anything he had ever felt before, but in a way, it felt good. Humiliating, but good.

Brie began to plunge the stiff cock-like silicone phallus deep into Jim's ass again and again. She was obviously enjoying the activity. She took a firm hold of his hips to steady both herself and Jim as she continued to thrust in and out of his virgin ass.

What Brie was unaware of was the fact that the dildo she was using to fuck Jim, was rubbing against his prostate as she thrust it in and out. In a matter of minutes, Jim let out a low groan as his prostate produced more of the milky substance through his cock and into the bowl below. It happened twice more before Brie finally tired.

"Can I stop, now?" she asked. "I'm getting tired."

Kathryn stepped up to her placing her hand gently on Brie's shoulder and said, "Of course you can, dear. And look what you have done." she pointed toward the bowl that contained all the fluid she had coaxed out of her husband's cock.

Brie pulled the dildo out of Jim's ass without so much as a thought for his comfort. It came out with a slight popping sound as she pulled it free of his anus in one swift motion. She leaned around to look at the bowl. "Oh, my!" she exclaimed. "Did I do that?"

"You most certainly did," Kathryn said as she helped the woman loosen the straps of her strap-on dildo in order to remove it. "That doesn't work for everyone, but in your case, you might consider getting yourself a strap-on to see if you can make it happen more often."

"Wow," replied Brie, "I guess I should."

Terri unfastened the straps holding James in place and helped him to his feet. "How do you feel?" she asked him.

"Humiliated," he replied. "But pretty good, other than that."

"Good," Kathryn said. "I have a surprise for you." She held out the keys to Jim's chastity belt on a necklace chain and said, "This is for you, Briana."

"The key to Jim's belt?" she asked with surprise in her voice.

"Yes," Kathryn replied. "Use it wisely. And for you, James, Terri will give you your diploma on your way out. Congratulations."

"Thank you," Jim said humbly. "I hope we don't ever have to come back here." He smiled as he said it.

Kathryn smiled back and said, "Well, not for treatment, anyway."

With that, the couple went back upstairs to the dressing room so James could get dressed.

On the way home Brie and Jim stopped off at a local diner for some coffee and to talk about what they had learned about each other and their relationship over the past couple of weeks. They ate some pie and drank some coffee while they talked. They agreed that they were both enjoying the changes that were taking place. Jim admitted to being turned on by the humiliation and even the paddling, to an extent. He was surprised at the changes he saw in Brie and admitted that he actually liked the idea of her being in charge. They also agreed that, from now on, the diner would serve as neutral ground since it was open twenty-four hours a day and they both felt comfortable talking openly there.

When they were finished, they drove home and retired for the night, exhausted from the evening's activities.

~ ~ ~

Chapter 7
THE WEB-TEASE

One thing Brie learned from Kathryn was that she needed to find ways to keep her husband aroused even when they were not together. She also needed to find ways to sexually tease and deny Jim when they were together. Denial of his sexual satisfaction was something entirely new to Brie. She was accustom to giving him sex whenever he wanted it and not getting satisfaction herself. But intentionally denying Jim satisfaction, or an orgasm, wasn't something she knew how to do. Brie studied the pamphlets Kathryn had given her on the subject. Though she learned a great deal from them, she wanted more. So she turned to the Internet to see if she could get some help there.

Brie figured as long as Jim had to be at the school at least until after four, she had plenty of time to find some ways of teasing and denying him that would, just maybe, be appealing to her as well. Actually, just the thought of getting Jim all worked up and then not allowing him to cum actually turned her on a bit. She didn't understand why, but the more she read about it, the more excited she became at the prospect.

Brie read several stories on the subject and some blog articles she found, but nothing really caught her attention until she found a web site that specialized in what they called 'web-teases'. She read through a few of them and decided that she could make Jim do one while she watched. "No," she thought to herself, "I can make him do it as if I were the woman in the tease. I'll give him the orders and watch as he performs the tasks called for in the web-tease." So she found one that seemed perfectly suited to her plan.

Briana planned everything out. She gathered the items needed for the tease session as called for in the web-tease she planned to use. She put the items in a small paper bag and then stuffed the bag in a drawer so Jim wouldn't find it before she was ready to play with him that night.

The Marriage Counselor

When Jim got home from work it was already after five o'clock. Brie served him supper in the usual way and then made him strip down and clear away the dishes while she prepared for the evening's festivities. She retrieved the bag of toys, and her best wooden hair brush. She placed everything on the coffee table in the living room and sat down on the couch to wait for Jim.

When Jim had finished clearing away the supper dishes and loading them into the dishwasher, he entered the living room to ask Brie if there was anything else he could do for her.

"You can get one of the dining chairs and sit across from me there," she said pointing to a spot on the far side of the coffee table.

"Yes, Mistress," he replied as he went to get the required chair.

While Jim was getting the chair she requested, Brie opened her laptop and waited for it to come back to life. She clicked the mouse a couple of times until the web-tease she wanted was displayed on the screen.

When Jim returned, and was about to sit down, Brie stopped him by saying, "Before you sit, let's remove that nasty cage. Shall we?"

Thinking she was going to remove the entire chastity belt, Jim hurried to stand in front of Brie on her side of the coffee table and said, "Yes, Mistress. I'd like that."

Brie leaned forward and pulled the key to his chastity cage out. "We won't be needing this while we play our little game, tonight," she said as she unlocked the tiny lock that held the cage in place, that confined his cock. Then she carefully pulled the cage off and freed his little cock from its confines.

"We are going to play a game?" Jim asked a little surprised as he returned to his chair and sat down.

"We are," Brie replied. "Now open the paper bag and place the contents on the table."

Jim opened the bag and dumped it out on the coffee table. "What's all this?" he asked, looking a little puzzled.

"That is everything you will need to play our little game," she replied picking up the deck of cards and removing the rubber band that held them together. As she began to shuffle the cards, she continued, "You can arrange everything neatly on the table while I shuffle the cards."

"Yes, Mistress," he replied, listening to her explain what it was all for.

"You are going to play a little five-card stud," Brie explained as she continued to shuffle the cards one more time. "The game is called 'Jacks or Better' and if you win you will be rewarded, but if you lose you will be punished."

"How do I win, Mistress," he asked still a bit confused.

"If your hand contains a pair of Jacks or better, you win," Brie explained. "If you don't even have a pair, you lose and a punishment will be assigned."

"What happens if I can't beat Jacks but I do have a pair of something, Mistress?" Jim asked.

"Well, that depends whether you can beat my hand," she explained. "Maybe you'll get both a reward and a punishment. Are you ready to begin?"

"I guess I'm ready, Mistress," Replied Jim.

Brie placed the top five cards, one at a time, face up on the table in front of Jim. He looked at them for a second and announced, "I have a pair if threes!" He was all excited.

Brie looked at the cards and said, "So you do. Shall we see what you get for that?" With that she clicked her mouse and quickly read the instructions that came up on the screen.

"What do I get?" Jim asked excitedly.

Brie picked up the dildo that was laying on the table and gave Jim his answer, "You get to suck on this for two minutes. I'll time you." There was a handy little clock on the computer screen provided for just that purpose.

"What?" Jim replied somewhat dismayed. "You mean I have to pretend this is a cock and suck it?"

"That's right, my little cross-dressing slave boy," she said, "you get to suck it. And for two minutes. Ready... Go!"

James loved the way Brie talked to him. It turned him on. It turned him on enough to make the game more exciting. He stuck the dildo in his mouth and began working it in and out as if fucking his own mouth.

"Times up!" Brie announced. "You can stop now."

Jim pulled the dildo out of his mouth and set it back down on the table. "That wasn't so bad," he commented.

"Oh, that was your reward for having gotten a pair," Brie said with a chuckle. "Now you have to stroke your cock for me."

"Really?" Jim asked. "I have to masturbate?"

"I didn't say that," Brie answered. "You have to stroke your cock very slowly three-hundred times. But you are NOT allowed to cum. Understand?"

"Yes, Mistress," he replied.

"Count them out load for me, too," Brie told him. "I wouldn't want you to slip up and miss a stroke or two. Go ahead. Start whenever you are ready."

Jim tentatively took hold of his cock with his right hand. It was hard enough, though it had been harder. "One... two..."

"That's too fast," Brie interrupted. "Do it more slowly."

"Yes, Mistress," Jim replied. "Three... four..." He was stroking at about half his previous speed and Brie thought that would be just fine.

When Jim had finally reached a count of three-hundred, Brie picked up the cards from his hand and placed them on the bottom of the deck as per the instructions from her PC. She dealt out five more cards face up in front of him.

Jim looked at his cards and said, "Not even a lousy pair, Mistress."

Brie looked at him with a sad face and said, "Aww," Then she perked up and smiled as she said, "Let's see what you've won, Jim." Then she clicked the proper link and waited for the screen to refresh.

"Oh!" she said as she read the instructions on the screen, "This sounds like fun! Here," she handed Jim a round shoelace from the table. "Wrap this around your cock from the base to the tip. Use it all."

"Yes, Mistress," Jim replied as he began winding the long string around his cock, over and over again, until there wasn't enough to go around it again. "Now what?"

"Now, pull it off in one smooth motion," Brie answered.

Jim pulled on the end of the string and his cock began swinging in a circular motion as the string rapidly unwound. "Ow, ow, ow!" Jim exclaimed as the last of the string pulled free. "That wasn't as pleasant as I thought it was gonna to be."

"That was neat!" Brie said excitedly. "Do that again!"

Jim hesitated. He said, "Mistress, I think once was enough."

"No, really," Brie said, "the instructions say you have to do it three times. So... Do it again, slave boy."

Jim began winding the shoelace around the base of his cock again. "Yes, Mistress," he said, not being very happy about doing it.

When he finished wrapping his cock, Jim pulled the string off without a word. "That is so cool!" Brie announced excitedly. I can't wait to do it to you myself. Okay, one more time,"

"Yes, Mistress," Jim replied, as he began winding the string around his erect cock one last time. This time Brie told him to pull it really fast. He grimaced, and complied.

"Oowww!" Jim practically screamed as the string unwound flinging his cock in circles. "That kind of hurts," he announced.

"Aww... I'm sorry," Brie said in her little girl voice. "But I still think it's really cool."

Brie looked back at the instructions on the computer screen and said, "Now give me one-hundred strokes any speed you want. Just don't forget to count them for me. And DON'T CUM!"

"Yes, Mistress," Jim replied as he took hold of his cock and began stroking it. "One... Two... Three..."

As Jim was stroking and counting, Brie picked up the last five cards that were dealt and prepared to deal another hand. "Come on," She said impatiently, "Hurry up so we can deal another hand." She wasn't really in a hurry, she just wanted to humiliate Jim as much as she could.

The second Jim finished his one-hundred strokes, Brie laid out the next five cards. "Aww... Poor Jimmy," she said when she saw that there wasn't even a pair. "You got nothing, again. Let's see what you have to do for me this time." And with that she clicked the proper link to reveal his next task.

"What does it say, Mistress?" He asked as Brie studied the instructions.

"It says, you have to put clothespins on your nipples," she began trying to conceal her delight. "And then you have to stroke your cock two-hundred times real slow. But on the up side, you get to use lubrication this time."

Jim wasn't too sure about putting clothespins on his nipples and remarked, "Can't we skip the clothespins, Mistress?"

"Oh, no," Brie replied with a giggle, "but I'll be happy to put them on for you, if you like."

"No, no..." Jim replied, "I think I can handle it, Mistress." He picked up one clothespin and carefully placed it on his right nipple. "Ouch!" he said. "That actually hurts."

"Well then," Brie said cheerfully, "I guess you'll want to hurry then." She handed him another clothespin and watched as he placed it on his left nipple.

"Here," She said holding out a bottle of lubrication. "Hold out your hand..." She poured a large amount of lubricant in Jim's outstretched hand. "Don't forget to count, and don't cum."

Brie was proud of herself for coming up with this web-tease idea. It was working out even better than she had hoped. Jim was humiliated having to do all this in front of her and it showed. She watched intently as Jim began stroking his well lubricated cock. She knew the lube would help to bring him close to ejaculating and that was what she wanted. Jim only paused once to keep from cumming. He had reached the one-seventies when he felt he might cum. He paused for about thirty seconds before finishing his task.

"What's the matter, Jimmy boy?" Brie chided. "Feeling a little edgy?" She chuckled at her own joke. She was finally feeling vindicated for all the stupid jokes James had told over the years.

Brie handed Jim a towel to clean off his hand and told him he could remove the clothespins that had somehow made his nipples feel numb. But when he released them, the pain shot back through each nipple as powerful as when he had first applied them. He couldn't help reacting. "Ouch!" he yelled as he bent forward and began rubbing his poor, sore nipples.

Brie dealt another hand and said excitedly, "Look Jim! You got three sevens! That beats a pair of Jacks. Let's see what you get to do this time." And she clicked the proper link.

"You get to masturbate for five whole minutes this time," Brie reported. "But you can't stop stroking. You can only slow down if you feel yourself getting close. So be careful." She reached across the table and poured a generous amount of lubrication in Jim's outstretched hand. "Are you ready?"

"Yes, Mistress," Jim replied.

"Go..." Brie said watching the clock on the computer screen. "Remember, not too fast or you will have to start all over."

Brie kibitzed him as he carefully, and slowly stroked his cock. Jim didn't want to accidentally cum because he somehow sensed that that would be a bad thing to do. He tried to pay no attention to Brie as she continued to humiliate him while he performed his latest task. He had to slow down three times but he made it through the five minutes without cumming.

"Times up!" Brie announced as the second hand on the clock passed over the twelve position. "You did it! You made it the first try. Good job, Jimmy boy."

"Are you ready for another hand?" Brie asked as she began to deal out five more cards.

"How many more hands do I have to play?" Jim complained.

"There's only a couple more," Brie informed him. "You can do it. I know you can. Besides, it's fun, don't you think?"

"If you say so, Mistress," Jim replied resigning himself to his apparent fate.

"Aw, you got nothing again," Brie said as she laid the last card down. "Not even a pair."

"Great," Jim said sarcastically, "what do I have to do this time, Mistress?" Brie clicked the appropriate link and began reading the instructions.

"Well," she began as a smile crossed her face, "first you have to put this up your butt." She held out the butt-plug that had been innocently awaiting use.

Jim took the object from her hand and remarked, "It's kind of big. Don't you think, Mistress?"

"It's the smallest one I have," she remarked. "I made a special trip to the sex shop especially for this game and you want to complain about the size of the butt-plug? Believe me, it was actually one of the smaller ones they had." She handed him the bottle of lubrication and said, "You'll need this."

"Thanks, Mistress. I think," Jim replied. He spread some of the lubrication on the plug and then on his anus. He stood up just enough to push the thing into his bottom, but not without a little difficulty. "There," he remarked when the plug was finally all the way in, "how's that, Mistress?" He turned to show her that it was, indeed, all the way in.

"Very good," Brie replied. "Now sit down, there's more."

Jim didn't want to sit down. He didn't want to feel that thing get shoved any further up his back side. It was uncomfortable enough not to mention the humiliation of it all. But he carefully lowered his bottom back down onto the seat of the chair, wincing as he did so. He could feel the plug being pushed even further up inside him. It seemed to fill him to capacity. But it wasn't so entirely uncomfortable that he couldn't stand it for a few minutes, anyway.

"Now you have to give me two more minutes of slow stroking," Brie announced.

Two minutes didn't sound bad. Jim figured he could do the two minutes and then he could get this anal invader out and be more comfortable. He began to stroke his cock once again. This time he was careful to go slowly enough that he wouldn't have to stop. He wanted to stroke himself fast. He wanted to get this ordeal over with as soon as possible, not to mention the fact that he really wanted to cum. It had been too long since he last had an orgasm. But, of course, that was not permitted, yet.

When he had finished his two minutes, Jim asked, "Now can I take this thing out?"

"Nope," Brie announced, according to the instructions you have to leave it in place until such time as you are told to remove it."

"Yes, Mistress," Jim replied resolutely.

Brie dealt another hand. There was a pair of fives this time. Not exactly a winner, but not a loser either. She clicked the appropriate link and read the instructions. "All you have to do this time is give me five-hundred strokes without edging yourself."

"That's not so bad," Jim said. "Then can I take this damned plug out, Mistress?"

"Not according to this, you can't," Brie answered. "Looks like you will have to keep it in a bit longer."

Jim put some more lube on his hand and began to stroke himself very slowly again. He was careful not to get too close to the edge. He didn't want to have to start all over again. Five-hundred wasn't that many strokes. He knew he could do it if he just took his time and didn't stroke too fast. He counted each stroke out loud as required. It helped him to have something else to concentrate on besides how much he wanted to cum.

When he finished, Brie congratulated him and dealt another hand. Jim got nothing. Not even a lousy pair.

After clicking the correct link, Brie announced, "This is your last hand, slave-boy. You even get to cum! How about that?"

The Marriage Counselor

Jim perked up when he heard that. He wanted to cum in the worst way and now he was going to get to. "Great!" he said with renewed vigor in his voice. "Can I take this thing out of my butt then, Mistress?"

"Well," Brie said, "Not until you have completed the task."

"Well, what is it?" he asked excitedly. "How many strokes, Mistress?"

"Ten," she replied.

"Ten?" Jim practically shouted. "There's no way I can cum in ten strokes!"

"Oh, sorry," Brie continued, "not that kind of strokes. I get to give you ten strokes with my hairbrush before you cum. Get over here and lay across my knees."

Jim wasn't as excited as he had been just a moment ago. He got up and rounded the table then laid across his wife's thighs. "Please be kind, Mistress," he begged.

"Yes," Brie said, "It's just ten, you can handle that." She looked down at Jim's upturned ass with the base of the butt-plug peeking out from between his cheeks. She thought how humiliating this must be for poor Jim. Then she smacked his right butt cheek hard with her hairbrush.

"Ouch! One, Mistress," Jim said wanting this whole ordeal to be over. There was another loud smack on the left side this time. "Two, Mistress."

When Brie had finally smacked his bottom a full ten times it was a bright red. She was proud of herself. She pushed Jim off her lap and said, "Now you can masturbate to orgasm. But..." she paused for effect, "you have to ruin it."

"What?" he said as if in shock. "What do you mean I have to 'ruin' it, Mistress?"

"I mean," Brie explained, "that just before you shoot your load you must stop touching your cock. You'll understand once you do it. But I warn you, if you don't stop in time, I will have to paddle you again. But this time I won't stop at just ten smacks."

"Yes, Mistress," Jim replied sounding a bit dejected. He sat down and began to stroke his cock. Brie encouraged him by telling him all kinds of things that she knew would turn him on. Things like, how she intended to make him wear his panties around the house and that he may even have to wear them to do some of the yard work in the back yard. Things of that nature.

It worked. In a matter of only a few minutes, Jim was ready to release his load. Brie reminded him that he had to stop the second he knew he was going to cum and he did.

Brie watched with excitement as Jim's cock strained and jerked but his cum only dribbled out of the end of his cock. Jim felt let down. He felt like he had been denied the release he wanted. Instinctively, Jim caught his ejaculate in the palm of his hand. And that's when Brie gave him the bad news.

"Now drink it, slave-boy," she said in no uncertain terms. "Drink it all down."

"What?" Jim was shocked at her request. "You really want me to drink my own cum, Mistress?"

"I have had to ever since we got married," Brie replied. "Now it's high time you tried it."

"I'll throw up," Jim protested.

"I doubt it," Brie replied, "but if you do, oh well. Drink up!"

Jim slowly raised his cum filled hand to his mouth. He looked at the creamy white liquid for a moment then closed his eyes and tipped his head back. He let the warm fluid drain into his open mouth and he swallowed hard. "Yech," he said when he had finished. "That was awful!"

"Really?" Brie asked. "Was it really all that bad?"

"Well," confessed Jim, "no, not really. I don't like it, but I guess it was more the thought of it that repulsed me, Mistress."

"That's right," Brie agreed, "it wasn't as bad as you thought it would be. Now was it?"

"No, Mistress," Jim replied. "It wasn't."

Brie said that the game was over and Jim could remove the butt-plug that still remained in his bottom. Jim had almost forgotten about it what with everything else that had happened.

All in all, Brie thought that it had been a fun evening and she planned to do it again sometime... Soon.

~ ~ ~

Chapter 8
THE PARTY

It was Saturday. Fran's party to introduce her dungeon to the guys was scheduled to begin at eight-PM. Brie had two hours to prepare Jim for what was to come. Little did he know, but Brie had volunteered him to act as the maid for the party. He was to serve drinks and hor'dourves to the other guests. As far as she knew, there would only be the six of them, unless Fran or Jane had invited someone else. The problem was, how would she dress Jim? Then it hit her.

Briana grabbed her phone and called the only adult sex shop in town. "Hello? I was wondering, do you carry any French maid costumes? You do? Great! I'll be right there. Bye."

As soon as she hung up the phone, Brie jumped in her car and drove to the Sex shop on the edge of town. When she stepped inside, a short, red-headed woman greeted her. "Hi, I'm Lisa. How can I help you?"

"Oh, Lisa," Brie began breathlessly, "I need a French maid's costume for my husband in a hurry."

"Sure," Lisa replied, "you must be the woman who called a few minutes ago. They're right over here." She walked toward the clothing side of the store and went directly to a wall of costumes. "Do you know what size he might be?" she asked.

"Yes," Brie answered, excited that she actually knew. "He wears a size 12 in women's clothes."

"That would be a large..." the red-haired girl said as she looked for the right size on the rack. She reached up and pulled one off the rack and handed it to Brie, "This is a large. Does it look right?"

"It looks perfect," Brie said holding it up to get a good look at it. "What accessories do I need to go with it?"

"Well, it comes with a head band, ruffled panties, and white stockings with black bows," Lisa said. "does he have shoes?"

"Yes," Brie replied, "he has lots of shoes. Oh, wait... He needs a wig, maybe short and blonde?"

"Sure," Lisa said, "wigs are right back here." She pointed toward the back of the store, not very far from where they were standing.

"Oh, I like that one," Brie said as she approached the wig display.

"This one?" Lisa said picking up the wig on the counter that was mounted on a Styrofoam stand.

"Yes," Brie replied excitedly. "That's exactly what I had in mind."

"Well, that was easy," Lisa said. "What else?"

"I guess this will do it, then. I'm in kind of a hurry." Brie said looking for a clock. "We have a party to attend tonight and I don't want to be late."

"I understand," Lisa said as she took the outfit from Brie. "If there is nothing else, I'll just ring this up for you."

"No, that's it," Brie said as they both walked back to the sales counter. "I'm so glad you guys carry all this stuff. I don't know what I would have done if you hadn't."

"Well," Lisa commented, "we have been looking for a larger place. But we can't seem to get the zoning commission to approve anything."

"That's too bad," Brie sympathized, "It would be nice if you were more centrally located."

"Yeah, well..." Lisa paused to reflect on the situation, "we are working on getting a place right down town, but I doubt we will get the zoning commission to allow it. They don't seem to want us around."

"Yeah," Brie agreed, "They are a bunch of old fuddies, anyway."

"That comes to sixty-eight dollars and 26 cents," Lisa told her as she put the maid's outfit into a large bag.

Brie gave her a debit card and waited for the machine to ask for her pin number. "Where down town?"

"I don't know for sure," Lisa replied, "it's just that this place is too small and the boss can't afford to add on. He was thinking of leasing some place."

Brie put her debit card back into her wallet and picked up the bag containing Jim's new outfit, "Well, I hope it all works out for you. Thanks. Bye"

Lisa said, "Thanks, and goodbye to you too." but Brie was already out the door. "I guess she was in a hurry," Lisa said to herself.

Brie was anxious to get home. She couldn't wait to get to the party and dress Jim up in the new outfit she had just bought. "He'll make an excellent maid," she thought as she pulled into the driveway.

When Brie entered the house, she looked at the clock. It was already six-ten and she had not picked out her outfit for the night. She set the bag from the sex shop on the nearest chair and picked up the phone and ordered a pizza. Supper would have to be quick and she didn't have time to prepare anything. This way, she could get dressed and eat later.

Jim was in the bedroom doing a little light reading when Brie stepped into the room. "You need to get ready for the party," she said realizing that he was not dressed, as per her standing order. "Oh, and by the way, I ordered a pizza. It should be here in about thirty minutes."

"Yes, Mistress," Jim replied. He was getting much better at using the proper etiquette. "Do you want me to wait to get dressed?"

"No dear," Brie replied, "you will find a bag in the living room. It's what I want you to wear tonight. Go ahead and get it and I'll help you get dressed."

"Yes, Mistress," he said wondering why she would need to help him get dressed. After all, he was a grown man. But when he retrieved the bag and saw what was inside, he realized why she said it. He carried the bag to the bedroom before removing its contents. He laid the wig on his pillow and the hanger containing the rest of his outfit on the bed as if someone were laying there and had magically disappeared leaving their clothes behind. Realizing he would need them, Jim went to the closet and retrieved a pair his black high-heeled shoes and set them on the bed as well.

Brie returned to the bedroom wrapped in a towel. She had just stepped out of the shower and wanted to get Jim dressed before the pizza arrived. "I see you found it," she said as she used a corner of the towel to dry one ear.

"Yes, Mistress," Jim replied, "I assume I am going as a maid?"

"Of course, you are," Brie said, "Fran needs someone to serve drinks and hor'dourves doesn't she?"

"I suppose so, Ma'am," Jim began, "but why does it..."

Brie cut him off short, "It has to be you because I volunteered you. That's why. Now get dressed and I'll help you with your makeup."

"Makeup?" Jim thought to himself, "Why do I need makeup? It's not like people aren't going to recognize me."

"Yes, Mistress," Jim replied aloud. He proceeded to disassemble the items attached to the hanger and laid them out on the bed side by side. He put on the panties first, followed by the frilly black and white dress, and then the stockings. "What do I do with this?" he asked, holding up the hair band.

That will go on after your wig," Brie replied. "Here, put this on." She handed the blonde wig to Jim. He pulled it down snugly over his own hair and asked Brie how it looked.

"It looks good," she commented, "but it will look better once we get your makeup on. Sit down over here." she said pulling out the stool in front of her vanity.

Jim sat down facing the mirror and Brie turned him to face her instead. "I have to see your face to do this," she told him. "Now hold still."

Brie applied what she considered to be the right amount of everything in order to make it obvious he was a man and that he was wearing makeup. She didn't try to hide the fact that Jim had not shaved since that morning. His stubble made it obvious he was a man and that's the way she wanted it.

Just then the doorbell rang. "Get that, would you dear?" Brie said walking back into the bathroom to put her towel away. "It's probably the pizza. I'll be down in a minute."

"Yes, Mistress," Jim replied as he headed for the stairs.

Jim reached for his wallet suddenly realizing he didn't have a back pocket. He stopped short of the door and looked down at himself. "God, the is embarrassing," he thought. He hoped it wasn't the kid from down the block who knows him. He opened the door and saw the delivery person. "Thank heavens," he thought when he saw a young girl standing at the door holding a pizza warmer.

"Pizza for James Galloway?" the young girl said.

"Uh... Yes, that's me," Jim replied, "Let me get your money." He looked around for Briana's purse in hopes that she might have some cash. He spotted it in the chair where she had laid the bag containing the outfit he was now wearing. He found a twenty and handed it to the girl. "Keep the change," he said as he took the pizza box she had just removed from the warmer.

"Thanks, mister," the girl said as she turned to walk back to her car.

"Damn!" he thought. He had hoped she hadn't noticed. Jim set the pizza box on the table and went into the kitchen to fetch a couple of Pepsi's. Brie had finished dressing and was just coming down the stairs when he got back.

"I brought your shoes down for you," Brie informed him as she set the shoes on the table for Jim. "I didn't think you wanted to go to the party in your stocking feet."

"Thank you, Mistress," Jim replied as he set a Pepsi on ice in front of Brie. "I'm not really sure I want to go to this party at all."

"Oh, you're going," she replied raising one eyebrow as she sat down at the table. "You're the maid! You have to be there."

"Mistress?" Jim asked, taking his own seat across from his wife. "You realize this is the most humiliating thing you have ever made me do. Don't you?"

"Oh, you love it and you know it," Brie replied. "Besides, you won't be the only one who will be humiliated tonight."

"What do you mean?" Jim asked.

"You will just have to wait and see," she replied. "Eat up. We have to get going. I want to be the first to arrive so that you can greet the other guests as they arrive."

Brie thought she detected a slight blushing as Jim answered, "Yes, Mistress."

When they finished eating, Jim and Brie drove to Jack and Fran's house to prepare for the evening's festivities.

As soon as they arrived, Fran took Jim into the kitchen and gave him his instructions for serving her guests. He was to make sure everyone's glass was never empty and he should serve the hor'dourves as soon as everyone was seated in the living room. He was also assigned the duty of answering the door and greeting each guest as they entered.

There were only two other guests invited to the party because Fran's dungeon just wasn't big enough to accommodate more than that. As soon as Jane and Frank arrived, Jim began serving the drinks and hor'dourves. The five other people at the party talked about how Kathryn had taught them so much and if it weren't for her, all of their marriages might have ended up in divorce.

Jack and Frank couldn't resist poking fun at Jim for having to wear a maids outfit. Frank even slapped Jim on the ass a couple of times as if he were trying to flirt with the maid. All of the women enjoyed the fact none of them had to take responsibility for playing hostess since Jim was filling that role. Jim never felt more embarrassed in his life, which was just fine with Brie. It was, in fact, what she had hoped for.

After about thirty minutes, when most of the hor'dourves had been eaten, Fran announced the reason why she had held this party in the first place. She wanted to show off her new dungeon. Of course, the women knew why they were there, but Jack was the only male who even knew about the dungeon but was sure that Fran wanted to keep it a secret. He was wrong!

Fran invited everyone to join her in the basement to see how she had "renovated" it. Once they all had time to look over the equipment, and marvel at her accomplishment, Fran made one more announcement. They were going to put the equipment to good use that very night.

Jack and Frank were both ordered, by their respective mates, to disrobe completely. Jim was told to remove only his panties, since he was more embarrassed wearing his dress than he would have been naked.

Fran took Jack to the St. Andrew's cross and fastened him securely with his back to the cross. Jane secured Frank on his back to the padded bench while Jim was fastened to the spanking bench with his legs spread wide and his high-heels still on his feet. Each woman carefully removed the cage from their respective husband's chastity belt so that free access to his genitals was made possible. Each woman had prepared a little demonstration for the others to witness.

Jane went first. She coaxed Frank's cock to full erection, which didn't take much since he was already getting hard just being bound in front of three women. Then she proceeded to tease his cock with an ostrich feather. It drove Frank crazy each time she would tickle his cock and balls with it. He would wriggle and strain in an attempt to obtain more stimulation than the feather could give. He was soon dripping pre-cum from the tip of his cock and the other women cheered Jane on.

The other men could see what was happening even from their bound positions. They knew their turns would come and Jim was afraid of what might be in store for him since he was the only one whose bottom was exposed.

When Jane felt that Frank had had enough of the feather, she took his cock in her hand and gave it nine or ten good strokes before stopping and pointing out how much Frank obviously wanted to cum. They all laughed when Jane informed him that was not going to be possible. She smeared a generous amount of numbing cream on his cock and rolled a condom down over that. Then informed Frank that she was going to ride him for as long as she wanted and that he would get nothing out of it except for the excitement of watching her breasts dangle above his face.

Jane removed her clothing and stepped over the bench to straddle her husband. His eyes definitely grew larger as she lowered herself onto his cock and came to rest against his groin. He could feel her weight. He could see her naked breasts jutting out from her well-formed body. He longed to touch them, but his hands were bound and he couldn't work them free, struggle as he might.

When Jane began to move slowly up and down the full length of his rock-hard shaft, Frank realized, for the first time, that his cock, though wrapped in Jane's warm, wet pussy, couldn't feel a thing. Jane was using him. She was using him right there in front of two other men and two other women. He now began to feel the full effect of his embarrassment. He watched carefully as Jane's breasts jiggled and swayed above him as she rode his cock to her first orgasm of the night.

Frank hoped for just a tiny bit of feeling to return to his throbbing cock so that he might get enough stimulation to have his own orgasm inside his lovely wife. He soon forgot that there were four other people watching as he was used for the first time in public. Well, semi-public, anyway. What confused Frank the most was that he was actually turned on by that fact. But even that was not enough to coax an orgasm from his poor, well used cock.

Jane had two more orgasms before she decided to dismount. Frank was utterly frustrated by the way he was used and yet prohibited from reaching

The Marriage Counselor

his own goal of ejaculation. He watched as Jane wrapped herself in a towel and then offered the use of his cock to anyone else who might be interested. But there were no takers at that time.

Fran stood up and removed her clothing as well. She wanted Jack to see her body and get even more aroused than he already was after witnessing his friend being fucked by his wife and not being able to cum himself. She stood in front of Jack and fondled his cock and balls with her fingers. She asked, "Did watching your friend getting fucked turn you on, Jack?" She didn't much care how he answered, she knew he had never been this turned on in his life.

Fran put some lubrication on Jack's cock and began slowly stroking it while she teased him about his current situation. She knew full well that Jack was turned on by watching Jane tease Frank the way she had. She asked Jack if he wanted to get fucked. If he wanted to squirt his cum all over her or maybe in her. She didn't care if he even answered. She knew she was turning him on just by talking to him in the sexy way she was.

In a matter of minutes, Jack was writhing and straining to be touched as Fran would stop whenever she thought he might be getting close to cumming. It drove him mad. She knew exactly how much teasing and stimulation he could take before she pushed him over the edge. But she wasn't about to allow that. Fran continued to tease and torment poor Jack until she finally tired of it. Then she offered to let any of the other wives have the opportunity to tease his cock as well. But no one took her up on it.

Now it was Briana's turn. She undressed like her predecessors had done, not so much because she needed to, but more because they had all agreed that they would. She stepped up behind Jim and began gently stroking his bottom with her fingertips. His arousal was obvious because his cock was trapped in a downward position by the edge of the spanking bench to which he was so securely fastened. He knew everyone was watching him closely, and as embarrassing as that was, it was strangely erotic.

Brie had a surprise for Jim. He thought he was going to be severely paddled, but that was not Brie's plan at all. Instead, she began smearing lubrication in, on, and around his anus. Then she retrieved a strap-on dildo that she had concealed in her purse before leaving the house. She pulled it in place and drew the straps up tightly. She applied lubrication to the dildo as she taunted poor James with the prospect of being fucked by everyone in the room, including the other men.

The fear Brie was trying to instill in her husband was working. His arousal grew at the thought of being fucked by the other members of the party, even if that included the men. He didn't understand why that was, but Brie knew. Kathryn had told her this might be the case since Jim was turned on by humiliation. After all, what was more humiliating than the prospect of being fucked by two of his friends and their wives?

Brie stepped up behind Jim and pressed the tip of the dildo against this ass. Then, when she felt his anus muscles relax slightly, she shoved it all the way into his bottom with one hard thrust. Jim let out a huge gasp. He was not prepared for such an attack. He was expecting Brie to take it slowly and gently. But such was not the case.

Brie paused for a moment and then started a slow, smooth pumping action. The dildo filled Jim's ass over and over again as Brie continued to fuck his most private of places. Brie continued this same rhythm until one of the other women mentioned that Jim's cock was leaking a great deal of pre-cum. With that, Brie sped up the pace. She shoved the fake penis in and out of Jim's vulnerable ass until she managed to coax a large amount of ejaculate from his body.

Jim was confused. He didn't feel like he had cum, but everyone was cheering and making lewd comments to that effect. The fact was, Jim's prostate was getting quite a massage when brie was pushing her fake cock in and out of his ass. So much so, that he ended up expelling his semen without having an orgasm. Though everyone else seemed to enjoy it, Jim did not. He felt cheated. He came, but he didn't. He didn't get any enjoyment out of what just happened. But that didn't seem to bother Brie. In fact, it was an unexpected bonus, as far as Brie was concerned. She was happy about it.

Brie withdrew the dildo from Jim's bottom and removed the condom she had placed on it earlier. She was very proud of herself, and with good reason. Jim had been thoroughly humiliated in front his friends. That, in itself, was enough for Brie. Of course, having been humiliated the way he was, it would be futile to attempt to humiliate him in that way again. No, she would have to come up with something entirely different next time.

The three women talked in private for a few minutes and came to the conclusion that all three men had been given enough pleasure, and disappointment, for one night. They got themselves dressed and then released the men from their bindings. The six of them returned to the living room for some more drinks and the remainder of the hor'dourves.

As they sat and talked, the men were allowed to get dressed. All but Jim, of course, who had to remain in his maid's outfit and was still expected to serve the others. They discussed everything they had just experienced and even some future plans for the use of Fran's wonderful dungeon. It was almost midnight by the time the party broke up and they all decided to call it a night.

~ ~ ~

Chapter 9
BRIANA'S GAME

It was Sunday morning. James and Briana were just finishing up their breakfast when Brie announced. "I have devised a game for you to play."

"What kind of game, Mistress?" Jim asked.

"A game that will determine when, or if, you will get to have an orgasm," Brie replied after taking a sip of coffee. "I think you'll like it."

"If it means I will actually get to cum," Jim said, showing genuine interest, "I like it already. How do we play this game?"

"We don't," Brie explained, "you do. Pour me another cup of coffee and I'll explain it to you."

"Yes, Ma'am," Jim said reaching for the pot. As he filled Brie's cup again he said, "So how do I play this game of yours?"

Brie reached into the pocket of her robe and produced a velvet bag. She held it up for Jim to see and said, "In this bag are ninety marbles. One black, two green, five red, and 82 white."

"Okay," Jim said letting his curiosity show. "And what do I do with them?"

"Each day," Brie began, "you will select one marble. If you get the black one you will get to have a full orgasm that day."

"Great, Mistress," Jim replied with glee.

"If you get a green one," Brie continued ignoring Jim altogether, "I will stifle your orgasm."

"Ouch," Jim commented.

"And if you get a red one," Brie said still ignoring Jim's comments, "I will ruin your orgasm."

"And what if I get a white marble?" Jim asked. "What then, Mistress?"

"For a white marble," Brie explained, "you get nothing. No orgasm at all."

"Wait, Mistress," Jim said suddenly realizing the implications, "you mean I only get one full orgasm every three months?"

"Those are the odds," she said in a take-it-or-leave-it tone.

"Those odds seem pretty extreme," Jim replied concerned, "don't you think, Mistress?"

"Not at all, Jimmy boy," she replied. "Personally, I don't care if you never draw the black marble. You will still get plenty of stifled and ruined orgasms."

"Gee thanks, Mistress," he said sarcastically. "I am supposed to be happy with seven ruined or stifled orgasms and one full orgasm every three months?"

"Don't worry," Brie said calmly, "I will give you lots of teasing. Besides, you enjoy pleasing me. Don't you?"

"Well, yes, of course, Mistress," Jim said still not seeing how that was supposed to make him feel better about it.

"I will allow you to please me orally and with vibrators and dildos nearly every day," She replied reassuring him. "You can get your pleasure from pleasing me."

"I guess so, Mistress," he said resigning himself to the realization that his wife was definitely in charge now. "So... Do I need to draw a marble now? Or what, Mistress?"

"We will start the game tomorrow," Brie explained. "Today, I have other plans. If you cooperate, you will get to have a full orgasm today."

"What is it I have to do, Mistress?" he asked. "Just name it."

Brie stood up letting her robe fall open. She was naked underneath it and she made sure James got a good look. "For starters, you can give me at least six orgasms. That is, if you want to." She headed off toward the stairs.

"Yes, Ma'am," Jim said eagerly as he quickly followed his wife up the stairs to their bedroom.

All the way up the stairs, Jim's cock began swelling. It quickly filled its cage, and by the time they reached the master bedroom, it was beginning to ache. He didn't mind. Jim loved giving his wife oral sex. He was good at it. At least in his mind. He was always able to make her cum that way.

Briana stepped out of her slippers and let her robe fall to the floor. She reached into the drawer of her night stand and tossed a condom, a large penis-shaped dildo, and a powerful plug-in vibrator on the bed.

"What's the condom for, Mistress?" Jim asked hopefully.

"It's for the dildo, silly," Brie answered as she lay back on the sheets and spread her legs wide apart. Now get busy. Start with the vibrator."

"Yes, Ma'am," Jim responded as he plugged the vibrator into a wall socket before climbing on the bed between his wife's outstretched legs.

Jim's cock was throbbing painfully in its tiny cage, but he didn't seem to mind. If there was one thing Jim loved most about his wife, it was that she still had a very sexy body, even after nine years of marriage. It had always been his incentive to keep himself fit. It was why he spent two days a week working out in the gym at the high school.

Brie's pussy was sparsely covered with fine blonde hair. She had never had much hair down there and Jim loved it that way. He flipped the switch on the vibrator and gently touched the head to the spot where Brie's clit lay hidden beneath the folds of her labia. Brie flinched, just slightly, at the first touch of the vibrator. She could feel the powerful vibrations all the way through to her clit. She had always been sensitive there, even when her clit was still hidden within her labia.

Jim knew what he was doing. He had done it so many times before. He slowly moved the head of the machine down toward that spot where Brie's inner labia spread out from between her outer lips. They were the most erotic shade of pink, and it always turned Jim on to see how bright they were against Brie's pale skin. He used the head of the vibrator to push the two inner lips apart and expose her reddening inner reaches.

Brie was starting to get wet by this time, and Jim took advantage of the juices that were beginning to flow from her honey pot. He pushed some of the juice upward, spreading Brie's inner labia and exposing her clit to the, now slippery, head of the vibrating invader. She squirmed as it passed delicately over her clit on its way up and then back down. She could feel each tiny beat of the vibrator as it teased her most sensitive spot, over and over and over again.

It was all Brie could do to keep her legs from closing tight. If it weren't for the fact that Jim was sitting between them with his legs over her thighs, she would have clamped them shut, blocking any more stimulation from that ever-insistent vibrator. Her eyes closed tightly. Her lips parted and her breathing became very heavy. Then it happened... Brie's body exploded in orgasmic spasms that filled her head with thoughts of being fucked by one huge cock after another. She fought to close her legs and escape the onslaught of the vibrating machine held tightly in place by Jim's own hand.

Her orgasm had only begun to subside when another wave of orgasmic delight washed over her entire body. Then there was another and another. Brie finally could not take anymore and reached down with both hands to pull the vibrator away from her sensitive vagina and clitoris.

Jim got the message and pulled the vibrator away. Brie's hands gently covered her own pussy as her climax finally reached its end. Her breathing was still heavy as she told Jim to put the condom on the dildo and use it on her. Well, she actually said, "Shove it in me! Shove it all they way in! As deep as it will go!"

She was obviously still wanting more, but now she wanted something inside her. She knew that unlocking Jim's cock at this point would simply take too long. She wanted to feel her pussy being filled NOW! Besides, the plan she had for him was going to be something especially sweet. So she couldn't unlock him just yet.

Jim quickly put the condom onto the dildo and pressed the tip against his wife's hungry vaginal opening.

"Put it in!" she yelled impatiently. Put it in NOW!"

Jim pressed forward and the silicone dildo slipped easily into Brie's waiting pussy. Her juices were literally dripping out by this time so there was little resistance to the fake penis as Jim pushed it in as far as it would go.

"Fuck me!" Brie cried in desperation. "Fuck me hard!"

Jim began pushing the dildo in and out of her pussy at a steady pace. He pushed it all the way in and and then pulled it out until only the tip remained inside. Faster and faster he moved the penis-shaped dildo until Brie, once again, began to shudder as another orgasm filled her mind and shook her body like a volcano erupting.

She reached down with both hands and pulled the dildo out of Jim's hands. Tossing it off the bed she cried, "Lick me!"

Jim moved as quickly as he could laying down on his stomach between Brie's legs. He buried his face in her vagina as she grabbed his hair with both her fists and pulled him tightly against her crotch.

By now, Jim's cock was pressing as hard as it could against the restraints of its cage. It was hurting. It hurt to the point that it was almost distracting him from his current activity. But it wasn't going to stop him from giving his wife the pleasure she so richly deserved. His tongue pushed into her juice-filled vagina as deeply as he could get it. Then he would withdraw it and rake it upwards across her sensitive clit and back down again. He repeated this procedure again and again, sometimes stopping to pay extra attention to that tiny nub that seemed to drive Brie crazy.

Jim kept up his onslaught until Brie began to cum once again. She began bucking and screaming and thrashing about, but Jim held on tight and rode it out until Brie finally pushed him away. She had had three more orgasms while he was licking and sucking her. He was proud of himself.

Brie lay still, breathing heavily, until her body returned to a normal state. As normal as it could after having so many orgasms in such a short time. She fell asleep without saying a word to Jim other than a breathless, "Thanks."

Jim relaxed with his head resting on Brie's pubic bone, her pubic hair tickling his ear. After about ten minutes, Jim climbed off the bed and picked up the dildo and vibrator. He removed the condom and tossed it in a nearby wastebasket before wiping them off with a sterile handy wipe. Then he put them back into the drawer where Brie had gotten them earlier. He returned to the kitchen to clean up the breakfast dishes and get himself

The Marriage Counselor

something to drink. He took a second to check how his cock was doing. It had leaked a large amount of pre-cum and soaked the front of his panties.

During all the time he spent cleaning the kitchen, Jim couldn't help but wonder why Brie had not allowed him to fuck her. After all, she had promised him a chance to cum that day. It bothered him a little and he started to feel cheated. Then he heard Brie calling him from the bedroom.

"Honey?" she called out. "I wasn't done with you. Can you come back up here?"

Jim ran up the stairs as fast he could, taking them two at a time. Suddenly, he didn't feel cheated anymore. She said she "wasn't done with him." He hoped that this would be his chance for that orgasm she had promised him earlier.

Brie heard him bounding up the stairs and waited for him to enter the bathroom. "Run us a nice hot bath, sissy-boy," She said as he stepped into the room.

"Yes, Ma'am," he replied breathlessly as he headed for the tub. Their bathtub wasn't exactly what you would call a garden tub, but it was slightly larger than your average tub, so there would be room for them both to get in it comfortably.

When there was a couple of inches of water in the bottom of the tub, Brie stepped in. The water wasn't too hot, but it felt good on her feet so she decided it would be safe to sit down. She carefully lowered herself into the water. "Won't you join me?" she asked James.

"I would love to, Mistress," he replied before removing his feminine panties and stepping into the large tub. He too sat down and the water rose to cover his crossed legs.

"I think that's enough," Brie said, "you can turn the water off now."

James turned to face Brie and reached for the controls that were situated above the center of the tub. "There," he said as the water stopped running from the faucet, "how's that, Mistress?"

Brie also turned to face Jim so the two of them were sitting cross-legged facing one another. "Put your feet on either side of me," she said as she scooted a little closer to him. "I want your legs apart so that I can get to you better." Then she removed the necklace that held the keys to Jim's chastity belt and unlocked the cage that contained his cock. She set the cage out of the way in the corner of the tub and replaced the necklace around her neck.

"Now," she began, "Scoot down so that your cock is a little closer and you're chest is under water."

"Yes, Ma'am," Jim replied taking the position she had requested. "How's that, Mistress?"

"Very good," Brie replied. "Now I can play with your cock and there isn't much you can do to escape."

"I wouldn't want to escape, Mistress," Jim said earnestly.

Brie gently took his almost erect penis in her hand and began to stroke it until it reached its fully erect state. "How does that feel?" she asked.

"Great, Mistress." was all Jim said in reply.

Brie continued to stroke his cock under the water with one hand while she fondled his balls with her other hand. She let her fingernails scrape gently over the sack that contained them while maintaining a steady rhythm with the other. As Jim became more and more aroused, she would stop stroking him for a few seconds and then begin again.

When she detected that he was getting close to ejaculation, she began a different method of stroking. She would give him five or six quick strokes and then release his cock for about ten seconds or so. Then she would repeat the process. Eventually, Jim was begging her not to stop stroking and allow him to cum. But Brie wasn't listening to him. She continued to tease his cock in this way for about twenty minutes. Until the water began to cool.

Then Brie decided that she wanted to end the bath and move everything back to the bedroom. They got out and let the tub drain while Jim dried Brie with a large towel before drying himself.

Brie, once her body was dry, went into the bedroom to prepare a few things prior to Jim getting there. She laid out the same dildo Jim and used on her less than an hour ago along with a condom and some lubrication. She also got a couple of short ropes she had prepared a couple days ago, to be used to bind Jim's arms to the brass headboard of their queen sized bed.

When Jim had finally dried himself completely, he returned to the bedroom where he found Brie sitting on the side of the bed, still naked. "Lay down on your back," she said the second he entered the room.

"Yes, Ma'am," Jim replied as he climbed upon the bed and lay on his back, ready for whatever Brie might have in mind.

Brie tied each of his wrists to one of the bars of the headboard. She knew she wasn't the best at tying knots, but that didn't really matter. She didn't think Jim would try to escape. Not while she was teasing his cock, anyway.

Next she pushed his legs apart and climbed between them putting her legs over his so as to hold them in place while she worked her magic on his cock. She applied a little lubrication to Jim's cock and then worked to spread it all over with one hand. Then she began stroking his cock with one hand after the other, each starting at the base and stroking up and off the tip before the next hand repeated the process. Every ten strokes Brie would stop and allow his cock a few seconds to rest, driving Jim almost crazy with desire.

After about ten minutes of this kind of torment, Brie moved her legs off Jim's so that she could push his legs up and gain access to his anus. She

The Marriage Counselor

applied a liberal amount of lubrication to his puckered hole and the surrounding area. Then she placed the condom over the dildo and carefully pressed the tip against Jim's tiny opening. After only a little coaxing she was able to push the dildo passed the initial ring of muscles and into his ass. She pushed it slowly until there was only about an inch left outside.

Then Brie began to slowly work the dildo in and out of Jim's bottom until he was comfortable with its presence. Then she pushed it in and lowered his legs back to the original position, placing her legs back over his to hold them in place once again.

Now, with the dildo placed firmly into his bottom, Brie turned her attention back to Jim's ready cock. She began to stroke it very gently. She was barely touching his penis as she stroked it. Jim began to writhe in an attempt to get more stimulation, but his attempts were to no avail. He could not get enough stimulation to make himself cum.

Brie began teasing and taunting him with her words. She said things like, "Poor Jimmy, can't you cum for me?" and "What's the matter, Jimmy, don't you want to cum for me?"

To which Jim only struggled all the more. He knew he didn't need to answer her, she was only trying to get him even more aroused. And it was working. But still not enough to get him off.

Brie continued to torment poor James until she thought he had had enough. When she stopped, she told Jim that she had other plans for him and that she didn't want him to have his orgasm, yet.

She finally released his bindings and allowed Jim to sit up. She made him climb off the bed and remove the dildo from his ass himself. Then, of course, he had to clean it up and put it back in the drawer from whence it came.

When he was finished, Brie told him to go to the kitchen and make them some tea and sandwiches which they would eat in bed. While he was gone, Brie turned on the television that was mounted on the wall opposite the bed and selected a movie she wanted to watch.

When Jim returned with their lunch, they relaxed while they watched the movie. When it was over, Brie told Jim that she wanted to take a nap and that he was more than welcome to join her. Either that, or she could put his cage back in place and he could clean the kitchen and living room while she slept. Jim opted to take a nap with her. They were both very tired and slept until after six that evening.

When they awoke, Brie suggested that they go out for dinner. She wanted to go to her favorite romantic restaurant in a nearby town. She even told Jim that he could go without his cage because she was not in the mood to put it on when she intended to tease him some more later that night. The truth was, Brie had something up her sleeve that she didn't want Jim to know about just yet.

Mistress Ivey

Brie put on a black teddy instead of her usual bra and panties, followed be a sexy black dress that Jim always liked because it was quite short and he loved Brie's legs. She also wore a pair of black, stay-up stockings and a pair of high-heeled shoes.

Jim had to wear a pair of black panties, khaki pants, a blue oxford shirt with a plain brown tie and his corduroy sport coat. He looked very handsome.

When they arrived at the restaurant, they were seated at a nice table near the center of the room. There were several other couples there scattered around the room. This was not a family restaurant. It was designed for couples. In fact, most of the seating was for two with only a few tables set up for four.

Once they were settled into their seats and the waiter had taken their wine order, they began looking over the menu.

Brie decided on the rib-eye steak while Jim ordered the chicken Kiev. Jim had just taken his first sip of wine when Brie interrupted him. "Hold on," she said, "I want you to do something for me before you dink too much of that."

"Yes, Ma'am?" Jim replied wondering what she could possibly want that would keep him from drinking his wine.

Brie leaned across the table and motioned for Jim to do the same. She whispered, "I want you to take that glass of wine to the restroom and masturbate into it for me."

"Say what?" Jim exclaimed.

"You heard me," Brie said raising her eyebrow. "Now go."

"Yes, Mistress," Jim whispered as he stood up with his wine glass in hand and headed off toward the restrooms. He was not happy about having to masturbate in the men's room, even though the thought of it had turned him on at first. But now, faced with the actual challenge of doing it, he was concerned that he might not be successful. He definitely did not want to face the consequences of failure. Brie could be quite sadistic, he had recently discovered, and he didn't want to feel her paddle for failing at this particular task. He was certain that she would be extremely upset if he didn't return with at least a little cum in his glass.

Jim found the restroom empty, which was a relief. He didn't want anyone to know that he had carried his glass of wine into the bathroom with him. After all, what other reason could there be for having done so, other than cumming in it? At least he assumed they would think that.

Jim chose the last of three stalls to attempt his task. He pulled his trousers and panties down and sat on the toilet seat to perform his task. It took him almost fifteen minutes to come up with the proper mental images in order to get his cock hard enough to masturbate. But he was, in the end, successful.

He was careful to make sure every drop of semen went into the glass. He swirled it around in hopes of mixing it thoroughly, but it failed. His cum didn't want to mix very well and could still be seen floating around, suspended in the wine, if one were to look closely at it. He pulled his panties and then his pants back up, tucked his shirt in and then exited the stall. He set the glass on the counter next to the sink and washed his hands. Then he picked up the glass, holding it down toward his side in hopes that no one would notice it, he walked out of the restroom and back to his seat.

He set the glass on the table in front of him and sat down. Brie studied the glass for a moment, checking to see if she could detect his semen in the wine or not. She could. She picked up the glass and stood up. She held it up and announced, "My husband has just masturbated into his wine. He will now drink it right here at the table." Then she sat down and handed the glass to Jim.

Jim had already turned several shades of red and was more humiliated than he had ever been in his life. He looked at Brie who was staring back at him with that one eyebrow raised, obviously waiting for him to comply with what she had just announced he would do. He took a deep breath, held the glass of wine up and stared at it for a few seconds, then he put it to his lips and tilted his head back. He took the entire contents of the glass into his mouth and, with one big gulp, swallowed the entire thing.

There arose a round of applause from everyone in the restaurant...

~ ~ ~

Chapter 10
EPILOGUE

Over the following months, more and more women were coming to Kathryn for her special marriage counseling services. Soon, more than half of the men found themselves wearing chastity belts. Of course, that meant fewer men were paying prostitutes for their time and, before long, they had all left town because the money had dried up.

Three months later Kathryn was overwhelmingly elected to the office of Mayor. She had a few changes in mind for the residents of her small town and wasted no time in implementing them. The first thing she did was to institute some new punishments for certain crimes against women.

During the next few years, the number of husbands in chastity rose to more than eighty percent. Crime dropped to an all-time low, and prostitution became non-existent in the little town of Northcrest, Ohio.

The reason was simple, anyone caught engaged in sexual activity with a prostitute, was placed in chastity and spent ten days in the county jail. Each day they would be subjected to four hours on the Venus for Men machine. The machine would be set on super slow for nine days in a row. Then, on the last day, it would be set to super-fast and every drop of semen would be extracted from his balls.

Public flogging and paddling were instituted for both men and women who committed other minor crimes. These punishments were often for such minor crimes as speeding, reckless driving, or public drunkenness. Driving while intoxicated, on the other hand, resulted in loss of driving privileges and a monthly public paddling for up to a year.

In spite of the new laws and punishments, the people seemed a lot happier and the crime rate dropped to nearly nothing. Most perpetrators were from out of town. As a result, newcomers were watched very carefully.

Once word got out about the new laws, people swarmed to Northcrest in order make it their new home town. Businesses grew and new industries came to town. It wasn't long before the population of the town grew to more than triple its previous population. And everyone enjoyed the new lifestyle. Male chastity was the norm, and women ruled with iron fists. Men knew their place and everyone lived happily ever-after.

###

End...

ABOUT THE AUTHOR

Mistress Ivey (Georgia Ivey Green), has lived as a female dominant since 2006. Before that she was a submissive to her current husband (and number one fan) where she learned what it means to be a dominant. She has been helping others to understand what a female led relationship (FLR) can be and how to make their relationships better. She has tried to educate people, and to dispel the stereo types that are normally associated with female led relationships that the Internet has, for so long, projected. She wants people to understand that a female can be in charge of a successful relationship without having to "dress" the part. That is why she started writing her blog "Becoming A Mistress" back in October 2010.

OTHER BOOKS BY
GEORGIA IVEY GREEN
(Mistress Ivey)

Taking back Your Marriage
How To Set Up An FLR
A KeyHolder's Handbook
Tips & Tricks For Keyholders
The Ultimate Guide To Tease & Denial
Mistress Ivey's Femdom Fantasies (Vol. 1 – 4)
Look for them at your favorite Ebook Store.

Check out Mistress Ivey's blog at:
Becoming A Mistress

Meet her on FaceBook:
https://www.facebook.com/mistress.ivey

Or on FetLife:
https://fetlife.com as "MistressIvey"

Made in the USA
Lexington, KY
16 May 2017